NEVERMORE

A twist to the tale

SHANEN RICCI

Copyright © 2023 Shanen Ricci
Cover designer: Lucas Weslet
Illustrations: Lucas Weslet
Editor: One Love Editing
Proofreader: All Encompassing Books
Formatter: Champagne Book Design

PLAYLIST

"A quoi sert l'amour? "—Edith Piaf

"Until I Found You"—Stephen Sanchez

"Spectrum"—Florence + The Machine

"Fat Funny Friend" —Maddie Zahm

"Love Story"—Indila

"Fairytale"—Alexander Rybak

"Be My Muse"—Aaron Taylor

"Electric Feel"—MGMT

"Heart of Stone"—Boombox Cartel

"Bring Me to Life"—Evanescence

"Dog Days Are Over"—Florence + The Machine

"I Wanna Be Yours"—Arctic Monkeys

"Rewrite The Stars"—James Arthur & Anne-Marie

"Lonely"—Justin Bieber & Benny Blanco

"All Of Me"—John Legend

"A Thousand Years"—Christina Perri

"Love Like You"—Rebecca Sugar

"Love Me Like You Do"—Ellie Goulding

"Infinity"—Jaymes Young

"Ghost"—Justin Bieber

"Just the Two of Us"—Grover Washington Jr.

"Unconditionally"—Katy Perry

Just because it's a fictional tale doesn't mean it's all false.
This novel is freely inspired by personal, real events,
experiences, and struggles.

For everyone who ever felt like the side character of the book, never
forget your story is worth telling, and you are worth shining.

NEVERMORE

CHAPTER 1

Aurore

"**D**ear Mister Asshole—"

"You didn't." My best friend, Emma, rushed out of the bathroom and froze by the doorway with my black-tie dress on. "You couldn't possibly have written that?"

I slumped on her couch in my purple pajama shorts and sweater emblazoned with the powerful message, *please do not annoy me or everything you say may end up in my novel.*

My phone in one hand, my tea in another, and in the mood for chaos, I assured her, "Oh, but I did. Do you want me to read the rest? Because I promise you it's worse."

"*Scheisse*, Aurore," she cursed in her native language, then dropped the heels she was holding on the ground. "Your personality will get you into trouble."

As always.

Emma took a seat next to me. If Emma was the epitome of the

blonde and exemplary princess, I was known as the contemporary fairy-tale godmother.

Not that I looked like an old spinster—even though I was definitely acting like it. I wasn't the hopeful one with warm advice either. No, that wasn't me anymore. I was the fairy godmother who arrived at an event and weighed down the atmosphere, often accompanied by evil crows. The kind that had the extreme talent of pushing people away with a fuck-off glare and who exchanged sunshine and rainbows for being embittered, like an angry cat ready to pounce at any opportunity.

I would be mistaken as lonely, reading romance books peacefully under my blanket. That was until I snapped and threw them across the room, some of them meeting my trash can, the others having pages ripped or succumbing to another tragic fate. Yes, I was that evil. I couldn't handle the couple's flawless happiness and how I was cast away from this ever happening to me in the land of boring reality.

My magic power was that I had built myself an infallible armor in order to protect those I love. And my curse, because there is always a curse, was that I was blessed with a permanent membership to Atlas' everlasting punishment, holding on my shoulders all the weights of my unsuccessful achievements. And if I were to let down my world, I'd let down everyone around me.

"I'm not the only one with a wretched personality for trouble." I showed her Spectre's Instagram page. "Read the latest article."

I handed her my phone so she'd tap on the link in the bio. Spectre, otherwise known as one of the most famous and revolutionary artists of our time or, as I called him earlier, asshole, was the only living person I entirely loathed. One I would gladly transform into a frog that no princess's kiss could save from my devilry.

He was a man probably coming from one of those privileged families who hid his identity like a coward. No one knew who that artist was, and that made him the biggest mystery of the century. He'd opened his social media account a couple of months ago and already had one million followers, yet he didn't show his face and posted only

TikToks and pictures of his studio, paintings, galleries, "accolades," and upcoming events. Events he never participated in, but the anticipation of crossing his path made people buy tickets at crazy prices to see him. I did my research correctly. Spying was an art, after all.

"Are you still reading?" I leaned toward the phone, impatient to get to the point.

"The article is talking about *The Sad Girl.*" She didn't lift her eyes away from the screen.

Here we go. The reason for Spectre's success was this painting, world-renowned as *The Sad Girl.* Enthralling title, wasn't it?

Well, I am The Sad Girl.

He made me The Sad Girl the day my villain era began seven years ago: dreams crashing into ashes, heart crumbling, and hope vanishing. That painting had exposed my so-not-healed wounds, and if I had to rank the worst days of my life, this one would top them all. Why? Because that was the day that started the downfall of everything around me, and I was unable to stop it, fix it, or make it all go away. And somehow, I made it worse.

All those years ago, Spectre had illustrated these devastating and weak emotions to perfection by releasing his biggest piece of all: *The Sad Girl.* A painting of which I became aware after the apogee of his career only a couple of months ago. I had waited for the right moment to write to him on the networks—but as usual, my timing was bad. Having your apartment lease ending in two months would do just that to you.

That was why I'd made it my personal vendetta to unmask the phantom that he was.

The Sad Girl portrayed a woman wearing a long midnight dress with a split down her leg. She stood on the verge of the Alexander III bridge under a starry night sky. You'd think she was about to jump into the void and end her life, the way her hair fluttered in the wind, and she didn't even try to balance herself with her arms as if all hope was lost. Lights, like the one of a lamp post, illuminated her in the surrounding darkness, and unstoppable tears flew down her vacant eyes—aka The Sad Girl. With her hand, she threw ripped papers that drifted away like an unreachable dream vanishing forever in the water.

I remembered this moment like it was yesterday, and it was a constant reminder of what I had lost and how much I had failed my sister. I promised myself I'd never cry again. I'd never expose myself to that vulnerability.

"The painting is exhibited in Germany." Emma's azure eyes flashed to me. "Spectre will be back in Paris. It said: Das mythische Werk *The Sad Girl*—"

"I know."

It looked like the painting was traveling more than I, which was the final strike for me to finally reach out to Spectre a couple of days ago. My sister knowing I was The Sad Girl was humiliating enough—I didn't need all of Europe to see my tears. "That's why I sent him that very polite Instagram letter."

Emma glanced at her watch, and a smile flickered across her face. "Léo is waiting for me, but I want to hear the latest carnage you did."

I led her to the page of my message. "Here you go. I know you'll disapprove, but this was therapeutic."

"You're supposed to burn the letter, not send it afterwards."

"Next time, I should try voodoo dolls by the postal office. Maybe that would work better and attract his attention." I curved my lips with sarcasm, and Emma shook her head in disbelief as she started reading.

Dear Mister Asshole,

I wouldn't flaunt your qualities as a liar, thief, and egomaniac, so I'll be cutting to the chase by introducing myself: I'm The Sad Girl—turned into a very angry one, in case you want to snap another picture of me and turn me into a world-renowned circus clown. I would be delighted to sue you for copyright infringement.

A thing I'd already researched but gave up doing. Spectre was almost untouchable. Money can buy everyone, and money wasn't something I had. So, I was following Spectre, being a ghost myself. I was his most faithful stalker.

But I'm kind enough to write to you first—something you've denied doing with me. If in your charming personality of swindler and fraud you have an ounce of humanity, you would do what is right. I await your response with great impatience. Wishing you a day of personal reflection and growth.
The girl who hates you bitterly.

"That man will never answer you." Emma barely bit back a laugh, settling on a cheeky smile. "Maybe if you had been nicer, and—"

"You know I don't do well with finesse and kindness." But I did do well with enraged letters written in the comfort of my hermit Parisian studio.

She pursed her lips together, malicious glee in her eyes. "Just like the time I convinced you to accompany me to my yoga retreat, and you were walking around with your computer and your three-meter extension cord, looking for the network, with your mosquito spray. I can still see you frightening the campsite manager on his misleading advertising of the high-performance Wi-Fi network."

"An uninspiring experience that I never want to relive." I brought a hand to my face. I was pretty sure my head was plastered on every trailer like a serial killer wanted poster. "By the way, you look beautiful as always. I hope Léo will keep his eyes on you." Léo was her French Prince Charming boyfriend of four years. "And beware with your heart—men can be deceitful. And if he still doesn't propose to you, you have to—"

"I know," she said as if she was bored of my constant warning. "He'll do it soon, I know he will, and it's gonna be the happiest day of my life."

"Or the day he traps you forever with him." I rolled my eyes. "I'll take care of your baby."

I shifted my stare to the English bulldog, Rosalind, or Rosie, who was slumped in her basket.

"Stop worrying. He's one of the good ones. Thank you for looking after Rosalind again, and for lending me your dress and doing my makeup. You're the best." Emma rose in the direction of the door. "My fairy godmother."

Wicked godmother. The first time she called me was when I was coming home from my weekend job at the amusement park Ever After. She used to be my downstairs neighbor and was having a breakdown at her doorstep because a giant spider haunted her living room. In a fit of weakness, armed with a broom, I strived to dislodge Peter the spider but instead, lost sight of him. As a result, I claimed to have slain him, but I can guarantee you that Peter was still alive and in top form. That's how, on a lie based on my inability to help, our friendship blossomed.

"No problem. I brought reinforcements." I dug the cookie dough ice cream out of my bag. "And plus, I have some writing to do. You can keep the dress, by the way."

Her eyes snapped open like a character in a cartoon movie. "Are you serious?"

"Yeah, I don't wear them, anyway." I could give her a piece of my unworn gown collection. She'd make better use of it. "This one is so you. It'll bring you luck."

"Wow, I—I don't have the words."

"Just leave," I ordered, my lips splitting into a cynical grin. "I have work to do."

She furrowed her brows. "Still no inspiration, huh?"

I was a romance author on a deadline. I had two months left in my apartment before being evicted, which meant two months to finish my book and to find a way to give it to the head of Ever After Publishing—all because I missed out on their international writing competition by a week. Once this miracle was accomplished, all I had to do was charm them with my almost nonexistent tale and hopefully earn enough money to survive and make my happily-somehow-ever-after come true before I went back to the countryside to help my family. *Easy enough.* This villainous plan was flawed, but it was the only one I had.

I made a promise to my sister, Luna, before everything, that I would write a fairy-tale story just like old times. Years ago, I signed my first and last publishing deal that allowed me to afford to live in the big city instead of being depressed in my small one, and this story resulted in the editors rewriting my book until the point it was a stranger to me.

Yet, I promised myself I'd prove to Luna that happy endings could exist; that if I could make my dreams come true, she could too. She always set me as her example, believing in me more than anyone ever did.

That's why I couldn't fail.

Even the antihero always had a soft spot for someone, and, well, she was mine. The only reason keeping me from being the town's depressed black soul.

She was nine years younger than me, and we used to sleep in the same room before I left, our country house being too small. Every night, we used to look at the star stickers we had stuck on the ceiling, and I'd regale her with bedtime short stories to help her sleep and keep the monsters away. Because that's what we're taught to believe—that no matter what, the story will end well.

"I can't disappoint Luna. With everything that happened to her, she—" I swallowed, ignoring the slam of sadness trying to wash over the reminders of my heart. *I wasn't there for her.* "She still didn't stop believing, and now, she's counting on me to keep my promise."

But I sucked. I couldn't write a fairy tale to save my life, and I had started thousands of projects that I ended up giving up and found excuses more outrageous than the others to her: *"Writing a book takes time, Luna. I'm almost done." "I wrote a chapter. You'll love it." "My computer died—I lost my project."*

"You don't have to be strong for her. She deserves to—"

"No," I cut her off. "I won't tell her that I'm working as a ghostwriter to be able to pay the rent for an overpriced apartment where I have to use the communal toilets on the landing. That my love life is lacking because I have higher standards, that any real-life man can't hope to fill at least ten percent, and that working at Ever After as a pixie is not leading me even close to joining their publishing company. I can take it. She can't."

Luna had an overdeveloped sensitivity; she took care of the well-being of everyone else before herself. If I were to tell her the truth, it would crush her and the wonder she still has, and my pride couldn't handle it if I failed her. Again.

I wouldn't condemn her happy ending because I couldn't get one for myself.

"But Luna loves you. Maybe you just need to get out instead of dating your ancient computer. You never know what or who you can find in the streets of love." Emma waved goodbye to me and wrenched the door closed.

True love was the biggest lie of all. It was something made up by people like me in books and movies. An escape from real life.

Love faded away, and my expectations in that register couldn't be met.

I was in love once. Only once.

But my heart had somehow managed to be broken more than once.

"Looks like it's just you and I, Rosie," I said to the dog, who at the same instant switched places with a grunt and laid her butt facing me as if I was annoying her.

I needed to kill that cookie dough ice cream if I wanted to finish my work tonight and find inspiration.

"You've been a bad girl, and I'll have to punish you." He trails delicious kisses the length of your collarbone, his fingers skimming across your shivering skin. You gasp when you feel his hard velvet shaft? Cock? Hardness?

I yawned and stretched my arms, the empty pot of ice cream by my side. It was almost midnight, and I hadn't moved away from the couch since Emma's departure, my eyes red from looking at the blinking cursor on the screen.

I was selling fairy tales on the weekend (more like sugar candies, but dreaming doesn't hurt) and selling kink tales during the week at the magical price of thirty euros for each short story imposed by my pervert of a boss, whose nickname was "Daddykink—the dad of pleasure." You'd think being an erotic ghostwriter was a dream job, but I could barely afford to pay my bills because renting a shithole in the heart of the capital was as expensive as a country house.

I had no recognition and no author rights, but I somehow still managed to convince my mother over the years that I was a successful author by sending her money to pay for the institution my sister had been recovering in, and now for her sessions with the psychologist and home lessons. My dad had cut us out of his life, and it was up to me to take on the role of mean big sister by bringing in the money, killing the vibe with my nasty remarks, and never being perfect enough for the standards everyone had for me until the point I was boiling, all my emotions locked inside. As my mother would say, I had an impenetrable heart of stone, resistant to any trial.

Little did she know a heart could bleed beneath a hardened exterior.

> **Daddykink:** Hi, my little fairy hands. Next week, I have a new blog short story for you about the dom/com sex scene. Ready to pay you 35 euros for 10k words.

I couldn't escape my nickname, but life was smiling at me with what people with a stable job would call a promotion.

"How generous of you," I mumbled, closing off the windows on the screen, done for tonight, with still no book written.

I turned up the volume of the villain playlist music playing on my gamer headset and rose up to stretch my legs, waiting for ideas to pop into my head, but I wasn't able to imagine myself as a main character other than the Evil Queen getting revenge by putting the head of a certain artist on a pike.

That's when I got lost in the black hole of anti-inspiration: swiping on my phone through social media before staring at the wall, wondering how I was going to get out of this writing block. I could write a novel in a month, but the blank-page syndrome had been persistent—despite that lame attempt at writing anything else but romance.

Rosie suddenly barked at me, and I snapped my eyes wide open, breaking away from my mental storm. She wagged her tail, her tongue out. That capricious dog.

"Gosh, right now?" I redid my half ponytail, tied up by my ivory-and-black ribbon.

Rosie barked again, and I surrendered, grabbing her leash. She went crazy, gesturing everywhere for a lazy dog.

I sprinted to the couch on my way to grab my jeans. "Wait, I need to change first—"

She barked again in hostility, and I shushed her. She would wake all the neighbors if she continued. Which she did until I put the jeans down.

"Fine, you win." I grimaced. "I can't believe you're making me go out dressed like this."

I jumped into my glitter pink flip-flops that looked stolen from a seven-year-old girl and unlocked the door. Arriving in the hallway after taking the elevator—because Rosie and the stairs didn't make a good duo—I took sight of my reflection in the enormous glass mirror. I looked either like a patient escaping from a psychiatric asylum for unicorns or like Chewbacca with my long, messy brownish hair.

My phone vibrated in my pocket. "Wait a second, Rosie. Maybe it's your mistress."

Emma was the crazy, worried kind of mom. If I didn't send her a picture of Rosie each hour doing absolutely nothing, she'd freak out, thinking her baby was sick or something. If only Rosie wouldn't make grumpy faces in each pic, maybe she wouldn't worry so much. Speaking of, Rosie wasn't waiting. She was scratching the door with her paw, wanting to go outside. She made me feel like a bad dog sitter as I unlocked my phone and—

"Holy shit!" It wasn't Rosie who woke all the neighbors, after all, but my scream echoing through the building. She even stopped scratching the door, her puppy eyes set on me.

I would have whispered that I was sorry if it wasn't for my throat being too dry to speak and the shock scouring through me.

I had one notification from Spectre.

One message.

One sentence.

 Only one.

I finally found you.

CHAPTER 2

Aurore

"What an arrogant jerk," I mumbled to myself in the middle of the deserted Tuileries garden.

I sauntered past the pink magnolia trees and manicured shrubs, the breeze wafting up the smells of summer blooms. Under the gaze of the statues and star-filled sky, Spectre's words looped above the sound of my audiobook.

I finally found you.

The worst part in that story was that I had left him on *seen* for several minutes, probably ten, unable to come up with any worthy comeback. First of all, I had found him. I was the one texting him; he was delusional.

A notification from my sister popped on my phone. Luna was still online at midnight, and my obsessive mind was already imagining the worst. My fingers flew over the screen.

Me: What are you doing online at this hour?

I went back to the discussion page with Spectre, already tapping out my message, when Luna called me. I picked it up at the first beep.

"Hi," my sister greeted me with a yawn. "I couldn't sleep, so I was drawing my manga. Mom is making a birdhouse in the garden because Duchess has befriended a hummingbird, and Mom just read on Facebook that hummingbirds bring luck."

My laugh echoed in the park. Duchess was the black cat I'd given her so she wouldn't feel so lonely. Our mother was eccentric, going on the eternal quest for love despite the numerous boyfriends she had after my dad broke her heart. She still believed each of them would be the one—but a simple online check had proven they'd all been liars, indebted, or still married. I didn't take after my mom's sunny personality, but Luna did.

"Duchess is the only cat who is friendly with birds." My smile faltered. "How is homeschooling?"

"Better than in the institute, even though I'm the one sometimes teaching new things to my teachers." Her voice grew thick and unsteady. "I'm just not eager to start in a new high school again. My therapist thinks I'm ready, that I'm making progress."

I felt an ache in my stomach. We were at the beginning of summer. September was still far away. We still had time. "First comes your birthday, which shall arrive very soon. Did Mom plan something?"

"She's throwing me a pity party with Madeleine and all the old people. It's gonna be hella boring."

I heard the sound of Luna's pencil strokes rubbing against her paper.

"Not boring since I'll be there." My voice was way too enthusiastic for this kind of event with all the hyenas craving the latest gossip. "In September, you won't have to go through all of this alone. I'll be back home. For good."

That thought alone sent a spasm of worry crossing my face, and I made a mental note to check the train ticket price, which would probably cost me a month of kink tales.

"You better be!" she chuckled. "And I know what I want as a gift."

"Anything."

"I know you've submitted your novel at Ever After, and I want to read it. I hope you didn't forget my dedication."

Anything but that.

"The fact you're not speaking means you're hiding it from me to offer it on my birthday, right?" She did that thing with her voice where it was full of mischief when she was about to uncover a great secret.

So, of course, I did what any responsible and mature adult would have done: I lied.

"How did you know?" My voice was pitched high, and my whole face scrunched up. I felt the stares of the statues in the park falling upon me with shame, urging me to stop right there. "You'll love it! I can't wait for you to read it!"

I can't wait to read it either.

I'm screwed. So screwed.

"You're the best. Counting the days!" She yawned again, and I heard her walk across her bedroom. "Well, I'm off to bed. Love you."

"Sleep well." The moment I hung up, I complained to Rosie, "Why can't I tell her the truth?"

The dog flared her nose at me as if she didn't understand either.

"But deadlines are good, right? Now I have no choice but to achieve my goals by using all my means, even if they are psychotic and stupendous." I gave myself a firm, tyrannic pep talk.

Speaking of pressure, I wasn't nearly done with Spectre. I glanced at our discussion page I was still locked on, only to notice he'd had the audacity to send me another message while I was on the phone with Luna, thinking about my next move. Preferably a smart one. So yes, I immediately read his message, and he knew it, which made me look desperate.

> **Spectre:** Scheduling a call tomorrow. Please, drop your number.

That was it. No hello. No beautiful, well-constructed sentences. Communication was definitely not his strong point—it was a time saver for someone so busy with his little self.

Nevertheless, contact with the enemy had been made. I shouldn't complain. Now, I had to act and think fast.

> **Me:** How presumptuous of you to think you found me while I'm talking with a phantom with no identity. It can't be one-sided, and with the past we share, I'd say we're close enough to be honest with each other. Care for FaceTime?

I just had the time to drop my number that he was already typing.

> **Spectre:** I heard your honesty, and I'm giving you the opportunity to insult me over a call. Let's not skip the steps.

My fingers crushed over the screen at full speed.

> **Me:** Coward.

"Did you hear him, Rosie?"

She snorted in a piggy sound, searching for whatever was on the grass as I switched to another chapter of my audiobook, letting myself be lulled into the story despite the fact I was imagining throwing golf balls at Spectre.

> **Spectre:** Save your insults for tomorrow, or you'll run out of them.

> **Me:** When it comes to you, I can be pretty creative and list an alphabetic version of everything you are.

Arrogant. Brute. Coward. Dick. Egomaniac. F—

> **Spectre:** No one ever did that for me. I'm flattered.

"Fucking jerk!" I screamed for the F letter.

> **Spectre:** Goodnight, Aurore.

Reading my name written by him made my blood boil. I refocused on the audio chapter narrated by a male voice. It had directly skipped to the steamy part, while I had no recollection of the chapter before.

"That's it, baby. I want to hear you scream from those precious lips of yours."

Another person would probably have a crimson blush spreading through their cheeks, but I didn't. I was listening to erotica with a straight, unapproachable face.

Rosie suddenly stalked toward the fountain at an athletic speed with the same excitement as if she was going to be reunited with her dog lover returning from pet jail.

"Rosie, what's happening?" I followed that stubborn dog, who now stood on the small ledge of the fountain, hurrying me up to tag along with her barks. "You're feeling adventurous tonight, huh?"

I stepped on the ledge, a breeze caressing my nape. On my tiptoes, I moved forward, keeping my balance with my arms like one would walk on a wire suspended in the middle of the void. "You got what you want. Now what?"

Rosie hated water. Logically, she shouldn't have tugged on the leash and chased like a boar in the middle of the fountain, splashing me without remorse, but tonight, she did.

"Rosalind Schneider, don't you dare—" I lost my balance, having the good idea to stand on only one leg. I stumbled backward, losing my equilibrium, and snapped my eyes closed. My fall was nearing.

But nothing happened.

For a moment, I thought this could be a dream if it wasn't for the fact an arm was wrapped around my waist in a strong grip, holding me secure. My balance was restored, and my heart fluttered at an extreme speed. The smell of white musk and cedar wafted up in the air like a citrusy breeze on a salty, stormy ocean. I safely opened my eyes, only to take in the sight of Rosie casually seated in the middle of the pool of water, her tongue lashing out in victory.

"I got you." The masculine voice of my savior leaped above the one in my headset.

His hand left my waist, and a shiver chased in its wake.

"I didn't need your help," I grumbled, finding a semblance of composure before reeling around to face the stranger.

Eyes the color of an obscure night were set on me. Dark hair was pulled back with class. The stranger was imposing, his posture regally straight. He had a squared jaw and chiseled face like those of the Olympian statues. He sure was the epitome of a book boyfriend coming to life, which meant I had probably fallen asleep, and this was a nightmare.

I pinched myself to test my theory, but nothing happened. He observed me in the midst of the growing silence with a detached expression I couldn't quite detect. I managed a friendly smile, and not even one of his lips lifted to return the favor.

"You sure looked like you did," he said with calm.

"I'm not a damsel in—" As I stepped away from the ledge to prove a point, my headset had the audacity to crash on the floor at this exact moment.

Oh no. My audio continued playing, this time out loud, and my shame ravaged me inside. I wanted to plummet myself to hell, already imagining what would be written on my grave.

"If you misbehave, you won't come." The audio broke through the silence, and I dipped to my phone to pause it and delete my existence. Unfortunately, I couldn't, and the audiobook continued with *"What a good girl you—"*

I finally shut it off and hid my phone in my sweatshirt pocket, pretending nothing had happened. I didn't notice until now how tall the stranger was. Tall enough to make me feel like a small moth, and I'd never defined myself as short. An unreadable expression plastered on his face, he was still scrutinizing me with a deadly coldness as if I was the strangest creature he had ever laid eyes on. He didn't speak, and that made the situation so much worse.

"I'm Aurore, and you are?" I held out my hand with the little self-esteem remaining in me.

"Ajax," he simply stated, skeptical of accepting my hand, which I retracted right away.

This man wasn't cold. He was ice-cold. The unapproachable, superior kind. I was either bothering him, or his aloof attitude was disturbingly casual.

"Ajax? Like the Greek warrior? The one who—"

"You're wet," Ajax cut.

"Wet?" I gulped, my mind wandering through the memories of the audiobook.

"Yes, your…" His eyes assessed my outfit, and recognition flashed across my features.

I was wearing purple unicorn pajamas.

"Attire," he described it as such. "Do you want to dry yourself with my jacket?"

A jacket he was already taking off to give to me. One from a fancy black tux that probably cost more than my rent. A jacket that seemed to have been ironed like a control freak. And he was offering it to me so I would use it as the fanciest towel of all time, to the point he couldn't possibly wear it afterward.

He held it to me, and I drilled my eyes on the sharp lines of the satin fabric of his dress shirt clinging tight to his herculean biceps and broad shoulders. Ajax. I was getting the name now, having peeked at his aesthetically pleasing muscles. *Focus, Aurore.*

"No, thank you, I'm fine. I like being wet." Damn it, that came out wrong. "I mean, it doesn't bother me. I like rainy, gloomy days, for instance. I usually walk everywhere, and, well, when it rains, I still do it. I find it pretty romantic and—" *Romantic? Abort. Now.* "Just saying a few drops of water won't kill me."

That monologue was mortifying. I had apparently chosen today to do a contest for the most embarrassing thing that could come out of my mouth, and I was breaking all the records. My dream was to be a novelist, and here I was, unable to put two words together to save my life.

Ajax simply nodded, keeping his devastating eyes on me as he secured his carefully folded jacket in the crook of his arm.

"You're an author?" That sudden interest destabilized me.

"How do you know?" Probably from the audio I was listening to, or was it the literal vibe I was giving? Or—

"Your sweatshirt. It says, '*please do not annoy me or everything you say may end up in my novel.*'"

Of course, the sweatshirt. *Hand me that gold medal right now.*

A ghost of a smile slanted his mouth ever so slightly, giving away a glance at the human underneath. "I'll make sure to remember that. I wouldn't want you to name your next villain Ajax."

"I like villains," I affirmed. "They're just misunderstood, interesting characters."

After all, I was much closer to the villain than the hero, allowing myself to be selfish and bad, too exhausted to reach perfection. Over time, I had lost my empathy and become unfiltered; even if I were to hurt people, I didn't care. Except when it was about Luna.

Ajax didn't reply, but that thin line stretching his lips didn't move away as the soft shimmering blue light of the moon licked through the sharp edges of his face.

"You have nothing to worry about. From what I saw, you're more of a hero in disguise. The dark knight in a shining suit." I couldn't just shut up. Thankfully, I hadn't referred to him as a look-alike Superman with a mysterious loner vibe.

I shifted my focus to Rosie, hoping to find some support, but the traitorous dog was sitting at Ajax's feet. She was unbelievable. Not only was she infatuated with this stranger more than she ever was with me, but she betrayed me, giving him the puppy eyes to charm him.

"And are you into heroes, Aurore?" His deep voice brushed on my skin like black velvet, the edge of sensuality prickling my senses at the sound of my name. "Or the misunderstood ones?"

"The nonexistent ones," I hastened to drop with raw sincerity. Romance was an art, not a reality. That's why living multiple lives through books wasn't enough for me anymore. I grew bitter over them and the false feeling of hope. Reality just wasn't like that.

"You write about romance." This wasn't a question but an affirmation. I was an open book to him while he was a shield, not letting anything pass through him.

"I do." I omitted the fact I was struggling with a lack of total inspiration. "And you? Are you into business or something? Or maybe your date ditched you tonight, so you're swallowing your sorrows in the park."

I made a mental note to my author-self to stop making scenarios inside my head and, worse than that, expose them.

"No. No date," Ajax deadpanned. "Why would you assume that?"

"You're alone at midnight in a park, dressed up super fancy. Your face is closed off. You're all serious and cold, so you don't scream *friendly*. You seem annoyed, even, with writing plastered on your forehead to leave you alone." I bit my tongue, and his brows slanted inward, processing my words. "So unless you work in the mafia or do some shady business, something is troubling you."

"What's troubling you, then?" he countered back.

"Oh no, I'm only here because Rosie needed to—" Realization flashed across my features. I wasn't holding Rosie's leash anymore. "Rosie!"

I searched on every corner to the point of having torticollis, only to see that my stranger in the shape of a living Greek warrior was holding her leash in his hand casually, to Rosie's grand happiness.

"Oh, thank god, I thought I lost you!" I scooped down to pet her. "I'm sorry, princess. I'll give you your nonfat yogurt once we're back."

Looking heavenward, I realized I was kneeling before a perfect stranger. My sight was at the uncourteous height of his zipper. His Adam's apple bobbed, and I rushed to get up.

"Thank you. Again. I should be heading back now," I rattled off like I had a train to catch.

Once standing, our bodies almost collided, leaving only a few centimeters of space between us. Our breaths intertwined, and that single microsecond was enough to make my heart skip a beat. I hurried to take a step back. His presence seemed larger and more intimidating. He exuded a raw magnetism, just like his scent, both masculine and sophisticated.

"Do you live far? I could call you an Uber," he offered.

"No, that's okay. Plus, Rosie likes to walk too." To that, she growled as if she knew I had told a lie.

Ajax handed me back the leash, and with the contact of our fingers brushing against each other, a small spark of electricity shot the length of them. He retracted his hand and spread apart his fingers in a tense move. Was I repulsing him? That was my cue to stop embarrassing myself.

"Well, Ajax, I hope you find whatever you were looking for tonight." I meant that. "Sunrise brings a new beginning and often an answer. Goodbye."

The corners of my mouth twitched upward, and I inhaled a deep breath, pulling away from him. I took the scenic way back home, the golden gate of the exit a few meters in front of me.

"Perhaps I already did." Ajax's voice breached through the emptiness, freezing me in place.

I reeled around, some meters now distancing us. It was my turn to scream, "What?"

"Can you two be quiet! I'm trying to propose to my girlfriend here!" a man yelled at us.

I searched through the illuminated streetlights, and looking closely, I saw a couple by the shadows of the trees. The man was on one knee in front of her, and the woman was seated on the bench with a bouquet. A phone was recording on a tripod, and I could see the small street orchestra waiting nearby for her to say yes.

"Oh, come on, you didn't rent the park!" I complained before mincing my way backward, but something in me couldn't stay quiet. *Leave, Aurore. Do not interact. I repeat, do not—*"I could snap you a picture? I'm good with a camera, and no offense, your tripod is not set up straight, so if you plan on doing a proposal only once, do it properly." I looked at the bride-to-be in question. "You don't have to say yes if you don't—"

"Please," the man hissed.

I mouthed, "Sorry," at him in a sarcastic way and swiveled my eyes back to Ajax. But he wasn't that far away anymore. He had prowled toward me, his gaze fixed on mine, not taking into account the couple at our side.

"I didn't even see you walk towards me. What do—"

"Would you be my date tomorrow night?" It was blunt. Direct. Efficient.

Ajax succeeded in muting me. My eyes widened, his question throwing me off guard since I couldn't tell if he was even interested in me.

"It'll probably be boring and formal." Jeez, he didn't know how to sell whatever it was. "I just arrived in town tonight for tomorrow's opening of a temporary art exhibition at the Louvre. My friend Isaac works in art."

For some reason, imagining this stranger being friendly with other beings was almost impossible for me. His gaze roamed my face in search of a reaction from my side, but it was my turn to not give him anything. Nothing came from my mouth. My right to speak was revoked. Plus, my relationship with anything artistic wasn't at its best.

"And I would like you to accompany me." The way he pointed that out felt as if acid was burning down his throat into admitting that.

"Why?" It was the only thing that slipped through my lips.

"Because having you by my side will make this event far less pain-ful." He smiled grimly. "And far more entertaining."

"I—" *Say something. Anything.* But my mouth was working against me, still hanging open.

"Think about it." He cleared his throat. "I'll be waiting for you in front of the entrance at 7:00 p.m. with the invites. The choice is yours, Aurore. Good night."

He walked off, cloaking the night, and I remained stone-still, taken by surprise.

That stranger wanted me to be his date.

"You should have said yes." The woman from earlier showed me her engagement ring, laughing and jumping into her fiancé's arms with an infatuation I struggled to understand. "It's not too late!"

The orchestra started playing music for the happy lovers.

It wasn't yet dawn, but something told me this day would change everything.

CHAPTER 3

Aurore

"There is a dude waiting by the arch of the park, and he keeps swiping on his phone." Emma's voice echoed through the speakerphone. "Oh wait, negative—he has a takeout bag. Thank god. I swear he was swiping on Tinder."

I stared at my ceiling, my feet resting on the wall in my high black socks. I was lying on the opposite side of my bed, hugging or, more likely, strangling my pillow, close to my chest. "Let's just abort. I'm not going."

"*Keine Chance!*" Emma only took her German voice when she was either angry or starving. "It's only 6:45 p.m. Tell me what he looks like again?"

This mission was a failure from the start.

I had the good idea to talk about my late-night encounter with the mysterious stranger with Emma, who, since that mistake, kept pushing me to accept his date as if it were some sign of the universe.

I was fine slumped in my bed, my computer open with a total of fifty words written in the space of three hours.

In the midst of negotiation with Emma, I had sent her and Rosie on a quest to find Ajax. I wouldn't stand alone in front of the Louvre without an invitation, waiting for a man that might stand me up. Nothing guaranteed that Ajax would come, and if he did, my lack of trust in human beings wanted to know if he would wait for me or if I was just a spare wheel of no importance. It was an evil plan, but better to be evil than a fool.

"If a Greek warrior like the hot version of Hades had a grumpy twin, it'd be him." I forced myself to stand, sauntering across my small apartment—which basically allowed me to take no more than five steps. "Only probably wearing a tux as dark as his eyes."

"So he's that hot?" The sound of Emma's footsteps quickened as if passing through a bush or something. "Rosalind! Stop eating everything you—"

The phone's microphone made an unbearably shrill noise, and a grimace formed on my face. "Are you okay?"

"Yeah, I'm fine. I'm getting closer to the Louvre. It's pretty crowded here. That event is super fancy. Wait, I'm sending you a video!"

Great. I swallowed when I received Emma's video notification on my phone. Unlocking it, I got a glimpse of the luxurious cars dropping off guests in elegant cocktail clothing. I would definitely ruin the vibe like an unwanted cloud ready to ruin the summer beach days.

I had a thing against artists: the story ending with Spectre and his Sad Girl, and beginning when I got fired from my temporary job for being a mediocre muse at Les Beaux Arts seven years ago, in comparison to the muse who agreed to pose naked with more cleavage than I could pretend to have with an extreme push-up bra. And let's not forget my beloved ex, Augustus.

Augustus. I used to believe his name made him sound like a prince. He was the epitome of the good guy, the popular, extroverted one that carried charisma with a full grin. I thought we were in love in every pastel romantic dress I wore by his side, with each tender gesture I allowed myself to feel, and with each beat of my weak and naive heart. I was the girl hoping for a man who would finally give her all the love she was yearning for.

But in the end, that prince of hers had broken her heart the day her world crumbled apart. Augustus had always been in love with *the other girl.* She wasn't the mean antagonist as you'd expect her to be. No, she was the one with shiny, silky hair she didn't need to brush, the girl next door that everyone adored, except for the villain who grew a feeling of jealousy toward her. Violette, featured in the list of "top 10 names for beautiful girls."

Violette and Augustus were the main characters, and I was the villain separating those young lovers from true love. And as a villain, no one will root for your happy ending. You're simply imperfect, selfish, and unworthy. Left out of the tale.

"Aurore?" Emma asked with her soft voice, probably not for the first time. "Did you receive it?"

"Yes, thank you." I cleared my throat, trying to deny the spike in my heart. "Emma, don't bother yourself. I have to—"

"What better things do you have to do, huh? To stay locked away inside your dark tower until you decompose?"

I snapped my eyes at my closed curtains and at the gloominess of my bedroom slash apartment. "It'd be a contemporary version of Corpse Rapunzel, where—"

"I think I found him!" Emma's shrill scream echoed in my ears, and I was convinced every neighborhood in Paris was now informed she was looking for someone. "Well, well, he's quite handsome, and I'm not into dark-haired guys."

I rose, alert, a whimper slipping free from my lips. "Are you sure?"

"Everyone is entering the pyramid except for him. He's alone, wearing a black and burgundy suit, and looks kinda lost, I have to admit. Understandable—it's 7:00 p.m., and you're not here. He's probably wondering where you are and if you'll *come*." The pun was intentional.

She snapped another video, which I jumped on my phone to see. That was him. Ajax, with his arms casually crossed on his chest, crushing the other guests with his imposing aura. A few female gazes turned toward him while his stare was lost in the opposite direction. He didn't blend in at all with the festive, smiling people. Poker-faced and cold as stone, my aloof stranger was there, waiting. And I was so not ready, neither physically nor emotionally.

"I hope your silence means you're getting dressed." Emma's voice turned sweet and caring. "Don't let this man pay for the wrongs others did to you. It's your time—don't let something that can be beautiful vanish away because you're scared. Look what happened to me and Léo."

"I'm not scared, and perhaps I don't want what you guys have," I muttered. "Love is not meant to be for everyone, and don't come crying to me when he breaks your heart."

"You're saying that, yet you're the one who's collecting modern princess dresses and never wearing them," she snorted. "Probably because, for some reason, you're waiting for the right moment. I don't know why you changed drastically. You're romantic, and whether your sarcastic self wants to admit it or not, you still believe in love. Even if he's not the one, don't miss an opportunity. This is not the same story and not the same ending."

I cast my gaze toward the object that took up the most space in my microscopic apartment: my closet. It was filled with ball gowns I'd never have the opportunity to wear, reminding me constantly of all the money I spent ridiculously. Therapy would say it was a sickness, but for me, it was my childhood hopes and dreams. It was as if I had locked the happiest part of me in that closet, and she wanted to escape, screaming for me to release her, but she couldn't be trusted.

Because that's the thing about being the antihero or the second character of the tale: the acknowledgment of being misunderstood is easier to admit on paper than in real life. We tend to hide our troubling parts from society to be accepted.

"Sweetie, it's 7:05 p.m." Emma's voice was almost imperceptible.

I was daring myself to go. Perhaps I could get inspired? I've been on dates, and even though the outcomes were disastrous with men who turned out to be in relationships, others who had a Don Juan complex, and those immature ones looking for their mothers, a flicker of hope was still there: that it could turn into something epic for a day. I knew the end of the story, but the beginning... Maybe Ajax could display a powerful beginning I could shamelessly represent in my fairy-tale story?

"What would I even wear?" Lately, my closet had been filled with purple and black since I didn't want to add the other colors back to my life.

"You're the one who's always helping me with this. I bet you already know," she quipped back with a laugh. "But please, no more black. Be friendly. Open. Don't scare him away! Let's go, Rosalind. Our mission here is done."

"I'm going," I firmly decided. "This could be revenge against my old, weak self. I'm stronger than that—I'll grab inspiration by the balls, and tomorrow, I'll have a chapter written."

"Yes! I'm so happy you've made the right choice," she said. "Even though I was expecting a more romantic answer. It sounds like you're going to war."

"Perhaps I am," I joked—not entirely. "I need to hurry. Thank you again, Emma!"

"Keep us updated! Lo—"

I hung up and rushed to my closet, opening it in one swift move. *Going to war.* I grabbed a mix of crimson and black to give me enough courage—for instance, while facing adversity, you should always wear red, and this way, Emma wouldn't complain. I wasn't all black, and she had said nothing against my leather biker boots with ankles that made me look like a gladiator in high heels—not that I knew how to walk with that.

I sprinted to the bathroom.

It was 7:10 p.m.

I was not dressed. Not wearing makeup. My hair was tied up with my clip in something that looked like a bun.

I was dead set on going, but the question was would he wait for me until then?

CHAPTER 4

Ajax

I was in front of the Louvre at 6:30 p.m.

I was always ahead; that was a fact. I left no detail to chance. I was in control of everything around me. My dress shirts were ironed. My clean cologne permeated my skin. My interest was dead set on the goal. I didn't waste any time with my lack of fascination for people. I had no desire to take part in any conversation, just like I had no desire to be here in the first place.

I took my antique vintage pocket watch out of my vest suit pocket and jerked open the top flap.

The time displayed 7:20 p.m.

I left it in the palm of my hand, a muscle working in my jaw. I'd been waiting for her for fifty minutes. The first woman I'd asked out in years had stood me up. I readjusted my cuffs, my gaze lingering on the next car arriving. But when a blonde-haired woman came out, my interest faded. Aurore's hair color was complex, similar to shades of autumn—it had a brown ochre base with gold oxide reflections.

The hand of the watch made another full turn, and I tightened my grip. Another minute had passed, and there was no sign of the girl wearing the unicorn pajamas of a six-year-old and with a beaming smile that could light up an entire city, in contrast to her killer eyes that could annihilate that same city.

"Ajax." Isaac came to disturb my peace, a flute of champagne already in his hand. "What the fuck are you doing alone with your solemn air?"

"Waiting," I deadpanned. The answer was obvious. "You don't have to stay with me."

"I can't believe you're still here." Judgment was etched in his tone. "Come on, she's not worth it."

I gunned my eyes to him. "This is not your choice to make."

"I've never seen you go through this much trouble for a girl. In fact, I've never seen you with a woman." Isaac, one of the only human beings I barely tolerated, thought it was the right time to joke. "*Sei pazzo.*"

"You're not Italian, Isaac." He only pretended to be because his second name was Fiore, and he was growing a light beard with his Van Dyke brown hair and thought that nationality would be his golden trophy to hook up with more people.

"I know, but it'd be much cooler if I was."

I checked my watch again.

It was 7:27 p.m.

She wasn't coming.

For a moment, something unwanted tried to flash across my features, and my index tapped on the rim of the watch at a speed greater than the spinning head. The scenario that something had happened to her obscured my already fucked-up mind in shades of menacing clouds before a storm. My brows pinched together, and I remembered the words she used to describe me. *Cold. Serious. Annoyed.*

"Am I that cold?" I didn't expect to speak out loud.

"You're not cold. You're iceberg frigid." Of course, Isaac didn't miss a beat, jumping on the opportunity. "The kind that can't get melted by lava."

I straightened my posture even more than it already was, coming across the stares of the new guests arriving, to whom Isaac returned their polite smiles. Next to him, I displayed no sign of friendliness, for the simple reason I wasn't friendly. I had no reason to fake it; the sight of their arrival did not please me in any way.

"So, you're expecting to let me go back in there all by myself?" Isaac complained.

"You like parties. You like people. I don't unless I'm obliged to."

My watch pointer was on thirty. She had made her choice, but I had other cards up my sleeve after just finding her again.

My gaze searched the crowd and swept far away to the large entrance arch, where there was a woman pedaling on her purplish bike at a frenetic pace. My lungs drew breath, and I commanded my legs to step forward. I saw, I heard, I smelled, and I disliked touching. I'd mastered each of these experiences, and yet none of those senses combined had given me anything, not even the skipping of a heartbeat.

It did now. She drove like the craziest version of a madwoman who would crush everyone in her path. Her feet were pounding like she had no gears, and she was leaning forward to gain speed. My date was certainly uncommon, equipped with a fiery temper and enough fuel to power an entire country.

I didn't move, observing her tossing her bike at the back so no one noticed she'd arrived in an unconventional way. She secured it by tying it up with a big chain I had no idea she was carrying and straightened her clothes with dramatic gestures. She then readjusted her half ponytail and flexed her fingers as if trying to calm herself. It was one hell of an arrival, and this succeeded in making my lips curl into the slightest ghost of a smile.

"Of course, the one you invited is the crazy one with a bike." Isaac chuckled. "In case you're both searching for me, I'll be—"

"We won't," I cut, my eyes devoted to her.

"You're a selfish prick, you know that? As I was saying, I'll be socializing and welcoming the VIPs and all that." He finished his sentence anyway, taking his leave.

Aurore was pacing in my direction with black pearl ankle boots and ebony tights. She made me think of Melpomene, the goddess of tragedy—the one holding a tragic mask in one hand and a sword in the other. She wore a skater skirt of the same color and a crimson top with large sleeves, displaying her naked collarbone. The day was fading behind her, and she seemed to carry the night with her. She was a painting of contrasts with a determined and sophisticated allure along squinting eyes.

My muscles stiffened. My jaw tensed. I felt the strange need to swallow as she arrived in front of me, carrying a smile around like a weapon that kills at sight. I craved to tell her she looked like a siren who could lure any man to destruction, but I've been known to upset people easily, so instead, I said nothing like an idiot.

"Is something wrong?" she asked.

Yes.

This was all a wrong, messy idea, and for some reason, I couldn't tear my gaze from her pursed plush red lips. They flamed like scarlet pigment. I didn't mind observing her. If it was up to me, I'd do that for the next couple of hours, but it wasn't, so I had to snap out of it. *Now.*

"No." I finally averted my eyes away from her. "Thank you for coming."

"I know I'm late. I'm so sorry. I feel terrible to have made you wait that long. I—"

"Not at all," I interrupted her. "I haven't been waiting long."

And here I was, lying to spare her feelings.

To that, she gave me a full smile, the corners of her eyes crinkling. "Is that a fob watch you're holding? I've never seen one. I thought those things were extinct."

I immediately put the watch back in my pocket suit. "It's my father's. He thinks he has lost it."

She nodded as if approving. I laid an arm behind her back without touching her as we strode to where the security guard was checking the names of the guests by the pyramid entrance.

She bit her glossy lip and mumbled, "I've never been here before. I mean inside. It's a first."

From the friction of her fingers, I could deduce that neither of us wanted to be here tonight.

"Your names," the security guard grumbled, not lifting an eye as we arrived next to him.

"Ajax Clemonte and—" I waited for my date to introduce herself.

She leaned on her tiptoes so he'd hear her amongst the crowd behind us. "Aurore Bardot."

A name fit for a queen.

The guard searched the list, and a brouhaha built up behind us. Someone was pushing away the crowd with his extremely irritating voice.

"Excuse me, I'm Bernard Dupont-Brillac, the artist."

My jaw clenched at the perched voice that screamed of bourgeoisie getting closer. Bernard tried to mince his way between Aurore and me, but he retracted when I shielded her next to me, keeping her away from that pretentious man. A tingling sensation ran through my fingers, but he had left me no choice. A normal person would have circled around us.

Bernard, as delusional as he was, tried to push me so I'd step aside as if he were the Prophet. He hurt himself by colliding with my back, and I didn't budge from my place, taking solid root on the ground. Bernard, on the contrary, stepped backward with the impact. I snapped my eyes down to him as he readjusted the round glasses he wore just for the style, wrinkling his nose in my direction. Wearing a filthy checkered suit of yellow and orange alongside his toad-green bow tie, Bernard was the most annoying artist of the century.

"Welcome back, Mr. Dupont-Brillac." The guard smiled fakely at Bernard, who was only a second-class artist, literally no one, and surely not the highlight of the show.

I knew him too well. After all, he had been my teacher long ago.

Distracted by his reflection in the mirrored doors, Dupont-Brillac didn't acknowledge anyone and took his leave while we were still waiting.

"You were checking our names," I articulated to the guard, my patience on edge.

"Right, Clemonte—" He searched through his list. "Sorry, your name is not on it."

I'd murder someone tonight. He was making me look like an impostor. "Ajax. Clemonte."

"No, sir, I'm sorry. We don't have a Clemonte or whatever your name is." *What a fucking mess.* "I'm gonna ask you to leave."

Another nerve twitched my jaw. I was arguing with a fool. The mask plastered on my face probably made me appear aloof while inwardly, I was burning. The idea of hibernating in Antarctica with penguins and to not have to deal with human interactions sounded almost appealing. I searched for Isaac, sweeping the crowd with a glance. I found him doing his social butterfly with everyone inside, like a clown distracting his audience at the entrance of the pyramid.

I waited for him to notice me, but when he didn't, my voice leaped above everything else, calling him. "Isaac."

At the sound of his name, his eyes widened, and he rushed directly to us, not wasting a second. He hooked a friendly arm around the guard's neck and switched his stare between the both of us. "Is there a problem?"

"Yes, that man's name is Clemonte, but I have no one registered under—"

"My bad, my mistake." Isaac gave him a familiar pat on the back. "Let them in."

Aurore remained silent, but her brain seemed to be racing, as if she were dealing with an equation. Finally free, we crossed the entrance, and in doing so, Isaac mouthed, "So, so sorry," to which I replied with a murderous stare.

"See, you didn't wait for nothing. She finally came," the asshole dropped loud enough with a big fucker smile on his lips. "You should have seen him, not wanting to leave his post."

To that, Aurore held in a chuckle by pinching her lips together. "Well, I'm glad he did."

"Isaac, this is Aurore," I introduced them. "Aurore, this is Isaac, my friend you shouldn't pay attention to."

"Your only friend, and the most entertaining." He bowed. "I'll let you two enjoy your date. It's not good for my career to spend more than five minutes talking with someone. No offense."

"Yes, you do so." My eyes were warning enough.

I turned to face the only person here who was stopping in the middle of the room to look at the transparent ceiling for a reason I couldn't picture. Maybe she was stargazing? She had a light smile and didn't seem to mind the glances of the people around her with their mortal boredom.

"Are you looking at something?" I asked.

Aurore's eyes fell back to mine, and she erased her smile. "Just the sky. We can see the stars through the ceiling, and it's making a weird shape like a—"

So stargazing it indeed was.

She breathed deeply. "Like a tufted deer."

"Tufted deer?" *What on earth was this animal?*

"It's a deer that has teeth like a vampire," she continued as if the answer was that obvious. "My little sister, Luna, tried to get bit by one once because I used to tell her it'd maybe make her immortal—you know, like turn her into a vampire—but it didn't work. Me, on the contrary, I tried to befriend him, but I found more success with geese."

I blinked. I had no idea what to reply and if any person was capable of formulating any semblance of an answer to something like that.

Faced with my silence, she opened her eyes and clapped her hands together. "Anyway, the sky was despicable. Shall we?"

"Yes." I showed her the way, wondering where she could have possibly seen that wonderland animal. "I'm sorry about all this mess, by the way."

She carefully stepped on the stairs. "Don't be. I always knew you had some secret identity hiding who you truly are. A disguise."

I remained blank.

"I'm joking." She raised a brow. "But anyway, the rude man who crossed us. That's why I hate—" She bit her lip before continuing. "I hate men who wear bow ties."

I couldn't be more glad I went with a simple tie.

We arrived at the bottom of the stairs, a billboard hanging in the middle portraying the opening of the art exhibition tonight and the room it'd be hosted in, the Apollon Gallery.

"Oh, I don't even know which artists are showing here. Let's see." She read through the billboard, and I remained behind her.

"Zekriev Morrinksky," she struggled to articulate. "Bernard Dupont-Brillac. The guy from earlier. And the exclusivity of the night is—"

Her face shut close, her enthusiasm disappearing as she slowly pronounced the last name as if it was the plague incarnated, "Spectre."

She froze in place for a moment and locked her fists. In the space of a breath, she turned to face me with a tight, razor-toothed smile. "Well, that sounds incredibly promising! Great. Loooooving it."

She didn't waste any time rushing inside the Apollon Gallery to saunter past its ornamented walls and masterpieces hanging on the ceiling. Following her, I knew I'd have to struggle with two things tonight.

One, to try to keep my gaze away from her.

Two, to hide who I truly was.

CHAPTER 5

Aurore

Flutes of champagne were served with toasts on golden trays to match the splendor of the event. Statues were aligned in a spirit of renaissance. The crowd was gathered in front of Spectre's wall, probably gossiping about his contemporary genius.

I had no desire to step further into either the crowd or toward that jerk's wall, so I remained by the Aries wall, crossing my eyes with Ajax from across the room. The intensity of his stare roamed over me without shame, making my heart leap into my throat. He was scorching me from across the room, his intention solely on me, contemplating me like an art piece. He attracted a few people close to him, most of them women, from whom he recoiled, sparing them a single glance. A grin shouldn't have tilted my lips, but it did.

And so I pretended to be busy admiring the artwork and, most importantly, eating all the buffet. I grabbed three toasts in a row, which seemed to displease the server, judging by his lips twitching downward as if it was impolite to eat the free food. Hell, it was free. And it was food.

"Those toasts are divine." I tried to strike up a conversation about the avocado, shrimp, and other fancy things inside that mind-blowing toast. "Don't worry, I won't go near the paintings with it." Except for Spectre's wall, but that would be wasting good food.

The server's lips stretched into a thin, tense line, and I swore he was about to scream, "Guards, take that impostor away!"

That was my clue to not monopolize the buffet anymore. I felt like a deer among hyenas, or more likely, a hyena among deer.

I positioned myself in front of the nearest painting and brought my tongue back against my teeth, hoping I hadn't caught a piece of food. Focusing on the painting and not my treacherous heart, I hooked a hand on my waist and analyzed the white canvas with a couple of black spots and a blue line in the middle of the page. I bowed my head to the side, skeptical. The description next to it was insanely long, and to be honest, I could have painted that. Especially for the price it was selling at. I could have made ten of each in one single day.

"What do you see?" Ajax's voice brushed my back when he arrived by my side, his face imperceptible.

"Honestly?" *That I should stop writing and produce money by splashing paint, an alternative therapy, instead of investing in a punching ball.* I raised a brow, considering my inner monologue. "I see a shovel with a splash of dirt. Unless the artist stepped on his canvas and swept it with his broom. In that case, the name of the painting should be *Sweeping the Dust Away* and not that speech about the universe and the degrees of human emotions."

"You have a wild imagination," Ajax replied simply, and a laugh slipped free from my lips at the thought that he wasn't seeing anything in it either.

"They should hire me to write their—"

"Excuse me." The man in the colorful plaid jacket faced us with the sharky smile of someone who wanted to sell you everything and anything. He was Bernard Dupont-Brillac—the rude artist who got sent off like a stray bullet after colliding with Ajax's back on purpose, and a man I unfortunately knew. Long story short, he was the teacher of one of Paris's most exclusive art schools, Les Beaux Arts. I used to pose there as a model to make some cash, and he indeed was the asshole who fired me. Hopefully, he didn't seem to remember me. But did it mean he heard—?

"Clemonte." The man in question nodded at Ajax, who had a hostile frown plastered on his face. Bernard then focused his attention on me with his vile little eyes. "I'm the artist of this piece you're contemplating. In case you were wondering, the line symbolizes the longevity of life. The boredom. It's a straight and long, monotonous routine, until the end invades us and we die. The tragedy of men and their loss."

"It's not really optimistic," I mumbled. "Life is not flat but, on the contrary, full of twists and turns. A line can't possibly describe it all. We go through so many emotions as human beings, right?"

Bernard's face snapped close, his nostrils flaring. A winning point for the *incompetent* muse. "And what do you know about art, miss? To admire a work requires a delicate openness of mind."

"Oh, I don't do delicate. I do direct and messy." I attempted a joke that no one laughed at. I could already hear Emma's voice in my head telling me to not cause a scene, but it was stronger than I.

I opened my mouth to speak again but was overtaken by Ajax, who had stepped in front of the man, overwhelming him with his imposing stature.

"Art is popular, and if you have to explain your piece with boring and over-the-top words, it means your piece simply lacks a message. Art speaks for itself. It shouldn't be imposed. May I say that you also deliberately plagiarized another artist's words with that sentence—" Ajax's jaw tightened, his eyes locking firmly on the man. "*Destiny has a way of connecting people. Sometimes the timing is wrong until it's right.* I believe that was the original sentence."

Bernard lacked words, his defense retreating with Ajax's fierce attack.

"My date—" The way he said it, possessive and strong, caught me off guard and sent a bolt of fire down my stomach.

It's me. His date. He was talking about me.

I was someone's date, and I wouldn't freak out. Both of them had their stare stuck on me as I held my hand to my throat, feeling like a piece of shrimp was stuck in it.

"Please continue." I waved at them, half choking with a semblance of a smile before swallowing a full glass of water from my lovely server.

"She saw a shovel, and you should be glad she was able to see the morbid message you failed to deliver, Mr. Dupont-Brillac."

"Art is subjective, after all." Bernard's sharky smile was weaker. "If you'll excuse me, I have other people to… enlighten."

Bernard disappeared in the blink of an eye from my field of vision. The way Ajax closed this man's mouth with brio was inspiring, but it also was the reason why I needed to keep my distance from him. I didn't trust this world, nor men, and he was definitely part of it to have memorized a sentence by heart.

"Did he truly copy someone else's pitch?"

"Yes," Ajax affirmed with all his aloofness. "Lots of people do to fill their lack of inspiration and hope to be in the shadow of the success obtained by someone else."

"Some humans have no morality, and yet, we still want to believe in the good in people. Otherwise, life would be too painful. The good news is that no one can steal your essence." I needed to find a way to stop this topic ASAP, or else I might tell a complete stranger about my family history and my everlasting list of every delusion I had. "So, you believe in destiny? No one quotes a sentence that quickly if it doesn't speak to them."

"I believe we're making our own, yes."

I hadn't realized we were slowly sweeping toward Spectre's

dreaded wall until now. I kept my anger in check and refrained from pouting at the elation of the people around it.

"And you?" Ajax's voice brought me back to reality.

Confronted face-to-face with Spectre's works, which were a mix of beautiful and tortured, portraying heavy emotions of love to hatred, I somehow managed to reply, "I'm a believer, so yes, for the better and the worse."

His artwork on the wall seemed almost inhabited—more alive than the ghost that he was. It felt like an angry wave that would wash over me at all times and crush me underneath the aphotic zone of the ocean. I didn't like the effect it had on me. I didn't like the pang in my heart. Fortunately, I had never come face-to-face with *The Sad Girl*.

In these paintings, their faces were almost imperceptible, if not for the emotion that increased tenfold, hidden by some sort of floating veil. On one, two people tried to join their hands, drawn by rough and thin lines. But the couple was separated by the precipice that dragged down one person. As for the other, he was consumed by the weight that fell on him.

In each of his works, there was a message. On another, it was a man who walked with swords behind his back, each of which symbolized contemporary elements like money, social media, betrayal… He didn't use realistic colors but sharp ones, like mixing navy blue with blood red and black with gold. He wanted to shock and make an impression. The last ones were morbid: from the grim reaper to one of a man sitting in the fetal position against a wall with words written like an impossible equation. The man was tearing off his face and screaming like a patient in a mental asylum. It was morbid. Morbid enough I had to hide the goose bumps on my forearm with my hand.

I disliked everything this man made me feel.

I held myself back from rolling my eyes and throwing champagne glasses at his art, when the crowd's point of view on his persona shifted, and my interest was piqued to the point I had no shame in eavesdropping on their discussions.

"We hadn't had a new Spectre painting in months. I think he was just an ephemeral trend," one older woman said to another.

"His work is so gloomy. Is it the only thing he can do?" she replied. "It's always the same thing. That man must be tortured."

"All geniuses are," a man interfered in the convo. "It's a shame if he were to be old news, but I fear he can't reinvent himself. It's truly a shame. Dupont-Brillac, on the contrary, is—"

"You seem offended," Ajax cut in, and I stopped eavesdropping.

"I'm not," I spoke too fast. "It's just I'm not really fond of Spectre's enigma." I quoted it with my fingers and a dash of sarcasm. "For me, he's just a man trying too hard to appear cool, while he sounds more like an egocentric jerk to me."

This definitely wasn't Spectre's night.

Ajax's eyes remained fixed on me, and a nerve flickered in his jaw. "Why would you think that?"

"He's a coward, not daring to show himself, and he created this whole thing about him like he's some kind of god or whatever. His art is—"

I gazed upon the paintings. No matter how much I hated him, this man had talent. A lot. The knot in my chest persisted, and those silly goose bumps had difficulty disappearing. But I couldn't admit it.

"Pretentious" was the word I settled for.

"Sometimes you're forced to go to lengths you're not used to taking to deliver a message."

I delivered a smile that probably looked more like a death threat. "Are you siding with him?"

"I would never dare stand with an egocentric jerk." I believed he'd almost made a joke.

We pulled away from Spectre's wall to stroll across to the other paintings in the room.

"Good." This time, the curl of my lips was genuine. "Why are you into art? You have knowledge, so you must like it somehow."

"I like the fact that an artist can immortalize an emotion, a moment, for life. It's very powerful."

I agreed with him, but a question hung on the tip of my tongue. "Do you work in this universe? Are you an art seller or something? Maybe a gallerist?"

Ajax stopped walking, deliberately ignoring my question, shifting his whole body in my direction. "Why do you write?"

"I write to make people believe in better days. To beautify life. It's like the need to breathe—I need to do it. I can't give it up. You know that everywhere I go, I carry a notebook with me so I can draft any inspiration that comes through my mind." I opened my little red bag and showed him my notebook and my pencil. "See? I'm always prepared."

As soon as I experienced something strong, I needed to write what I felt like to capture an emotion and make it stay in time. It was like a personal diary in a way where I was free to expose my flaws and thoughts without judgment—maybe it was my way to be seen and heard.

"Why didn't you write anything tonight? Are you not inspired?" He closed a few centimeters between us, and I couldn't step backward, or else I'd have collided with the barrier behind me that prevented people from getting too close to the paintings.

The distance between us was not socially acceptable, and his smooth, subtle scent of musk and a fresh aroma made me travel to a sea of silken sheets. Clean and proper, it sounded just like him. My heart missed a beat. If I were that kind of girl, I'd blush. He was dangerously attractive, and on top of that, Ajax looked like a human shield—one you'd want to lose yourself in his embrace.

"I—I haven't been able to write anything for a very long time. You can't write what you don't believe in anymore." And here I was, gasping for air as if the room was deprived of it by his mere presence. "I mean, I do write for my job as an erotic writer, but it's different. I'm a ghostwriter, so it's not my work." He waited for me to continue, probing me with that devastating stare of his. "And now, this is my last chance to have a stab at my dream to publish a novel. One that would prove that I was right to believe. That happy endings do exist."

But for that, I had to become the person I'd been before.

"If you could write anywhere, where would you be?"

I thought this through.

"I think I'd like to be by the ocean, the sun radiating on my skin. Nothing else but the sand. This way, I could bring an oversized hat and a black bikini, holding a juice in my hand and pretending to be all rich and powerful in a villa way too big for a single lady." A smile tipped off my lips, and a laugh slipped free. "That, and starlight skies."

"I can inspire you." He was dead set, wearing a poker face as if he was carved from marble.

I wasn't sure if he was overly confident or if he truly believed he could solve my problems like some charming knight. *Wrong target.*

"Let's get out of here." His impulse caught me off guard. He went from a controlled Ajax to someone striding across the room, ready to fire up this place.

"But—where are we going?"

He stopped on his way, drilling his midnight eyes into me. "Do you trust me?"

"No, I don't." I wasn't that foolish. "I barely know you. Plus, trust isn't something you give away and—"

He gave me a scowl that almost stretched his face like a normal person. "Good. You shouldn't, but I need you to pretend just for tonight."

"Pretend?"

"Yes." His voice brushed my skin like soft velvet. "Let's pretend just for one night. Give me one night to change your mind and be inspired."

I lost any notion of time. The sound of what was happening

inside of me leaped through the crowd. The thumping of my heart. The fear in my gut. The desire growing in my core.

"I'm sorry, I should go. It's late." It was ten, and even if Cinderella had until midnight, fairy workers, evil or not, had to wake up early. "Thank you for everything, but this is not my place. If I'm honest, I probably agreed to go on a date with you for the wrong reasons. Not that I used you—you're great. I just have issues. Lots of them. You don't want to deal with them and—"

"I get it, Aurore." He didn't seem offended. "Grant me two hours. Let's say until midnight."

My heart was beating faster and faster like a pressure cooker about to combust, and I wished I could just shut it down.

"Please," he said. "At the first strike of tomorrow, I'll disappear, and until then, let's pretend we're not us. Not our pasts nor our fears. Just two characters."

He was speaking directly to my author self. "The words you're using are so not fair."

"I can be convincing when I want something." A thin line etched its way across his face. "I know a place that can inspire you."

"Don't tell me it's your apartment because I'm not into that, and that's a creepy line," I countered.

"My apartment is average, so no, that isn't it, nor something implying to have sex with you if that's what you meant." He loomed closer, and my eyes came to the height of his broad shoulders, which stretched the fabric of his suit that clung tight to his very well-defined biceps. I immediately lifted my chin so I encountered his stare back. "I'm a patient man, Aurore. I'm not in it just for that."

Just for that? What was he in it for? I tried to probe his soul with a skeptical gaze and made a decision I was sure to regret. "Fine, let's get out of here."

The next few minutes were blurry in the grip of adrenaline. We rushed outside, heading in the opposite direction of everyone else to step out in the dark of night.

"It's nearby. We can go by foot." Ajax readjusted his suit, observing his surroundings. "We'll pick up your bike right after."

My lips parted, and the fresh breeze didn't lower my body temperature. My bike? No way. He had seen me arriving on the verge of a mental breakdown. My moment of shame was cut by my phone ringing in my bag. I searched for it in the midst of the mess, dropping a few curses. People knew better than to call me because I was most likely to never pick up the phone—unless I was in a very shit mood.

"It's nothing. I—" I shut it off, and alongside the missing call, I had a Google call invitation that was in the US time zone, asking me to hop on a call with Spectre at 4:00 p.m. *his* time, which meant 10:00 p.m. mine. "Damn it!"

Ajax's brows slanted inward. "Is something wrong?"

The number called again, and I had never been more determined to pick up my phone. "I'm sorry, I really need to take this. I won't be long."

He simply nodded, giving me enough privacy to deal with the jerk.

One beat later, I picked up my phone. "Hi."

"Hi, Miss Bardot? This is Spectre's—"

"I'm glad to finally be able to put a voice to the man who stole my image, and don't try to impress me—I'm not. Do you know how I felt when you portrayed my private moment? Don't you dare—" I unleashed a flood of hatred that was cut off by the older voice.

"I'm sorry, Miss Bardot, but I'm only Spectre's agent." *Of course.* "I'm calling you because I'd like to schedule a meeting with you to discuss *The Sad Girl,* and I'm hoping we could come to an agreement. I'd like to know your availability for next week. I'll be back in Paris."

"I'm pretty much available. How's Sunday afternoon?" This would give me enough time to prep after work and not enough to stress and kill myself with anxiety.

"How about 4:00 p.m.? I'll email you the address."

"Perfect. Have a great night." We hung up, and that's why I loathed phone calls—this would have easily taken two seconds by text message and wouldn't have made my heart race.

I walked over to Ajax, who was also busy typing something on his phone with his forehead creasing. The moment I arrived back to him, he put his phone away in his suit pocket as if he had felt my nearing presence.

"Is everything okay? You look tense."

"It's just an issue I'll solve very soon. Now, let's see your place." I shut my eyes for an instant. "Not your place as in your apartment but your special place."

"I'll lead the way."

"So, this is how I got elected Miss Ballerina of my hometown."

Telling Ajax about my personality-shaping childhood stories wasn't part of my plan, nor was telling him about my weekend job at Ever After while we passed by the lit-up art galleries under the vaults of the columns.

"What did you wear?" And somehow, he still didn't seem bored by them.

"My mom sewed my tutu. It was awful because first, it was green, her favorite color, because we were short on purple, and she was terrible at it. I looked like a bush instead of a daisy." I chuckled, remembering my teenage years. "And then, I had to perform a dance. This was my main-character moment. Luna was recording everything on the camera, and I—"

Only then did I realize we were standing on an arched bridge that spanned the Seine. My heart raced at the sight of the gilded sculptures, the nymph reliefs, and the belle époque architecture. It was the Alexander III bridge. One of the streetlights was flickering, the light about to go out.

My face closed up, and my lips thinned, flashbacks trying to pierce through me.

This was the bridge of The Sad Girl.

"Aurore?" Ajax called.

I faked a smile and continued crossing that damn bridge, balling my hand into a fist.

"Then, the day of the show, I slipped. The floor was wet, and I broke my ankle. End of the story. I'm not even sure I was that good." For all I knew, it was more proof that I wasn't meant to be the main character.

I struggled to breathe under the weight of my heavy heart. I had avoided this bridge like the plague for years. I couldn't tell if Ajax had answered me or not, the wind whistling in my ears and my footsteps crossing each other faster and faster until we stepped off the bridge. We plunged into small cobblestone alleys, and Ajax stopped in front of a small back door that seemed to lead into an abandoned gallery on the street corner. No one was in sight.

He turned the handle of the door, which squeaked open with a creaking sound like in a horror movie. "It's always open. No one knows about this place."

And for good reason—this place looked creepy as fuck. What was I doing? I'd be on the news tomorrow with the discovery of my corpse. All of that trouble to have followed a man who looked too good to be true.

This didn't stop me from entering, already thinking about my obituary and the words people would say during my burial. I had always thought my eulogy would be "To the one who followed her dreams." But now it would be "To the one who followed the Greek warrior and for what reason? None other than stupidity."

Ajax took the looping old iron stairs and leaned on the ramp, dust coming away from it. "It's on top."

Step after step, we trudged higher, passing broken windows and creaking sounds. Crossing the final stairs, he slammed open a door with a forbidden warning sign, and the light of the moon radiated in shades of blue. Ajax advanced on the mansard roof, holding out a hand to me, and I thought I was dreaming. Windows with golden lights and the illuminated Eiffel Tower contrasted with the darkness of the landscape.

"This is wonderful!" The wind blew into a breeze as I joined him in the center of the roof. "I'm so glad I didn't stand you up and that you didn't bring me here to murder me."

"I used to come here during my teenage years. I was more of a rebel."

"You?" *Undemonstrative, clean-cut, arctic him.* "A rebel?"

I took my shoes off, balancing on my tiptoes. A slight smile slipped away for a brief moment, and I carried my heels in my hand. I ambled on the line of the roof, exploring the immensity of the world just for ourselves.

"You can't drop something like that and expect me to not follow up on this," I added, the weight of his gaze on me trying to destabilize me. "How were you as a teenager? I told you my story; now tell me yours."

I tripped over, wanting to keep my gaze on his, but he caught me with one strong arm hooking me in his embrace. He pulled me to his chest, the moon shimmering on half of his face. I had trouble breathing when I muttered, "I'm okay."

My two feet touched the ground safely, and we pulled away. A knot formed in his jaw as if I were repelling him or triggering something unwanted.

"I used to work temporary jobs to survive, hoping I'd make it on my own. I was a different man."

So, Ajax had grown up poor. Perhaps we weren't that different.

"That must have been hard. I understand the struggle." But something about the way he said it, almost robotically, showed he was hiding something. "What changed, then?"

"I got exactly what I wanted and became who I wanted." His hand flexed for a second. "And that turned out not to be enough."

"What do you mean?"

"Most humans are a disappointment."

"I agree, but this can't be the case for all of them," I said, his scars calling out to me, his stone heart beating in harmony with mine. "That's why you're all closed up? Your past made you this way?"

He waited a moment, so I added, "It's much easier sometimes to confide in a stranger."

Someone you'll never see ever again.

"I've never let my past shape me. I'm in control of who I am, not the others." His eyes read into mine, inking a powerful message within me. "And what's your story, Aurore?"

"Me?" I laughed, half-apathetic, half-desperate. "I was like every kid, I suppose—happy and so hopeful, imagining countless stories. I was the good girl with ballet slippers, ruffled pastel dresses, and ribbon in her long locks of hair. The hopeful one who believed in the promise of happily ever after and the lies that it could someday be her turn. I wanted to become legendary and be a storyteller that would inspire the ugly world. For me, nothing was impossible as long as you believed. How cliché."

I sounded ridiculous. He must have taken me for a naive freak with the way his whole face tightened, probably wondering why he'd bothered to ask.

"I did witness love in its pure and magical shape, growing up with parents who couldn't keep their eyes off each other at the dinner table. My father used to bring yellow dahlias to my mom every time he was back from his business trips, just like he'd carry me on top of the packs of hay and calculate the age of ladybugs with me and my sister," I added, confiding in a stranger that couldn't care less about my backstory or had no desire of becoming my personal psych. "But all those memories were a lie I created to blind the obscure truth."

The one where my father had abandoned my mother, my sister, and me—and our fairy-tale life.

My mind rewound through the memories. At the dinner table, Mom would hold her fork until she broke it to hide the ugly truth from us. My father brought my mom's favorite flowers, hoping she'd forgive him for having a double life and breaking her heart all over again. He took me on a walk so Mom could cry alone and clean excessively to remove all traces of the other woman and the kids he had elsewhere. The family he chose over us.

One bad news always brings another, and my sister paid the price for my father's lies.

"Something happened, Aurore," I remembered my mom sobbing on the phone. "The school called. It's Luna."

My heart thundered, the memory so vivid.

"She got into a violent fight, and… I didn't know. She never told us… This has been happening for months."

"You speak in the past." Ajax's voice saved me from falling deeper into the void, his eyes searching for the truth underneath.

"Because I've been hurt." I admitted my vulnerability for the first time before letting my heart solidify again. "I mean, we all get hurt, right?"

"I suppose," he stated simply. "How did you know it hurt you this way?"

What a strange question. "Because as much as I want to be that person again, I can't, and that's my problem. Now I'll probably end up as the hostile old woman children whisper scary tales about. The one who wears a long, fake-fur coat and writes dark crime novels with a diabolical laugh," I joked with a nervous laugh, to which he didn't even give me a semblance of a smile.

"This is how you see yourself?" His tone was dry.

"You know—" I played nervously with my fingers. "—that life has been taken away from me. I became who I needed, someone strong and fierce, someone I could rely on in order to survive. If I go back to being that naive girl, I'll sink. Does that make sense?"

Our eyes met, and the steel barrier around my heart broke slowly. "It's nothing. It doesn't make sense. I—"

"You needed a hero in your life, but you had no one to take care of you, so you became the villain." He put into words what I couldn't explain. "I get that, more than you think."

"What makes you one?" For the first time, I felt free to be who I was. A side character who didn't have what it took to be the hero, who slowly turned into the bitter, pathetic villain of her story.

"I sacrificed everything to become who I am, and I'd do it again, selfishly." He cleared his throat. "Tell me something about you. Something that is a part of you but you'll never say out loud on your own. Like a secret. A confession. I want to understand you."

If I were to tell him and we ran into each other again, it'd be embarrassing, but then again, it was unlikely to happen. We seemed to belong to the same category: the ones who don't get happy endings. "Fine, but only if you admit something too. And something very personal."

"I will," he promised.

I joined my hands together and admitted my vice. "I have a collection of fairy-tale dresses. Ball gowns I never wear. And I think I do that because I would love to take the place of a romantic heroine inside a book. It's stupid, I know, but I have no choice but to be stubborn and fight to prove that life is not all sadness and broken hearts. That it can also be wonderful and magical. I want to continue to believe in it from all my soul, even if I'm incredibly mad at happy endings. But is it too selfish to want the same happiness as those heroines?"

Well, well, well, it looked like that part of me wasn't buried as deep as I thought.

"That's noble," Ajax said. "But sometimes, life is empty."

Empty. That word echoed in me like a knife cutting me piece by piece. Life was empty, meaningless, without a dream and love. Empty and lacking inspiration. Just like me.

"Life would be too depressing without a dream. Sometimes, it's hard to believe, but you have to force yourself and continue, even if you don't want to, and one day, it'll pay off. We forge our reality." *I hope.* "When I used to tell stories to my sister, I thought I had a superpower. It was an escape from reality."

His lips turned into a thin line I interpreted as a smile. "That's very main character of you to say."

"But I'm no main character. She'd be the perfect one who has the whole world at her feet with just a glance. The one everyone would declare a mondial war to save her. I'm more of the sarcastic side one who will hunt you to death if you break the heart of someone she loves. The one with a bad temper and a tendency to fuck things up and serve only as moral support to the main character. The one you don't go to war for."

"And don't you think that side character deserves her own story? Sounds way more appealing to me than the other." His voice made me believe he was interested in reading into me. "Those characters are fools if they don't go to war for you. Because with you, they could win."

"You don't mean that." I shook my head, my skin prickling like a barrier, ready to defend me, but he didn't budge with all his seriousness. "All right, your turn, Mister."

He cleared his throat. "All night, I had one thought that I couldn't get out of my head. One that consumed me."

"Which one?" My voice was weak.

"About the taste of your lips."

"My lips?" I repeated, my nerves racking.

"Yes."

Time floated in the air, a mystical pull drawing us together, closer and closer. We inched forward, the starry night our only witness—like a black curtain enveloping us under its veil, keeping the secret through time. Just one night. All my senses became alert, inhaling his scent like the last day of summer and a goodbye kiss.

We were close enough so we could breathe the same air. It was the part where I'd close my eyes and hope for the magic of that first kiss, lust melting with angst. But it didn't happen. The moment was broken when Ajax pulled away. His inscrutable mask was on again, to the point I could believe this was all a figment of my imagination.

Of course, that perfect kiss fantasy wouldn't happen. Because life just wasn't like that.

"We should head back." His tone was drier than usual.

It took me some time to get my spirits back. "Wait, a second, I think I want to write something."

"You're inspired." He paused. "I'll wait for you by the stairs."

Alone, I dug out my notebook and pencil. Tonight, I had something to say. A moment to magnify.

That feeling of déjà vu. Once, a cruel and sad moment, and another one so beautiful and enchanted that the first stroke of midnight would come much too soon. Is it better to stop it now before the disillusion?

"You didn't have to bring me home, you know?" I turned my keys in my hand. "I have pepper spray in my bag."

Cold and stern, Ajax was holding my bike on his shoulder like it weighed nothing to him until we arrived in front of my apartment, a typical Parisian studio with expensive rent.

"I still have two minutes to share with you." He positioned my bike on the ground.

I stood up on the ledge, and yet he still managed to stand taller than me. "It was nice to meet the real you tonight, Ajax Clemonte. I'll be sure to search for you online properly when I'm home."

"I have no doubts. Thank you for accepting my invitation."

The tension between us was so unbearable that I immediately made a dramatic bow and dropped like an idiot, "Maybe in another lifetime, we will meet again."

Thirty seconds remaining.

I didn't give him my number.

He was staring.

I was panicking.

Ten seconds.

I wrenched open my door and—

"This is not over, Aurore. It never is."

At midnight, Ajax disappeared through the cobbled path, and I closed the door on the most enthralling night I'd ever had.

A night of reverie before jumping back to reality with only reminders, the butterflies in my stomach, and the pound of hope.

"Come on, Aurore. Don't be fooled. It doesn't last. It's ephemeral."

But for a moment, I let myself be transported, rediscovering the desire to be inspired.

CHAPTER 6

Aurore

"You can't go on like this, Emma! This guy is a misogynist who makes you cry in the toilet. He's a bully. Two people on your team have already quit. You need to stand your ground. You're too kind for this garbage!"

Emma's eyes bulged out from their sockets, and it was only then that I realized I was screaming in the middle of the candy palace shop located halfway between the swan rides on the magic river and the giant's lair.

I mouthed, "*Sorry,*" and ignored the stares of the judgmental people buying cotton candy and ice cream. I was done with my shift, plucking the crimson flowers out of my hair. I covered my purple pixie dress with a black sweater with some voodoo dolls on it and threw my wings on the table, getting out of character.

"It's okay, I can take it. He's just a coworker. I can ignore him," she convinced herself.

This was why I could never be part of a team like she had—they were organizing all kinds of events, each one more dazzling than the others, and battling for the spotlight, especially that now they'd landed a yearly event planning with Ever After.

"If you want, I could wait for him in the dragon alley with a shovel if he's crossing his way to the enchanted forest. I bet Pegasus' statue would even help me ship him to Zeus' trial, and we both know he's not as lénient with men as he is with pretty women," I came up with a three-act revenge plot in the space of two seconds, and still no happily ever after in sight.

"This is a little villainous for Ever After." She chuckled. "And that's the reason why you should be writing. Where are you at with your manuscript?"

I lingered on the scenery of the fairy-tale fairground with its colors and the promise of happiness on the smiles of hopeful families. I wanted all of that, but now, I was jealous and envious of them. "I'm at a place where I'll make the rise of the villains and kill the prince. I doubt they'll want that. I'm not exactly selling fantasy."

I had nothing left to lose, so trying to come face-to-face with Ever After's publisher seemed infinitely simple in my mission-impossible plan. But writing the manuscript, that was the tricky part. Especially since I had been rejected once during my online applications years ago; and because I wasn't the kind to take no for an answer, I decided to work here to force destiny—little did I know destiny was stronger than my will.

"Speaking of fantasy." Emma clasped her hands on the table. "Tell me about Ajax. Did something else happen?"

"No, it was only one evening." My palms soaked up the warmth of my cup of tea. "Sometimes it's better to end the story before it begins. This way, the memory is sublimated."

Lesson number one I'd learned from my side characters' mates: people always leave, and stories don't always end on a happy note— so by rejecting the possibility of more, you're not the one who's abandoned and hurt.

"What if you missed out on something beautiful?" My best friend didn't share my opinion.

"I'm not naive, Emma." I lifted my chin. "There is a difference between a moment and a story. Sometimes it's not meant to be. Plus, I did look him up online afterwards."

And, might I add, I was pretty good at looking people up online. I could have been hired as Cupid in disguise. When Léo and Emma started dating, he had to pass all of my tests to be worthy of her. Looking him up online, I had found his whole astrological theme, analyzed all of his identified Instagram pictures—and do not get me started on his followers list. As I always said, better be prepared and not lose your time. I didn't have trust issues; I used my skills to be aware of scammers, liars, playboys, and Don Juans who would suck everything out of you like leeches.

I inhaled a deep breath, loosening my grip around the cup.

Point was, dating was a battlefield, and true love was rarer than getting struck by lightning.

"And?" Emma waited, ready for me to spill the dirt.

"And I didn't find much on Ajax Clemonte, but he was promised an impressive soccer career during his teen years with the whole scholarship package, which stopped abruptly for no reason. After that, nil, apart from the fact he owns some art galleries. His name is alongside one of his friends, Isaac, who I briefly saw at the art exhibit. So maybe he's some kind of art collector, but—" I paused for dramatic effect, wondering if I shouldn't have confided to Emma that I was on the verge of building a report on him alongside a complete slideshow. An attitude that was either control freak or crazy—or both. "I did find a lot of things on Léon Clemonte. One of the best and wealthiest surgeons, actively involved in charity giving with his prodigy soon-to-be surgeon son, Archibald. And would you believe me if I told you he was the Sagittarius version of cold Aquarius Ajax? Plus, they have a fucking castle in the middle of France."

"*Was ein Plottwist!*" sweet and shy Emma screamed in the middle of that dreamy pink place—which was my plot twist of the evening.

She leaned forward, trying to mince herself like a mouse. "So he's from this kind of family?"

"Yep, French royalty." I raised my cup and in my haste burned my tongue while taking a sip. "And he had the audacity to tell me he struggled to be who he is now. How pretentious is that? Thank god, I didn't get mixed up in all of that."

"You know you're judgmental?" Emma, of course, didn't burn herself drinking her tea. "He's not in the big family internet picture. That means something. You should be the one to know that sometimes your family can be a weight to carry."

"It can be a weight to carry when your absent, lying, piece-of-a-father has a double life and is still surfing on big occasions to ask for tickets to Ever After so he and his other children can have fun. Not when your father is richer than the president in an eighteenth-century castle," I deadpanned, a bit louder than expected under the impatient stare of my fairy coworkers, who were wondering what I was still doing here since my shift ended an hour ago. *I have no life—get on with it.*

"I know you didn't deserve what happened to you, Aurore, but you can't condemn everyone. Léo's family didn't accept me at first, and they are strongly against us getting married, and I think that's the reason he doesn't want to propose to me." She managed a smile. "And you were the one who told me this would make our love stronger and that one day I'd show those fools they were wrong. You promised you'd be here as my maid of honor, annoying them about how happy we look together."

"Well, back then, I had more faith in people."

"You mean more faith in you?" Emma hinted. "You accomplished a lot."

"You mean all the sex scenes I've written? At least I've brightened up the evenings of women dissatisfied by their selfish and unfaithful men." I raised my cup, which made Emma laugh. "Anyway, I have to go if I don't want to be late for my appointment with Spectre's agent right now. I need to ace my game."

"Good luck. I have no doubts you'll be the killer that you are."

I handed her that killer smile in question.

If being the villain of my story taught me anything, it was that chaos could be my middle name.

Spectre's agent and I had an appointment in the lobby of a fancy hotel—the supreme place for business meetings, and I was in the middle of an awkward moment. The one where you're waiting in the middle of the room for your date to arrive—one you don't even know what he looks like—trying to appear busy and confident, not lost and frightened.

I ended up sitting on the green velvet sofa, straightening my back and crossing my legs on the side because I had the exquisite idea to change out of my pixie work dress and into a long black one with a split, thinking I would look classy after I ditched my creepy doll sweater, while I looked like a permanent member of the Addams family. A notification popped on my phone.

Spectre: I'll be reachable at any time during the meeting.

I furrowed my brows. Why would he do that? Was he scared, or did he want to throw me off my game?

Me: Yet, you're still playing hide and seek.

Spectre: Maybe I'm looking at you right now.

I lifted my head, glancing at the crowd around me. After smiling at two wrong men, one old enough to be my grandfather and one who was married, I decided to stop trying to guess. Both of them thought I was flirting, and one of them offered me a mimosa. I won't tell you which one. And I won't tell you which finger I childishly raised.

Me: You're not here.

Spectre: How would you know?

Me: Your eyes will tell the truth about who you truly are. I'll unmask you.

Spectre: You're bold and honest.

Me: Virtues you're certainly lacking.

Spectre: Maybe I don't seek to be virtuous but simply human.

Me: You're bad at it.

Spectre: I agree.

I found myself laughing. What on earth? I immediately dropped my smile and started tapping again when a man with a gray suit went through the stairs, almost running, eyes stuck on his phone. He was dynamic. Definitely in a rush. Probably in his forties. He had an East Asian look in him, with short, silky silver hair and deep-set eyes. He looked like the badass hero in an action movie, carrying a briefcase. And he was coming toward me with heavy, determined strides yet was still elegant.

I didn't lose my composure, remembering the man was on Spectre's team. I shouldn't be impressed. I locked my phone, not letting Spectre's distraction get to me.

"I'm Eric Wén, Spectre's agent. It's an honor to meet the woman who inspired *The Sad Girl*, Miss Bardot." He gave me his hand to shake and sat in front of me, readjusting his suit in one swift move.

"Likewise," I replied with the same politeness, my voice managing not to break at the mention of that wretched painting. This was the moment I'd been waiting for.

"I'm gonna cut to the chase and be honest with you." He crossed his legs, posing his palms on his knee in a position of power. "Spectre has a generous offer for you. One I'd strongly advise, considering, and one I strongly didn't advise him on making. I'm sure you're aware your case isn't strong enough to make it into court, and it's best for both parties if *The Sad Girl* remains a myth."

He was good. Confident good. Arrogant good. But I wouldn't let myself get swallowed up. "I have no desire for the world to know me as *The Sad Girl*, but trust me when I say that if Spectre's offer isn't appealing to me, I will go to court. A scandal would be enough to ruin his reputation, and even if I don't win, the damage would be done."

My nerves were racking. I was bluffing, my legs ready to flee and my heart about to combust.

Eric dropped his rigid business mask and laughed. "You're good, but we don't have to go to those extreme lengths, like I said. I'm here to make an agreement with you, not to start a war."

"And why would I believe your word? You're on Spectre's side, and you're just here to buy my silence." I was no one to them, just a means to an end.

"It's true." He leaned forward. "But I'm human too, and I witnessed your hatred."

Right, when I screamed at him on the phone. Not my best moment.

"I'm sorry for that, but you have to know this painting belongs to the past. It'll never go away. You'll never be able to make it go away."

I knew, and I could live with it if I had my revenge on him, on life, on something. I wanted to stop feeling like a failure.

"That said, Spectre is offering you an extremely large sum of fifty thousand euros." Eric flashed a smile. "For your image. But that's not it."

Holy shit.

Fifty thousand euros.

With this money, I could change my life. Luna could visit me. I could give her the life she deserved and—

"But there is one condition. He wants you to be his muse. He's open to negotiating and—"

"No fucking way!" I jumped abruptly from my seat. "I'll never pose for him."

He gestured to me to calm down. "Please, Miss Bardot, hear me out."

"I'm sorry, but if Spectre thinks he can play with me once more with—"

"He's ready to offer you another fifty thousand euros for you to be his muse, which gives you a total of one hundred thousand," Eric said.

I dropped—no, slumped—on the couch, not knowing what to say, as if the weight of the money was pulling me to the ground.

Looked like I had no principle left whatsoever.

"All he's asking for is for you to be his muse for one project. He's open to working with your rules." Eric's dark eyes plunged into mine. "It's a way to scratch the past, and frankly, he's quite generous to the point he won't make any profit on this project, for a reason I completely ignore."

My mouth thinned, hatred consuming me. I needed money, so of course, I was considering it. Who wouldn't? I was proud, but I was also realistic and materialistic, my bank account barely staying above ten euros at the end of each month. But making a deal with the man I hated—who probably was an old pervert—would be a nightmare.

But as the proverb says, keep your enemies close. I would discover what the monster looked like and unravel that coward Spectre to get the closure I needed. He thought he was buying me, but if I was smart, I'd use him to get what I wanted. Revenge on life, and perhaps get inspired—the heroine does need a retreat in a sweet little cottage house, and, well, I needed a nemesis to battle.

"I have conditions," I affirmed with determination, refinding my devastating fire. "If I were to accept, I need to know more about the nature of the project, no more stuff behind my back. I have the power of decision. Plus, I want to meet him before I make a final decision. And don't come up with a smart way like him wearing a phantom mask or something. No more hiding."

I needed to know who he was, to put a face on the man who stole my pain to create a masterpiece. This vile psychopath.

"Spectre reveals his identity on rare occasions within the framework of a professional partnership. You cannot hope for—" Eric's phone rang, and he stopped talking, his eyes set on it. He snapped his lips shut, reading whatever he had just received. "After all, that could be arranged. But you'll have to sign a confidentiality agreement to protect his identity. And this is not negotiable."

He raised an eyebrow, pointing out that last aspect, and I wondered why Eric had suddenly changed his behavior about meeting Spectre.

"Fine." I rose. "And also, no nude painting or any weird, sexual, non-classy thing."

"Of course. I'll email you the location and other information regarding our matter once you've signed the NDA. This is it, alongside the contract that you're in no obligation to sign now." He handed it to me after searching through his briefcase. "You can take a couple of days to think this through. I'm open to rediscussing the terms of the contract beforehand if necessary."

"I will. I'll be in touch." We shook hands strongly. "Goodbye, Eric. You have a lot of courage to work for him and defend his interest."

Eric gave me a real smile this time. "I hope you'll accept our offer."

I slipped away from the hotel and collapsed on the wall outside, letting go of all the breath I didn't know I was holding. My hand was shaking. My heart was sinking. My eyes were closing.

I was going to find out who Spectre was. My fingers flew over my phone, tapping out a message that would change everything.

> **Me:** I accept your conditions. Prepare yourself to meet me.

His response was instantaneous.

> **Spectre:** I'll see you soon, Miss Bardot.

And that terrified me.

CHAPTER 7

Aurore

To: Aurore Bardot
From: Eric Wén
Subject: MEETING

Dear Miss Bardot,

Thank you for sending over the signed NDA. Spectre will meet you in his studio. He believes you'll be able to evaluate his work in order to make the decision to be his muse and that knowing his place of work will reassure you. You will find the address attached at the end of this email. A car will pick you up and take you to your destination at our expense (and back home, rest assured).

As agreed, our driver will be waiting for you in front of your apartment at 3:00 p.m.

Do not hesitate to contact me if you have any difficulties.

Cordially,

Eric.

I had three reasons to freak out.

One. I had taken the modern carriage sent by Eric, or, more precisely, a luxurious black car, which took me to my destination.

Two. The destination in question was a picturesque seventeenth-century harbor ringed with buildings from the Middle Ages, timbered houses, and impressionist artists. I was in Honfleur, a two-hour ride from Paris. The bastard was living in a fairy-tale town. Which brought me to my third but not the least reason.

I was on my way to meet Spectre.

Spectre, in his natural habitat, and I was the willing prey coming to him armed with my jeans, crop top, and black platform shoes with reinforcement on the heel. Here I thought I had everything under control coming here, but truly, only a non-mentally sane human would have accepted.

After passing the small streets of the town center and a large number of galleries, most headlining this odious artist, we arrived along the white sand beaches. The car began to slow, and I calmed my nerves by pressing my palms together. Now was not the time to get anxious and remorseful.

After gaining height on the cliffs at the edge of the beach, we turned down a small alley. An elegant iron gate opened, and we drove inside a typical neat French garden. The property was a little over-elevated, resembling a mansion. The brick walls were beige, with white terraces giving a sumptuous panoramic view of the ocean. The neighboring mansions stood a bit further away, giving some privacy.

Don't be fooled.

This three-floor house was the lair of an arrogant jerk, not a fairy-tale house, and no pretty sight would make me change my mind.

"Miss, we're here." Spectre's driver peered through his visor at me as if it was the third time he was informing me of this.

"O-Okay, thank you," I mumbled and left the car, unsure of what to do next.

Several hundred images swirled through my mind as I tried to imagine Spectre, terrified of unmasking the man who had exposed my pain. He was definitely an old man rich enough to afford this kind of house. With the little bravery remaining in me, I decided it was now or never. If I started to think and not act impulsively, I'd crawl back to my blanket and drown myself in cookie dough ice cream and binge TV shows.

I made my way up the marble stairs and went around the house to follow the small cobblestone path that led to the backyard garden overlooking the beach. At the very end, surrounded by foliage, there was a white balcony giving a seafront view, with a man standing erect in the middle from behind.

I stepped forward, the salty oceanic air calming me, despite the fact my nemesis had never been so close. He was here, wearing a black shirt rolled up on his forearms, and seemed somehow tall and well-built—nothing like the image I had made of him.

"So, we finally meet." My voice was quivering, and that wasn't the moment. "I can say all that I have in my heart. How you—"

Spectre turned around to show his face, and my world collapsed.

I felt like a knife had poisoned my heart, and I screamed, "You!"

My lips turned into an expression of disgust as I eyed the man in front of me. "It's you! I can't believe this!"

This was a nightmare.

Spectre was the man I had shared the most beautiful night with.

The one I had made a fool of myself by confessing to him the tales of my heart.

Ajax was the most despicable man on Earth.

"I can explain," Ajax—I mean Spectre—said, walking casually in my direction.

I shook my head. "You're a fucking liar! I can't believe this. I can't believe you! What a jerk you are."

"I never lied to you." He thought he was smarter, a muscle in his jaw clenching. "I never lied, Aurore. All I told you was the truth."

Maybe he didn't lie, but he had omitted the truth that changed everything. "You were playing with me! You're a maniac. Did you have fun watching me make a fool of myself and confiding in you? I can't believe this."

I wanted to smash everything. Ajax was the same man who'd painted me. He'd been the one watching me on the bridge that night. He'd witnessed and immortalized everything. And on top of that, Spectre was the stranger I'd deliberately told my most shameful confessions and fears to.

I was ridiculous, and the spark of hope he had created that night turned into gunpowder.

"Aurore." He tried to hold out his hand to reach mine, but I stepped back. "I couldn't tell you who I was. I'm sure you're aware of the risks. I'm taking one at this moment, with you."

"So you decided to play with me? Bringing me to one of those art events to test me? Make fun of me?" Betrayal burnt my throat. "And what about coming across the bridge? Another joke of yours? You're a sick psychopath! Was it all a scheme because I reached out to you?"

"No, I wanted you here with me. Meeting you was a coincidence, and—" He swallowed harshly. "It was to show you that not everything will end up the same way. That it can look alike but be completely different. It was to help you to—"

"Don't say another word to me!" I gritted out, accusing him with my finger. "You lied. You and your money can live in peace. You won't buy me." I searched my surroundings, on the verge of throwing the nearest object at him, but all I could find were those fucking blooms. "Why me? You want to paint me again because I'm such a mess to you?"

"No," he said simply in the midst of the few seconds of silence I gave him. "That night, you had known me for me, not for..." He lowered his voice. "Spectre. Am I such a bad guy to show you who I am behind the mask so you'd give me a fair chance before hating me?"

"You don't deserve a chance, Aja—Spectre."

"Let's go inside so we can talk and—"

"The great Spectre is used to having everything he wants, right?" I hissed.

He dragged his eyes to the old grandmother taking a sun bath on her rooftop balcony very far away. I had to squint to notice her. No doubt she couldn't see us.

"I would appreciate it if you didn't shout my name for everyone to hear," Spectre gritted between clenched teeth.

He meant everyone, but the beach facing his house was private, and the neighbors were almost vacant. That jerk had probably never lived in an apartment, where you hear what your neighbors are watching and their daily fighting.

"Right, because you protect your privacy with an NDA but not the privacy of others. How selfish of you." I narrowed my stare at him and walked back to the gardens to get the hell out of there.

"Aurore, I know that you're mad, but you have to stop insulting me."

Spectre followed after me, and in the middle of the garden, I turned around and waved my hands sharply, on the verge of knocking a bee on the way to forage the flowers. "Why, Spectre? Because it hurts your feelings? Oh, wait, you probably don't have any, judging by—"

Crap.

Water washed over us, splashing us, and in a moment, we were soaked from head to toe. The automatic watering had started. With my hands, I removed the water obscuring my view and couldn't be more thankful my black liner was waterproof.

"This is just my luck." Did I forget to add that my crop top was white and my bra blue? At this point, I might as well hand myself over to the white sharks.

"Let's go inside to dry," he offered in his aloof tone, keeping his composure as if we weren't still standing like two idiots in the middle of the water jets. He should have been as ridiculous as me, but his attitude didn't scream embarrassment like mine.

"No, I'll dry by the sun." Or the lack of it. Either way, I didn't want to give him nor the water the right to wash away my fire.

"Aurore." And here was my name escaping from his lips like a hot, desperate moan. "I know you like getting wet."

Damn it, he remembered our awkward talk.

"But I'm offering you a chance to get dry and to dirty up my neat house all you want, and something tells me you'd like that very much. There is free food."

He had a point. Two points. The driver was gone, and I was trapped in this hell with him for probably an hour meeting or so.

I jutted my chin up and, out of solutions, admitted, "Fine, but you let the devil enter your home, don't be surprised by the result. That does not mean, in any case, that I accept the contract. I need answers."

Once his front door was open, I detected white stone statues by the long corridor of the entrance. The inside of his house was empty, with a few boxes on the side as if he was either moving in or out. The huge white walls and large bay windows let the sunlight enter. It was stripped down to a minimum with only the necessary furniture.

The marble floor was covered with a glossy varnish, and I stared at my muddy shoes. "Do you have a cleaning lady?"

"No." Spectre delivered from behind me the answer I was waiting for.

"Good." I entered his mansion with my shoes on, making a mess—a thing I would usually never, ever do, but my nerves were pissed.

Spectre's curious gaze fell on me. "You'd have to do way more than that if you want to spark my temper. If nothing else, this is nothing but amusing to me."

I thinned my lips, and to that, he scowled.

CHAPTER 8

Ajax

If eyes could kill, Aurore's would murder the ebony black shirt I was holding.

Her fingers tapped impatiently on the corner of the beige sofa she was seated on, and her legs were crossed together in hostility.

"What's in your hand?" Her brow rose slightly. "You really thought I'd wear your shirt?"

Obviously not. Her accepting my hair dryer and a towel was already unexpected. I readjusted the cuffs of the ink-black shirt I switched into after the sprinkler incident and sat across from her on the chair.

"No, I thought you'd be pleased to ruin it into pieces. It's by far my favorite." I demonstrated the same sarcasm as hers.

"By all means, then, I'll take it." She leaned forward, grasped the unlucky shirt in question, and observed it with disdain. "It's nothing special. It's black, like the one you're wearing. I bet you're the kind of control freak who sorts his shirts by color in his closet?"

"By shades, you mean. From raven black to white ivory." Always in the same order.

She squinted her eyes at me as if I were the Collatz conjecture before focusing on the toasts on the transparent coffee table—one of the only pieces of furniture left in this place.

"It's the same toast as the gallery opening I went to with *Ajax*."

She meant me, yet I believed she was referring to someone else. Someone worthy of her memory.

"You liked them." I hooked a foot around my knee and prepared myself for her new flood of speech that should come in one, two—

"*The Sad Girl*," she dropped, resisting the food with a new will that surprised me. "You were one of Bernard Dupont-Brillac's students seven years ago. That's where you saw me. At Les Beaux Arts, where I was posing as a muse."

She linked her slender fingers together.

"Yes." It was never my intention to lie to her. I was on her side; she just didn't know it yet.

"I don't understand." She shook her head, her voice breaking ever so slightly. "I never saw you at the classes."

"You don't remember" was the only clue I could give to her.

For three weeks, I had seen only her and the long dresses she wore for the class.

And she never glanced in my direction.

She was part of my canvas, but I was the outsider, painting the artwork.

"It doesn't matter. And then you followed me that day on the bridge for what? Impressing your artist friends that the weird girl was crying?" I let her assume that. "Don't tell me that Augustus sent you that evening as some kind of sick joke!"

Augustus. That despicable human. "A sick joke?"

"Yeah, the one who broke up with me the day after my life fell apart because he was in love with all-too-perfect Violette."

I snapped my brows. She seemed pissed.

"That day you so kindly illustrated for the world to witness," she finished spitting her venom. "Anyway, I searched for your family name, Clemonte. No wonder you had to struggle in a chateau in the middle of France."

She didn't know what she was talking about.

"You want me to apologize for being born into the Clemonte family?" I remained calm, not having any desire to expose any part of those years.

"You're right," she mused. "I shouldn't have said that. That was off topic and pretty much insensitive."

"Was that an apology?"

She fired her eyes at me. "You're the one owing me countless apologies. Don't you dare hope for one, or you'll die waiting for it."

"As I told you, I can be very patient, and I don't have a problem apologizing about hiding my identity from you."

"I need to know why you painted me. Why me?"

I cracked my knuckles. "On the bridge, you seemed tempestuous and soulful—"

"No, I was heartbroken and sad, Spectre. And on top of that, you're making fun of my misery with over-the-top words."

I couldn't perceive what I had said so offensively. It was the truth—why would she believe I was making fun of her?

The world was blank in grayish monotone colors. Uninspired.

But she was life. The incarnation of it. A rainbow of emotions.

"You have succeeded in externalizing emotions that some people are unable to get out." I thought this through. "And I knew that such pure and vulnerable emotion would touch the world. I didn't paint your weakness but your strength."

Her chin shook, but she remained proud, as if a block of ice was keeping the torrent locked inside her. "Why am I truly here? You want to impress me with luxury so I would accept your contract?"

"You said you wanted to be by the ocean."

Her eyes doubled in size. "I don't understand."

"To be inspired," I added. "You said you wanted to be by the beach. This is my place of work. I want to show you my studio, and I hoped for you to be inspired since you're lacking it."

"Way to rub it in my face." She chewed on the inside of her inner cheek. "You're certainly not on the highlight of your blossoming yet short career. Have you read what every newspaper says about you?"

"I don't stoop to paying attention to criticism. Especially the nonconstructive ones."

"You can't pretend this doesn't hurt you," she affirmed as if she could feel for me what I didn't. She then rose up, crossing her arms. "Show me that studio of yours, then, even if I bet it's empty judging by the fact you haven't been able to paint anything in six months."

So, she'd spied on me.

She probably found some flattering articles announcing the end of my career if I didn't reinvent myself with something brand-new. My old art pieces were defined as "déjà vu" and too macabre for the audience. And now, I had become even more ghastly than usual, unable to produce anything that would see the light of day.

"Follow me."

Not that I gave her a choice when I stomped to the end of the corridor and unlocked the door leading to my studio, my hand nevertheless remaining nailed to the handle as if I was forced to bring a monster into my home.

I knew it'd be a terrible idea from the moment my brain tried to mix shades to reproduce the exact color of her lips. It'd have taken me easily an hour at most if my brain cells in question hadn't been hypnotized by guessing the taste of them, leaving me with a growing frustration between my legs. The contact of her subtle touch had left my skin tingling for several days. If she were to enter my studio, she would stay here. At least, the memory of her would. An idea that I couldn't tell if it was pleasant or not.

"What are you doing?" She was frowning heavily. "It's like you've seen a ghost that doesn't want to leave you in peace."

"Well, maybe that's exactly it." Except for the fact she wasn't a ghost, and I needed her.

"Great. Looks like the ghost and I are gonna be great friends."
She pushed the door open and crept into my atelier.

Here we go.

"Okay, this is enormous. How many easels do you need? You have
like ten of them? I see broken canvases, tables like those of architects
with rough, unfinished sketches. It'd honestly look like a worksite if
it weren't for the large windows—" She burst into a laugh out of nowhere. "It's a mess. Who would have thought you were messy? I took
you for an android incapable of emotions."

My Adam's apple bobbed as she stepped into the middle of my
"mess," as she had described.

Her stare was locked on the paintings hooked on the walls. "*The
Sad Girl* isn't here."

"She's still in an exhibit." And I wouldn't risk bringing Aurore face-
to-face with my painting, or she'd burn it into ashes, my career with it.

She did not go further on the subject. "You read my conditions?"

"Yes. You'll have the power of decision, and no—" My eyes traveled to her, a nerve working my jaw at the sole thought of—"nudity."

Her nudity, to be exact. A very disturbing thought that would
probably reduce my sleeping schedule for the upcoming weeks.

"Right." She gulped and drifted her eyes toward my artworks in
progress. "Everything you've done lately is pretty morose and dark,
might I add."

Her eyes landed on the portrait of a man I'd painted with a liner
brush. Like in all of my paintings, except for *The Sad Girl*, his identity wasn't perceptible. Most of the time, it was by a game of contrast,
but this time, his eyes and forehead were hidden by messy lines. Tears
leaked, and a silent roar escaped his lips. Only one of his bleeding fists
was visible, hitting an invisible enemy. Maybe she was right.

"You don't like it?" As if her feedback had any importance to me.
I shouldn't care. I didn't care. I wouldn't care.

"It's unsettling." She focused on the artwork by squinting her eyes.
"It's like when you're angry and want to scream all your guts out, but
you just remain silent in an argument because you know it's pointless.

The lines form some clouds, circling as if his brain is exploding by a flux of emotions, eating the man alive. It's like a void. Emptiness." She blinked away, becoming her stormy self again. "But that's not the point. It's still morose and even morbid."

Morose. Morbid. All of those words were negative.

"That's why you're here, to brighten up and fill my days with that sunshine temperament of yours." I demonstrated the same sarcasm as her.

"Your days?" Her loud voice echoed across the room. "How long will it take to make one painting exactly?"

"As long as it's needed, and I never implied it would be a painting. I'd probably only sketch you. It'd be faster and more veritable." My shadow blanketed her as I loomed over her. "I want you as my muse. I have a deadline in a month, so we have a month. We may finish early if you inspire me."

"If I inspire you?" she screamed. "Have you seen me? I'm trying to be the complete opposite of that nightmare you're painting! If you expect me to cry again, I—"

"I don't. I need you because you're the—" I searched for the right words. "You're the strict opposite of me. I've been given an opportunity with a deadline, but for that, I need to paint something 'happier' and more in that hopeful spirit of yours. I need to reinvent myself, as you must have read somewhere."

An opportunity I had been refusing for months despite Eric's complaints until meeting her again.

"Do I look happy to you? I want to murder you, Spectre! I'm not the right flowery person you need!" She waved her hands hysterically. "Plus, from where you stand, you're already pretty much inspired for an exhibition in a haunted castle."

"I need to see the world through you," I said. "My art is declining. If you look closely, half the canvases are broken. I haven't been able to paint anything decent in months, and you are the opposite of transparency and boredom. That's why you're here—to stimulate my creative intellect."

"Creative intellect? That's how you define inspiration? It's not something you can control or a set of skills. It comes from your cold business heart, Ajax." That was the first time she'd called me Ajax. "So, you're telling me I'm stuck with you for up to a month, where you'd be sketching me until your 'creative intellect' decides to cooperate?"

"Yes. I've made a room ready for you. The days we'll work together, you can sleep here so you won't have to travel back and forth. We'll not lose any time, and we'll be able to work in better conditions. I won't have to worry about where you are and what happened to you."

"You, worry? Art is not an army commando." She gestured with her hands, and I sensed the disaster nearing. "Wait a minute!"

She hit the canvas next to her, and thankfully, I was quick enough to save it from its downfall, but my can of paint was not equally lucky and crashed to the floor, tinting my overpriced Richelieu shoe indanthrone blue. My frigid stare hit her, and she minced her way backward. "I didn't do it on purpose, I swear."

"It's fine." One of my shoes was blue. Clownish blue. I looked like an idiot, and the smile curving her lips was living proof of it. She nevertheless continued walking backward, two steps away from colliding with the life-size Greek statue behind her. "Aurore, I'd advise you to be careful, or you'll collide with Icarus."

"Are you speaking in metaphor? I'm not trying to reach the sun and—"

I didn't give her enough time to explode my unfinished sculpture into the ground as I hooked an arm around her waist and made her spiral back against my chest, dodging the disastrous tornado that she was. The smell of her hair, like orange blossom and cashmere wood, intoxicated my nostrils, my heart skipping a beat. The moment she realized she was in my embrace, she parted away, and my fingers tingled with something new. A feeling of awareness, perhaps. It was similar to the one I'd felt on the rooftop when she slipped into my arms. Again.

"Right. It wasn't a metaphor."

"No, it wasn't."

She faced me, a strand of her hair falling in front of her burnt umber and phthalo-green eyes. Her face had perfect symmetry, but there was something different.

I never noticed she had freckles before on her cheeks and on top of her small button nose. She must have been hiding those behind her makeup for a reason I didn't understand. People would pay millions of euros for a piece of canvas speckled with paint—and not one of those paintings compared to her.

I wanted to get to know every freckle of hers.

"Anyway." She rubbed her hands along her body and fixed her gaze on mine, regaining her hostility. "You can't expect me to sleep in your mansion. Us, in the same house, it won't end well, Spectre. I work on the weekends. I still loathe you. I won't make you pancakes in the morning. First, because I don't even know how. Second, because I'll burn them on purpose so you get food poisoning. Instead, I'll be using all your hot water tanks and emptying your fridge. Because when I'm pissed, this is the kind of villainous fairy godmother that I am."

"I have a big water tank." By the way her eyebrows rose, I deduced it was my turn to share the same clumsiness as she with my words. "And you're definitely more menacing than whatever villainous fairy godmother you're referring to. Your room will be seafront, with a private balcony and bathroom. You can have your weekends and days off if you're busy. You won't see me apart from our work agreement unless you want to eat my pancakes because I do know how to make them, and I'm not opposed to sharing if you behave."

"If I were to accept, it'd be only for the money and the fact that a little luxury cannot hurt," she deadpanned. "Especially at your expense."

"Very well, then."

She blazed her eyes at me. "So, let's get this over with. When do we start?"

"You're not in the mood, Aurore." My lips curled in an attempt to look friendlier, which, judging by her frown, made me look indeed scarier. "It's me who chooses when we begin."

She seized the contract out of her bag, took a pen with haste, and signed it in a rush.

"Oh, Spectre." She accompanied the hostile, fake smile plastered on her lips by slamming the piece of paper on my chest. "You're not ready for me. I'll make you regret wanting me as your muse and for having ever painted me. You chose the wrong woman."

As she was striding out of my atelier, I knew she couldn't be more wrong.

I would never regret painting her.

And more importantly, she was the right woman.

"And, Aurore," I called her back. "I'm breaking a rule here. I shouldn't tell you this information about that happy project I need you for, but I'm no liar. I'm the artist selected to collaborate with Ever After for their hundred-year anniversary."

CHAPTER 9

Aurore

"I'm not entitled to say more, but all I can guarantee is that Spectre is the manipulative, frigid, egocentric jerk I always thought he'd be," I said firmly, closing my luggage and slumping on my bed with a deep breath.

I'm the artist selected to collaborate with Ever After for their hundred-year anniversary.

Spectre's words were inked into my brain, the memory of what happened next so vivid. The way I craved to snatch the contract from his hand, to tear it and Spectre into pieces, but I didn't do any of that. I had given him a sly leer, concocting a new plan at top speed, because it was too late to regret divulging to Ajax that night that I was indeed working at Ever After. My ego had taken another stab. This was the true reason he needed me: not because I was a fairy tale or muse material but because I was working there. But my feelings didn't matter; they'd pass and die, just like the ones before.

"Aurore?" Emma called out.

Spectre wanted to use my knowledge. Well, I'd use him, too, to get my happy ending.

So a deal had been made.

I accepted his contract and swallowed my pride in exchange for him delivering my unwritten novel to the director of publication of Ever After by the end of our collab. He accepted without complaints, and I was on the verge of making my impossible mission barely possible.

I had the opportunity, a way in to my fucked plan, and all I needed to do was to write that stupid novel.

"I don't like when you remain silent. It means you're up to no good." Emma joined me on the bed, her eyes brimming with curiosity. "I wish you could tell me what he's like. Is he actually old? Creepy? Tell me just a clue, please!"

"He's—" *Annoyingly handsome at every angle for such an evil soul.* "Okay."

"*Willst du mich verarschen!*" She was offended. "I'm your best friend, and all you can say to me is that he's okay? And is that a blush on your cheeks?"

"No, it's not!" It wasn't a blush. It was rage.

"At least you're forgetting about Ajax."

"You'd be surprised to know how hard he is to be forgotten with his ironed shirts and 'I'm a decent guy' bullshit attitude, with his superior stare that us common mortals should be so blessed to receive." She couldn't understand my sarcasm alongside my high-pitched tone.

My phone rang with a notification from Spectre. Emma knitted her brows in response, probably lost in the midst of my tantrum.

> **The Devil incarnate (skull emoji):** The car is waiting for you.

I decided to ignore his message and threw my phone on the bed.

She was now facing me with her arms folded over her chest in something that would have looked authoritative on everyone else but not on her. "Do I want to ask who the Devil incarnate is, and what was all that with Ajax?"

I gave her a smile that meant *you don't want to go there right now.* "So, anyway, what are you guys doing here in my way-too-small apartment to have three people in?"

Léo came back to us, stopping pretending to be busy on his phone to give us privacy to talk. He hugged Emma from behind, who giggled, which made me instantly roll my eyes at the display of affection. Great, they were contaminating my apartment with their love germs.

"I—I want to ask you for a favor. And I came up with a full plan last night." I didn't like the sound of that nor the look of Emma's glittering eyes. "You remember that my event planning society organizes a charity ball each year?"

"Of course, I do." I snorted. "Like the one you did last year with the bidding auction when the depressive man who was divorced twice couldn't stop speaking to me, and you made me bid for him because you thought he'd cry onstage if no one wanted him. He even tried to kiss me and accused me of slutty temptation because I refused him. What are you—"

Seeing her face twitch and Léo grinning, the realization hit me. "No fucking way!"

"Yes, please!" She gave me puppy eyes. I was a master of that game. She couldn't fool my purple heart. "It will be different this time, I promise. And you did punch him and—"

"He was trying to touch my breast to see if I was the same bra size as his ex!" I inhaled deeply. "I'm not going through this nightmare twice. Singles are at the mercy of psychopaths during this type of event, and I don't have money to bid on yachts and romantic trips for two!"

"But I thought of everything!" she screamed in that little voice of hers. "We're gonna auction five guys and five girls, all respectable people who either work with the association we're raising money for or our department."

"Great, so this year you want me to be auctioned like some kind of object?"

"Kinda." She grimaced, seizing both of my hands. "Someone

pulled out, and I need a replacement, or else my career is ruined. My colleague, the rude one you wanted to hit with a shovel, would gloat at my failure and complain to our boss. Everything has to be perfect because last year it was a nightmare, and you know how much speaking in public already stresses me out." That was a low blow. Emma was vicious. "As my fairy godmother, you need to protect me. Plus, it's for a good cause for children in hospitals. This year, we'll have elite guests. It's so important I don't mess things up."

"Why do you think I'd care about a good cause?" It was my turn to cross my arms across my chest with a deadly stare.

"Because the Aurore I know would."

"Perhaps she's dead, and this Aurore doesn't like the idea."

"It's for children." Emma batted her eyelashes.

I pursed my lips.

"And the person who bets the highest price on you will only win an opportunity to help the cause at your side for one afternoon. It'll all be supervised and secured. Plus, I have a plan to save you." That was her argument. "Please, please, please."

"What did I do to deserve this?" This was going to be a nightmare. "Don't count on me to smile and wave like Miss World. I'll come as Dracula, and I won't smile unless I truly mean it. And there better be food."

"You'll help children who don't have a fairy godmother like I do." She played on my heartstrings.

"You'll end up having a wicked witch if you continue down this road." I fired my eyes at her, knowing I would sell my soul to that good cause because the little angel on my shoulder couldn't say no and leave me in peace. "What's that plan of yours?"

Emma exchanged an accomplice look with her boyfriend. "Léo will bet on you no matter what. This way, you'll not end up with someone weird like the past year. You'll be condemned to absolutely nothing. See, genius, right?"

"Allow me to express doubts about this wobbly rescue." When a prince rescued someone else other than his soulmate, it most of the time ended up badly for the person.

"I promised Emma I would vote for you," Léo said. "We'll not let you down."

How could I say no? All I had to do was to put on a smile and a dress—that wasn't from my collection because I was definitely not ready. "Fine, I'll do it. When is it?"

"In two days. Nine p.m."

"You're kidding me? You're telling me this only now!"

"Thank you so much, Aurore. You're the absolute best." She went in to hug me, and I swallowed the fact I'd be going to a ball.

After this whole apocalyptic mess, I was on my way to meet with Spectre with hatred in my gut to begin our collaboration. During the ride, I went through my unread messages from my family.

> **Luna:** You're going to a ball??? I'm so jealous! You better be dancing with someone.
>
> **Me:** I'd prefer to dance with you.
>
> **Luna:** That wouldn't be so fairy-taleish, right? Wait, Duchess just stepped on my watercolor painting, arghhhh!

Luna was painting now?

I received a text from my mom at the same moment.

> **Mom:** Hello, honey! I hope you're still doing awesome, my bestselling prodigy! Don't forget about your old mom. Ps: Thank you for the payment for Luna's psychologist sessions, but you sent me more than expected? What would I do without your help…

My father never bothered to check in with his daughter, who seven years ago was in the hospital, between life and death. He never took responsibility and let us down—the first time when my mother was pregnant with Luna, and the second when his double life was exposed.

My mom, on the contrary, was living in her own world, one with butterflies and mystical creatures. She occupied herself with activities crazier than the others. It was her own way of coping with the real world. So I had to reply to her as I usually did: pretending that everything was great because she was counting on me.

> **Me:** I am! I'm so busy working that I made more money than usual.

> **Mom:** The creative visualizations I did for you finally worked!! Honey… Could you lend me two hundred euros to make a safe haven for bees? It's for the planet. It'd be nice if you gave back the extra money you made. The karma will thank you.

That was my mom in all her splendor. After all, with the fifty thousand Spectre had already sent me, I would be able to change my life and the lives of the bees apparently too. A win-win for nature and me.

> **Me:** Sure, anything for nature.

> **Mom:** They'll thank you!! I'll send you pictures. Did Luna tell you about the party I planned for her?

She sent me a selfie of her doing a thumbs-up, wearing the new cosmonaut costume she'd bought, I guess to extract the bees' honey. Another notification popped on my phone at the same time.

> **Luna:** So Duchess has rainbow paws now. I need to clean her up. I'll talk to you tonight. xo.

> **Me:** Mom, cancel Luna's birthday party. I'm sending her tickets for Ever After. I'm taking care of everything.

It tore me up to admit it, but Spectre and I had two things in common. One, we were both on a deadline, and two, lacking inspiration. But for Luna, I'd succeed in writing that novel because, in contradiction to him, I had someone to love.

> **Mom:** Really?? She's gonna be so happy!

The car stopped in front of Spectre's mansion. I hurried outside, my suitcase wheels getting stuck in the cobblestones. I lowered the handle and crossed the front door, swinging the suitcase inside to see Spectre staring at me. He was already waiting behind it like a freak. His ironed dress shirt let me peer at his muscles underneath, exposing his Greek warrior body that was contracting in the most destabilizing and annoying way.

"Only one suitcase?" he said, not letting himself be put off by my loud arrival.

"I'm not moving in for eternity." Not that I would mind if he wasn't here. "Plus, in two days, I need to head back to Paris, and that's not negotiable."

"I'll be busy too. Do you need any help?" he offered, glancing at the luggage and to one of the wheels that was squashed on the ground, filled with pebbles.

I immediately tightened my grip on the handle with determination. "So, what do we start with?"

His dark eyes assessed me. "I don't suppose you have in that luggage of yours some clothing that could fit with something rather artistic."

"Only things you'd strongly disapprove of."

"Fine, we're going shopping, then."

"Shopping?" my voice echoed, and I let go of my grip on the handle, my luggage dropping to the ground.

"Yes. For the sketches." He paused. "I won't draw you in just anything. I want a visual. Unless you want to be naked?"

"No." I sucked in a sharp breath, almost coughing on it. "Clothes. I need clothes. What do you have in mind?"

"I'll know when I find it."

"That's quite pretentious," I mumbled. "You just have to tell me who you want me to be and act upon. After all, when I was posing as a muse, I was just a statue."

"I don't want a statue. I want you to be you. Do not hold back."

Why would he want someone like me for Ever After? "But I—"

He prowled toward me. "You can't see yourself like I see you, so please don't argue with me on this."

"I doubt you see me in any positive light though."

I was a means to an end, one he certainly didn't want to need. Just like he was my only way to get me out of the mess I was in—soon without an apartment, currently without a novel, and let's not forget, without contacts in high places and without money. At least I could scoff at those last two items on my list and not worry about the first since I'd be heading back to the middle of nowhere after being graciously expelled from the big city. All I had to focus on was inspiration.

"You'll just have to find out." He passed in front of me, his car keys in one hand. "Let's go. I'm driving."

"And you're also paying for everything." I squinted. "And everything can be a lot."

"If you think that should bother me, you're wrong." He strode to the Aston Martin parked in front of the gate and opened the passenger door for me. "Aurore, you can waste my money all you want. I don't care as long as I obtain what I want. In that case, you, as my muse."

"You're unbearable," I cursed him.

"And you're delicate, an example of rare amiability."

"I'm only a reflection of your warmhearted and welcoming amiability," I attacked, entering his car.

"You and your arsonist personality are about to light up a fire every time you're around me." It was his turn to step inside, warming up the engine. "Your seat belt."

"It may be to thwart you from icing the world." I crossed my arms. "I'm usually a sunny and very nice person." Or, more accurately, I used to be.

"You're atypical." His hands tightened on the steering wheel. "Where did you learn to have that personality?"

"Well, I was raised by my hermit of a mom in the middle of nowhere in the countryside, making up imaginary characters for friends, so I guess that helps."

"I understand better. Can you please put your seat belt on?"

I snapped my eyes to him menacingly. "You understand what better? That I'm a peasant to you?"

"No." He cleared his throat. "It makes sense why you're so free and you. You do come out from a fairyland, after all. I envy you."

"Yeah, right." I shook my head. "Anyway, are we gonna leave this parking spot someday soon or wait for the car to magically transport us to the destination?"

"I'm waiting for you to put your seat belt on. Safety first."

The seat belt. Right. I did as he asked. "Better?"

"Yes." He thinned his lips. "My fairy."

He revved up the engine, that smug, thin line still plastered on his face. Was it Spectre's attempt at making a joke?

"I'm not a fairy and certainly not yours," I deadpanned.

"There are different types of fairies, right? From the pixies to the banshees. I'll let you guess which one I was referring to you about."

He sped up across the road, and I smiled. Well played.

"There is no way I'm wearing this!" I called out through the changing room, watching my reflection in the mirror.

This was my sixth try-on. To the first four, Spectre had remained like marble, sitting on the girly visitors' couch. As I showed him the outfits like a brooding catwalk model, he had addressed me with just one head nod. One head nod that meant no way in hell. He didn't like, or most likely tolerate, anything. Was that surprising? Coming from a man with impossible standards and a control freak attitude, not so much. At the fifth one, he had given me just one dismissive sign of his hand. Even the saleswomen were terrified of him, not daring to offer him any kind of help.

And right now, I was the one chickening out.

I was wearing a long dress in a rainbow of colors from crimson red to dark purple, passing by a shimmering red and a soft pink at the bottom. It was enchanting. The neckline was plunging. The lace fell on my shoulders with golden ornaments, giving it a romantic and somehow dark vibe with the austere shoulder pads. Tight at the waist, the fabric slipped over my rather wide hips, with an open split on my leg—my tan line was visible from it, and I had to pull my panties up so they wouldn't be seen. These were the kind of dresses I could add to my collection. But this one was even worse. It was exactly me, and that's why I feared the meaning behind the dress.

"Are you coming out?" Spectre called out from behind the curtain.

"No."

I heard him rise up from his seat and felt his imposing shadow looming behind the curtain. "Aurore, let me see."

Why did I have a silly passion for ball gowns? Because they made me hope for a life I couldn't have. One that was only meant to be fiction and not reality. Wearing them, I allowed myself to feel like the main character, and the idea that Spectre could read me terrified me. It'd mean he was part of my tale, and a fragment of my heart feared rejection. Perhaps I had impostor syndrome. *Why do I suddenly care?* I snapped my fists the length of my body, inhaling deeply. I wouldn't care about what Spectre thought.

"No, let's try a new one." Something that didn't make my heart beat across my chest like a cloaking bomb.

"If you don't open the curtain, I will," the bastard insisted.

"Don't you dare! I said we—"

He did it anyway, and through the mirrored glass, the heavy weight of his stare fell on me. Panic took possession of my conflicted heart in the shape of hair hissing on my skin. I didn't like the way he was stealing my oxygen. Why on earth was I feeling this way? Spectre didn't impact me. I loathed him. And this was just a dress. Nothing else. No fairy-tale bullshit. Nothing.

His eyes dipped down and lingered on every part of me for seconds that felt like painful hours. Only his pupils were moving, and in that moment, I'd have preferred to be naked. I wouldn't have felt so vulnerable and exposed.

"This is the one. We're taking it." His dry tone didn't display any emotions.

I used to tie symbolic moments to some dresses. With this one, I imagined dreams coming true, castles in ruins, and a second-chance trope. It created a spark of inspiration and hope, and I had no idea if that was actually a good thing.

"It's too see-through and plunging. It's not the one," I made excuses. "I look like a villain."

"Aurore, look at me." The rasp of his voice prickled at my senses, and I braved meeting his eyes through the reflection in the mirror. "If you don't believe you're the main character, I will make you one. You can't hide from me. This dress, it's—"

"Me," I finished in a whisper.

"Perfection," he dropped at the same time.

A mere flash of surprise etched its way across his features. It didn't last long as he concealed it with his throat bobbing and usual aloofness when he said, "I'm going to pay for the dress. Get changed."

He closed the curtain, and I leaned against the mirror wall to take a shaky breath.

I'll make you one.

My heart hadn't beat that much in forever.

Spectre and I had one common point.

His lack of emotions bled through every action he did to the way he dressed and spoke—the precision of his words, the coldness of his gaze, the sharp lines of his black dress shirts. It was as if he was dead inside, but appearances can be deceitful.

I, on the contrary, felt too much, and I didn't know what to do with the surge of emotions that dragged me into the abyss.

And in the end, we were both hiding who we were through our art.

Nonexistent and haunted.

CHAPTER 10

Aurore

Shopping with Spectre was efficient.

Everything was timed. He knew what he wanted, and he wasted no time in getting distracted. He was a man on duty. When I tried to hold him back by asking, "How about that?" he gave me an icy look, followed by, "Take what you want, but in two minutes, it will be too late."

In the end, I made him buy useless things like fridge magnets with a seagull, three cookies because I was starving, and what I was most proud of: a pink teddy for his car.

"There, that's perfect!" I finished hanging it on the rearview mirror, the pink bear swinging from side to side. "It immediately has more style."

"It's horrible," he said without taking his eyes off the road. "You're aware the moment you're gone from my car, I'll make it go away, right?"

He still wasn't annoyed; I should have got the pink bubbly car seat cover as well. After all, I was the muse, and I planned on install-ing a dictatorship.

"You don't have to be so grumpy about everything. We have your dress and all the things you need to the point I bet everyone thought we were prepping for a parade."

"Maybe if you hadn't stopped at every aisle and held out ridic-ulous things to annoy me, we would have avoided stares. But you, Aurore, are a show all to yourself." He pressed on the accelerator, overtaking the lazy drivers.

"At least I'm a sunny spectacle, not a robocop on duty. Do you ever smile, Spectre?" I gave him a beaming smile full of sarcasm that would warm even his frigid heart.

"Occasionally." He put on his blinker. "And you, Aurore, do you sometimes let your guard down, or is 'attack' the only word in your vocabulary?"

"You have the talent to attract all the most negative aspects of my personality. It's as if all my flaws come together in a group meeting just for you while my qualities are taking a sabbatical." I inched forward to retrieve my phone, which I had clumsily dropped. "Shit, where is—"

The car came to a halt, and I felt myself rock forward, but I was held back firmly by Spectre's arm, which kept me glued to my seat. A car cut us off, running through a red light. My heart was stuck in my throat, hammering at full speed, grateful I didn't crash into the window. Spectre's arm was immobile and rigid like a shield, his eyes firmly set on the road.

"Be more careful."

As if it was my fault people had murderous urges.

He retrieved his hand before I could thank him. Not that I would. I had a seat belt. He didn't need to show off his strength nor make my stomach knot with the fact that perhaps Spectre could care.

We were exiting the small town of Honfleur, pedestrians flock-ing to the picturesque streets. On my right, a crowd was concentrated around a tree inside a park. Small multicolored papers were stuck on its trunk. People were depositing some others inside, and my interest was piqued. A wooden sign was suspended above the tree, where it was written, The Wishing Tree. *As if it were that easy.*

Old me would have wanted to get out of the Aston Martin and head for its colors, except Spectre sped away from the place, continuing on the road leading to the beach. He took a right, and we somehow reached the park entrance from the back. He pulled over, and I widened my eyes at him.

"You wanted to go, right?" He unbuckled his seat belt, and I was sure my mouth was hanging open like a carp. "You remained silent, and I know you're always carrying papers and pens."

He exited his car, and I couldn't be more shocked. I didn't waste the opportunity and followed after him in the midst of a group of children, and teenagers recording a TikTok, until we arrived in front of The Wishing Tree. It was majestic. On the plaque next to it, it explained the belief that once upon a time, lovers were reunited by the tree after the Second World War. She had written him love letters that she had secured inside the holes of the tree trunk, hoping he'd come back to her, and he did.

My novelist heart contracted, touched by the story. Another happy ending. My grip tightened on my bag, a simple wave of hope surging through my veins. I used to be a sucker for things like this, so I didn't hesitate. I went against my defensive self and tore off a sheet of paper, which I handed to Spectre, who had his hands in his pockets and gave me a puzzled look.

"It's for you. To make a wish," I insisted.

"I don't believe in those things," he dared. "But I'm surprised you're offering and want whatever dream I have to come true."

"I'm not evil, Spectre. I'm not going to deprive you of that. Plus, I know you secretly want to do this, but you're afraid this would hurt your cold-as-stone reputation—which you already protected with that NDA of yours, so now, accept before I regret my gesture." When he was about to grab the paper, I retracted it. "And this better not be something shady or negative. I didn't wave the white flag."

He took the paper and the pen that I handed him and froze for a moment, carrying them as if they were unknown objects to him. He was an artist. Surely, he knew what to do with them.

"This is just paper. Don't look at me like that." My throat went dry, and my skin bristled. It was time to break our eye contact. "Well, I'll step aside to do mine. I'll leave you to it. I have a second pen."

I squatted on the ground away from the crowd and fluttered my eyelids closed as if I was about to do a sacred ritual to get closer to my deepest wish. I smiled, projecting what my life could have been: writing in my long-sleeved feather black robe with a beach view from my mansion before going on a book tour. Visiting castles with Luna. Dancing with my one true love. And for just a second, I eclipsed reality, and I believed I was worthy of being the hero of the tale.

I wish to be who I used to be, to make my life a fairy tale, and for Luna to have everything her heart wants.

I couldn't be short, so the tree would hopefully understand the vibe of my dream. I lifted my eyes to Spectre, who was standing erect and, to my grand surprise, focused on whatever he was writing with dedication.

Look at him, being invested in a childish activity.

The scene almost stretched out my smile, but when his eyes captured me and his pen strokes quickened, I dropped it. Was he drawing me? I tucked my paper inside my hand and rose up to face the tree.

I didn't have to turn around to feel Spectre stalking toward me— maybe I recognized him by his scent as if he was just out of the shower on a crisp spring day, or I had developed a warning radar at his approach, my whole body rebelling for an inexplicable reason.

"Did you make a wish?" I turned to face him, still undecided about where I would put my paper.

"You could say that in a way." He folded his paper carefully before tucking it inside his pants pocket.

"You didn't." I narrowed my eyes. "And you're supposed to hand the paper over to the tree."

He crossed his arms, and I swore a light smug, satisfied expression crossed his features, unless it was a product of my imagination. Either way, I wanted to erase it.

"You were drawing." I faced back to the tree trunk, wondering what would be the best way to climb it. "The tree inspired you, huh?"

"I drew you."

"Me?" My eyes widened. "But it's been a second!"

"For once, you didn't have this barrier. You seemed free for a moment."

"But you didn't make a wish!" I stood on my tiptoes, trying to reach a hole. "Damn it, I'm too short."

"Do you need my help?" he drawled, his voice smooth with a rough edge. "I could carry you on my shoulders."

I considered it for a moment. But no way in hell. Climbing on the back of an ogre was much more preferable and far less dangerous. I didn't give him the pleasure of replying and climbed the trunk, leaning on the first branch to reach the same height as him.

"I want to be like them! Me too, I want to go there," a little girl screamed with excitement, and I wondered what made her think it was a good idea.

The mom next to her, who was way shorter than I, kneeled in front of her daughter. "It's not possible, darling. I'm not tall enough."

Just when I was thinking about offering to climb my way up with her wish paper in my hand and calculating the possibility of it, the cold and ruthless Spectre appeared in my vision, carrying the child to the top. She locked her paper in *my* tree hole with the brightest smile, trusting him way more than she should.

As for me, I remained glued to the tree like a koala—and not the most agile.

"See, Mommy, the strong man helped me fly." The girl ran to her mother's arms when he made her reach the floor safely.

Spectre and I locked eyes, and I bet behind his aloof attitude, he was grinning inside.

"You're welcome," he said with nonchalance, mother and daughter already heading to the next activity.

As for me, I resigned myself to putting my paper where I could reach it: at the bottom with everyone else.

"I'm guessing if I were to ask you again if you need help, you'd tell me to fuck off?" This was addressed to me.

"You'd think right." I succeeded and descended from the tree. I could hardly believe that I got there without falling in the dust and making a mess of myself. "See, I didn't need you. By the way, do you work out, or is it natural?"

I had said that. I did. I should think, then speak, not the opposite, and no holes were big enough for me to plummet under right now.

"I do," he confirmed what I already knew. "I used to play soccer before."

I hoped my poker face didn't transmit the fact that I had looked him up online much more than an emotionally well-balanced human would. "Why did you stop? Was it an injury?"

"A lack of passion."

"Oh, that must have been a hard decision." Spectre was an enigma: he had literally everything everyone would have dreamed of, yet he was hiding behind an identity. "When buying a book, I used to scroll to the ending to know if it had a happy ending, and if it didn't, I used to change it and—" *Change the subject now.* "Luna always told me I have a pretty wild imagination. When I was young, we didn't have money to go anywhere, so I dreamed instead."

"And sometimes people with money stay in their comfort and stop living. They're enslaving themselves."

My interest was piqued. "Is this what happened to you? Why you became… you know?"

"I'll wait for you by the car. We're done for today." And just like that, he was gone.

I ripped out another paper with the desire to immortalize the feeling burning in my heart and the mystery that was Spectre. So it was with my soul that I wrote:

It's only deep in the catacombs of your heart that a wish resides, and that's where we can read one's soul.

CHAPTER 11

Aurore

I woke up this morning with a stab in my heart because today was the day Spectre was sketching me.

The idea of getting buried under the blankets was tempting, the satin sheets smelling of tuberose and jasmine. Everything in Spectre's guest bedroom was cleaner than a five-star hotel and meticulously organized, despite the huge computer cable hanging from one side of the room to the other, but that was mine. I didn't have the displeasure of meeting with him after we came back from shopping yesterday, but judging by the noises coming from downstairs, I deduced he was either busy painting or doing some super-rigid activity in that messy studio of his.

For some reason, my legs led me to the kitchen in search of comfort, because last night I decided to play the polite card and pretend that I wasn't hungry so as not to meet again with my icy roommate.

And I wasn't ready for this.

Any of this.

"Aurore." *Not even a good morning, how did you sleep?* Just "Aurore," as if my presence behind him was something he'd rather dismiss.

"Spectre." I followed his lead, my nostrils flaring at the smell of pancakes.

My attention shifted to the colossal lunch, with a variety of jams, chocolates, and fruits. And if that wasn't enough, Spectre turned around, two glasses of freshly made smoothies in his hands.

My eyes doubled in size. I must have jumped into a parallel dreamy universe. He was shirtless, depicting ripped muscles and abs of iron without shame. Greek warrior indeed. He was annoyingly attractive. I wasn't used to being attracted that easily to a man, but with him, it was like I'd been carried away like a dead leaf in a tornado.

He had the kind of charisma that made me want to be held in his arms, which was unnerving. I didn't like to be held. Why on earth was I burning? Maybe it wasn't a hormonal attraction but the idea of him being more vulnerable without his layers of fancy clothes.

"Is there something wrong?" Displaying one of his doubtful frowns, I couldn't be more thankful that he didn't have a clue of what was going through my mind.

"No, everything's impeccable. Optimal." *Optimal?* Now he must be certain something was indeed wrong.

"You were staring." He didn't let me go that easily.

"Well, you'll be staring at me for the next couple of hours. I think that's worth the little glance I shoot you." I was proud of myself for my remaining repartee.

"You're right." He placed the smoothies on the counter, taking two plates out of the cupboard. "But there's one main difference. You probably find me repulsive, judging by your hatred for me, while I do not."

"I—" *Could he really think that?* "I do not find you repulsive."

I snapped my mouth shut before I revealed more than I should.

"Breakfast is ready." He handed me a plate so I'd sit on the opposite side of the counter to face him.

"I'm not hungry. I can eat after you, and—"

"Sit, Aurore." This was an order. "You squint at the food. You're hungry. You need to eat."

"Did you make that for me?" I asked, my throat drying up.

"I made breakfast. It's not a wedding proposal. It's nothing. Just a part of our *contract*. Now, please, would you sit."

I complied and sat in front of him, trying to make myself as small as possible on the chair.

I drank the smoothie, and on the first bite of the pancake I mixed with half the jar of chocolate, I came to a dangerous conclusion. This was the most erotic thing I'd ever eaten and felt in a while. "It pains me to admit it, but you're a good cook. It's delicious."

"I'm good at other things too."

I swallowed a huge piece of pancake that went the wrong way.

"Other things?" I repeated.

His eyes roamed over me, stopping on my lips. "Yes."

"So." I switched the subject, snapping my hands on the counter before my heart decided to explode like a ticking bomb. "Where did you want to get inspired?"

"At my atelier."

"So you never paint anywhere else than your atelier?" I took another bite. "Before, I used to write outside so I'd get inspired by switching scenery. But now, I can't because my computer battery is dead. You should try. I think it'd help."

That was my first advice as an official muse. One he didn't seem eager to follow.

"I like when things are organized, peaceful, and prepared. Plus, I wouldn't want people to stop and look at my work and disturb me with unsolicited questions."

"And let me guess, you also have a very strict routine for each day?"

"I do," he said. "I have an hour-by-hour plan and objectives."

"And that's probably why you're uninspired. Your whole process is boring," I dropped in a half laugh. "It's too academic to be in a studio, posing like a store mannequin while watching the clock ticking.

We'll go to the beach today. It's deserted, and the sun brings vitamin D." A thing Spectre would certainly need since he had skin as white as Dracula, and according to my mom, the sun also brought positivity and good energy, so here's hoping.

"I won't draw on the beach." He refuted the idea immediately.

"I'm here to break your stoic routine, and you have already seen the carnage of which I was capable in your workshop." I rose up from my seat, done with my breakfast and determined to get the both of us inspired.

He cleared the dishes, and with lethal calm, he said with burgeoning irritation, "You can't be serious."

He was obviously against it; that's why I was so eager to make it happen. "I'm very serious. Please."

One second passed. Then another. And it was then the silence became heavy. I had to accept defeat.

"I'll accept if it makes you more comfortable." His voice held me in place. "But next time, I'll be the one in control."

"Yes, Spectre." I raised a brow. "I suppose I need to wear yesterday's dress?"

"There is no need for it now."

I hated the way his eyes bored into mine with intensity, and the melody of the pounding in my heart.

I jutted my chin up. "No need?"

"I've already memorized it on you from every angle in the fitting room."

That sent a shoot of steam alongside my belly, and I exhaled deeply, ignoring his comment. This was his job. Not that he ever looked at me that way. "Why did you buy it, then? Why not just sketch me while I wear it?"

"Because it fits you. You should own it," he said casually. For another person, it'd be a compliment, but coming from Spectre, it was like a cold shower or something devoid of feelings.

"I—" I stammered, gesturing to the stairs. "I'll wear something of mine."

"We'll start in half an hour."

I hurried up to my bedroom, getting over this tension as quickly as possible. I shut the door behind me, making a mess of my luggage to find a white crop top with purple tulips and a black slip skirt. I selected a ribbon of the same color for my hair.

"Things you don't have to do to create a good story," I mumbled, hoping to find my old self back.

Half an hour later, I came downstairs, where Spectre was already waiting for me with an iron-gray dress shirt rolled up on his forearms and gray trousers that were way too sophisticated for the beach. His hands were in his pockets, and under his armpits, he carried a small leather briefcase that probably hid his sketches and pencils.

We remained analyzing each other, probably brainstorming how different we were. We didn't even look like we came from the same century.

"I packed sunscreen." I showed him said sunscreen just in case he didn't know what sunscreen looked like. *How idiotic of me.*

He nodded, and in silence, we crossed a little path beneath his house that led to the empty beach. The first moment I grazed the sand, I stepped out of my shoes to feel its friction below my feet. I faced him, my back against the calm sea, a light breeze wafting up my hair backward. "You don't sit?"

He opened his suitcase, preparing his paper. "You expect me to sit on the sand?"

"It's sand, not acid. Plus, you won't draw anything like that."

His Adam's apple bobbed, and he sat straight on the sand despite himself. His pencil between his fingers, he annotated something and brought his hand up to his chin, gazing at me.

"So, inspire me," the arrogant man had the audacity to say.

"What?" My voice pitched. "Just like that?"

"We're at the beach. I'm sitting like an idiot. It's your turn to do your part."

I chuckled darkly, craving to smash his face with the nearest pebble. "So you expect me to just do a cartwheel and do crazy stuff until it hopefully sparks something in your stone heart?"

"Indeed." A thin line drew on his lips as he tapped his pencil against his sketchbook. "I could direct you, but you won't trust me yet. I'm letting you do this your way."

"I'm not a clown, Spectre!"

"No, you're my muse."

I balled my fist, wondering how good it'd feel to throw sand at him. "And don't you dare sketch my temper! This is not what—"

I stopped, my eyes widening at the show in front of me. A seagull had landed on Spectre's shoulder. Spectre, who was as tense as ever.

"Oh my god! I can't believe this!" I brought my hand to my mouth, trying not to laugh out loud.

"Get this seagull off my shoulder," he threatened with clenched teeth.

"Are you scared of them? I'd have never thought that'd be the great Spectre's fear." My laugh sparked to life. "I think she likes you."

"Aurore," he warned again.

"I'm sorry, this is too good. I need to—" I searched for my phone. "Wait, where is it? Please, don't move!"

"Don't you dare take a picture."

The seagull didn't agree, and her high-pitched squeals and predatory swoops vibrated for the furthest crab on the beach to hear.

I finally found my phone and snapped a picture of Spectre giving me the deadliest look. "Here, beautiful!"

"You're blessed with excellent ideas, Aurore, truly," he deadpanned, lifting his shoulder to chase the seagull away. She didn't move, so he used his other hand, but the stubborn seagull still didn't move an inch.

I squatted in front of them. "Who knew you were an animal lover? You look like a pirate."

"I don't want to hurt her," he gritted out. "So please, get her the fuck off my shoulder."

"Fine, I'll help you out." I approached the animal, using the cutest voice I could think of. "Hey, cutie, you're scaring the big man in front of you and—"

The gull screamed and flew in my direction as if she was about to attack me because I was separating her from her new lover. I fell on my back, losing my balance, and it was my turn to scream. I protected myself with my arms, and I closed my eyes shut. *That jealous bird.*

"Aurore."

Opening only one of my eyes to see through my arms' protection barrier, I wrinkled my nose and took notice of Aja—*Spectre*—on top of me, hiding the ray of sun piercing behind him and shielding me from that psychopathic creature.

"What are you doing?" I furrowed my brows. "Did you jump to protect me or something?"

"No," he immediately replied, pulling himself together by standing up. *He did. He actually did.* "Your rescue was a failure."

The bird had flown away in the sky, sand was in my hair, and I realized how ridiculous this whole situation was. "It really was, huh?"

I had the first unstoppable laugh in a long time, unable to stop myself as he retook his sitting position with a small grimace. I got to my feet, dusted myself off, and turned in circles before I brushed my hair to remove the particles of sand.

Spectre had his eyes on me, and this time, his stare didn't make me want to flee like a story you want no one else to read. He was already starting to draw, his hand having a mind of its own.

"You're drawing?"

"Yes. What you're doing is—" Lines were drawn on his paper, and something in his eyes had changed. He was inhabited. "Acceptable."

I began to walk like a tightrope on an invisible line and mused, "You see, my methods are efficient."

"Your methods are uncomfortable."

"You know what's uncomfortable? Hiking for five hours straight just because it led to a valley of four-leaf clover because your sister asked you for one for Christmas," I countered. "I embarked on a fantastic epic quest."

"Did you find that four-leaf clover?"

"Oh, I did," I said with pride. "But once I got home, it was all crushed and dead in my hand. I cried for a week. She was the one who offered me one in the end, right before I left for Paris. She stuck it on one of my journals for good luck. Did you ever get one?"

His eyes didn't leave his sketchbook. "Once."

"The child in you must have been happy, or were you as frigid as you are now?" I found myself joking.

"I wasn't a child. My father kept us too busy with schoolwork to go on such meaningless activities."

"That's sad," I dropped. "It's not meaningless."

"Why is it sad?" The eye contact was the most intimate connection we could have with another person, and he was trying to pierce through me again, sketching my every movement at a frenetic pace.

"Because everyone deserves to have a clover. Even you. Did you search long for the one you got?" I tucked a strand of my hair behind my ear.

"It was offered."

Of course, him searching for a clover somehow didn't make sense. "I bet you were the genius kid busy with fancy painting classes all day long and—"

"Do what you just did with your hair again."

I wet my lips, playing with my hair once more. I lost myself in the abyss of his eyes, his glance empowering me, and somehow, my heart calmed down. Shivers spread on my skin, and I studied Spectre's features. From the knit of his brows when he wanted to get something right, to the slightest tilt of a corner of his lips, to the way he squinted his eyes to capture every detail.

"No. My father tore up my drawings as soon as he saw that I was enjoying them. It was a waste of time. I learned late, taking lessons with Dupont-Brillac."

There was more to Spectre's backstory. One I shouldn't and wouldn't be interested in.

His attention dropped to my neck and my hair, and it felt like phantom kisses on my skin. My belly coiled. His stare was switching between me and the paper, a battle working inside his eyes as if hundreds of emotions were submerging him. His pencil strokes became much more fierce and imposing, like a sort of trance, and everything accelerated.

He had this look. A haunted one. As if he wasn't a master of his fate any longer, as if he was battling something inside of him that was tearing him apart behind his mask of indifference.

And at one point, he put down his pencil and closed his sketchbook, shutting off the emotions building within him. "We're done for today. We'll continue in the morning."

"Right." Tomorrow afternoon, I had to go to a ball and get auctioned off, and I couldn't be less excited about it, but at least anything else was better than staying here, Spectre stealing my breath and my common sense. "I'll stay by the beach a bit longer."

He walked away, tensing his hand, and I let myself fall on the sand. I'd let my vulnerability drop, and that wouldn't happen again. "You hate him, remember, Aurore."

CHAPTER 12

Aurore

"You're entirely mine." My fingers flew over my keyboard as I mumbled the words out loud. "You taste like—"

The outlet of my charger came off with a brutal blow, and my computer shut off, my document page being replaced by a black screen.

"No!" I tried hitting all the keys to turn it back on, but it was too late—the incredibly loud fan had become quiet, and the only thing I saw on my black screen was my shocked face, even though I knew this would happen. The price I had to pay for having clumsily unplugged my computer for a second was losing an hour of writing, and even worse, having to face the wrath of my own dragon: daddykink.

This was what I got for having a computer older than seven years.

"You're mean to me, you know that? I'm so screwed!" I cursed, exiting the balcony of the bedroom in defeat. I thought it'd be a good idea to write under the stars and the melody of the sea, but it was mission impossible—I did have a fairly large extension cord though.

I entered my bedroom at Spectre's place—or more like the vast display of beige and white—and texted my boss, my hands tightening on the screen. It was exhausting to be a ghostwriter. I needed the money, but now that I had it, nothing was holding me back from quitting that job. Nothing except the already signed contracts for stories I had to finish for daddykink because I was not the type to quit halfway, especially not with a lack of inspiration escaping like a dandelion with the wind. I had to be patient. A thing I wasn't any good at.

I had a request for a new follower on social media.

"She didn't!" My mother had created an Instagram account, where she had already shared twenty pictures of her safe haven for bees. She was posing with her thumb up in each of her selfies. She had only one follower, my sister, who had added a profile picture of hers on social media for the first time.

I immediately liked it, only to notice the commentary of a teenager named Ryan, who quoted a gothic poem. My brow lifted as if I was drawing my sword, ready to attack my opponent.

> **Me:** You look gorgeous and… Who's that Ryan?

> **Luna:** He's a boy I met at the psychologist… I like him. We've been talking every day lately.

My heart thundered across my chest. Ryan was a teenage boy, dark hair with a bad boyish vibe, judging by his profile picture, but his account was private.

> **Me:** Why was he there? Be careful.

> **Luna:** Here we go again with the doubtful questions. I knew it. That's why I didn't want to tell you about him.

> **Me:** I'm just being cautious, Luna. He's a stranger and you went through a lot already.

I was ready to endorse the role of the bad guy to protect her. I didn't care if she hated me; I wouldn't let the story repeat itself twice. I wasn't there when she needed me the most. That wouldn't ever happen again.

Luna: He went through more than me, and life at home isn't even better for him. He's the only one who can understand me.

Luna: You can't control my life. You're not even here!

And there it was, that slam of guilt coursing through my veins and shrinking my heart into a knot. My father had left my family, and I'd done just the same. For my dreams. For the money. For a better future for all of us. But everything I had done wasn't enough. No matter what, I couldn't win.

Luna: I didn't want to be mean. It's just… I can't have you as my only friend. Do you remember how it feels when someone makes you smile? Well, he makes me smile.

I grimaced, picturing that grotesque smile I used to have on my face when I believed I was experiencing true love. I hadn't truly smiled in a long time. I smiled a lot, with sarcasm, fake politeness, or the one where you're pretending everything's perfect. But a smile that lit up your face with happiness as if you had everything you needed right here with you, that one would probably never appear again.

Me: I'm the one who is sorry. I'm happy you've made a friend. You'll tell me all about him when we meet, okay?

Luna: Yes!! I can't believe you got me tickets for Ever After, you're the best sister!!

If only.

The doorbell rang, and I instantly jumped to my feet to run toward the stairs.

"It's for me!" I screamed toward the entrance, already feeling my stomach growl at the idea of the four-cheese pizza I had ordered.

I slammed the door open. "This is for—"

It definitely was my pizza.

In the hands of another man.

Spectre's best friend, Isaac.

My eyes remained stuck on my pizza, held hostage by him, and my nostrils flared at the smell of goat cheese. Next to him was Eric, who eyed me from head to toe. Yes, I was in my unicorn pajamas, and I had pink socks with multiple crowns, and yes, in another circumstance, this would be embarrassing if I wasn't starving to death.

"We met the pizza guy on the way. Perfect timing," Isaac said. "It's fitting that Ajax ordered one. I was starving."

I gulped, feeling myself get all fired up. There was a missing slice. A fucking missing slice.

"You ate my pizza?" My tone sounded like I was going to summon the darkness to blast him to the spot.

"Just a slice." He grinned, and oh my—

"Aurore doesn't share food." Spectre appeared from behind me. "It was her pizza, and she'll most likely murder you for the crime you committed."

His friends laughed, thinking he was probably joking, but it was true: I didn't share food. Ever. My eyes were still magnetized to the missing slice of pizza, and their laughter subsided.

"It's fine," I lied to not appear like the selfish eater that I was. "I just don't share with him, but as long as it's no more than a slice, I won't be offended."

Isaac grinned. "I'm sorry. I should have known that fucker would never order us pizza—it was too good to be true. I bet he forgot we were coming tonight."

"I'm happy you accepted the contract," Eric switched the subject.

They stepped inside Spectre's house as I hugged my unfortunate pizza. That annoying artist towered over me, interrupting the reunion between us. "I'll order some more. What do you want?"

"Salmon for me!" Isaac yelled before throwing himself on the couch in a lazy way, like he owned the place. "And for Eric, a honey one."

Spectre closed his eyes as if he wanted to keep his nerves in check or kick them out already. "And you, Aurore?"

"Nothing from you." My stomach didn't thank me for my pride. "I should leave you to your soirée. I have work to get back to."

"Nonsense, you're staying with us!" This was from Isaac. "I promise we'll tell you all the embarrassing and bad things about Ajax—it'll be fun. Damn, this apartment is empty as fuck. Where is all the furniture?"

I reconsidered everything, hearing Isaac mumbling from afar. I opened my pizza to eat a slice and suppressed a moan. "Fine, I'll stay."

Spectre's jaw tightened, and I took the remaining free space on the couch alongside his friends, understanding rapidly who was who in the group. Isaac was the funny, social one. Eric was the serious and considerate one. As for Spectre, he was the cold one with a heart of stone. The despicable one. One who couldn't stop observing me on his armchair with his hands intertwined like a businessman about to win over a six-figure contract.

"Like I said before, I've never seen Ajax with a woman. That's why when he said you were to be his muse, I was shocked. Even Eric didn't understand why, quite frankly." Isaac spoke too much, so I wasn't surprised the moment Spectre fired his deadly stare at him, shutting him up with a single glance.

"We are the only ones close to him to know his identity because we've been working together for years, and he didn't admit it to us directly," Eric tried to catch up on Isaac's excess of information.

"I think I know why." I raised my chin. "The first painting made him famous and probably won him a lot of money, so naturally, he hopes to have that again."

The room fell silent, and my nemesis's lips curled into the slightest line. "Maybe it's for your charming mood."

I bit into another slice of my pizza like a savage. "I'm sure you will not fail to illustrate my bad temper in your happily ever after sketches."

"It's like they're doing some weird foreplay," Isaac whispered to

Eric, but Spectre and I reeled around to face him at the same time. "Relax, guys, all tastes are in nature. I'm not judging here."

"Why did I even invite you here tonight?" Spectre threatened in a dry tone. Good to know he had the same amiability with everyone else.

"You didn't—we invited ourselves because you're a fucker." Isaac pointed his finger at him. "You're such a loner you need us to put sparkles in your life."

"Sparkles?" His stare dropped on me, and I was convinced he was about to make a comment about my unicorn pajamas or my rainbowish personality, but he didn't.

"We can discuss your departure to—" Eric tried to speak, but Isaac interrupted.

"No work talk. It's a fun time, guys."

"Departure?" My voice cringed despite myself, my eyes stuck on the muscle working in Spectre's jaw. "You're moving out?"

That would explain the boxes and lack of decoration.

"Yes," he deadpanned. "I'm in the process of moving to the US permanently after the end of our contract, so you won't see more of me."

That was good news, right? He would be gone, *The Sad Girl* with him, and I'd be somewhat rich, back to my hometown, and hopefully with a publishing deal. That was our happy ending. And why did I feel something twitching in my stomach? I loathed him. My nemesis was leaving.

You have issues with people leaving, Aurore.

"Who will expose the tears of the sad girls from our country now?" I joked. "Perhaps your old mate Bernard Dupont-Brillac?"

"He's nothing but a fool." Spectre's face curled into an expression of disgust. "And he's not looking for a muse, in case you wanted to apply."

I rolled my eyes. "That's such a pity."

He gunned his eyes to mine. "Would you have preferred to work with him?"

"I hate that guy." But at least he didn't make my heart feel like it was about to combust in my chest.

"So that's what jealousy looks like on Ajax's face? Unbelievable," Isaac commented in a failed whisper.

"Good, because you're my muse for a month, Aurore. Don't forget that." There was an inch of cruel amusement in his voice.

To that, I grimaced at him as he made his knuckles crack in his way-too-perfect tailored suit, his clean fragrance overpowering the smell of my cheese pizza. It felt like Spectre and I both wanted to kill each other, our eyes fighting instead of our fists, for a reason I completely ignored. It felt like a need. Like breathing. And I wasn't ready to let all the anger I had for him vanish because he was leaving. I wanted to hate him some more. That didn't make fucking sense. Was I—

"Anywayyy," Isaac cut the tension between us. "Shall we play a game?"

"I'm in." Eric smiled. "What do you have in mind?"

"The game of 'for how much.' A player estimates 'his price,' a figure up to a maximum of fifty once the bet or question is asked. He then chooses a number within the amount, and if the opposing player guesses it, he has to do the bet."

"Eric, when will you ever learn that we shouldn't let Isaac decide? It always ends badly," Spectre said.

"Oh, right, because you never play, Ajax—you're a bore. Aurore, will you play?" Isaac's eyes sparkled.

Usually I would say no, but the way Spectre's fist locked, I couldn't resist. "I'm in."

"You don't have to," Spectre insisted.

"But I want to," I quipped back.

"Isaac, for how much will you admit one of your deepest secrets?" Eric asked.

"I'm going with five. I'm not afraid."

They both counted to three.

"Two," they both spoke at the same time before laughing out loud.

Eric nudged him in a friendly way. "Spit it out."

"Fine, fine." Isaac pretended to think of something, but the grin on his face betrayed the fact he already knew what he'd admit. "I slept with a famous actor, and I was the one to never call him back."

"That's not really a secret—we all knew this. We saw you." Eric's eyes turned to Spectre, who nodded in reply.

"Okay, then, I don't have secrets. I'm sorry I'm an open book, nothing to hide." Isaac's attention drifted to me. "Aurore, for how much will you step into the sea, up to at least the hips, and scream something about Ajax?"

"That is ridiculous and dangerous," Spectre cursed between clenched teeth.

"For ten," I said in a burst of courage.

We counted to three and—

"Seven," I said.

"Three." Isaac thought he could have won this one, judging by the way his eyes lit up. "Damn it, your turn. Maybe we should have played cards instead?"

"Spectre." I locked my gaze on Spectre tightly as if I was about to fire a missile. "For how much will you say something nice to each of us?"

"Fifty."

We counted and—

"Thirty-three," I aimed.

"Thirty-four," he shot at the exact same time as me before his lips turned into a ghost of a smile. "Aurore, same thing as Isaac said. For how much?"

"Is it me, or are they gonna ditch us to play together?" Isaac again failed at whispering.

"Fifty." I gritted my teeth. A war had officially started.

We counted to three.

"Twenty-seven," we both said.

Everyone laughed except for us. I didn't move or react. I couldn't believe the Greek warrior in a suit did me dirty.

"You don't have to do this, Aurore." He pulled himself backward on his seat, squaring an ankle over a knee as if he was untouchable. "Like I said, it's a ridiculous game."

Isaac raised a finger. "Oh no, no, no, rules are rules!"

"She'll not go inside the water, Isaac. It's nighttime, and the sandbar is unreliable at this hour," Spectre roared at him.

"There is no tide here. I've done it thousands of times already! Nothing will happen to her with water up to her hips! I'll go with her if it's what—"

"I'll do it." I rose firmly from my seat, sorely about to regret my choices. "A game is a game."

"Aurore," the man with a heart of stone, ground out like a menacing storm.

"You can watch me, Spectre."

With a decisive step, I passed the front door and went out in the direction of the gardens leading to the ocean. I crossed the small gate and descended the slope to arrive in front of the sea, which was simply lit by the crescent moon. What the fuck was I doing? Just to counter Spectre. This was stupid. Childish. Everyone followed after me with the light from their phone and Isaac's laughter breaking through the darkness.

It was summer, and I had grown up in a small village not far away from the sea, but still, this wasn't an excuse for a moonlight bath.

"Don't forget to say something about Ajax!" Isaac called out from the sand, standing in the back with Eric, who looked skeptical.

Spectre had his arms crossed and I'd guess a murderous look.

"You can do this, Aurore. It's okay," I mumbled before bringing my toes to the water. At least it wasn't frozen; the temperature was even agreeable.

I had to walk some time on the sandbank for the water to reach beyond my knees. I sank a few meters further offshore in the black water, my heart throbbing as it finally reached my hips. I tucked my stomach in, the water lapping above it. I turned around to face them, taking another step back.

"Ajax! Behind your obnoxious attitude, I know there is a beating heart," I screamed, realizing they were far away and that I should get back ASAP. I couldn't even clearly distinguish Spectre's menacing shadow.

But like all the adventures of my life and my bad luck, I felt something slimy caress me under my feet, and I backed up to avoid it. I did avoid it, except that my feet no longer reached the sandbank, and I found myself under the water all of a sudden, cursing this accursed tide and this childish idea.

Submerged under it, my body adapted to the shock of the cold water, the sound of waves hitting the sand echoing in my ears as I held my breath. I felt like I was buried in a nightmare. I emerged while coughing because I had swallowed the wrong way. Another wave slapped me under, and salt water stung my nose. I couldn't find purchase on the stupid sand; the water was too deep.

Before I could swim to the shore, the sea stirred as if someone had joined me in this apocalyptic idea. It was just a matter of time before hands grabbed me and pulled me out of the water. I collided with a strong and wet torso harder than a rock. I held the balance with my arms as those same hands skimmed across my waist to keep me steady.

I craned my neck and blinked twice, close to swallowing sea water again. "Ajax? What are you doing here?"

"You are impossible and unconscionable."

I was. But Spectre had stepped in with all his clothes, which meant he was as crazy as me. His hands were still wrapped around my waist, even though this time, I was able to reach the sandbank with my feet.

I somehow didn't pull away from him. "Like I said, you provoke the worst in me."

"Why in the goddamn world do you have to be so fucking stubborn," he cursed. Spectre cursed. "You're infuriating."

"Why do you have to be so austere?" I quipped back.

"The way you hate me, it's as if you're trying to convince yourself to not feel anything else other than hate. You want to make me your villain."

"You're wrong." I took notice of my hand on his heart. A hand that I immediately withdrew. "You're the one I can't figure out."

"Because you don't search within. You only see what you want to see. You need to blame someone when, Aurore, it's not me or my painting that hurt you that day. I'm not responsible." He paused, his hands tightening on my waist as if he didn't know if he wanted to pull me closer to him or further apart. "You're driving me insane. I can't think straight. Why is everything complicated with you, and why on earth do we end up in the water all the fucking time? Is that a habit of yours?"

"No, it's not, and I don't know either." My heart slammed in my chest with the recognition that our bodies were locked. It sent a tingling sensation down my spine, a mix of fear and adrenaline coursing through my veins. I knew it wasn't healthy, and I couldn't explain why Spectre was the only person on earth I loathed. But I loathed him. I loathed him to the point I didn't want to stop. "I didn't ask you to come inside nor to make that weak rescue attempt. I'm not your princess to save, and you're surely not a prince!"

"You provoked me, Aurore. You knew I'd come because I don't have a fucking choice."

"Right, you can't lose your muse." I lifted my chin, inching my lips to his.

"I can't lose you," Ajax dropped with raw vulnerability. One that made me skip a heartbeat.

In the space of a brief second, he blinked before putting his mask on once more.

"What on earth are you talking—"

Our lips crushed together.

Salty and wet met with need and desperation.

His soft lips invaded all of my senses, like an unstoppable tornado taking everything away on its course. His hands cupped my cheeks like this was a kiss you'd been longing for for so long that an eternity couldn't possibly satiate you. The moment our lips locked, it rushed a cocktail of hormones through my system. It was as maddening as my near-bursting heart.

I kept my eyes half-open for a moment, zeroing in on his. His forehead was creased as if he himself didn't know what on earth was happening between us. The taste of his lips alone was erotic and hypnotic. It wasn't shy. It wasn't magical. It was a need, like breathing. A heart-fluttering need.

And so I gave in to that strange bond between us, closing my eyes. My brain shut down, and our tongues swiveled together. He claimed my mouth, desperately and in total abandonment for a man who didn't portray any emotions. This kiss felt nothing like him. It was a consuming, ever-bright flame. This could reveal only one dangerous thing. I was wrong about Ajax.

A sound escaped the back of his throat, half moan, half growl, and the hair on my skin hissed in reply. My knees buckled as he draped his arms around my frame, small compared to his.

"Your lips pouring over mine have the power to take away and give back life," he muttered in an almost inaudible way, like a confession you want no one else to know.

The lack of oxygen, my shredded breathing, my throbbing clit—I was going to explode. My stomach twisted into a knot. This was the unknown. This blistering heat took me by surprise, and even though I knew I should stop it, all I wanted was to stop time. My fingers sank into his skin before roughing through his silk hair. My heart jumped, like a warning, like it was time to say farewell. He was opening each of my wounds, infiltrating himself into the deepest areas of my soul, and I wouldn't allow it.

I pushed him away, finding back the breaths he had stolen from me. I took a step back, as if it would erase this moment that should have never happened. His eyes bulged in recognition for a fragment of a second, seeming as lost and empty as I was.

"You can't just kiss me, *Spectre*. I don't want this!" I pointed to the both of us. "This, this will never happen ever again!"

"You kissed me back." A nerve worked in his jaw as if I shouldn't have kissed him back. As if I was the one who'd complicated everything.

"I don't want to kiss you," I articulated, killing all those butterflies dancing in my belly and all the feels from that kiss. I couldn't kiss him. He was nothing but heartbreak and sad endings. "I'm just a contract. We're just a contract. Plus, you're leaving, and I'm not some quick fuck. I despise you, so please, don't steal more from me than you already did."

The harshness of my words made my stomach twitch even more, but he simply nodded. This moment would remain buried in the past, and just like the waves hitting the shore around us, it would disappear into a fleeting memory.

"You're gonna catch a cold." It was his turn to retract from me, the warmth of his body missing. "You're free to leave tomorrow in the morning. I believe you have somewhere to be."

"Ajax," I whispered, but he was joining the sand, not turning back.

I followed after him, still in shock at what had happened and, even worse, what it had triggered in me. What if hating someone was the easiest option? The one masking the void inside of me?

Maybe I judged him too quickly.

No, Aurore. He's Spectre.

Ajax reached the shore and walked with heavy stomps back to his house as I arrived on the sand next to Isaac and Eric.

"I'm sorry for the bet," Isaac excused. "I was just trying to provoke Ajax, Aurore. This is my fault. To be fair, I didn't think you'd do it."

"You didn't force me in." A bitter taste stuck in my throat. "I don't even know why I did that."

"Maybe because you're trying to prove something to yourself." Eric handed me a towel. "Or to him."

Actions meant more than words, but this didn't make any sense. I approached my partnership with Spectre as a war for power for a selfish end. "I didn't ask to be rescued, nor did I have the need to."

"You didn't have to ask to be rescued, but perhaps this is what you truly wanted. Ajax cares, even if he'd never show it to you. That's how he is."

No, I didn't want Spectre to be part of my fairytale other than being the villain.

The villain I wanted this deal to be over, not want or be inspired by.

"I don't think Spectre is capable of caring."

When these words escaped my lips, I knew they felt wrong. I was a liar.

Because by the way he kissed, he betrayed what lay deep within him.

And by the way he left, he was probably capable of hurting.

CHAPTER 13

Aurore

I slammed the bedroom door behind me, taking in a last deep, intense breath before rushing to each corner of the room with my soaked hair.

I threw my wet clothes on the ground and tied up my hair with a towel from the adjacent bathroom, remaining in my underwear. It was always in the moments of anger that you hurt your little toe against a piece of furniture. Which was exactly what I did, swearing some insults at Spectre's commode. I stuffed all my belongings into my bag, trying to squeeze in as many things as possible without folding them.

In the middle of my mess, I had left one of my notebooks on the floor. I always took them with me, hoping to relive an emotion and be inspired in some way. I knelt down to pick it up, coming across the date stamped on the page it was open to. It was my diary of the year that had changed my life. Seven years ago, from the time

I had left my hometown. A time that seemed so distant with painful memories that I hadn't dared to go back into it.

I plunked to the ground.

Our first official date!!

Augustus is the most romantic (soon to be architect) man I ever met… he organized a typical French picnic (in a real basket) for us to eat by the Seine. He told me to dress casually, which I did, putting on a plaid midi dress with a hair bow, because no one wears a bow anymore.

Augustus told me I was sophisticated, and his eyes settled on me for long minutes the moment I arrived, which I guess is a good sign. After that, I accidentally crushed the picnic basket by smashing it with my heel, not noticing it on the floor because I was too excited to see him. And what did I do? I laughed. Augustus, on the contrary, did not. Then, I invited him over, but he found out I was a terrible cook, so we made love. I didn't orgasm twice like in those novels, but he did, once. I like him a lot, and I think he likes me too, because he cuddled me afterwards. It was like in a book. And here I am, writing this to myself instead of sleeping in the comfort of his arms. Maybe it's true love like mom and dad's?

I laughed at my old self as if she were someone else, so stupid, foolish, and naive. I was failing at being perfect, and I had no idea.

I turned a new page. "Let the villain era begin, my dear."

Augustus had to work on a uni project with a girl with a beautiful flowery name. Violette, I think. I met her—she could be a model but isn't one. She was kind to me, and they already had inside jokes. She seems like a good friend. But all I felt was jealousy. The way his eyes bored into hers was nothing like he ever looked at me. He had a stupid corny smile on. My heart wanted to combust. I think I'm in love with him… Maybe he'll love me over time? I'll do anything to fight for true love. Maybe she's the villain behind her angelic facade?

"Well, that was embarrassing." I spared myself from reading how

I tried to hold Augustus close to me, trying to be as perfect as possible, but I was insufficient. I was not the chosen one. I faded over time, and my smiles filled with jealousy and envy toward the sweet and kind Violette. I had believed for a few months that I would experience what I craved the most: a romance of my own.

"She was not the villain," I sang in a high-pitched tone as I went back to the beginning of the journal, having no desire to remember Augustus and flower girl's love story.

I was the one in the way of their one true love, and now they were happily married, living the Insta life.

"Assholes," I cursed before I stumbled over a different handwriting.

A note was tucked in the middle of my notebook.

Please, continue to inspire me with who you are.

My brows knitted at the title. It was the day I'd met Augustus at Les Beaux Arts seven years ago.

"Wait, I remember that day." I gazed at the handwriting, plunging into a memory of the past I hadn't thought about all this time.

I had arrived early at Les Beaux Arts, except that on the way, my long dress had caught in a thorny bush, like an unfortunate irony. It was torn, and pulling it didn't help its case. I had left my belongings in the studio where I was working as a muse, and I had locked myself in a kind of storage room, hoping to find a thread to repair the seam, when I heard the group of students arriving.

Long story short, they went through my stuff and read my unfinished novel, making fun of my characters and describing me as "the corpse bride who paraded through the halls like an evil ghost."

My finger slammed across the page of this day.

I just wanted to get out of that stupid closet and give them a good lesson. But I had to keep my job, so for a moment, I mumbled in my corner about how I'd get out from this mess, thinking that I was alone among the vast tall shelves filled with odds and ends—from unused globes to wooden mannequins to learn poses, and sheets of all sizes and old art books. A window covered in cobwebs lit up the path with dust in a blinding orange light.

I ducked down to see the other side, but all I saw was a boy, or rather a raven-haired man drawing on his canvas. He was leaning on the ledge of the vault of the other old window with a crack, dressed in holey black jeans, and had no problem sitting down in the dust. His bag was old, with hanging threads. I wondered if he was a student—he certainly didn't have the attitude. His dark gaze fell on me, and I immediately took a step back.

He was threatening, but I threw him a "What? I'm surprised you're allowed to be here too."

He deigned not to answer me, and his disinterested gaze returned to his canvas as if I was boring him to death. It didn't help calm my nerves.

I wanted to go out, but the latch dropped in my hand. This building was so old that nothing held in place. I complained and knocked on the door, and that's when the rude guy decided to get up.

I thought he was going to help me or say a word, but he stared straight ahead, not glancing at me, his hair falling in front of his eyes. He was strange, believe me. Tortured, even.

He, on the other hand, managed to open the door without the handle and, for once, dared to look at me from his side profile. "Wait here."

I was about to protest, but he closed the door behind him and left me in this critical situation. I knocked on the door, insulting him from inside. Whispers coming from the studio echoed, and I stopped kicking the door to eavesdrop. The words "freak" and "beggar" escaped the incomprehensible hubbub.

There was a noise from the table, another one, and laughter. Soon, footsteps headed in my direction. I stepped backwards, a shadow forming under the door.

My notebook slipped underneath, and I grabbed it directly, clutching it to my chest. "Thank you, but I'm stuck. I can't get out," I said.

I glanced at my book, and a note was added inside.

Please, continue to inspire me with who you are.

The latch clicked, and the door opened slightly, and I put the note back where it came from and rushed outside.

The strange, tortured man.

He was walking away, hands in his pocket. He'd given my novel back to me. I was ready to run after him, to thank him, but a voice interrupted me.

"You lost something, love?" A man with a devastating smile gave me back my bag, his elbow leaning on the doorstep. "I don't think that old closet is suitable—nobody goes there. Are you okay?"

"Who is he?" My stare locked on the rude stranger from the closet, who looked back in my direction for a moment before continuing his way through the corridor and disappearing. I wondered if I would ever see him again. "I met him in the storage room."

"Him?" he chuckled. "Don't pay attention to him. He's a freak. I'm not even sure he takes classes here."

My eyes then swiveled on the stranger in front of me. He was charming with high cheekbones and brown, tousled hair.

"But he gave me back my journal." I raised a brow.

"And that's why he's running away instead of having a pleasant conversation with you?" The man knew how to smirk, and he had a point. "So maybe you could thank me over a walk later on? I promise I won't bite, and I'm known to have excellent conversation skills."

Dear diary, this day was a sign of fate, I know it.

And I'd made the right choice.

"Aurore." I held out my hand to the man in front of me. "Sounds like you're my hero."

"At your service." He kissed my hand. "Augustus."

I smiled.

"Augustus. You sound just like a prince."

I had met the man who would undoubtedly steal my heart and make it vibrate and fly through the air.

I closed the notebook, looking vacantly at the floor in front of me. *How could I have forgotten about all of this?*

I remembered searching for that stranger the following days by going to the storage room.

I never saw him again. Not once, to the point that I thought I had made it all up.

"Fuck," I dropped in a whisper, my cold heart decaying.

There were similarities that were incomparable, starting with the ghostly presence of the stranger.

Spectre.

Ajax, could it be you?

And why didn't I remember you sooner, erasing this part of the story?

CHAPTER 14

Aurore

"Can you take care of Miss Jenkins?" Emma sprayed her neck with thermal water, stressing out in her sparkly dress. "She's on her fourth flute of champagne."

My eyes flitted to the old lady flirting with the servers and abusing the free alcohol below the arches of the old renaissance monument. "Don't worry, I'll take care of it. You go do your thing."

After all, this was Emma's gala or, more accurately, a foundation created by Ever After in partnership with L'espoir, a children's hospital foundation. But she was the reason I had a little black evening dress on that made me look like I had all of my life pulled together and, as a bonus, very long legs. At least my crimson lipstick and pulled-back hair didn't make me look like I'd been to a funeral beforehand.

My best friend seized my hand in a strong grip that almost broke my bones despite her small frame. "You look great, very adult, very formal."

"I promise I won't pull an evil, wicked fairy godmother act," I reassured her, omitting the fact I truly hoped Léo had my back because I had pepper spray in my bag, and I was ready to kick off my heels at any time if a drunk guy tried to grab me.

"I need to announce the beginning of the auction." She started to leave but turned around as if she had forgotten to tell me something essential and important. Which didn't reassure me. "Oh, did you know we have a Spectre painting tonight?"

My smile was frigid. That colossal mistake I had kissed was everywhere, haunting my dreams, entering my mind with wild scenarios and unwanted thoughts and questioning. This morning, a driver was waiting to drive me back home, and I hadn't even seen Spectre since the night we had kissed. Thankfully, he wouldn't be here tonight—his aura and paintings were more than I could handle.

"Well, I hope he'll make you earn a lot of money."

"I hope so too." Her excitement vanished the moment she bulged her eyes at Miss Jenkins, who was showing something on her phone to the server. "Aurore, can you—"

I lifted my hand and headed toward the old lady. "I'm on it."

I passed through the crowd to arrive at the buffet with my biggest marketing smile on. "Miss Jenkins, they're waiting for you backstage."

She chuckled with malicious glee, whispering to my ear, "They don't have champagne backstage."

She was smart, but I was smarter. "Maybe not, but I bet this charming man would accompany you, and between us, there are a few jewels put to auction that you could try on before the other women."

Her eyes sparkled. I knew how to talk to materialistic drunk old ladies. "Why not keep this information to yourself, then? I'll choose the most dazzling ones."

She was serious, and this secretly scared me. *Would I end up like that, too, with my temper?* She was wearing a funeral dress, and she was antisocial. A potential villain.

"Maybe I want you on my team."

She laughed. "You make me remember a bit of my younger self."

Oh dear god.

"I'll teach you all that I know." On that note, she complied, and I gestured to the server to help her walk backstage.

I gave a thumbs-up to Emma, who was onstage. She was still spraying her face with thermal water as if she was under a burning sun, her fingers shaking. The gala hadn't even begun, and it was already promising to be exhausting.

"A flute won't kill me." I seized the glass from the bar behind me and swallowed it whole with a grimace. I needed something to help me cope and—

"I think we've met. Your face is familiar to me."

I spat out all the rest of the alcohol I had in my mouth and coughed, wiping myself with the towel that served to keep the champagne cool. I squinted my eyes, trying to place the person behind the voice—it was pretentious, edged, and definitely familiar.

"Right." This sounded more like a "fuck" as I turned around to see Bernard Dupont-Brillac with a bow tie with multicolored caterpillars and a navy suit. "At the expo, you were the artist."

Bernard analyzed me from head to toe. "You were with Clemonte. What's your name again? After that night, I learned the kid didn't quit and had followed a small meaningless career in art with his troublesome friend."

On top of that, this asshole didn't even remember me.

"I'm Aurore. You must be proud as his teacher." And here I was speaking too much, too fast, instead of shutting my mouth and hiding behind whatever objects I could find.

"Hmm," he dropped in a high-pitch snort. "He was destined for boredom from the start. It was even a miracle he got accepted there in the first place. A real misfit." He smiled as if remembering a funny joke. "He didn't have the artistic gene, so I could never do anything for him. Unfortunately. It's one of my biggest failures."

That was actually mean. Really mean.

The kind of discourse I'd heard most of my life: *Fairy tales don't sell. We're not interested in your work. You have nothing special. I'm sorry I couldn't love you.* So many rejections. So many cracks in my heart.

"Maybe it was your teaching that was flawed." I gave him back his sharky smile. "But again, I don't think it was a failed artist's dream to end up embittered as a professor who's obviously jealous of his students."

I slammed the champagne glass on the bar, and Bernard's eyes widened at the fait accompli that I had a mouth as big as my ego. I had no reason to defend Spectre, yet Bernard's insults sparked something bitter in me.

"I won't permit you to say atrocious things to me." He furrowed his brows, inching closer to me. "Clemonte wasn't following the rules, wanting to always do things his way as if he was some kind of genius. His art was technically pleasant but so bland. So empty."

"How was he?" I hated the fact my voice sounded intrigued.

"He refused to paint on an easel. He stooped to draw almost on the ground like a savage wanting to use his own material, and on top of that, his gear was worn-out, as if he had found it inside a trash can. He had no respect for my teaching nor for the other students. He was acting as if no one was in the room. He didn't care."

I smiled. I smiled the same way your boyfriend's parents tell you touching stories of their son during his teenage years. Only, this wasn't anything like that, so I had to kill that stupid proud smile on my face and the image of the boy from the storage room in my mind. The one with his flyaway hair, tortured gaze, and ripped jeans. A silent outsider.

"One of my paintings is being put to auction right now, so if you'll excuse me, the failed artist will be the highest bid of the event," Bernard concluded.

"After Spectre's, you mean." And there it was again, my big mouth and that stupid smile. "Enjoy your evening, sir."

"Are you working here or something?" His look was disparaging.

I cracked my knuckles, chewing my inner cheek. "No, I'm getting auctioned for the cause."

I thought this would make me sound strong and fierce, but I appeared desperate.

"Oh," he chuckled, readjusting his ugly bow. "Wonderful."

I ran away from him to head backstage, wondering how this event could go even more wrong.

"Hi, everyone." I heard Emma's shy voice on the microphone, and displayed a grimace, scared she'd pass out in the middle of the scene. She wasn't at ease, and the stress derailed her voice like a stutter. "Thank you for coming here today to support hospitalized children and the foundation L'espoir. To start the charity event, we have the pleasure of announcing to you that this morning, we received a signed shirt from the football player Darek Smither and two unique pieces of art to be auctioned. One from BDB and the latest piece by Spectre."

I rolled my eyes instantly, knowing that Spectre's painting would go for a higher price than me, and BDB would laugh at my certain humiliation.

I was definitely screwed.

CHAPTER 15

Ajax

I could affirm with certainty that I loathed these events.

I didn't have the slightest idea why on earth I accepted to come here. Everyone pretended to be here for charity, but most of them couldn't care less—just like the Clemontes, they were here to reduce their taxes.

The golden gala was just the coronation of elite families and future world changers. Families like mine. All of that circus served with silver platters, exceptional service, and bespoke tailors.

"Ajax, I'm glad you came. We haven't seen you in forever." My younger brother, Archibald, drew me into an expressive hug, one I had no choice but to comply with.

And here was my reason for my appearance—his constant whining about reconnecting the family years later.

"Being the black sheep of the family has its privileges." One being to not attend these events.

My brother was the golden boy of the Clemontes, a talented

surgeon with a brilliant career ahead, Mom's piercing blue eyes, and Father's money and support.

"It's about time we make amends, don't you think?" Archibald grabbed a flute of champagne, displaying a seductive smile to the servers. He hadn't changed a bit. "Father misses you."

"By that, you mean that he's intrigued that his failure of a son managed to somehow earn more money than him in something as meaningless as art," I deadpanned, and we sank into the heart of the event, taking a seat in the far back for whatever was planned to begin.

No one in my family knew I was Spectre, apart from my mother. They certainly thought, like everyone else who would search for my name online, that I had a little art gallery with Isaac. For my father, everything linked to art wasn't a career. I took my pocket watch out of my suit for a moment. I had only been there for five minutes. The evening was going to be long.

"Probably, but winning Father's respect is hard." Archibald's jaw clenched. "Since you left us, I graduated top of my class, did the best internships, and it's still not enough for him."

"I had no choice." That was a fact. I had left my brother in the mouth of the crocodile, at his mercy. The same one who'd named us both with the letter A because it was the first one of the alphabet.

"It's okay, I'm better than him now. Look at what I've become." He opened his arms as if I was supposed to see something new behind his sharky grin. "What made you change your mind about coming here?"

"You actually did," I said, analyzing a crowd I hadn't seen in forever. They looked at me as if the Clemontes' son had been resurrected from the dead.

"Hi, everyone," the blonde lady on the microphone said in a frail voice, rubbing her fingers together. "Thank you for coming here today to support hospitalized children and the foundation L'espoir. To start the charity event, we have the pleasure of announcing to you that this morning, we received a signed shirt from the football player Darek Smither and two unique pieces of art to be auctioned. One from BDB and the latest piece by Spectre."

Some people in the crowd gasped. The charity event had officially begun. I wasn't opposed to giving to charity, even one sponsored by my father. Not that I had many paintings to give. Most of them were thrown into the trash or remained as blank as I was.

"If Father were here, he'd cringe," Archi gossiped.

"How so?"

"He hates Spectre's artwork. He says he's mocking us, that he's a disgrace." That made me smile. This wasn't surprising. "Mom, on the contrary, adores him."

"What about you?" I asked, focusing my attention on BDB's piece that was getting auctioned at the moment.

"I—"

Archi was interrupted by an old man's voice leaping above everyone else. "Twenty thousand!"

The blonde lady tapped once, twice, and BDB's art piece was sold for that price. I adjusted my tie. I had to do better.

"And now the latest piece by Spectre," she continued with way too much enthusiasm for something as boring as this auction. Truth was, the piece that was displayed at this moment was an unfinished one, dating from a year ago, and was called *Disillusion*—as Aurore would say, pretty morose. "A 40x30 cm linen canvas, made in oil painting."

"Five thousand!" a woman screamed.

"As I was saying, when have I ever been entitled to have an opinion different from Father's?" Archi finally finished his sentence, smoothing his tie.

"Certainly not since you touched your trust fund money," I implied.

"I didn't. I don't need his money, Ajax." He drew another of his sharp smiles. "That said, I've learned a lot from Father. I understand why he was such a ruthless bastard to us."

"Twenty thousand!" someone else yelled, which had just matched the bid for BDB.

"Looks like he's making you his own puppet," I said. "Do you even like medicine?"

"I'm not doing this for him, and you'll thank me when I'm saving your old ass later in life."

The battle continued for the painting before being sold at thirty-five thousand.

"And now, these are our five single women and men who agreed to participate in the auction. The highest bid will win a date with his/her chosen one at the L'espoir foundation. Don't be shy with the money; it's for a good cause, and who knows, perhaps you'll meet your soulmate. Let's begin with the ladies!" The blonde presenter was probably the most excited person in the whole crowd, desperately trying to sell her things.

Speaking of desperate. How desperate did you have to be to agree to be auctioned in the middle of—

"Are. You. Fucking. Kidding. Me," I roared out loud, my eyes stuck on one of those five *single* women.

It didn't surprise me that she'd gotten herself involved in this mess.

"What's wrong?" Archi asked, having not the slightest idea that Aurore, my muse, was standing on the podium.

She had a mars-black dress on, one short enough to display her legs and accentuate her curves. Yet she didn't wear one from her collection of dresses she was talking to me about. She wore scarlet-red lipstick and heels that very much made my hardness pulsate in my trousers, her hair pulled back in an elegant ponytail.

That woman would be the chaotic death of me.

I had the sudden urge to jump on this fucking podium, put her on top of my shoulder like a caveman, and get us both the fuck out of all of this. But instead, I swallowed that lethal urge and pained to remain in my self-control.

She seemed lost, talking to the old lady next to her, who must have been nearly ninety years old. She could barely walk and had her hand locked inside Aurore's. The woman pointed her other finger at Aurore's hairpin, and a second later, my muse was arguing with her, which made the old lady pout, snapping her eyes at Aurore, offended.

Then, my muse took out her hairpin and gave it to the drunk old lady with a grimace plastered on her face because she couldn't say no to save her life. The woman grinned in victory, and Aurore tapped her foot on the ground so fast I feared she'd make a hole and plummet herself right off the stage and—

"Ajax?" Archi called again. "Did someone catch your eye?"

"No." I didn't leave a place for hesitation.

"The first lady is Miss Jenkins. She's the oldest lady here. She knows how to cook, and she has the best sense of humor. Miss Jenkins, everyone!"

Aurore helped the old lady walk onto the podium, curving her back so she'd put herself at her height. Despite myself, a ghost of a smile stretched my lips. In the middle of the catwalk, she took off her heels, probably having too much difficulty walking with them and taking care of Miss Jenkins at the same time. Arriving at the end of the podium, Jenkins gave a dismissive gesture of her hand at my muse, wanting the spotlight all for herself. Aurore let her go and ran back to her place, a hand clutching her dress so it wouldn't lift.

To others, she might have been out of place.

But to me, that girl was butterflies and rainbows in a rainy, cloudy town.

"Damn, she is nice, don't you think?"

Something hot spiked in my veins, a raging feeling spreading in my core at my brother's comment.

"I wasn't in the mood to give away money, but perhaps I should reconsider. I rented a room, and I have to admit, coming back with that pair of legs and mouth wrapped—"

"Shut up, Arch," I snapped at him. "Don't speak of her like that, or I'll have no choice but redo your portrait that even surgery couldn't arrange your face afterwards."

"I knew it." The bastard laughed darkly. "This promises to be fun. Well done, brother. You're finally ending your solitary reign."

"You're a jerk," I hissed between clenched teeth. "You don't date either."

"But it's not about me, is it? Just a thought though—it's weird your lady is about to get auctioned by some creepy dudes."

"She's not mine." That felt bitter on my tongue.

"But you wish her to be?" Archi didn't drop the case.

"A hundred euros for Miss Jenkins? Someone?" The blonde lady's smile dropped, and the old lady curved inward, the realization no one wanted to bet on her clouding her features.

"One thousand euros!" Archi screamed, attracting all the attention to him. "I'll take that beautiful woman."

My brother for once did a charitable thing at my expense when Aurore's eyes doubled in size and snapped to me, looking rather murderous. She became crimson red before blazing her eyes at the blonde presenter. *Do they know each other?*

The old lady winked at Archi, who turned to me with his flirtatious grin on. "I always had a way with women, compared to you and your austere vibe."

"And here I thought you didn't have a heart," I deadpanned.

"And here I thought you weren't capable of emotions."

He won this round.

"The second lady of the night is Aurore Bardot." At just the sound of her name, my cock pulsed in my trousers as if I was a horny teenager. Pitiful. "She's a writer with thousands of stories to tell, a real sunshine."

She stepped in, still blazing her eyes at the presenter, and whispered something to her. The blonde lady opened her eyes even more in return and gave her a head nod toward the catwalk. Aurore continued her model walk, her heels still in her hands. I couldn't be more thankful to not be standing in the first row, or else no doubt she'd have thrown them at me, and I'd have bet she wasn't the kind to miss her target. She fired her stare between me and someone in the front row and stopped at the end of the podium, a hand poised on her hips and a frigid fake smile on.

"One hundred euros, anyone?"

Someone raised a hand. I shifted my head to peer at whoever the fuck the man in the front row was. All I could tell from where I was standing was that he was blond. Aurore smiled at him. What the—

"Two hundred." Another man of a certain age, judging by his grayish hair perceptible from the back, raised a hand.

"Three hundred," the annoying blond man outbid him.

My lips were twitching backward. She gave him weird puppy eyes full of hope as if he was some fucking knight in a shining pearl-white suit. My fist balled.

I was supposed to be discreet. One of my paintings was here—I couldn't risk attracting the attention on me, especially since everyone here potentially knew I was the son of Léon Clemonte, and on top of that, Bernard was here. I couldn't do anything stupid or irrational.

"One thousand!" the older guy continued to bet on my muse.

The blond one hesitated, exchanging a glance with Aurore, who was gunning her eyes to him in a way that meant "don't you dare let me hang in there, idiot."

"One thousand five hundred!"

The prices rose higher until her chivalrous knight had a win for three thousand, and the old guy retracted.

"Three thousand? Once, tw—"

"Five thousand," I lashed out without thinking, and Aurore's eyes widened even more like a sociopath about to murder me.

I was supposed to observe, not act. I didn't even know if it'd be safe to have a date with her, to get closer to her, just like I had no idea why I had kissed her. She created an impulse in me. For my sanity, I needed to remain far away. Yet, here we were, unable to step back. I couldn't let her be at the mercy of one of those assholes.

All eyes of the crowd were on me, and Archi didn't help, showing his dimples with an asshole grin similar to Father's—the one that showed he was living only for the quest of money, financial investment, and emotional detachment. Not that I would blame him.

My muscles stiffened, and I blazed my eyes at Aurore's knight, who gulped his feelings away. He would not win this round. That was the perk of having money.

"Five thousand two hundred," he nevertheless continued, smiling at me with determination.

I'd annihilate him. "Seven thousand."

He hesitated, glancing back at Aurore, who was imploring him with a look. *She wishes.* "Eight thousand."

I was tired of this game, a nerve flickering in my jaw. I readjusted my cuffs, my tie, and I spoke loud enough for all of them to hear and for silence to own the room. "Twenty thousand."

The crowd gasped, and the blond man snapped his mouth shut, returning back to his chair in defeat.

"And to think that I could have missed this." Archi was still having a blast.

The blonde presenter had a huge smile plastered on her face when she looked over at me, which made me frown doubtfully. "And Miss Bardot goes to Aja—" She cleared her throat. Interesting. She knew my name, and by the way Aurore shut her eyes as if she was about to combust, I deduced she was probably one of her friends. So she had talked about me, which made me feel idiotic. "The man in the gray suit in the back."

I readjusted my lamp-black, not gray, suit, waiting for Aurore to come to me with heavy stomps.

"I have a question on my mind though. How did you do it, to be able to afford this?" Archi became serious. "All those years ago, you left basically homeless. Léon had disinherited you."

"I worked, Arch." I had no interest in continuing this discussion, focusing on Aurore walking like a firecracker toward me with flames ravaging her eyes.

When she arrived, she snapped her finger in my direction. "What the fuck are you doing here?"

I cracked my knuckles. "I could ask you the same. I didn't know one of your hobbies was to be occasionally auctioned."

"Just like I didn't know you liked to buy ladies in your free time."

"You mean rescuing you. It's a full-time job of mine."

"I didn't need rescuing. I had someone betting for me, and he should have won." Now I was truly burning up with a need to smash something. That was unfamiliar. "You spent twenty thousand euros on me. Why on earth!"

"Who is he?" I sounded jealous and pathetic, a possessive need washing over me like a tide that couldn't be tempered. I had no imagination for my next painting, but enough to imagine this man in question touching her, and that thought alone made all my muscles rigid. None were good enough for her. Not Augustus, not him. Not me. None.

"I don't think that concerns you," she had the audacity to reply, folding her arms.

Her gaze darted in the direction of the man in question, and she shook her head sideways to him, as if she was warning him of something. I reeled around to lock my eyes on the man, who continued to stare at her as if she was his. I remained stoic. What did that fool want? He got up and came toward us, and I was mentally ready to obliterate him from her field of vision.

"Oh fuck, no," she sighed.

"Afraid to introduce me?" I teased.

Blond knight arrived at her side. "Is everything okay, Aurore?"

Blood pulsed in my veins. "Yes, Aurore. Won't you introduce us?"

"I—humm." She hesitated, swallowing. "This is Léo, Emma's—I mean, my *very* close friend. We're very close. Yep." His stare stabbed her, and in reply, she took his arm before saying with a much less sweet tone, "This is Ajax, my former nemesis, and the one with a smug look on his face must be his brother. The family resemblance is quite visible."

"It's him?" Léo exclaimed, and Aurore's nostrils flared. "I mean, you never mentioned him until now."

She pinched her lips even more.

"Enchanted," Archi said, taking pleasure in this messy situation. "But between us, I'm the more handsome brother."

I rolled my eyes.

"It's fine, Léo. I can handle him," she assured him.

Blond guy nodded and offered me his hand. "It was a nice battle out there, but I couldn't risk bluffing my way up there anymore. Thanks to you, you've made my girlfriend's night, helping her raise tons of money."

Girlfriend. Probably the blonde girl onstage. I accepted his hand, which displeased Aurore, making her frown. "Nice poker game. I fell for it."

"I like him. Better to have him on your team than an enemy." He pointed to Aurore and took his leave.

She was pouting with her mouth clamped.

"This wasn't smart to try to make me jealous. Léo seems like a nice man. I would have hated to do him wrong," I said.

"I didn't try to make you jealous." That smile gracing her lips was a big lie. "I agreed to go in there because Léo, my best friend's boyfriend, agreed to bet on me so I wouldn't find myself in an awkward situation again where I have to go on a date with a freak."

I delivered a cunning line. "And here your plan failed again."

"You're right, because you just can't help it." She then turned to my brother. "How did you handle him as a child? He must have been infuriating!"

"What do you want? I'm a saint," he answered in an all-business voice I wanted to tune out. "If you give me your number, I can tell you all the stories about that loner Ajax."

"Hu-hum, I'd have to refuse. One Clemonte is more than I can deal with." She crossed her arms. Good girl.

Archi jerked his head backward. "You're right. He's the better brother, and that's why it pleases me to hear you give him such a hard time. I love it."

"Don't you have anywhere to go, Archi?" I implied.

"As a matter of fact, yes, I have a date with an old lady, after all." His attention went back to me. "By the way, Father wants you to come to dinner to celebrate my newfound surgeon career, and Mother would love to have you back. If you don't do it for me, do it for her. Her heart has been broken since you left. So please, come with Aurore."

I was about to reply with a bland no when he cut in. "Think about it, okay? I'll tell them you'll come though, the both of you, so hopefully, you'll do the right thing. Aurore, it was a pleasure."

He left to mingle with the crowd, and Aurore's eyes questioned me. "I believe if I were to ask you what's the deal between you and your family, you'd switch the subject, correct?"

"Correct. Would you care to dance?" I asked her bluntly.

Her lips parted. "What? Why?"

"Because at this kind of event, you dance." The auction was over, and music had started to rise in the back, couples already forming.

"You want to dance with me?" She still pretended to not understand.

"Yes."

"Like right now?"

"Yes."

"Okay," she admitted simply.

I gave her my hand, and we stepped into the middle. I ignored all the gossip around us, my stare fixed on her. I laid a hand on her lower back and brought her closer to me, something tingling in my fingers. I didn't like proximity and physical touch, and yet I had invited her to dance. Especially since I was certain that I hated dancing. A waltz played, and we had no choice but to spin.

"I didn't know you knew how to dance," she mumbled in the middle of a turn. "But then again, I barely know a thing about you."

She collided with my chest, and I heard the frenetic beats of her heartbeat. "You know more about me than I've ever told other people."

"You must not have formed any bonds with other living things on this earth," she replied with sarcasm.

"Indeed, I have not." My hand cupped her waist, and I lifted her in the air so she'd whirl. "I've always been private."

"You mean invisible." Her stare defied me, and she arched her arm in something that looked like a crown. It'd have been a gracious ballet move if I hadn't had to dodge her hand almost slamming me in its descent because of the momentum she took like a spinning top.

She, then, probably confused by the way I was trying to interpret how to match her moves, looked back at her feet for a moment, swallowing.

"Is it your ankle?"

"You remember." Of course, I remembered her ballet story she told me about that night. "No, it doesn't hurt. I just feel ridiculous."

"You're certainly not."

"How do you do this, Ajax?" She called me Ajax. Not Spectre. "To make me confess every single thing about me so easily."

"Perhaps because I see you." *I see you in a way you don't see yourself.*

We stepped, slid, and stepped, turning in circles, her body swaying in ways I've never seen anyone dance before. Her eyes backfired on me, and she unleashed moves I had to dodge, as I remained blank, unable to come up with something similar. Her dancing was atypical and somehow indescribable—a mix of the carefreeness of a child, waves with her arms like what I would picture an octopus seducing his mate would do, all of that thrown into some kind of Amerindians sacred ritual dancing style. But nevertheless, this was the first dance in my entire life I was tolerating—even if at this point, I was only standing watching her perform around me.

"What?" My fairy stopped her fairy dance and lifted her chin proudly. "Is something wrong?"

"No, I like looking at you."

"That's not how a dance works."

"Perhaps I was having a better view from here," I said, noticing only now my lips had stretched into a thin stupidious line all this time.

I came back to her, and my breath brushed over her nape. "How does this charity date usually work?"

"The bidder and his date usually go on a charity date where they do something fun for the kids. Last year, it was an animal charity, so I worked at the shelter for a day. Its goal is to sensibilize the rich and the coldhearted. You know, people like your kind." She smiled, and we started dancing once more.

My hand traveled lower on her back, static electricity at my fingertips. "I want that date with you."

"This doesn't have to be a real date," she mumbled.

"Go on this date with me."

"I doubt it'll be your scene."

"You don't know that." Her back collided with my front after a spin, and I inched my mouth closer to her nape, a hand on her waist. I sensed the goose bumps on her skin, and my muscles stiffened at the feel of her.

"No." She shook her head, parting away with another whirl that would have sent her hair straight into my face if I hadn't had successfully avoided it. "You don't strike me as the kind to go on dates."

"You're right, I don't. Dating is a waste of time, and my expectations are described as too high."

"Oh, I believe you. You must be impossible to please, wanting nothing but perfection." She painted a mocking smile. "Must be so painful for you."

"Perfection sounds about right." My eyes dropped to hers as we continued to occupy the space.

"No one would be good enough for you. We're imperfect and flawed."

"It must be hard to look into a mirror," I countered back. "You're as exigent as I am."

She lifted her brow. "So, we're both meant to die alone and be the villains of our stories?"

"Me, perhaps. You, no." I closed my fingers with hers. "I told you I was failing at being human, so teach me."

She circled her arms again as if she had wings, not letting me take the lead this time. "On a date?"

"Yes."

"You're not ready for that. People have fun on dates. They laugh, they sometimes cry, and feel a lot."

"Most dates are just about getting dinner with boring polite questions to hook up afterwards," I was stoic, yet I did make her somehow laugh.

"You're right. Romance is not what it used to be, but what matters is the emotional connection, the pounding of your heart when your fingers brush and—" Her stare dropped over my shoulder, and she furrowed her brows, the life that inhabited her leaving.

She parted her lips, but no sound came out. I shifted around to see what was causing her to stop sparkling and I caught a glimpse of Bernard making his way through the crowd with a satisfied smile on.

"I'm sorry, I need to go." She stepped backward, the song fading away. "I'll go on the date alone; you don't have to worry. We don't want to blur the lines, and I—I'll see you soon."

She pulled away from me for the second time in less than twenty-four hours. My self-control was escaping me. I couldn't stay away from her.

And so I stayed like an idiot in the middle of the dancing scene, wondering what on earth had happened, and in what world she had propelled me with her.

CHAPTER 16

Aurore

"You're dressed as a fairy. Are you good or evil?" The little princess in front of me squinted her brows as I grabbed the scoop of ice cream and put it on the cone.

"That depends on who you're talking to." I leaned over, displaying a sharky smile. "I used my magic powers to put fairy dust in your ice cream. One of your wishes will come true."

The little girl's face lit up, and she closed her eyes as if she was about to blow out a candle to make a wish. The way she ran away from the store to go back to her mommy to tell her the story about how she met a real-life fairy made me grin in the empty space. We weren't opening for another fifteen minutes, but I made an exception for her because, believe it or not, I was somehow in a joyful mood.

I went back to my computer—which I had plugged in instead of the hot chocolate machine because choices had to be made—and continued my short erotica story using my remaining free time. It was a new dom-neighbor-next-door trope—because my story about fae kings got refused by daddykink.

Bending over the counter, I typed the story, sentences flowing across the screen, kicking off that empty white page.

"You'll take it," I whispered, immersing myself in my role. "You'll take it like the good gi—"

"Aurore," a husky, deep voice echoed, and my fingers crashed on the keyboard.

A draft passed, and I didn't move, too afraid to look at who was behind me. I cleared my throat and shut down my computer, finding a semblance of composure. I glanced at the ice cream clock. We'd only opened a minute ago—that customer had an annoying sense of punctuality.

I shifted around to meet Spectre, dressed in his usual morose gray, looking out of place in the candy-pink scenery. It was as if he was coming out of a sexy Halloween parade to jump inside an enchanted forest for unicorns.

"Ajax. Do you have some kind of meeting with Ever After, or are you here by some unfortunate circumstance to torment me?"

"I came for you."

I blinked. "For me? How did you know I'd be here?"

"You told me you work here," he said simply, as if I had made him a detailed plan on how to find me in this maze. "I just had to search for you and your purple aura emanating like a tornado in the middle of this pretentious pink world, my fairy."

I snapped a fist on the counter, leaning toward it like a gangster about to draw their gun. "So, you bought a ticket for Ever After, while you could have just waited to see me like on Monday?"

He moved forward with that confidence and regalness of his. "I don't like waiting while I can take matters into my own hands."

"What matters?" I gulped, pretending to be busy readjusting my already too perfectly arranged counter.

"Our date," he affirmed. "Our mandatory date."

"I believe I already refused." I managed a crisp smile, the images of our heated kiss making my hands moist. "I'll go alone tomorrow. It has already been arranged."

"I know." A fine cunning line was on his lips. "I'll come to pick you up, and I wanted to make sure you wouldn't bail on me. That's why I'm here in person."

"What you're doing is psychopathic and villainous."

"I thought if someone could understand psychopathic and villainous, it'd be you. You said you liked villains." His tendency to remember everything I'd ever said was starting to irritate me, and worse, it was attractive. Like a game you couldn't stop playing even if you knew it'd end badly for you, because the more you played, the more you had to lose.

I hate him. I hate him. I—I took a deep breath. "You're incredibly stubborn for someone who is too busy to date and with the emotional sensibility of a stone."

He leaned on the counter, and his approach made my hair hiss alert like a warning to not kiss him again. "You should take that as a compliment."

I laughed. "Why do you want that date? You can't possibly really want this? Do you even like me?" I gunned my eyes at him, but he didn't budge, his Adam's apple bobbing out. "You like me? You do?"

"I tolerate you," he gritted out.

"Right! Probably because the great Ajax is used to disliking things, not liking them." And again, my lips quirked up at the sight of his grumpy self.

"People get bored of the things they like. Liking is not a compliment," he grumbled, but that didn't matter.

"You *like* me," I played with him in the hope that maybe he would let all of this go away, and begged for my heart to stop hammering like this was some romantic moment. "That's why you can't stay away from me."

"That reverse psychology won't work on me. We—"

"Excuse me," a woman cut us both off, and I felt a blast of

annoyance. "Are you ordering an ice cream? Because we're waiting in line, and if you aren't, please step away."

I bent my neck to the side to see a line of people waiting behind Ajax. Crap. I had never had this many customers before.

"My apologies." He offered a charming smile to the lady, one that made her smile in return and made me want to slap him with a mixer. Ajax never smiled; he always wore a hostile growl. "I'll take an ice cream."

"Which flavors would you like, sir?" My hand tightened on the ice cream scoop.

He searched through each flavor. "Are you ready to accept my order?"

"No," I deadpanned, which made me sound impolite while we both knew we weren't talking about ice cream.

"Give me a good reason to refuse."

"Choose your ice cream balls." I slammed the scoop against the palm of my hand, which startled the lady behind him. "Sir."

A knot formed in his jaw. "I'll take the—" He lowered his voice. "Rainbow blue one."

"Rainbow blue?" I screamed in a laugh for everyone to hear, which made Ajax's face twitch. "I'm sorry, it's just hilarious."

"Are you making fun of me?" He looked around him, and if I didn't know him too well, I'd say he was embarrassed.

"Yes, I am." I couldn't stop laughing. "I took you for a classic ice cream kind of guy, but you, Ajax, the grumpy man with a black soul who never gives a real smile, ordered a rainbow one. It's ironic."

I took the cone and threw two scoops of rainbow ice cream inside, a grin not leaving my face. I added two candies to make a little snowflake man like I did for the children.

"I prefer ice cream with weird names and candy flavors. My brother used to make fun of that too." Ajax wasn't offended. "It's ridiculous, isn't it?"

I handed him the ice cream. "No more than an old spinster who collects fairy-tale dresses. The ice cream is on me. The sight of you with it is making my day."

Someone cleared their throat in the background, growing impatient, and yet my eyes remained glued to Ajax.

"You're trying to get rid of me."

"Perhaps." I raised a brow. "You're not the only stubborn person here."

Cold and invisible Ajax turned around to face the woman behind him, and with a deadly tone he said, "I'm paying for everyone's ice cream."

The crowd gasped.

I gasped.

Even the clock hand stopped.

Ajax was serious. And he wasn't going anywhere.

"There. I believe I bought us a couple more minutes." He took a seat at the counter, readjusting his suit in a professional way if it wasn't for that blue ice cream in his hand. "Place your order, Miss. I'm just here to hand over the credit card."

I held out a chuckle, and Ajax kept his word. He paid for ice cream for everyone in the line, to the delight of the parents and children but to my biggest displeasure. We didn't even talk but stared at each other until the end of my shift, which arrived some hours later at the time of the night show. The worst part in all of this was that time flew at a pace it never had before, and the knot in my heart spread wider, encrusting itself like a virus.

The crowd long gone, I was cleaning the tables as Ajax lifted himself from his seat. He was about to talk, but I capitulated first. "Fine. Tomorrow, I'll let you go with me on that date. But don't get your hopes too high. It's a fake date."

"Very well." He didn't give me a smile, as if he wasn't even satisfied with the outcome.

"Are you not happy about it?"

Done with my work, I grabbed my stuff and exited the store, following behind him. We walked the cobblestone path in the midst of the people gathering by the castle and fountains to watch the show about to begin—the swans would dance on the lake, the characters would take life, and fairy-tale magic would charm everyone as fireworks would signal the end of an inspiring story.

The last couple of months, watching the night show, I used to want to burn the whole thing down in a scream. It all felt stupid and pointless. But today, it didn't bother me to see the happiness on everyone's faces and the promise of a forever happily ever after. It made me hopeful. Again.

"But you are." Ajax analyzed me, being a stranger in the middle of a universe that wasn't his own. "You look happy right now—even though I'm next to you. What do you feel?"

"Peaceful, safe, and almost inspired." I drew a mere smile for a fraction of a second and retreated in the opposite direction of the show, away from the rush of excitement around us. "My sister will be coming here for her birthday. She's gonna love it. My goal is to write everything this place is conveying. This kind of bliss. Of dreams."

"Why don't you?"

"I can't." My sigh was carried away by the music of the parade. "I told you, I don't believe in it anymore. It's not for me."

"Then, write what is truly you, not what everyone including yourself is expecting of you." He paused. "You don't strike me as someone who stops believing. I wish I could understand your elation with all of this."

I met his stare, the lights of the fireworks tainting his face with hundreds of colors. Colors that almost made him look like some misunderstood prince. "You don't find this magical?"

"It's not real."

"Doesn't mean it can't be. It may not be real, but your emotions and what you feel are real, so who cares?" I defended. "Reality or dream, it doesn't matter. It's the same."

"You're seeing the world in a strange way," he said. "And I mean it as a compliment."

"Maybe that's the reason I'm lonely."

The crowd laughed, carried away by the spectacle, while here we were, turning our backs at this moment, cut off from it.

Ajax noticed this too, and he furrowed his brows, towering over me. "It may feel lonely to live in your own world, but at least you're not powerless over living in the world others created for you. You're making your own tale."

I swallowed, his comment leaving goose bumps on my skin.

"Believing is not always easy; sometimes I just want to give up, but if I do, it'd feel like I'm dead inside, and I don't want that. So, I feel stuck between those two parts of me."

The orchestra played the melody of love in its splendor inside the park, but did true love truly exist? All that love brought me was disappointments and failures. Every time I had loved or those around me did, we ended up getting hurt over and over again. Everyone leaves, so it's better to reject the possibility of getting hurt again before being abandoned. That's why I needed to kill each butterfly I allowed myself to feel with Ajax before the story repeated itself.

"You should enjoy the show and get inspired. After all, it's what our contract is about, right? An alliance toward our goals." *What I am to you. A muse with an expiration date.* "This is truly what you want— to leave for the US?"

"Yes." He didn't think twice. "If I stay here, I'll get buried underground. It suffocates me. It's my only solution if I want a career worthy of the name."

"Looks like you have something to prove to the demons of your past," I whispered. "I need to go back home to work. I'll see you tomorrow."

He nodded. "You have hope for everyone else, yet you don't allow yourself to be who you truly are."

"Because I'm broken, Ajax. And you painted it," I snapped. "You immortalized the day that broke me."

His face remained closed off. I drove further away from the fireworks rising in the sky, and blossoming happy endings.

There were different versions of one storybook tale.

For the endings, some were happy and touching. Others were gloomy and tragic.

Some delivered a message of hope as others warned us against the big, bad world through darkness.

I thought I could make my own tale, but perhaps I was stuck in the wrong story all along.

CHAPTER 17

Aurore

I rushed from one side of my studio to another, cleaning everything I could find and removing all my Post-its from the wall, listening to a rather steamy audiobook—one I couldn't help but picture Spectre in.

I had built a very heavy file on him in the hope of satisfying my hatred in the shapes of lovely pink Post-its. I might as well write a crime novel now. Even though I was starting to wave the white flag, if there was anything my father had taught me by constantly messing up and being a liar all this time, it was to not trust my heart completely.

I stopped for a moment, trying to clarify the mayhem that was happening inside my head.

I had replied to my mom, made the payment for the bees, and hopefully restored my karma. I went on Luna's Instagram account to spy on Ryan, who still had his profile set to private.

Now, I was waiting for Ajax to arrive at my apartment because this arrogant guy had wanted to pick me up for our "date." The date for which the charity had just thanked me, where I would be delivering a fairy-tale lecture. Not that I was aware of it. It was a brand-new surprise, where I would not only have to tell stories to the kids but also perform as the fictional bookish version of me—if that made sense. I blamed Emma. She had probably told them I was a fairy-tale fanatic, and now they wanted us to play dress-up. She strongly denied this, but I knew it was her.

I eventually forwarded the message to Ajax, who messaged me back: "I'm not getting dressed up, but I can't wait to see your costume." And to that, I replied: "You better find something. I'm not doing this alone."

"This is gonna be a nightmare." I would either fall or make jokes no one laughed at or, worse, be unimaginative. And lately, I hadn't been able to write anything that didn't include the words "penis" and "orgasm," which I doubted would be fitting for the context. My lease was ending soon, and just like Spectre, I too was going to move out and leave this part of my life. It was my last chance to fulfill my dream, and if that didn't work, I'd stop crushing my soul again and again for good.

"Greaaat." I kept on adjusting my outfit, which screamed, *I didn't bother to try seducing you, yet I spent one hour searching for the perfect ensemble to wear.* Typical. It was the kind of outfit I'd regret. The one that makes you look good in the morning with a flat stomach, but after eating barely anything, here it goes again, bloating. "I need to change. I need to—"

My doorbell rang; it could only be him, half an hour early.

"Coming!" I screamed like a boiler that was about to explode.

I slammed the door open. Not to my surprise, Spectre was dressed up in a full black three-piece tailored suit with his pocket watch attached and his typical Italian loafers that screamed of money. It was an outfit that looked similar to the one he usually wore but perhaps a bit more morbid and fancy.

"You were supposed to find something fairy-taleish."

"I'm the grumpy villain," he stated simply, entering my place without waiting for an invitation.

I made an overdramatic hand gesture that meant *please, come on in.* "You're dressed up as the grim reaper."

"I could work with that." His eyes roamed over me in a way that my one-hour outfit search was all for nothing. "And you?"

"I don't have anything." Liar. Liar. Liar. I'd been ready for this moment my whole life.

Ajax turned to regard my whole studio, which took him no more than ten seconds, taking in everything with a tight line. His eyes then shifted to my closet. "Is this where you hold your dresses hostage?"

"It's private. Plus, may I remind you that I didn't even invite you in."

"Aurore, we won't leave until you wear one of your dresses, and that's an order."

"No. You know I won't." I folded my arms on my chest. "And I don't receive orders from anyone."

"I'm not just anyone."

"Pretentious, exigent man with a cold heart counts in the anyone category," I countered back.

"Aurore, I'm serious." He towered over me, making me feel short compared to him. "You're my muse, and as my muse, I demand to see you wearing one of these dresses."

And now I was thinking his authority was hot. What on earth was happening to me? "But it's a date, and as a date, it's pretty screwed up on your part to not compliment me on how gorgeous I naturally and effortlessly look instead of asking me to change my outfit. Very douchebag move."

"So now you're acknowledging that this is a real date?" He didn't miss the beat.

"I didn't. I—"

"The kids are waiting for us. You wouldn't want to let them down." He looked at his old-fashioned vintage watch. "My cold-blooded heart doesn't care, but I bet you'd have regrets explaining to them why they all waited for nothing. At this age, you don't forget being—"

"Fine, you win. You're the evil one, manipulating me like that." I eyed my closet, my heart palpitating. "It's like pretending something that I'm not."

"Isn't that what writing is about?" He leaned on my closet. "And trust me, you act like a character coming from a storybook every day. You're definitely like that. Now, don't force me to watch you change because I will. I will even put that dress on you if I have to."

"You're a pervert on top of being a narcissist psychopath."

"I know each of your curves already. I have a good memory." He dared to tease me with that placid attitude of his. "Plus, I brought you a small gift."

My eyes doubled in size at the mention of the gift. "What is it?"

From inside his vest, he handed me a box. "It wasn't expensive; it's even ridiculous."

I opened it with haste. It was a crown. An evil queen kind of crown with black rocks and sharp edges. There was a wand too—a fairy godmother wand with a darker twist.

"I can't believe you bought this." I couldn't help but laugh. "I love it. That's actually touching."

"You seriously like it?"

"Of course."

"Then, allow me." He crowned me. "Now, I want to see you wearing one of those dresses of yours. I'll sit on the edge of your bed since you don't have a couch."

My heart increased its tempo, but he didn't leave me any choice. "Okay, I'll do this, but if you dare laugh, I'm going on our date wearing my unicorn pajamas, and you'll be the one with the princess gown."

"We have a deal." He sat on my bed and crossed his arms,

bringing out the muscles in his biceps. "Not that I'd fit in any of your dresses."

I lifted my chin and opened my closet. I needed a dress fit for the charity. I opted for a lavender one that left my shoulders bare, with long sleeves and puffy at the hips. Going into the bathroom, I put the dress and the crown on, accessorizing it with my wand. I applied a darker shade of gloss and added dark purple sparkles to my eyes.

"You got this, Aurore. You're not defined by your family, your failures, or by others. You're you. You're not ridiculous. You're—" I contemplated my reflection. "You're certainly weird for a twenty-five-year-old woman, but it's about time the fairy godmother becomes the main character. You deserve this. Luna would be proud."

Finishing my pep talk, I snapped a picture and sent it to my sister.

> **Me:** Can you believe that I'm wearing this?? Going to the charity date I was telling you about.

> **Luna:** OMG. You look so pretty!! Your life is a dream. Are you going with some man, though?

A blush crept on my cheeks.

> **Luna:** Don't you dare leave me on seen! It's a man, isn't it?! I need to know everything about him!

> **Me:** We'll talk later ;)

> **Luna:** You're vicious... and here I am, stuck doing homework during summer break. You better tell me everything or you're not my sister anymore!

I shut off my phone and exited the bathroom. I bowed dramatically in front of Ajax as if I was introducing myself in a royal court, the sound of the bathroom door creaking behind me before clicking shut.

"How do you find me, my dear nemesis?" I teased with a

taunting smile. This wasn't terrible after all. Being seen. Daring. Lifting my boundaries.

"I find you…" He became serious, a cryptic expression on his face. "Beautiful." He paused again, clearing his throat. "Or, as you put it earlier, naturally and effortlessly gorgeous."

"Thank you." I managed to keep my breathing in check. "Those dresses mean a lot to me. It's like the promise of a story that could be mine, a dream you don't want to let go of. It's hard to find a place to wear them. Well, I used to wear them for art classes when I modeled."

"I remember," he said.

"What?" Stupid hammering heart.

"The fabric of your gown, it was mesmerizing." His eyes locked on mine, but this time, he was the one to look away first. "Where would you wear them now?"

"I don't know. Beautiful places. Inspiring ones. For instance, I always dreamed of visiting the place I used to call 'the castle in the sand.' I don't remember the exact name, but I pretended this was my castle as a child, and my sister pretended she was my fiercest warrior. Anyway—"

"I'll bring you there," Ajax deadpanned, and it felt like all the air in the room had been stolen. "I'll bring you to those places until you wear each one of your dresses until the last one."

"Yeah, right." I snorted, but when he didn't budge, I asked, "Are you serious?"

"Why would you believe I'm not?"

His comment tightened the knot in my heart, and I hated the feel of it. The pound of hope. A crack in my already damaged heart.

"I—I bought cupcakes as well. I hope they'll like them." I obviously didn't try to bake them myself, following the recipe of a child on YouTube.

As I headed toward the exit, I felt Ajax's fingers brushing on mine. "I'm not lying, Aurore. I'll prove it."

We somehow made it to the hospital, where Veronique from L'espoir was waiting for us. All the shades of white around me made me uncomfortable, phantom ants scattering on my skin. I hadn't been to a hospital after what had happened to Luna, and being there again brought all the feels back.

I managed a smile, facing Veronique, a forty-year-old brunette with a kind expression, and handed her my box of cupcakes for the kids.

"Thank you for coming. They're waiting for you in the common room." She greeted us with a beaming smile while I hadn't been this stressed-out in my entire life. "I love how you're dressed up. I was expecting to see you as a princess."

I chuckled nervously, stroking my arm at the realization I had tried to be the princess but failed again. Veronique opened the door, and flashbacks struck me. I saw myself running with all the air in my lungs in my long dress in the cold hallway. I remembered the doctor's diagnosis. My mother crying. My absent father, who didn't pick up my calls.

My hand slammed to my heart as if I wanted to stop it at the view of the group of children, between six and thirteen, sitting in a circle. *Some of them are the same age Luna was back then.* It felt as if my heart shattered into thousands of pieces. Some of the children couldn't breathe on their own, had scars on their skin, or were in wheelchairs. A loud buzz echoed in my ears. I couldn't handle it, a wave of pain washing over me. I balled my hand, and I remained blank, unable to move or do anything. I was petrified.

"I can't do this," I whispered to Ajax, panic seizing my throat.

I couldn't play the princess and act like sunshine while they were the true heroes and I was the impostor. I wasn't the person to help them. Tears lashed the corners of my eyes, and I sprinted to the opposite side, disappearing from the room. I rushed to an empty white corner of a hallway and exploded into tears.

I had a hypersensitivity hidden underneath, and today, I couldn't hold on. This was unfair. No one deserved this. No one—

"Aurore," Ajax's voice called me from behind.

"I'm sorry, I need a minute." I struggled to breathe in and out, and before I could think, I collided with Ajax's chest, hard and desperate.

He held his grip on me, wrapping me against his strong frame. I sought a comfort I never received. I never dared to be that vulnerable before because I needed to remain strong for everyone else, but today, I couldn't. Ajax stroked my hair, and I let it all go, the pain and the remorse.

I wasn't there for Luna.

"I feel like an impostor. When I saw their smiles, despite the pain and fear they must go through, I couldn't step inside. I don't have the slightest idea of what they went through, and here I am, how can I help?" More tears fell. "I'm just parading in a silly dress— this doesn't help. This doesn't change the fact I—"

"Aurore." Ajax's hands met my cheeks, and I had to crane my neck to meet his eyes and show him my tears. My weakness. Silly tears. I hadn't cried in forever. "You can help. You're ingenious, creative, and you have such a caring personality. I've never seen anyone like you. If there is one person that can make others believe your life is one of a storybook, it's you. Hell, you inspired me. The foundation is named Hope for a good reason."

"You don't understand…" More tears flowed. "My sister, she—" I tightened my hands on his vest until it crumpled. I'd never said the words out loud before. I was never able to speak of it again because it tore my heart. "My sister was bullied hard at school for years, and I wasn't there."

My lips trembled, and I shut my eyes. "I was in Paris, too busy to listen to her or care for her. They made her go through hell— she no longer ate anything in the canteen and hid in the toilets because they humiliated her. They hit her, and she lied to us about the marks on her skin, pretending it was nothing because she was ashamed. We knew nothing of the hell she was going through. Nothing." I bit on my lower lip hard until it bled, my nostrils flaring from rage. "The school knew my dad was unfaithful, and a group of kids used that to hurt her. They created a social media group and page to shame her and even pushed her into a river one day, treating her as less than a stray dog. And the day my mother called me—"

My hands shook, and Ajax's arms pulled me even closer to him like a protective shield.

"She was at the hospital with cuts on her wrists. She had tried to—" My voice dropped, and I fell on the floor, curving myself around my knees.

I was responsible. I'd let that happen to Luna by being in Paris. She had no one but me, and I'd failed her. I didn't respond to her messages after hours, dodging her calls when I wasn't in the mood. I even told her she was a drag when we were younger, tired of being the big sister and the pillar of the family who had to handle everything. I wasn't with her when my family exploded and my dad's true colors showed. She was alone.

She hadn't been back to school since that day. She was now scared of meeting new people her age and shut down all of her social media accounts before bringing them back a couple of weeks ago—probably because of this Ryan. In September, it'd be her first year back to school, and I was terrified the story would repeat itself.

I breathed deeply. "She thought her life was meaningless and that no one loved her. When I thought I had lost her forever, I promised myself I'd never let anything bad happen to anyone I care about. That's why I need to prove to her that happy endings do exist. I can't let her down again. My little sister has the kindest soul. She deserves her fairy tale. Not this. And I'm a failure at that too."

I crashed my face on my hands, and Ajax crouched down in front of me. I felt his fingertips brushing over my hands before he separated them to expose my tears. He stroked a strand of my hair behind my ear in a touch that was caring and affectionate, but his face didn't reveal anything.

"Aurore," he whispered. "I'm not good at this... dealing with emotions, but I—"

"It's okay, Ajax. I'm not asking for pity or—"

"Your sister is strong. She survived, and she believes in you. You don't have to be invincible for her—just be you. She hasn't lost hope. You need to forgive yourself and stop feeling unworthy of her love. Life may not be fair, but we have to make it the best we can." He snapped his lips shut, frowning. "When my mother was diagnosed with Alzheimer's and dementia at an age younger than usual, my father treated her like a patient, as if she was a stranger to him and not the same human as she was. She isn't unhappy—she's a fighter, and she doesn't want to be looked at with pity. Your sister simply wants her sister back, and for that, you need to heal, just like she does."

My eyes widened, and I tried to erase the new tears forming. "You're actually very good at this."

"The expensive appointments at the shrink my father paid for will have been useful for something." I believed he was trying to make a joke. "I left too. I left my brother at the mercy of my father, and I'm not even sure my mother remembers me. So I think I understand how you feel."

"It feels like climbing the top of a mountain, and as you try to reach higher, you have to take off the arrows stuck on your back, your hands so blistered that it burns. A storm tries to kick you off alongside the falling stones, but if you fall, you crash and die. It feels like you have no choice but to continue, carrying your loved ones like a weight so they won't fall with you," I whispered. "It feels like you'll never reach the top of the mountain, but you don't have a choice."

"It feels just like that," Ajax added. "Except that I dropped the weights and didn't look back like the unemotional man that I am."

"Ajax…" My eyes bored into his, and I hesitated to reach for his hand. "I'm sorry about your mother. That is heartbreaking."

"The day I left, she was only at an early stage, just messing up with names and not remembering what happened minutes ago. Sometimes, she'd walk at night without remembering where she was. She's the only one who used to know I'm Spectre. Now she's forgotten, but she still loves my art," he confided. "That's why I paint. Because I want to immortalize moments so they are never forgotten. Our brains can die, but not what we feel watching an art piece. No one and no sickness can take away our essence and how we feel. That's why those children and your sister need you. They need your creativity. Your feelings. They need to remember how it feels to be alive. They need to remember they are strong, loved, and that they are allowed to dream. To have the future they hope for. Those happy endings of yours."

"I thought you didn't believe in that." I wrinkled my nose, snorting like a kid in need of a Kleenex. "You said life is empty."

"And you're proving me wrong."

"You're—" *Perfect.* My chin shook, my hands trembling, witnessing a part of Ajax I'd never seen before. A part I connected with more than I thought I ever could with another being. "You're right."

I erased the tears with my knuckles. "I'm sorry. Oh god, I haven't cried once in all these years, and today, I can't help it. The tears don't want to stop."

"Never excuse yourself for feeling."

I took a shaky breath. "I'm not used to being vulnerable."

"I won't hurt you," he said as if I had offended him.

"I really want to believe you." I calmed myself down with some breathing, looking at my surroundings with a new peace. "I'm ready now."

"I'm right behind you."

He lifted himself up, and he kept his promise, walking behind me. Our hands brushed together when I stepped into the room once more. The chatter stopped, and beautiful wide eyes were on us. Ajax gave me a head nod and parted his hand away from me. *I got this.*

"Hi, everyone!" I waved at the children, my mascara probably dripping down my cheeks. "Today, I'm alongside the—" I looked at Ajax, who stood next to the board. "The misunderstood knight. And we'll tell you a fairy-tale story, but it's not a story like any others. This is ours. I recognize all of you—you were the heroes of Alandia."

"And to help you remember the tale, we brought outfits to help you choose your characters," Ajax cut in, showing the bags tossed to the side of the room.

The children rushed to the bags. Inside, there were either swords to be knights, crowns to be princesses, and other disguises to be witches, magical creatures, or superheroes. All of them dressed up, Veronique helping the ones who couldn't get dressed by themselves. I had no idea where the clothes and accessories came from. Ajax had said "we." Was it he who brought this?

A little girl dressed as an Amazon warrior said, "But you, who are you?"

"You're no princess," another one with a crown added.

I locked eyes with Ajax, and a smile tilted my lips, accepting my character. I brought a hand to my Evil Queen crown, and Ajax made drawings on the board. It was my cue.

"Some would say I'm the villain of the tale, but that's because they don't know my story," I narrated, my eyes probably sparkling with mischief. The children gossiped, and some gasped. "I'm your evil fairy godmother, and I'm here to make you remember the magic in you. It all began with once upon a time, forgotten by everyone else…"

I improvised a fairy-tale story with every character the children were dressed up as. This way, they'd all either act as villains or heroes in the tale. There were no secondary characters, only main ones. Spectre was illustrating every scene in the back, as I lost myself in a storytelling of adventures, magic, and love. The choreography slowly took place, and blank pages were written. At the sound of their laughs and the sight of their eyes immersed in the story, I knew I couldn't give up. I couldn't let them down. I couldn't let past events define me. They were all like Luna, strong dreamers, and so was I. I still felt that passion warming my heart and shattering the thorns.

I was worthy of a happy ending.

"And that's how you guys were the heroes of Alandia, saving it from misery and sadness." I bowed, and the children clasped their hands.

I exchanged a look with Ajax, whose lips were curling into one of his emblematic scowls.

"Fairy godmother!" a girl in a princess dress called me, tugging on her ribbon. "Is he your boyfriend?"

"No," Ajax and I denied together at the same time.

"The way he looks at you, it's like love. And you, you're red like a tomato," she insisted with a laugh.

"No, I'm not." If I couldn't feel my blush before, I could definitely now, and I wasn't the kind to blush.

"You're blushing!" other girls screamed at the same time.

I crossed my arms and squinted. "Stop now, or I'll curse you."

But my threat made them laugh even more.

"Knights don't love." A boy brandished his sword to the sky. "They conquer."

"Their hearts are brave. They love, and they protect each other." I displayed a smile. "My sister is a knight. She always has my back."

"Will the evil fairy godmother come back to tell more stories?" the boy in the back under a ventilator asked.

"Me?" I literally gasped.

"Yeah! We want to know your story," another one added.

"You're funny," the girl with the ribbon said with a beaming smile.

I swallowed, feeling uncomfortable. They wanted

me—grumpy, sarcastic, side-character me. My stories and I were chosen.

"I'm sorry, I don't think I'm the right person," I refuted with hand gestures.

"Please," they pleaded in a group.

"We can identify with your stories. It feels real," the boy in the back dropped.

"We have a place in them, even if we are imperfect," one of the kids whispered.

Imperfect.

I peered at each of them. All with incredible stories to tell, but they didn't feel like the main characters. They felt imperfect because it was what we made them believe with stories not representing them.

"You're right." I smiled, recognition flashing across my features. "You know what, I'd actually love to."

The children put on satisfied smiles as Veronique clapped her hands. "It's time, guys. The knight and the godmother have to go now."

"But I'll be back with more fairy tales. I promise," I added in a high-pitched tone as the children started to gather back to their daily schedule, complaining about it.

"I have a question." The pretty girl with the princess gown rolled her wheelchair to be next to me. "Are you truly a fairy godmother?"

"In a way." I crouched on my knees to face her. "I mean, we can be everything we want to be, right?"

"I want to walk someday again. Can you help me?" Her eyes shone, and I parted my lips, shooting a glance at Veronique.

Veronique's brows knitted together, and she gave me a head shake, her hand over her heart. That child would never walk again, but I couldn't let her lose her dream—the feeling was too painful. If we could dream it, we could make it happen, one way or another. There was always a way—that's what Luna taught me.

"I'm sorry. I cannot do that," I said to her.

Disappointment washed away her features, and her hopeful smile dropped. "Oh, I thought so."

I seized her hand. "But I promise I'll make you fly."

Her features lit up again. "Really? Could you do that?"

I laughed. "Yes! Yes, I can do that!" Evil godmothers had plenty of resources to carry out their evil schemes, and I was a tenacious one. "What's your name?"

"Clara."

I stood up. "Clara, I'll make you fly. That's a promise."

We exchanged a last smile, and Veronique came to see me alone once the kids all left. "They loved you."

"Thank you. I would like to help more often." I paused. "My friend Emma mentioned you wanted to produce a theater show for the kids? Perhaps I could help with the storytelling and the organization. I'm still in Paris for a couple of weeks, if that's enough."

"Oh yes, we were looking for a volunteer to get invested in a theater show, but we still haven't found anyone. It would be a pleasure if we could have you, and I'm sure parents would love it." Parents liking me was another battle. "I'll contact you about your availability and schedule a free time for all of the children."

"It's perfect. Thank you so much." Ideas came to my mind, and a wave of new hope surged through me.

"I should be the one thanking you, and your—right, not your boyfriend." She glanced at Ajax. "When he told us you were a writer and could do a fairy-tale reading dressed up as a real-life storybook character, we were so happy. Plus, the children love the outfits you guys brought today."

"He did that?" My mouth hung open. He was the one who'd called them, not Emma. That sinister Ajax mincing his way into my cold heart had planned everything.

"He did." Veronique grinned. "I should head back to work. We'll keep in touch, Aurore. Glad to have you on board."

I couldn't detach my eyes from Ajax, who was prowling toward me, removing the bits of chalk that had landed on his jacket.

I lifted a brow. "So, I heard you were the one responsible for me dressing up like that."

"You needed a reason to wear your dresses, and now that you've done it once, you won't just look at them in your closet."

"Thank you for everything you did today. For me and for them. You're not as selfish and coldhearted as I thought you were."

"Is that a compliment?"

"I think it is," I teased. "I think you even helped me find my inspiration."

He leaned closer, and it took all the willpower in the world not to jump into his arms. "And how so?"

"I have tales in my head. Life is too depressing without a dream, and like you said, I can't change my view of the world. Life is not empty, and if I succeeded in proving you wrong, I can do it with everyone else. Life can be a true fairy tale—this is not my ending yet." I removed the crown that he had offered to me from my head and analyzed it, excitement coming in a wave that couldn't be tempered. "I want to fight for all those who haven't seen their story written. I want each person to find themselves in my books. I want myself and everyone else like me to feel that they have the right to that happiness too."

And here it was, my biggest confession. I'd been searching for inspiration outside of myself while I had it in me all this time. Everything I felt and lived, everyone around me fighting battles of their own: I had a story, one inspired by reality. I had to use all the emotions within me, not only the light but the blackness too. Just like fairy tales are born from the dark and the gloomy to bring out light and joy.

"I'm very pleased to hear that." A thin line sketched his lips. "And what would your Aurore fairy tale look like?"

I thought this through. "She'd wear a tight black bustier dress, with crossover lines to add some textures, an open slit on the leg, long black gloves, and a veil a shade of purple resting on her shoulders. And this crown on her head."

"Her clothes are what came first to you?"

"Obviously." My lips turned playful. "You can tell a lot about her by the way she dresses. For instance, this one, she'd be the misunderstood evil queen. Happy endings are not the same for everyone."

"Well, I look forward to reading it."

"I'll inspire you too, Ajax. I'm your muse—you'll see. I'll help you get what you want," I promised to the man who had given me back the spark I had lost.

I was finding myself again.

I had cried, but I was rising up from my ashes.

And in the end, I wouldn't overcome my past with hatred and revenge but with love and forgiveness in my heart.

CHAPTER 18

Aurore

Spectre's art studio didn't feel like a battlefield.

Classical music rocked my heart in a symphony worthy of a final act. A light breeze escaped from the half-open window behind me, swinging my dress toward Spectre. A ray of sunshine hit part of his face, and his gaze raked over my body like sensual adoration. His pupils widened, dedicated to the task. The way he observed me didn't feel intrusive but way too erotic.

His dress shirt was unbuttoned at the top to show off his fair, muscular chest. It was the first time Spectre wasn't so neat and strictly dressed, despite wearing his fancy trousers.

Posing for him wasn't a burden, even if I bit on my lip so hard to contain my heart racing like a clock out of order. His pen went back and forth over the canvas with hard strokes, commanding his brain. Sometimes, out of nowhere, he'd tear up what he'd drafted and start over again. Other times, he'd remove one of the sketches to save it, and redo another, moving his easel to another angle.

But his eyes—his eyes were solely mine.

"I have a question," I cut through the silence, changing my pose by lifting my dress as if walking in a valley of flowers—even if I was picturing myself crushing them one by one.

He just hummed, informing me I could go on but too dedicated to his work to speak.

"*The Sad Girl.*" My trust issues were spreading again, the need to unravel Spectre's intentions stronger than anything before I could let myself fall into the rabbit hole. "Why don't you sell *The Sad Girl?*"

"Because I want the world to see it. No one else gets to own it."

I made that a second question. "How did you remember every detail of me? Did you take a picture?"

"No." He took out a charcoal, his eyes setting firmly on mine, giving me his full attention. "I can remember every detail of you. I don't need a picture."

"So, why did you ask me to become your muse? Why not use a picture?"

"Because I work with emotions. I want to witness the moment and memorize it. With your hatred of me, you showed me only a side of you. If I were to take a picture of you back then, it'd be you giving me the middle finger, and that's not what I wanted."

"But I could just have pretended with a smile or something. We wouldn't have to spend all this time together." For some unknown reason, my heart hammered at the sight of Spectre stalking toward me and cleaning his hands with a towel. I was finding excuses to escape the tension. Another excuse to run away.

"Precisely. We wouldn't have." He paused for an instant, lingering so close to me. "Contemplating a picture isn't enough. I need to unravel your truths and know everything about you as my muse. Obsessively explore your many facets."

Another step from him made my heart pulsate in my throat, and a horde of goose bumps made my hair stand on end. "It sounds like you're asking for my soul, something far more intimate than being a simple muse."

"Simple?" he breathed, the corner of his lips lifting up. "I heard the relationship between an artist and his muse is intuitive, peculiar, visceral, complex."

Until he got bored and set his sights on another muse. My father had loved my mother a long time ago; he had courted her with many dates and shared her life for twenty years. He did all of that only to betray us, hiding his true colors all this time. Augustus chased me to fall in love with someone else. The moment I gave in to Spectre, he'd flee, just like a memory.

"We have an expiration date." I lifted my chin. "I'll do my best to help you with your fairy-tale project because it's what you pay me for, and after that, you're leaving, right?"

I'd noticed that the boxes in his house were already packed.

"Yes," he dropped. "I'll be heading to the US."

And meanwhile, I'd be headed to my small town, going back to where it all started.

"Why are you leaving?"

"I have nothing left for me here." His finger skimmed across my jaw and stopped on its course. "Can I?"

I nodded, and he pushed my hair slightly away from my collarbone, stroking the naked, shivering part of my skin delicately.

"What are you running away from?" I recognized the look in his eyes. I'd had the same when I wanted to give everything up. The emptiness. The void. The past.

"I've been given many opportunities, lots of money, and expansion—that's if our collaboration is successful. If I were to stay here, this would be the downfall of my career. I've seen everything I had to see. I'm done, and my latest pieces are…" He cleared his throat. "Either terrible or absent. All the money I'm making is from my investments, not so much from art."

"The eternal quest for inspiration. And do you feel you'll be able to have a new beginning if you hide who you are?"

His eyes dropped to my lips, and my belly melted like lava. "It's part of the myth."

"That's why you don't want to stay in the same place? You believe people will unmask you?" *Why would it be too bad? He's a walking dream.* "But you'll always be alone because if you were to create a link with anyone, everyone would end up knowing someday. It's inevitable," I mused out loud as a warning that nothing good could come from giving in to temptation.

His fingers had stopped on their course. "I'm used to being alone. I'm better left alone. It's the best for everyone."

"How can you live like that?" My lips inched closer to his, having a mind of their own. "How can you cut everyone from your life and live like a ghost?"

"It's what I feel inside."

"Emptiness," I said, and he frowned. "I've looked at your studio and artwork. I'm the only painting whose face is visible—you usually never paint people in a way we can recognize who they are. They are always hidden. Why?"

Our bodies were attracted like magnetic electricity, a few centimeters from colliding. This was dangerous—not in the exhilarating, playing-with-fire kind of way but the destructive kind. The kind that gets you submerged underneath water, that feels so calm and needy, but it'd choke you to death if you stayed longer.

"Because you were the only person I met who didn't hide who she was or her emotions. It was pure. Raw. Beautiful. You did what others couldn't. That's why *The Sad Girl* spoke to the world. They could identify with you. They could feel. You made others feel. Do you know how gifted you are? No one thought you were weak, Aurore. Broken, maybe, but never weak."

"Broken isn't any better," I snorted.

"Broken means you survived. It means whatever life threw at you, you were stronger and beat it. It means you won."

I'd hated him for so long, but I was healing. I was growing, despite the fact it left a scar on me. The scar that my close ones would see as proof I wasn't strong enough. The scar that exposed my imperfections and this feeling of *not being good enough, not worthy enough.* I'd been reborn that day, because *feeling meant being alive.*

"I had no muse until you. Only you."

I felt his hot breath brushing over my lips, and my stomach coiled.

"I-I can't do this," I shrieked in a low moan.

"Aurore." At the sound of his voice, my eyes drifted to his. "I can't control the urge to kiss you."

Before I could snap an answer, our lips had crushed together and sent me to another world with him.

His hands roamed my skin as our kiss grew hot and passionate by the second. It wasn't the one described in fairy tales but the kind that ravaged your soul and ignited your whole being. One that sent you to the top of the stars. Each flick of his tongue was possessive as my hands latched on to his jaw, the need for more growing like a heated volcano. His strong arm hooked around me and held me steady in his protective embrace. His body would have felt like stone if it weren't for the beating of his heart—which was beating as strongly as mine.

It was like ice meeting fire, a combustion of elements forming an electrical shock.

When we pulled back, neither he nor I seemed to realize what had happened. Ajax, usually so controlled and frigid, had eyes like a storm, ready to ravage me, passion consuming him whole. As for me, my hatred had transformed itself into an inferno of lust.

"I have to write." I pulled my spirits back, breaking the kiss. I felt inspired. And now, I needed to go.

"We're done for today," he said at almost the same moment, as if we hadn't just kissed like a very scorching moment in a book.

At least we agreed, right before I almost tripped. Again. "I know I'm a walking disaster. This happens when I'm either flushed, awkward, or angry, and I can't seem to help my case by talking."

"You're flushed?"

"You just kissed me." As if that should be my best defense. I'd kissed him back too. Hell, I almost bit him. And worst of all—he inspired me.

"But you told me you didn't want to do it again."

I wished I could read him.

"I don't because there is no us." I defended a lost cause. "You shouldn't have kissed me again."

"You're making it hard for me." He didn't seem to have listened to me, lost in whatever rigid universe he was coming from.

"You're leaving, and I'll be leaving too, for what it's worth, and I have a story to write, and you're drawing me for a project I dreamed of making mine. That doesn't scream healthy, earth-shattering romance." I pulled away. "And worst of all, I'm under contract with you, Spectre. You can't have anyone in your life because you live like a ghost, and I'm The Sad Girl."

"I need to protect myself."

"From me, because you don't trust me, and I get it. I don't trust you either." I managed a smile. That was why this whole thing was doomed from the start.

"Do you still hate me?"

I thought this through, the taste of his lips still inked on mine. "This answer belongs to me only. Now, if you'll excuse me, I have an appointment with my bed and unicorn pajamas to get some writing done at my home."

He nodded, and I pinched my skin, promising myself to stop making impulsive mistakes with Spectre, or else he might give me the biggest heartbreak of all.

I only had one thing on my mind the moment I crossed my front door—and it wasn't to finish off the leftover chocolate fudge in the fridge that I had saved for the occasion but to open my notebook.

I didn't even bother to sit up on my bed; my nose was already diving through the pages of my past in search of a specific moment.

The one where I'd probably first met Ajax unknowingly in an abandoned storage room.

"Where is it, damn it." I turned the pages with speed every time I came face-to-face with the name Augustus—this asshole filled my notebook.

I slammed my finger on the paragraph. "That's it!"

I was beginning to believe that the tortured man I had met was a ghost. One who haunted these remnants of the past with his presence. This was the sixth time I had returned to the storage room looking for the stranger. But he had never come back, while I was leaning against the same broken window through which gave a view to the gardens. I began to write in the middle of this dusty place with the smell of old books, and dear journal, I found proof that the stranger was real. I found sketches made on some kind of parchment hidden in the windowsill. The pencil marks were dry, stiff, hard, and unerasable.

It was the same drawing over and over. A barely sketched man's face, proportioned with circles and squares, which displayed several expressions on his face. The same emotions had been drawn several times in different ways, as if we could guess someone's personality just by the way he smiled, before being scratched out. He had added the words empty, fake, not it, *all around. He approached them almost in a scientific way, like an actor trying to reproduce them. But most of the expressions were overdone—they didn't seem real. Except one. It was the only girl present in the sketches— or more or less only the woman's gaze, because only her eyes were drawn. She had a lost look, half-sad, even if her eyes seemed to squint as if she was smiling falsely.*

I even thought for a moment that she looked like me, but she had beautiful eyes full of sweetness that could be read like an open book, and I was the kind to hold everything in. I put the sketches in the corner. I had no more time. I had an appointment with Augustus, who was returning from his architecture class with Violette at this moment. Maybe she was the girl the stranger had drawn?

I hurriedly pulled out the letter I had in my pocket addressed to "the dark stranger" and tucked it in with the rest of the sketches. I had written the sentences:

'Dear ghost, I hope we'll meet again. I'll be waiting. Not just for your name, but who you truly are. My sister gave this to me for luck. I don't need it anymore. It's your time to make a wish, stranger. The girl from the storage room.'

Inside the letter, I had given him my most prized possession, hoping that Luna wouldn't hold it against me.

My four-leaf clover.

I don't even know why I did it—no one knew about that man, except rumors that he was some 'freak,' but something inside me pushed me to find out the truth.

The door cracked open, and I ran towards it. I had ten minutes left before I posed as a muse. Augustus had come in and asked me why I was standing in this dismal storage room. Again. Violette gave me a wave and a smile, which I didn't return.

"We still have five minutes before I start working." I pulled Augustus by his collar and kissed him in front of her, looking her straight in the eyes before slamming the door, displaying a sharky smile that I had won. I hate her, dear journal. I hate the way she makes me feel like—

"Argh!" I shut the notebook. I didn't know if I was more repulsed by how ridiculous I was or by the regret of not having sent them both to the bushes nearby before shipping them to a land with no happy ever afters.

A couple of days after that, the storage room had definitely been closed. Rumor had it students were making out inside at the risk of damaging the material. My jealousy had cost me to lose the safe haven of that stranger and the possibility of ever seeing him again.

"Which meant he probably never got the four-leaf clover." I thought this through. "But Ajax said he got one."

Had the four-leaf clover sent me to him all along, or was my imagination playing tricks on me?

CHAPTER 19

Ajax

Productivity was a word I adopted in my daily routine. Everything was meticulous. Organized. Detailed. I left no place for anything colorful or anything that would derail my peace. Except for my fairy—the reason why I ended up, for the first time in my life, in front of the TV, a remote control in my hand and my fingers tapping out "fairy tales" in the afternoon.

A knot formed in my throat. This was all ridiculous. I had work to do, and yet, I was about to do absolutely nothing, trying to understand the phenomenon that she was.

She had been raised with this idea of the world, a world that was unknown to me. I rented the first movie, about to suffer through a marathon of princesses and all-too-perfect Prince Charmings. I sat straight on my sofa, the orchestra announcing the happy ever after to come, a weird sensation attacking my vital organs.

"This is ridiculous." I was ridiculous, on top of being unproductive and obsessed. I could convince my lying self I was doing this for my

Ever After project, but the truth was I couldn't care less. I was doing this for one desperate purpose.

Lost, I grabbed my phone instinctively, watching her name on the screen. I could do anything, but I was using the little free time I had dedicated to searching for why she was like a fairy in this gray world.

I ♥ pathetic men

Loser me: I hope you have those unicorn pajamas on.

I texted her. I did it. And it was probably the worst line someone could think of. To help my case, her answer was instantaneous.

"My"

My fairy: As a matter of fact I do, but I'm in the middle of a movie, regretting my choice right now. *crying emoji*

That makes both of us. I lifted my eyes and watched the prince make his entrance with a song and a costume that screamed carnival. She was into that, while I was similar to the abandoned castle of the wicked witch in the gloomy background.

Me: How so?

My fairy: The dog is about to die, and I feel so sad. He SHOULDN'T die!!

Her emotions seemed strong. Overwhelming.

Me: It's just a movie.

My fairy: You have the emotional sensibility of a robot. No wonder why you're oblivious to my suffering.

She sent a bunch of emojis again, and I froze on the phone. She was about to cry for fiction. She was feeling through fiction, and here I was, blank in the real world.

My fairy: See, you don't even know what to say. When was the last time you cried? And don't say never!

Me: Probably as a child. I don't remember.

My fairy: I'll make you watch and read all the saddest books and movies I know. I'll get a tear from you someday!

Here's hoping.

Me: You're wasting your time.

I refocused on the fairy tale and watched the fairy godmother appear, my lips twitching. She was weird. Aurore wasn't like the old lady but more like a youthful eternal bloom. *And you're a corny asshole.*

> **My fairy:** You're the one who's texting me. Do you feel lonely?

I glanced at the void around me. If this was being lonely, I think I enjoyed it. At least, I wasn't bothered by it. It was white and empty but familiar.

> **Me:** Do you?

> **My fairy:** Sometimes.

At the same time, my brother sent me a text.

> **Archi:** Are you coming to the family dinner? And don't play the busy card, I see you online, asshole.

I rolled my eyes and threw my phone further away. The sweet and caring prince was fighting for the princess, while the villain was failing in achieving his goal, being selfish and having almost no allies. I swallowed hard, inching forward to watch the TV.

I spent the rest of my day binge-watching the whole list, getting somehow closer to understanding Aurore's personality.

But what all of this taught me was that in that universe, I identified with the emotionless villain dead set on his goal and hurting everyone around him.

Aurore

Spectre had left me on seen.

I had no idea why he had texted me in the first place, but this was fun, and I wasn't ready to let him get away with it that easily. Taking another bite of my chocolate cake, I sent an impulsive text.

> **Me:** How's the whole art stuff going?

> **The Devil incarnate (skull emoji):** I took a break today.

> **Me:** You never take breaks. Are you sure you're okay??

I laughed, slumping further on the bed, my computer giving me a nasty look over the two hundred words I had written—but at least my nails had been done in a pitch-black color. I had found a semblance of a plot for my fairy-tale draft, one including our cold, grumpy anti-hero living in a dark realm, the sister wanting to participate in a knight contest, and the main character, a fairy godmother made evil queen who had no magic whatsoever. A dream cast.

> **The Devil incarnate (skull emoji):** I'm not the one crying over movies.

> **Me:** Hey, I don't cry. I don't shed a tear, I just hurt myself.

> **The Devil incarnate (skull emoji):** Why on earth for? Is it pleasurable?

> **Me:** You're soulless, but it's okay. I'm ready to share a part of my soul with you.

The doorbell rang, which was unusual. I wasn't expecting anyone. I lifted myself from my place of work and ambled toward the door with incoherent mumbles about not wanting to be disturbed doing absolutely nothing. Someone knocked on the door again, and I re-thought my life choice about not adding a button where I could flush the unwanted stranger out of my apartment through an ice shower.

"Impatient." I unlocked the door with a deadly stare, and I came face-to-face with my avid texter: Ajax. My eyes doubled in size. "What are you doing here?"

"What are you doing right now?" He purposely ignored my question.

"I'm in my pajamas, probably with leftovers of cake around the corners of my lips and—"

"You don't," he deadpanned as if that analysis was important.

"Great. At least I didn't embarrass myself even more, but as I was saying, I have a freshly manicured hand holding a spoon, so I think this pretty much displays what I was doing."

"So, you're not busy."

"This is a full-time activity, and it's very draining and consuming," I quipped back, readjusting my hair despite myself.

"Would you come with me to a family dinner?" He switched the subject bluntly.

"What?" I dropped the spoon on my little toe and didn't even feel pain, still in shock. I didn't expect my nemesis—the nemesis I'd kissed like a beast earlier—to want me to meet his parents.

"I know it's last-minute, and we'll have to leave in an hour."

"One hour?" My voice was shrill, probably awakening all the neighbors. "And you're asking me this only now? I don't know what to wear to meet a family of surgeons and doctors who have a castle in the middle of France!"

Yes, I felt like a peasant meeting the aristocracy.

"It's not a castle," he corrected with his annoying tone. "You can wear one of your dresses. And I'm only asking you now because I just made up my mind about eventually going, and I drove to your place, led by this impulsive move."

"Only now?" My eyes flared. "What made you change your mind?"

"An impulse. Probably a mistake," he grumbled.

"A mistake? You have to be there for your mother, and your brother seems to care for you. Why would you hesitate?"

"Does that mean you're coming?" He paused. "My fairy."

I crossed my arms, leaning on the door. "Maybe, but only if you beg." *squeal*

"Please," he growled. "If you need me on my knees, I'll even bow to you."

"That's tempting." I chewed on my inner cheek, holding in a laugh. "Fine, but I have questions and—"

aaaAHHHH-

He glanced at his pocket watch. "The car ride is pretty long, and I know how much you can talk, and you have only fifty-eight minutes to get ready. Are you sure you want to get into this right now?"

"You're right, no time to waste." I hurried into the room, but to do what? I was meeting Ajax's parents. Plus, Ajax was leaving soon. I froze. "But Ajax, what if I don't fit?"

I didn't expect the scowl on his lips. "This is what you're worried about?"

"Of course, I am. I like when people like me. I want them to like me." My childhood issues about wanting to be the perfect one sparked up. "Except for you. I didn't care if you did or not."

"How privileged I am." He didn't enter but, on the contrary, parted away from the main door. "If you feel uncomfortable, we'll get the hell out of there, but I have to warn you the Clemonte men's genes are hard to get rid of. You've seen my brother."

Was this his attempt at joking? "No one sparks my temper as much as you do, and if there is one person who isn't afraid, it's me. Now, I'll go put on my war armor, then."

I closed the door in Ajax's face in a draft, and I believed he remained waiting for me behind it. I rushed back to my bedroom and tied my hair with a bow. I put on a dress up to my knees with some frills like a ballet tutu. The fabric of the top was in pastel lace. It was halfway between the kind of dress the princess lost in the woods would wear and the one the villain would wear at a fashion show. To that, I added heels and my small fluffy bag.

One hour and a few minutes later, I was ready and descended the countless stairs to meet with Ajax by his car. A car parked like an asshole in the middle of the Parisian street. The Greek warrior wore, for once, a white shirt underneath a marine blue suit as his eyes roamed over my dress.

"I think it's castle-worthy, no?" I said. "And me dressing up this way means nothing! It's just that I doubt your parents will appreciate me if I were to wear my big black leather shoes and arrive like a cloud of black fog. Now, say something."

Vibes fr

"I think you've been raised by fairies in an enchanted wood and eat flower nectar for breakfast." Of all the things he could have said, this was the first thing that came through.

"I know that wasn't supposed to be a compliment, but I'll take it anyway."

He knitted his brows. "Who says it wasn't one?"

"Because for you, enchanted wood and fairies probably scream of immaturity and a curse at your daily silent meditation, and don't get me started on flower nectar."

"Or perhaps you're the colorful painting in my dull blank canvas, Aurore." He opened the door for me to step inside, and that's how I embarked on a journey I didn't expect.

I second-guessed my choice when Ajax revved his engine. "Am I crazy to have agreed to come with you?"

"You definitely are, to my greatest pleasure."

"At least I'll know where you come from. It'll be a fun social experience." Even though I was stepping into the midst of family issues, a part of me felt I was about to discover more about the origin of Spectre. "I have a tendency to attract chaotic situations."

"The Clemontes are anything but fun, but we know chaotic," he mused, and there was no turning back when we departed. "Thank you for coming."

I didn't answer as we moved away from the capital to race into the unknown. I waited only until we had crossed the highway toll to ask my first question.

"So, what's the deal between you and your father? And before you say anything, I want to remind you that I'm in the car with you and that I deserve a reply. And yes, I'm nosy—deal with it," I said with finesse.

"Long story short, I'm my father's biggest disappointment," he dropped, his eyes focused on the road as the car exceeded the speed limit.

Ajax was breaking the rules; it wasn't in his temper.

"And the long story?" I contemplated with a proud smile, my pink teddy bear bouncing. He still hadn't removed it from his car.

"I used to be his favorite son, but as I grew up, we never got along. He had always been demanding. For him, art was not a job for a man. Especially for a Clemonte, and he showed it to me multiple times when I was a kid by replacing my free time with anatomy studies. He had a future set up for me before I was even born, to follow in his footsteps and become miserable for the rest of my life." He spoke as if he had no feelings whatsoever, as if this didn't pain him.

"That must not have been easy growing up. How did you face him?"

"I didn't, at first. I grew up wanting his approval. I stopped painting because real men don't do such foolish things, and I stepped into line." His grip on the wheel tightened. "With my father, everything was a competition between my brother and I. He put us against each other so we'd annihilate one another to become better men instead of working as a team. The winner had a gift; the other was a disgrace. I was the eldest, so I was stronger, but I couldn't keep doing that to him. It would have destroyed him."

"So you protected him," I whispered.

"I tried but failed. I promised my father I'd do what he awaited from me, on the condition he left my brother alone and let him do what he truly loved. We had a deal. And so, my brilliant career in football started, and I was one of the best students in my first semester at university. Of course, I studied medicine, and I loathed it." Ajax almost chuckled but in a dark and twisted way. "But Archi being Archi saw it as an offense. He thought I was stealing the spotlight from him, and our relationship changed. Father had exactly what he wanted—us to be rivals. That's when Mom's first signs of Alzheimer's appeared."

"Your father sounds more like the evil witch to me than a dad, but it's noble the sacrifice you tried to make for your brother. I always knew you had a heart behind your armor of muscles and mask of coldness," I joked, but when Ajax remained silent, I had to push deeper. "How did you become Spectre, then?"

"I faced my father. Told him the truth about who and what I wanted to be. He told me if I decided to embarrass him, I should just leave and never come back. So, that's what I did. I left my family and my trust fund and never looked back." His jaw clenched. "I was basically homeless at eighteen. I took a couple of jobs to survive, mostly as a server in Paris, and that's when I took Bernard's classes with the little money I had."

"What a rude jerk!" My leg snapped on the car dash. "Did your father excuse himself afterwards?"

"I haven't seen him since that day. He disowned me from the family."

"What?" I snapped again, my knees hitting the car in a way I'd have bruises for days.

Ajax furrowed his brows. "Are you okay?"

"Yeah," I groaned, stroking my knees. "You're telling me we're going to see your father right now and that you haven't spoken to him for like, what, ten years? And you brought me into this mess?"

"Correct."

I let my head fall back. "This is a nightmare. Is this why you brought me? Because you knew your father would hate me since I represent basically everything weird? Is this some kind of revenge plot or something?"

"It's actually thanks to you that I changed my mind about going." *To me?* "I have no doubt you'll either charm him or make him do his loser face. The face I've only seen once in my entire life. The one where his two eyebrows rise and where he chews on his inner lip. It means he is beaten by his adversary. But if he displays a full, sharp smile, it means he's about to annihilate you, and I suggest you run."

"Jeez, thank you for the tip." I rolled my eyes, making a mental note to focus on the lip biting and another to watch out for the display of teeth. "Does he know we're coming?"

"I believe so. He tried to reach out to me since he had learned from my brother I was on my way to beating his fortune. I suppose he found me worthy of the family name suddenly and realized he had another toy to his game in the wild."

"You know that you're describing your father like some kind of tyrant. Not the kind of villain we like." We, meaning me and the heroines of my unpublished novels.

"If this is any consolation, we have a fountain." His eyes met mine in something malicious. "In case you wanted to get wet again."

"You know that thing about not wanting to hate you? Well, it can come back ASAP if you push my buttons. Plus, it's always your fault that I'm wet and—" I bit my tongue. Damn it. "I'll. Not. Go. Inside. Your. Fountain. That's all I'll say."

"Trust me, Aurore." His eyes set on the road. "Next time I make you wet, it won't be because of a fountain or the sea."

That comment made me choke on my breath. Ajax saying this seemed unlikely, and yet, he had. He implied what I think he did.

"You do know how to calm my nerves. This way, I'm sure to not embarrass myself or you in front of the entire Clemonte legacy. Or maybe I'll just hide in your dungeon or something."

"We have a cave." A thin smile slanted his mouth. "Fairies aren't supposed to hide but have magic powers."

"And knights in shining suits are supposed to save the damsel in distress, not bring her to the dragon's den."

"But I'm no knight, just like you're no damsel in distress, Aurore. We already established behind these layers of blooming sunshine you have spikes like the sharpest sword."

"Afraid I'll make your heart bleed to death, Mr. Clemonte?"

"You have no idea."

CHAPTER 20

Aurore

"Are you kidding me? So you do have a castle!"

I blinked twice, taking in the view of the Clemonte estate: a stone chateau with a large expanse of garden lost in the countryside. Undoubtedly something that belonged to the historical heritage. The pictures I'd found on Google Maps didn't do it justice.

"And it looks like my father invited all of his colleagues." Ajax readjusted his suit, eyeing the guests. All the men were dressed in elegant dress shirts, probably in their fifties. As for their wives, they were either wearing suits or square and formal dresses. Beside them, I looked like a marshmallow or a psychopathic cheerleader. "It's not my brother's big day; it's Léon's. Again."

I dug out my phone and turned it into a selfie position. "Come here, let's take a selfie. It's just for my sister."

He frowned dubiously. "A selfie?"

"Yes, that thing people do when they have fun and make

memories, you know? Okay, get ready. One. Two—" I snapped the picture with a frigid, nonsmiling Ajax and sent it to my sister. "It looks like it's your first selfie."

> **Me:** Look where I am!!! (Yes, he's the one I went to the gala with, his name is Ajax, and it's kinda his castle).

"Perhaps it is." Ajax seemed somehow worried. "What did your sister say?"

> **Luna:** Wow, did you pull him out from one of your novels?? By the way, there is an angry-looking old man in the back.

"She said there is an angry-looking old man." I tried to zoom in on the picture, seeing if I could photoshop that man away.

"She thinks I look like an angry-looking old man?" His frown deepened.

"Not you, but—"

"It's not a tourist attraction here." The angry old man in question faced us.

"That's him," I whispered to Ajax, seizing his arm under the gunning stare of the man otherwise known as Ajax's dad, Léon—thanks to my prior stalking research.

Here I thought they'd greet each other, but Léon decided to turn away to continue his conversation with his guests.

I swallowed the cold shower we just took. "Did he just ignore us?"

"That's Léon, trying to make an impression."

"You came." Archibald, dressed in a beige suit, gave a nod to his brother. "I can't believe I will have to work with those pricks. I can't stand them." He then turned to me with a sharp smile, halfway between Ajax's scowl and that of a lawyer who would annihilate you in a case. "Today is like a wedding day for the Clemontes. My marriage with medicine."

I laughed. "Sounds quite atrocious to me, but hey, congratulations. May you and your wife change the world."

"Thank you, Aurore. I bet you're the one who convinced my brother to bring his ass up here."

"I'm more of the reason why we're late," I admitted.

"And you look totally not fitting with the scenery here, which I like very much. Imagine Father's face when—"

My eyes opened wide as Ajax cut in, "Where is Mom?"

"Léon asked her to change into another type of outfit, one much more fitting than… pajamas. Someone is helping her."

"Ajax?" a frail voice echoed from behind us. It was coming from the woman standing by the door. "You're here."

His mother. She had the brightest smile, with light makeup and family jewels on that made her look elegant like an aristocrat or some royal family member, her hair delicately put into a bun.

"Mom, it's nice to see you," Ajax said when his mother went to take his hands. I stepped away, ready to give them some space, but he introduced me. "This is Aurore. She writes about romance, like those books you love reading."

She turned to face me and analyzed me with a kind expression that proved that fairy-tale mothers-in-law couldn't all be evil, and— *Mothers-in-law? He's not my boyfriend. Ajax is not my—*

"You're so lovely, and your dress… You seem familiar." She had seen my alias, *The Sad Girl.* "Oh, I'm so happy to finally meet Ajax's girlfriend."

Girlfriend? Oh god!

"None of my boys ever introduced me to anyone before, and I prayed to god to have a daughter one day and—I hope I'm not scaring you."

I couldn't help but chuckle. "I'm the one who usually talks too much, and you look radiant, Mrs. Clemonte."

"Call me Hélène, dear. And Ajax—" This time, she faced her son. "I want to know everything."

Neither he nor I dared to say anything about me not being his girlfriend.

"Ajax." That voice froze everyone in place, coming from behind me like a dark, monstrous aura. "I had to greet some guests."

I tried to shorten myself, getting away from the shadow by

mincing my way up to Ajax's side. Léon was back with closed-up features, gray hair, and a square face. A physique that screamed of rigid-
ity and left no place for imperfection.

"Léon," Ajax hissed, his stare darting to his father. "Always busy."

Hélène's arm wrapped around Léon's back in a way that betrayed
the fact she was probably still in love with her husband. "That beautiful lady next to him, it's Ajax's girlfriend."

He didn't spare me a glance nor take the hand I was handing
him to seize. I had no choice then but to pretend to readjust my hair
awkwardly.

Hélène didn't give up, and she graced me with a genuine smile.
"Let's go inside, dear. I'll show you the place."

"Hélène, I don't think it's wise to—"

"I know I'm sick, Léon, but that's no reason to treat me like an
incapable person. Let me be the mother-in-law. It's a wedding day."

Wedding day? My eyes drifted to Ajax, feeling terrible that they'd
fight over me, but his stare remained locked on his father.

"Mom, we're celebrating my upcoming career, not my wedding
day," Archi corrected with kindness.

"No, silly. It's a wedding." She put a hand on his shoulder and
chuckled, her Alzheimer's messing with her memories. "Come now,
Aurora."

I followed after her, leaving the Clemonte men together by entering the castle, or more like the den of medicine with renaissance
paintings of medical implications. For someone who seemed to dis-
like art, he sure had a lot of it to accompany the tapestry and wooden
furniture.

"I read a lot of erotica during my youth." She chuckled again, and
something told me I'd love that woman. "We need creativity in this
world. My Ajax was very good with pencils as a child. Very talented.
I think it helped him. He was so shy. Always alone."

"Ajax was shy?" So he'd had it since childhood, his aloof attitude.
Through the open door, I noticed that strange man in question, still

conversing with his father. His jaw was rigid, and something in my heart tightened despite myself.

"My son was always in his own world, and he shielded everyone else from it. It's like we never existed. I knew he cared, but he was… well, distant."

I remembered when I used to create a fantasy world where I was the queen with a unicorn ghost for my best friend before the birth of my sister. "I can relate to that."

"Of course, you do. That's why you're together." Her smile faded, her expression growing serious. "Tell me, do you care for Ajax? He has a lot to give and a big heart, but he doesn't know how to open himself sometimes."

I didn't know what to say. I didn't loathe him, or at least, it felt wrong to. "I—To be honest, I hated your son at first." *Here we go.* Not the answer she was expecting. "He was rude and used to stare at me as if I was crazy, but with time, I've gotten to know him. He's quite…" Ajax and I locked gazes from afar, and it made me feel peaceful, secure. "He's caring and somehow different from the other men I've met. Your son actually inspires me."

"Blooming love is priceless."

Blooming what? No. No. No.

"I'm not sure I'll remember any of that, as he probably told you about my condition, but I want you to know that I'm so happy he finally found someone to share his lonely life with. He needs to heal, and by the way he's looking at you, I know I don't have to worry anymore. I—" She furrowed her brows, rubbing a hand on her forehead. "What's that word again?"

Her phone rang, and I remained speechless. Never in my life had I been accepted for who I truly was. She trusted me while I felt like a fraud.

"Oh crap, I forgot to take my pill," she said, and I peered at her phone, where she had a lot of alerts to take a pill, to drink or eat. "I'm sorry. I—what's your name again?"

"Aurore." My lips curled up. "I'm with your son."

"Aurore, like the aurora borealis. I don't remember if I ever saw one, but it had always been my dream." She observed me. "And I see you today. Archibald is lucky to have you."

"Archibald?"

She insisted with a beaming smile. "Yes, my son. He's here today."

My heart broke into tiny pieces as I muttered, "I'm here with Ajax."

"Ajax? I haven't seen him for such a long time. I don't think he'll come."

Ajax slipped to my side in a flash. "I'm here, Mom. I'm not going anywhere."

"Oh, Ajax!" His mother exclaimed, hugging him as if she hadn't seen him in forever. "You're sleeping here, aren't you? I have the room ready for you and Aurore and—"

"We can't, I'm sorry," Ajax cut her off, clenching his jaw. "Léon will not approve."

"I see. At least I got to meet her. We will remember this moment." She maintained a smile, but I could sense she was pained to not have her son longer. "You should show your old bedroom to her before dinner."

"Very well, then."

Hélène headed in the direction of the kitchen, whispering things to herself as I noticed a wheelchair placed in the corner. Did it belong to his mother? I called after her, "Your alarms on your phone rang. You have a pill to take."

"Oh, right! Thank you." She smiled, but her gaze had changed. She seemed lost, as if she was physically present but mentally absent.

I ignored the slam in my gut, and we prowled up the wooden stairs leading to the rooms. In the middle of the hallway, there was a door to a room open where a big board was standing up, displaying a family tree with the names of each member of their family. It was probably a memory exercise for his mom. An exercise where Ajax's name was scratched from it.

"Your mom is lovely. It just breaks my heart to see this happening to her," I confided in him. "She told me a bit about how you were as a kid, and I have to admit, I'm not surprised. I bet you were all cute being your aloof self."

Cute? Did I just say cute? Hand me a shovel to dig my grave right now.

"I was weak." Ajax's mask was on again, probably because of the talk he'd had with his father. This was how he'd built an armor of coldness around him so he wouldn't be that happy kid his father despised. "I know you didn't ask to be here. I'm sure you had other plans."

"You'd be surprised that I didn't. Except for working and ignoring the constant emails from daddykink telling me to rush at three in the morning," I snorted and realized I'd never mentioned his name out loud. "Daddykink is the name of my boss. Anyway, I'm happy to be here."

Ajax wrenched the door open next to him with a lack of excitement. "That's the room."

I stepped in. It was pretty basic, certainly not what I was expecting from a child's bedroom. It had sports trophies and medals from science contests, but aside from that, the decorations were nonexistent in the midst of the boring display of gray.

"Your old bedroom is no fun. Mine used to have star stickers on the ceiling and a lavender wall because it's my favorite color." His was probably classy and unsmiling black. "I was expecting something with pirates, maybe superheroes or awkward posters."

But the room had a private bathroom attached. It was another type of fancy. I sat on the bed, and Ajax took a seat on the sofa, as if he couldn't stand to stay in the same room as me.

"So, you didn't bring any women back, then, as a teen?" I leaned on the bed, stretching my arms.

"No, I didn't. You're the first in my bed."

I jerked up, almost choking on my breath. "But you did it before, right? Unless you're a—"

I couldn't say the word *virgin*.

His lips quirked up slightly. "I've had sex before, Aurore."

"Right, of course." And now I was embarrassed again.

"Was that an invitation?" → same

"In your dreams." *And in mine.* "I could sleep next to you in that bed, and nothing would ever happen."

"Because I'd take the ridiculous couch and let you have the bed, is that right?" He entered my game.

"Not quite. Let's say if you were to try anything, I'd have to throw a punch," I joked to hide my nervousness at the thought. Especially since Ajax was big and the bed was minimal. Sharing a bed with him and feeling his body underneath mine would— I LOVE this game

"If you say so, Aurore, but I sleep shirtless."

I gulped. "If you think that scares me, you're delusional. I can sleep shirtless too, and we'll see which one of us will—"

His eyes lit up. "I would like that very much."

I threw a pillow at him. "Jerk."

He threw it back at me with minimum strength. "Quitter."

I opened my jaw, pretending to be offended. "Oh, I'm gonna annihilate you, Ajax Clemonte. Get ready to be smashed in a pillow fight!"

I rushed at him like a rugby player with a ruffled dress in the middle of a scrum. And that's how Spectre the Untouchable destroyed me at the pillow fight. We made a racket, chasing each other around the room with my high-pitched cries. My bow dangled in my locks of hair, and I collapsed on his bed, Ajax caging me under him. I couldn't stop laughing, not because I liked losing but because I felt alive.

He locked our hands together, and if this wasn't sufficient to make my teenage hormones finally spark to life years later, my belly contracted under his fresh, all-male fragrance. His eyes dedicated to me, he hardened his grip on me, as if his cells were bubbling, on the verge of exploding in contrast to his impassive exterior.

I reversed the situation and changed our positions so that I would be the one on top of him. I was sitting on his crotch, and I realized that my panties were brushing directly on his growing hardness through his pants. I could have thrown another pillow at him and won, but I didn't. Instead, I plunged my eyes into his and hated myself.

I wanted to silence my heart and our gasping animalistic breaths. We couldn't fight this attraction anymore.

"Aurore, about that kiss earlier—"

"Let's pretend this didn't happen," I panicked. Perhaps because I was afraid to admit the link that drew me to him or to be rejected and called a mistake. He made me feel a wave of hope like I'd never felt before. *I don't want to end this dream. I*—"I don't want to read much into that. It was a moment, that's it."

"That's all you feel?" A spasm twitched his face. "That it was a mistake?"

No. "I—"

"The truth, Aurore."

I bit my tongue. "It's just that it's scary, okay? I'm freaking out. That kiss was good."

"Those kisses. We kissed twice," he corrected with arrogance.

"Right. Those kisses. But you—I don't know if I can trust you with my heart. I don't know if I can trust myself around you. I'm conflicted. I don't know if I want to punch you or kiss you, stay far away from you, or breathe the same air. Hell, I don't even know what you think of me. I feel like a complete mess every time I'm around you. You're always staring at me with intensity—I feel like I'm a freak to you. Now, it's your turn."

I finally could breathe after lashing out a monologue, my heart jumping in my chest. It was his turn to reverse the situation, and he wrapped his arm around my waist before pushing me back onto the bed, him on top of me. My lips yearned to taste his, but he remained in position, his body on the verge of closing on mine, a nerve working in his jaw. Silly brain. Silly me. Silly—

"First of all, those kisses deserve more than a 'good.' Second, I don't think you're a freak. I'm trying to contain myself to not tear off your clothes and make you mine right now because you're frustrating me every fucking second. It's infuriating. Annoying. Consuming. I didn't want to want you, Aurore, but I do, and I have no control over it. I'm trying to take this slow because you already ran away from me.

One second, you're difficult and impossible and pushing my limits. Next, you're brave and beautiful, and trust me when I say next time I'm kissing you, I'll not let you go again because there is a pull that draws me to you that I cannot ignore. I tried, and here I am again, spellbound."

I didn't expect that. To see vulnerable Ajax. For his monologue. For my heart to hammer like it was beating solely for him, for my core to burn, and for each fiber in me to react to him.

"If something happens between us, it'd be an unsolvable mess," I concluded, my voice low and agonizing. "We don't have the promise of a happy ending."

"If nothing happens, it'd be an everlasting empty one."

"So you want me for a steamy one-night stand?" Another crack in my heart formed. "Already did those when the Prince Charming vanished to let the ugly frog take place the next morning. So not into them."

"And knowing this makes me want to annihilate them for being unworthy of you. It makes me want to smash something. It sends acid down my throat. It's not pleasurable. So, no, one night won't be enough."

"You're leaving," I continued. "And so am I."

"I know. I thought about that." He paused for a moment. "But I want to continue feeling what I feel when I'm with you."

"What do you feel?" I gulped, my heart on the verge of combustion.

But my question threw him off guard, and I knew him enough to conclude by the way his Adam's apple bobbed in defiance that he would not reply to me. His impenetrable mask was on again, and his brows slanted inward like my question was painful to him.

"Ajax, Aurore, it's time to—" Archibald entered the room, observing us both with a smug smile. "Oh, I interrupted something. Never mind, lovebirds."

He left, and we both immediately pulled away. I readjusted my dress before I walked away from that damn bedroom.

CHAPTER 21

Aurore

There wasn't just one table covered with a white tablecloth and silver cutlery under the veranda where we dined but several. One for the family. One for the doctors and surgeons. And another for their wives. It was bigoted. Ajax and Archi had to offend their father for me to be accepted at the family table, and here I was now, at the very end, left with a small angle to eat despite the vastness of the space. But no doubt, if it was up to Léon, I would have ended up in the kitchen with the staff. Not that I would mind—they were my people.

"I would like to raise a glass to my son, Archibald, the only heir of Clemonte. I'm proud of you for continuing the family legacy," Léon raised a glass, standing up from his chair. "No doubt you'll have a flourishing career, following in my footsteps. I always had faith in you. You're my biggest accomplishment. May you be an example to your older brother."

Both brothers had their jaws clenched and an impenetrable mask

plastered on their faces. It was the guests' turn to applaud, and Léon
sat back in his chair like a king celebrating with his crowd. On the spur
of the moment, I seized Ajax's hand under the table, which made him
tense even more.

"I don't suppose you want to say anything to your brother, Ajax,"
Léon attacked, serving himself some lobster and vegetables.

Ajax raised his glass, his icy gaze locking on his brother. "To Archi,
may you not follow this path just for Léon's approval."

"Archibald told me you're making a good living. How does managing a failing gallery allow you to acquire such money?"

"Honey," his mom tried to interfere, not touching any of the food
on her plate. "I'm tired, please."

I tensed my hold on the silver fork. He didn't know who his son
was. He hadn't seen him in years, and this was the only topic at the
table: money.

"Why? You want me to lend you some?" Ajax bit on the broc-
coli, squashing it.

"You're doing nothing meaningful in your life apart from flirting with whom I supposed is your intern." He glared at me as if I was
a meaningless toy that he wished to make disappear into smoke right
away.

I let my fork slap down on my plate. "I'm no intern. First, because I couldn't handle working for him—it'd be a mess and—" *Not
the point, Aurore.* "And because I feel like you're trying to insult me
with a job position that is honorable. It doesn't define my value. And
Ajax is doing something meaningful. You're wrong about your son."

"You shouldn't be here at this table. You weren't invited," Léon
said with lethal calm.

"Don't talk to her that way." Ajax tensed.

"Father. I invited them." Archibald tried to defend me.

I swallowed my whole glass of water, wishing I could become a
phantom. Léon was giving me a full, pristine, white-toothed smile,
and this meant he was about to annihilate me. I drifted my eyes away
from him, but it was too late.

"Aurore. It seems I judged you too soon." He was terrifying with confidence like none other. "What are you doing in life? You're working in an Ever After parade, perhaps?"

It usually would have flattered me, but coming from him, it meant I was coming from a distant galaxy he had no pleasure in discovering.

"Like the aurora borealis. It's such a pretty name," Hélène commented, putting her hand on top of her husband's.

"Thank you, Hélène." I smiled, thankful I had her by my side. "I'm an author."

"Of philosophy? Theses? Have I ever read your work?"

"No, I've been traditionally published once, but it didn't work out. I work for an online company in a way." I paused awkwardly. I had no choice but to be honest. "So I doubt it. I write about romance and women's pleasure. Steamy scenes, you know. I either make people dream or very—" *horny.* "But you weren't wrong about the Ever After parade. I do work there, too, because I have a thing for fairy tales. I mean, I grew up in a barn, so I was connected with animals and all that." I stole Ajax's drink in a panic and finished it in one go, feeling awkward. "I'm planning on writing a novel very soon, thanks to your son's help."

Everyone stared at me as if I was crazy, except for Hélène, who displayed a huge beaming smile. She made me believe I was her new favorite person.

Léon swallowed. "Lovely."

And that's how I made a promise to myself to not say another single word until the end of the dinner.

"So this is how you spend your time, Ajax," his father continued. "Do you know why I called him Ajax? It's after the Greek warrior. A tyrannical hero. He was a leader. Now, all I ever see in him is weakness. I wonder what I did wrong raising you."

Ajax sat straight up in his seat. "You're afraid I've become better than you, *Father.*"

"My head hurts," Hélène whispered.

"Father, please," Archi took another stab at rescuing the conversation.

"What? He's sitting here like he's a part of our family with some girl he found at a circus show, and I should stay quiet? He's the one who left and shamed our family name."

Ajax's fist clenched. "This is the last time you insult Aurore, or I promise you, Léon, I will make sure all of your colleagues here know your true colors."

I mumbled an "it's okay" that no one heard.

"I was a great father to you." He raised his voice, a vein popping up on his forehead. "You've always been my biggest disappointment. I taught you how not to be weak, and yet here you are, quitting everything you ever started. I spent countless amounts of money on shrinks trying to cure you. I bet she doesn't know?"

Léon fired his stare at me, but I did not hold his gaze. What did he mean by *she doesn't know?* Ajax's fist tightened even more, to the point that his veins stood out, his whole body tensing.

"My head hurts," Hélène mumbled to herself.

"You didn't change a bit." Léon's lips turned into an expression of disgust. "I don't even know why you came back here. You're parading like a peacock, but I'm ashamed of you. You're no man. You're pitiful."

Ajax had a deadly smile on, and it was enough for me to break my vows, blood thrashing against my cells.

I hate bullies.

"How could you say that to your own son? You know nothing about him because you don't pay attention to anything," I unleashed like the evil fairy godmother spreading misfortune.

"Aurore, you don't have to do this," Ajax tried to reason with me.

"No! I'm sorry, but your home is full of paintings and sculptures, and you dare say you didn't want that kind of future for your son? On top of being a selfish man, you're a fucking hypocrite, Mr. Clemonte."

"Hypocrite?" he articulated, letting out a dark chuckle.

"Damn yes, you are." I leaned forward, my chin and mouth quivering. "You're frustrated with your life, so you're blaming others for your misery. Your son is nothing like you, and thank god, he's actually passionate, caring, and he has a will like no one else. I've never seen someone as meticulous, organized, and ambitious as him. Hell, he ran away from you!" I slapped my hands on the table, and it was my turn to laugh. "He gave everything up so he could be someone. He did it on his own, with no help. You must be proud of him, and if you loved him, you'd open your fucking eyes and know what your son is capable of and who he is."

My breath caught in my throat, and I breathed like an animal hunting prey, my hair raised on my neck like spikes. My aura must have been dark purple. The crowd had fallen silent, and remorse started to cloud my features if it weren't for Ajax's scowl on his lips. He wasn't mad at me?

Léon's face tightened, and he chewed on his lower lip. I remembered what Ajax told me: it was defeat. I had beaten him. I did it. I won. I made him KO.

"You should leave, Ajax. You're dead to me."

"Léon, stop this," his mom cut in.

Ajax rose from his chair, straight and regal. "I'm dead to you, but I'm haunting you every day."

"You can leave now. It's not like your mother will remember you were ever here in the first place."

"Father!" Archi roared.

Ajax towered over his father, his dark eyes gunning at him. "Don't you dare hurt her feelings. Memories last forever—don't forget what she used to say. Mom is here, she's not dead, so treat her with the respect she deserves and not like a fucking patient of yours. She's your wife."

Ajax stormed away, and I followed right after him, exchanging an apologetic smile with his mother. "It was great to meet you. I'm sorry for everything, Hélène, and I—"

I ran after Ajax, who was walking away from the garden with heavy stomps. He stopped by the entrance of the house, the cicadas singing their evening song.

"Ajax!" I screamed, catching up with his pace.

He turned around to face me, anger clouding his features. "I'm sorry I brought you into this mess. I thought he'd changed, but I was wrong. You didn't deserve this."

"It's okay. I understand what it is to have family issues. I get it."

He observed me for a moment and shifted abruptly in another direction. "Come."

I didn't ask questions, and we went a few meters further, heading toward a rowboat anchored beside the river. He removed the knots that tied it to the ground and pushed the boat onto the water. He stretched out his hand to me, one foot on it to hold it in place. "Let's take a ride."

A puzzled look spread across my features. "We're about to be surrounded by water again. You know it's risky territory."

"I'm ready to take the risk. You coming?"

I accepted his hand and sat down at the end of the boat, trying to fit all of my puffy dress inside. Ajax sat down across from me and took off his suit jacket to roll up his sleeves. With the paddle, he made us drift on the calm lake, surrounded by a horde of old trees on each side—weeping willows, their long branches falling into the river, the birds taking shelter to make their nests. They were my favorite trees because despite their macabre look, they harbored life.

Ajax stopped rowing. "Do you really believe everything you said about me?"

"Of course, but I thought I'd save your flaws for another time." I smiled, the boat turning in the middle of the lake slowly as if in a magic moment. "I know how it feels to be rejected and have the world against you. If I didn't have my sister, I'd have given up on my dreams a long time ago. Did you have someone?"

"Isaac believed in me; he had what I didn't. He was sympathetic, and he knew how to attract a crowd and be the center of attention, obviously."

"I regret we—" My phone vibrated. Once. Twice. Then, the ringing stopped, and a couple of messages from daddykink offering me a new ghostwriter job for a novelist popped up. I was on the verge of throwing my phone into the lake. "You know what? I think I'm done."

"Done?"

I chuckled. "Yeah, done. I'm done ghostwriting for daddykink, and I'll focus on my dreams. I'll get selected by Ever After. Why shouldn't it be me, you know?"

"You're entirely right," Ajax said, taking the control back of the boat. "Your story deserves to be told."

"How do you know? You've never read anything I've written." I snorted. "Perhaps I'm terrible."

"I actually did. It was… adorable."

"Adorable?" My eyebrows rose. Adorable wasn't good. Adorable meant cheesy, predictable, and—

"I read your first published book. It wasn't you. It was nice and sweet, but it's not—" He paused, searching through his words. "You didn't use your emotions; you did what is expected. And I believe if your writing is a part of you, it can therefore never be boring or terrible. You're anything but that, as long as you don't try to imitate what is expected from you. Your writing didn't look like you."

"I wrote something that would sell because Ever After never wanted my stories. On top of that, all the big publishing houses rejected everything I wrote after that book, and I lost the desire to tell stories." I curled my knees on my chest, the water leaping on the bark. "I'm not even sure the story I'm writing now will be any different."

"What's a great story without some deceptions, rejections, and failures?"

The wind blew, and I caught in my hand one of the leaves that had landed inside the boat. "At the charity gala, I met with Bernard. He spoke to me, and he said he thought of you as a failure. What's your story, Ajax?"

"Bernard always said my art couldn't convey a strong message. I was an artist with no soul. He always used to mark the center of my artwork with a thick red cadmium brushstroke, and he said that the stroke would haunt me all my life as a symbol of my incompetence, so I guess I wasn't his favorite student."

"That's abusive if you ask me." I squinted my eyes. "It was bullying. He had no right."

"I—" He cleared his throat. "I shouldn't have brought this up after what happened to your sister."

"No, on the contrary." I found myself smiling for some reason. "It's like I misjudged you all along."

"The reason you were crying on the bridge all those years ago, it's the day you learned she…" He didn't say the rest as we passed under the branches of the weeping willow, which caressed my skin in a gentle touch. We were safe, in a place where we could confess our remorse and failures.

"She almost died, yes." I swallowed. "It wasn't the first time. The first time, it was all my fault."

"Your fault?"

I crumpled my dress, tightening my hold on my knees. "When I was a teenager, my mom told me to watch over my sister at the pool. She didn't know how to swim well, but I wanted to hang out with the other girls. I was tired of constantly taking care of her. So I gave my sister some inflatable things, and I left her alone, even though she begged me not to. I called her a stupid drag. Some minutes later, I heard my mother screaming. Luna had almost drowned, and it was because of me."

"It wasn't your role to be a mother to her," Ajax added. "I don't think less of you, Aurore."

"Perhaps because we've both made mistakes." I gave him a shy smile.

"I'm not the right person if you seek pity or heavy emotional support." He darted his tongue and wet his lips. "But I can listen to you without judgment."

"You want to be my therapist?"

His eyes didn't budge from mine. "I want to know what and how you feel."

My fingers intertwined together. It was just us at this moment. I could confide in him because he was as flawed and imperfect as me—and yet, for me, he was approaching a dangerous kind of perfection.

"I grew up with the perfect happy family, but it was all a lie. I thought my father was the Prince Charming, and I was much too similar to the annoying main character who got everything she wanted like a little princess. I lied to myself so I wouldn't see the ugly truth. The day my mother became pregnant with my sister, my father left for three months without any signs of life. I prayed for him to come back, and he eventually did, but during that time, he had already given up on us. I pretended we were reunited for the happy ending. My mom changed over the years, since he had been cheating on her all along, and she knew it. She stayed with him because of us."

I took a deep breath, caressing the leaves of the weeping willow. "I left my hometown to follow my dream——the one to win the Ever After publishing contest and become an author—but I didn't even make the first cut. That didn't stop me—I kept striving for what I wanted, even at the price of not picking up my sister's calls because I was too ashamed to tell her the truth. The birth of The Sad Girl began the moment my mother called me in the middle of a Les Beaux Arts class. My sister had come back from school earlier than planned, before her lunch break, and had caught the violent fight between my mom and my dad. Her world had collapsed at her feet. She texted me, but I didn't see her texts. She went back to school in the afternoon, and for the first time, she stood up against her bullies, tired of everything."

I curled my fingers, drifting my eyes away from Ajax. The wind blew again, and I closed them for a moment, feeling like a knife was cutting my already bleeding heart. "She lost the fight, and so she locked herself in the school bathroom, and she tried to…" My voice quivered. "Luckily, the principal found her, and she was brought quickly to the emergency room. That day destroyed my sister and me."

I let out a shaky exhale, Ajax watching me without an ounce of emotion. I continued, too late to back away. Tears wanted to form, but I didn't allow them to overpower me. "After the phone call, I was done with believing. My entire life was a lie, and real life was shit. I couldn't even go back home to be there for her because I had to stay here and earn enough money to support my family. I think they did not realize the sacrifice I had made. To them, I was only being self- ish. I didn't tell them about how lonely and hurt I was, nor about my failures and fears, because it meant admitting that life was hopeless."

Ajax knitted his brows. The memory was so vivid. I snapped my fists on my legs. "A few days later, I went to see Bernard to excuse my- self, but he told me I was fired for a new model. Apparently, some stu- dents got into a fight because of me. I called my father, who never went to see my sister at the hospital. He didn't care, yet a year later, he came back, asking me for a ticket reduction at Ever After, after seeing one of my posts on social media. And on top of that, Augustus, my first love, broke up with me the day of the call because he fell in love with that perfect girl. So, that's my story and why I used to stand away from the fairy tale, trying to strengthen my heart with ironclad lead armor."

I was brought back to reality by the sounds of laughter echoing from the other side of the river, where small lanterns lit up a sort of gazebo covered in ivy.

"You can take more than you think, Aurore. You have talent in you. You can't let them win." Ajax parked the boat near the roots of a tree. "As for your father and your ex, they were assholes who are not worthy of being part of your life. Promise me you'll write that novel. Not for your sister but for you. You're perhaps not the same person you were seven years ago or the perfect character you wanted to be, but you're still you. You're…" His Adam's apple bobbed. "You're per- fect to me."

"Ajax," I breathed.

"Your story is not over. Look at the emotions you stirred in my father tonight—you won. Look what you did with me and for the kids at the foundation. You deserve to tell your story because no one else can do it for you. You know about fairy tales—surely you know what happens after you beat the dragon." He got out of the boat and held out his hand to me.

I seized it for the second time and stepped over the water onto dry land. "Look at you, not cynical but optimistic."

"And you're a dreamer. Perhaps you're too inspired while I'm not enough."

"You're a world-renowned artist," I chuckled. "Surely you're inspired."

We headed in the direction of the gazebo with the lanterns hung around it. The crowd had left, so it was ours, and my novelist heart warmed up at the idea.

"I'm not. I stole emotions from people, just like I did with yours. I'm an impostor in a way."

"You're a storyteller," I changed his words. "But you see the world as if you're not worthy to be in it. You put this barrier between you and the real world. You don't allow yourself to feel."

Ajax's eyes landed on mine. "Perhaps I just don't. Perhaps I'm unable to."

"Oh, I don't believe that." I smiled. "But if you want, I can feel enough for the both of us combined."

"You're a fairy in humans' land, Aurore. You're the main character for me."

The sky rumbled as my hand landed on the white wood of the gazebo. "What do you see in me, Ajax?"

"I see life, Aurore." The sky roared again, stormy gray clouds approaching. "It'd take me an eternity to paint every facet of you."

I pulled away from him and started circling around the gazebo. In the absence of my notebook, I wrote a note on my phone to fill in the fearless and violent beating of my heart. It seemed to be stitching itself together every minute I spent with Ajax. And now, I'd write the line my evil queen would say to her magician in my novel.

I'll feel for you, but would you dream for the both of us? You resurrected my magic, but would I have enough fairy dust to protect my heart from you? I'm afraid of what you stir up in me.

I passed my head between the bars of the gazebo, my hands above them, to find myself face-to-face with Ajax, who was on the other side.

"Spectre."

He put his hands on top of mine.

The sky rumbled once more.

"My fairy."

I knew I had to ask the question. The one that'd been haunting me now. I needed to know if he was the boy from the storage room. "Were you the—"

A heavy downpour fell on us.

In a split second, we were soaked. I glanced heavenward at the sky. A black cloud was above us.

"Are you kidding me?" I laughed, pulling my hair back.

He grabbed me by my waist and led me inside the gazebo, locking our bodies amid my chuckling. We took shelter under the small space, the rain beating harder and the smell of wet grass wafting up through the air. An invisible pull was attracting me to him, and against all odds, the storm had struck us together, sealing our fate like an electrical shock that couldn't be pulled away. Our eyes plunged into one another, reading our souls in the midst of something so devastating that felt so peaceful.

I was the one to inch closer this time. I laid my hand on his chest, and I heard the pounding of his heartbeats slamming at full speed. It surprised me. His face was aloof, but his heart was about to combust. "Your heart, it's beating so fast."

I wet my already wet lips, and Ajax's hand traveled the length of my waist, his scent invading my nose in a need for lust.

"What do you feel now?" he asked.

"I have tingling all over my body, and I feel like my heart wants to plummet away from my chest, like I want to flee." My lips parted slightly. "I'm terrified."

"Terrified?"

"To kiss you again." *Of what it could mean.*

"Do you want to?"

His lips grazed mine in the slightest of touches.

"I shouldn't."

Heartbreak, my heart warned.

Sadness, my mind warned.

Need, my soul spoke.

"I'm desperate, wanting you obsessively." His words echoed within me, and I made the choice to listen to only one part of me.

My soul.

On my tiptoes, I crushed my lips on his.

He held me close against him, his tongue dancing with mine in an inferno of emotions. He pinned me against the gazebo, and we kissed each other under the melody of the rain. The devastating weather was nothing against the flick of our tongues and the contact of our skin. It was nothing compared to the way his fingers explored my legs wrapped around his torso and the way I was grinding my hips against him like an animal. No, it was nothing compared to the way he cupped my jaw, possessively and needily, as his other hand descended to grasp my butt cheek with no shame. The way I felt his hardness brushing against me and, in response, the way I bit and sucked his lip. This was destructive with an uncertain outcome. It was forbidden.

"You know what this means." He brushed over my nape. "There is no coming back from this."

"You know how the story ends for people like us," I whispered, craning my head backward.

"Terribly." He sealed this accord, kissing me again like he didn't care about the consequences.

Ajax

"I'll race you." Aurore pulled off her heels, her eyes sparking up.

She was hurrying back to my parents' house to get the hell out of there as fast as possible, and I was following behind her, walking casually despite the fact we were both soaked. By now, I was used to being in odd situations with her. She jumped backward with a smile on her face, and mascara dripping down her cheeks, not that she seemed to care. She was a mixture of tragic and beautiful, and if my canvases were waterproof, I would have immortalized her as I saw her—trying to ignore my pulsing hard-on.

"There is no way you'll make me chase after you like some—"

"Last one is a loser! Go!" she screamed and raced to the house, not caring that her bare feet landed on the dirty wet ground.

I finally did run after her on impulse—maybe it'd dry my soaked clothes since the rain had stopped pouring a couple of minutes ago—but there was someone in front of my parents' house. My mother. She was standing in the middle of the gardens wearing her ghostly night-gown, scrubbing her fingers together. She was searching all around her. She was lost.

I passed in front of Aurore and ran toward her, my vitals feeling heavy for some reason. "Mom, what are you doing here?"

Taken by surprise, she laid a hand on her chest and approached me with trembling fingers. "I was looking to feed the kittens some milk, but I couldn't find Mom. What are you doing here, Léon?"

"I'm Ajax." A muscle in my jaw clenched. "Grandma died years ago. You're at your house, and it's the middle of the night."

I didn't like the look in her eyes, the way her pupils twitched, trying to solve the maze of memories inside her brain. "Ajax, you're here. We have to tell Léon. We have to—"

"Mom." My jaw clenched again. "You need to go back inside, or you're gonna catch a cold."

"No, the kittens! I can't." She pulled herself away from me, re-tracting her arms warily against her body. "I won't go back inside. Don't force me."

"Mom, you need to—"

"Ajax!" Léon came through the door, rushing like a madman to-ward his wife in his pretentious silk pajamas. "Hélène, are you okay? Go back to our bedroom. I'll be right there, okay?"

"How can you let her go alone at night?" I roared. "She could drown herself in the lake or get lost in the woods."

"Don't tell me what to do!" my father screamed. "You're gone from our lives. Don't pretend to care—you can't care about anyone but yourself."

"And who taught me that," I deadpanned, striking my eyes to him. "You're too proud to admit that Mom is sick in front of your colleagues, pretending to have the perfect family, but you're the one who broke us down."

"Hélène, would you like to go inside to search for the milk with me?" Aurore kindly asked, probably trying to spare my mother the scene.

"Who are you?"

"I'm Aurore. I'm here with your son."

I enjoyed the sound of that. More than I should have.

"Like the aurora borealis. How beautiful." And here she was, seducing my mother over again with ease.

"Don't talk to me like that," my father spat his venom once my mother was out of reach. "I'm doing everything I can. Now, I don't ever want to see you again. Get out of my house. She's sick because you left."

I felt a nerve spiking in my chest. It hurt. "She was already miserable. You saw your own sons as a personal project, and you didn't care for her, only about your career. These may be your last moments with her, and yet you still don't realize you've lost a son, and now you're about to lose your wife."

"My wife is already dead." My father showed his true colors. "She doesn't remember. She's not Hélène anymore."

I sensed Aurore glancing at me from inside the house, and for a moment, it destabilized me. "To me, she looks exactly the same, and it's better she doesn't remember you so she won't notice the pitiful man you've become. She'd be ashamed. Everything you're feeling inside will never go away. You're the one who killed her from your heart, just like you did with your children."

My father's frown deepened. "You don't know what it is to feel. You know what pain is, Ajax?"

Pain is tears. No, that's sadness.

Pain. I focused on the definition of the word. *Pain is unpleasant.*

My nostrils flared. *Only someone without feelings wouldn't know what pain feels like. Pain is*—My jaw clenched. *Pain. Pain. Pain.*

"It's what I thought," my father snorted. "Get the hell out of here. I don't want to see you ever again."

"Gladly."

With heavy clomps, I headed in the direction of my car under the weight of my father's stare. Aurore came rushing after me and had the strange politeness to wave goodbye at my father and, worse, to address him with some words.

"I think you're a good man and that deep, deep down, you love your son and your wife. I'm sorry this happened to you." What the heck was she doing? "You can't do everything alone. Don't be afraid to ask for some help, or else you'll have regrets. Goodbye, sir."

"Wait—" my father spoke to Aurore. "You deserve better than my son."

"And he deserved a better father, but it's not too late."

She stepped into the car, which made my father's frown deepen even more. He had just met my Aurore. I sped the car away, and through the rearview mirror, I glanced one last time at my father in front of his beloved house. I slammed the mirror and tightened my grip on the steering wheel.

A new wave of acid was trying to annihilate all of my cells, leaving me with a never-ending flame inside my core. I wanted to smash something.

And in the midst of my apocalyptic torment, Aurore did the unexpected.

She put her hand on my leg, and something warm appeared in my chest. It was different from the warmth of before—this felt like the first ray of morning sun. Nice and calming. The shard in my guts felt less painful.

"I have a question," she said, hesitant. "Why, Spectre? Why act like you're a phantom while you sacrificed everything to become who you are right now. You're acting as if you're…"

Dead. She was about to say dead.

She cleared her throat, her doe eyes meeting mine. "If I were you, I'd scream to the world that I am, you know… I'd terrorize the world with my accomplishment. Look at your father—you let him speak to you like that. Why do you hide your identity that much?"

"I do not hide," I deadpanned, tightening my grip on the wheel as I focused on the road, wanting to gain speed and lose myself in it. "I reinvented myself to be who I wanted to be. If I were to be Ajax and Spectre, everyone would look at me differently. They'd think I became successful because I was a Clemonte, and for the others, I'd attract people interested in my money or fame. I want my freedom and to be able to trust people."

"I call bullshit."

I aimed my eyes at her.

"Maybe that's true," she added. "But it's like you stopped existing. You have literally everything, and you call yourself Spectre, like you're some ghost, a memory of yourself. Why?"

Aurore was as smart as she was feral, and she was reading me better than I'd ever read anyone. "That's a discussion for later, my fairy."

"You have to give yourself space to exist. During the days we have left together, I'm ready to open my heart wide enough to let you see what you're losing."

"So you'll give your heart to me?" I frowned. "Beware, I'll be eager to take everything."

"For now," she countered. "I don't want you to flee away from happiness."

So this was how it felt to be happy?

When the constant void became warm, and if time would stop eternally, I wouldn't mind.

CHAPTER 22

Aurore

"So, what do you think?" I glanced back at Ajax with pride shimmering in my eyes.

He was squinting behind me, and the only thing he dared say was "How's that thing still alive?"

I protected my computer in offense, hearing the motor wheels spinning and being careful not to unplug the power cord, or else it would shut down in shock, having no battery left. Admittedly, it was old but had survived for many years.

"Not the point, Ajax. Just don't touch anything. We never know."

"I don't see the word with that big line in the middle of the screen." Right. Sure, it might be ancient, but it still was working.

"It's a 'frustrated viper,'" I said with my biggest horror smile.

"I'm glad to know I wasn't the only one who had a taste of your magnificent letters." Ajax tilted his lips slowly. "I'm *happy* you did that. I'm sure he deserved it."

Happy on Ajax's face translated with a heavy frown.

Today, I had made the decision to stop writing for the company that was paying me lower than the minimum standards, and stopped being under the constant pressure of daddykink exploitation. So, that's how I made the impulsive decision of writing a *you made my life a living hell* letter.

"You don't think the writing in purple is too much?" I was provocative on purpose. "And what about the heart and rainbow emoji?"

I reread my masterpiece.

Dear Mr. Daddykink,

I'm enchanted to announce to you my resignation! I don't have the strength to battle your dragon's demands any longer for that low price. I'm wishing you, nevertheless, all the very best and hopefully to not turn into a frustrated viper—because that's what this job does to you, and I doubt no frog can help break the curse. Writing should be creative, and it's just painful with your company. Anyway, a new chapter is turning, one where I'm free of this consuming job. All my very magical best. Signed: not your little fairy hands.

"This is very you," Ajax concluded. "What did he say?"

That was the moment that I wanted to shrink back in my chair and hide.

"That I was still under contract for the last short story and that after, he'd be glad to get rid of me because I was no fun and, frankly, terrible. And also, that my letter was probably the best writing I ever did, which wasn't a compliment." I laughed. "One week of torture and I'm done, and I have an outline for the fairy-tale story and a semblance of a beginning."

His gaze dropped to the doc titled "messyfirstdraft-unknown." "To celebrate, I'm inviting you out tonight. And before you ask any questions, it's to get inspired."

"Aren't we supposed to work on your sketches?" My eyes opened wide. "If I recall correctly, our partnership contract ends tomorrow, and I'm not even sure you have a piece ready for Ever After."

"I know." That was the only thing he said as he exited my room.

He returned with a package carefully wrapped that he placed on my bed. "For you, for tonight."

Before I had the chance to follow after him, he was gone, and I fell onto the bed, excitement rushing through my core. I eagerly opened the package and read the writing on the card: "It's time to make your entrance."

Inside, I contemplated a midnight-black bustier dress with some crossover bands on the shoulders.

"Oh my god! It's hers!" The way I screamed, I was sure Ajax had heard me from downstairs.

I pulled out the dress from the package to view it on top of me, heading in front of the mirror. It was exactly her. The dress I pictured for my evil queen, the main character of my fairy tale, and Ajax had found it. He did. He really did.

"I have goose bumps. I have freaking goose bumps!" I shrieked again.

The dress was long and hit my feet, tight around the hips and waist, and had an open slit on the side. There was a midnight satin fabric from dark purple to cheerful lavender to wear over the arms and deep black gloves. I jumped on the bed, snapping my legs in the air, feeling my chest contracting.

He understood me, and that's why out of all my dresses, this was probably one of the most meaningful.

You know that moment where the heroine descends down the stairs under the desire-filled eyes of her date? The one that has your heart blossoming with new feelings?

Well, it wasn't like that.

I was rushing to every corner of the room, having failed my eyeliner line, so I had to restart from scratch. This was what was happening in real life. You messed up your perfect night with the perfect dress. After the fourth try, I did it, my hands moist with anxiety and my eyes red and swollen. On the verge of a mental breakdown, I was ready to smash all the mirrors. Everything had to be perfect.

"Aurore, is everything okay?" Ajax was behind the door since I was late by twenty minutes, spending the last fifteen with that fucking eyeliner and the other five dying of anxiety and rethinking my life choices.

"Yes, yes I am."

He didn't believe me. The door was opening up. My mind processed these two pieces of information at full speed, and I aimed for the door and slammed it closed with my back. *He's gonna think I'm crazy.*

"Aurore?"

"Can you wait by the car?" I asked, biting my inner cheek.

"Why? What's wrong?" He didn't make it easy for me.

I turned around, my lips brushing against the door. "I want to make an entrance. If you're behind the door, it'll ruin everything."

My fairy-tale heart was already ruining everything, but Ajax didn't insist and drifted away from the door. Now, this was the moment. I put on my heels and inhaled deeply, doing the final touch by tightening my hair with the bow.

I descended the stairs, watching carefully that he wasn't hiding somewhere nearby. Through the doorway, I glanced at Ajax leaning on his Aston Martin, wearing a three-piece burgundy suit that screamed of elegance, and the coward in me begged to flee. Being the main character wasn't as easy as it appeared. I would be fine battling any enemies or defending my friends, but when it was about me and love, I was a totally different person. One weak with trust issues.

I took a step forward, then another, until his gaze assessed me, and I stopped. His expression would be unreadable if it wasn't for the way he gulped and the growing bulge in his trousers that he hid with his hands in a smooth maneuver.

I reeled with a doubtful raise of a brow to break the tension. "How do I look?"

"Like mine." His answer was instantaneous, to the point his own possessiveness surprised him.

I felt the weight of his stare upon my lips. "Yours?"

"Yes," he said, his mouth a thin line, before repeating, "My muse, and more if you let me."

"Am I bringing you to your knees, Mr. Clemonte?" My voice was playful.

"Unfortunately, yes." He wet his lips, and something throbbed inside of me. "I'll kiss you the way you'll have the taste of me for weeks before fucking you with adoration if you allow me. And then, when I get off by the sound of your racking orgasm and your legs shaking, Aurore, you'll be as much mine as I'll be yours."

My mouth hung open.

"Who are you, and what have you done with Ajax Clemonte?" I was playing with fire, and I blamed it on the dress.

"What you made me." His brow rose, and he opened the car door for me. "I may have listened to that audiobook of yours. Or should I say 'spicy' audiobook, as you guys say."

I didn't know if I wanted to hide, share my lists of books with him, or simply get spicy together. "So you switched from classical music to spicy steamy romance? Get any inspiration from it?"

Shut up. I didn't say that. I did. I—

The corner of his lips lifted up. "This is not even a quarter of what I've been dying obsessively to do to you for the past weeks we've shared together, my muse."

My clit throbbed, and I stepped—no, I rushed—inside his car, or else I'd do something I would most likely regret. I could apparently listen to smut with a straight cold bitch face, but I couldn't listen to Ajax talking about smut without feeling a heated wave ravaging me from within. Ironic.

Ajax being Ajax thankfully didn't insist, revving the engine and driving out of the city. He might be a gentleman, but I was certain he had evaluated the possibility of doing some things in the back seat of his car. Not that we could—he was too tall, too big, too—

"You're quiet."

"I'm just thinking about…" *You, railing me.* "Plot issues."

"You can lay them on me if you want."

Overthinking and sharing my useless thoughts, that I knew how to do, and this was the task to which I subscribed during the rest of the trip.

We arrived in a small traffic jam; there was a sort of event at an illuminated gallery in the middle of the closed shops. A crowd was waiting at the entrance, and the main poster displayed… Spectre's latest artwork. The one with the man who had black lines instead of his brain, who was currently exhibiting here for this week only. It was opening night.

"Is this where you're bringing me?"

"I could, but we're not going there," he said without taking his eyes off the road, and at the roundabout, he took the opposite direction of the gallery.

"Why? Aren't you supposed to be there? You're the artist, after all."

"No one will ever know if I was here or not. I have better plans for tonight."

One question went through my mind. Why would he not go to his own exposition for a date with me?

"I guess you won't tell me where we're going, right?"

"No. You'll just have to wait, and if you ask too many questions, I'll blindfold you until we're there."

I had no doubt I'd end up this way, the questions on the tip of my tongue.

Either way, it made my belly coil.

"We didn't have to do this, you know," I tried to bargain with my cold Greek warrior in a suit, his hand blindfolding me from the view in front. "Plus, it means I have to trust you, and I'm not one to be guided by—"

He scooped me up with one arm in a caveman move, walking on what seemed to be sand.

"Ajax, where are we?" I didn't like his silence nor the feel of the last ray of sun leaving my skin for the night to rise.

He set me on the ground, his whisper behind my neck. "You can open your eyes now."

I did, the view in front of me taking the shape of a fairy-tale castle.

"It's the castle in the sand," I dropped, goose bumps on my skin. "You remembered."

"Of course, I did."

Ajax continued on the path in the midst of the sandbanks leading to the gravity-defying, gothic-style Benedictine abbey held within the fortresses of the Mont.

"Why would you do that for me?" I beamed, the golden lights calling me to nestle with them.

"I told you I'd get you inspired."

I made a mental note to snap some pictures to share everything with Luna later on. "My sister is gonna freak out!"

We visited the village that grew up in the shadow of the imposing walls. It was picturesque, almost deserted, animated with only a couple of shops open. A few people dressed in costumes like harlequins, and children held balloons running on the narrow cobbled streets. Harmonica music was playing in the back with the smell of burning wood like a campfire. The atmosphere was one of the summer nights with spectacles and traditional celebrations.

"This is beautiful!" I took the scenery in, walking in front of Ajax, turning in a circle.

"Let's go to the top." He laid an arm around my lower back, and we passed people dancing flamenco and eating grilled meat.

The dancer approached me with her hands outstretched, and I joined her for eight counts, no more, no less, dancing under the imperturbable gaze of Ajax.

We crossed a small park below the abbey to admire the night view of the bay of the sea from the balcony of the fortress. I leaned on the ramp, and just one firework rose up in the sky to mark the beginning of the festivities.

"You have to make a wish." I pinched his arm. "And don't ask why. It's my tradition."

"Why?" he obviously asked. "It's just teenagers playing around, not a real firework."

He was right. It stopped right away and vanished through the night into smoke.

"It doesn't change anything. I used to believe fireworks were fairy dust, and so I'd make a wish. I'd imagine they'd carry it with them in the sky like a shooting star. I believed if my thoughts were strong enough, it'd come true," I mused. "Ajax, can I ask you a question?"

"Anything."

It was finally the right time. "At Les Beaux Arts, did we meet?"

"We did." His voice was deep, serious. "But you don't remember. I was invisible to you."

"So, it was you." It confirmed my suspicions. Everything made sense now. "The man in the storage room. The one who gave me back my journal."

He didn't say anything, but his eyes spoke for themselves.

"I—" I swallowed. "I'm sorry I didn't thank you in person. I never saw you at the art classes."

"You were busy." His jaw clenched. "You were with Augustus, and I was the stray dog of the class, so I didn't exactly want to be seen. I was far in the back, behind my canvas."

"You're not a stray dog, Ajax."

"I was." His face closed, the obscurity darkening his features. "The first night I came to Paris, I didn't have any money or place to sleep, so I slept at the train station. I didn't know where to find help. I had no family, and I didn't exactly have tons of friends back home. I preferred to be alone. My bag of belongings was stolen. I lost everything except for my father's pocket watch. I remembered feeling so dirty, like less than nothing. Some days later, I had the chance to find somewhere to work and met Isaac, who got kicked out of a bar for being drunk. Unexpectedly, he rented me his apartment."

My hand gripped his, his gaze following the motion as if no one had ever taken his hand before. As if he didn't know whether to be hostile or not, not trusting the meaning behind it.

Before I could think of what to say, the next words escaped my lips. "I think you're incredible."

His stare fired back to mine. "It's humiliating, Aurore."

"No." I shook my head. "It's brave. You're brave."

"I—" His mouth slapped shut, and he glanced away. He was opening up to me, and this time, I wouldn't give up or let go. This was my last chance to discover the man behind Spectre.

"How did you get into Les Beaux Arts after that?" I obviously couldn't take a delicate voice, so this sounded more like a police interview.

"It was some years later, during an open class, after I had saved enough money. I spent everything I had on Bernard's class. Truth was, I didn't like it. It was too scholarly for me, but when I saw you—" His Adam's apple bobbed, and I felt his hand tightening under mine. "I was fascinated by you. You were the epitome of life, living in your world among people who were gray and placid. I wanted to find you again. I never heard your full name until you wrote to me on Instagram."

"But I—Why me?"

"I remember that I felt something strong seeing you. I couldn't describe it or tell you what it was, but it was good and raw. It was overwhelming. I remembered the man you were with. It twisted my stomach at the thought he didn't deserve you."

Destiny did exist after all, even if the choices were ours. "So it's like we were connected by the stars."

"I came back to the classes every day for you." He shifted his body so he faced me, the dusky night reverberating in his irises. "Even though you were there only once a week, I came to all of them because I didn't want to miss you. You inspired me."

"Your paintings," I whispered. "They all have veils, like my dresses. Is it because of me? Of the dresses I was wearing?" Again, his silence hid the truth underneath. "I wish I had known. I wish I had found you."

"I didn't want to be seen just like I didn't want you to get to know me. I had nothing to offer you back then. I was nothing."

"Your heart would have been enough, Ajax." I took a shaky breath. "I wanted to see you, but you didn't let me."

He reached into his jacket pocket and handed me his watch. "Open it."

I did as he said only to see a clock ticking. "I don't understand."

"Open the hidden compartment below the clock."

I did, and my eyes doubled in size at the sight of what was inside. Phantom ants scattered through me.

My heart missed some beats.

I'd been blind. All this time.

"You found it," I gasped.

I brushed the four-leaf clover with my fingertips. Ajax had found my letter all those years ago. He had kept my clover all this time.

"I didn't forget what you did for me," he said. "And you were right. My wish came true."

I closed his watch and handed it back over to him with a shaking smile full of emotions. "You became Spectre."

"No. I saw you again."

I was his wish.

Oh, my heart.

My heart stopped.

I froze.

Breathing was hard.

Stupid tears threatened the corners of my eyes.

This feeling in my gut. I had to lay a hand on my stupid heart. I'd wanted to feel that my whole life, and now, I was freaking out.

This couldn't be it, could it?

My heart wasn't mine anymore.

A deep frown was on his forehead. "I hid some things from you."

"You can tell me," I somehow managed to reply, my body impossible to control or be tempered.

"Growing up, Archi and I were opposite. He was the rebellious, reckless kid who got himself into trouble, but I had problems identifying with emotions. I didn't know how to express them, name them, nor feel any empathy. I was a void but very sensitive to my surroundings. My parents brought me to a shrink, who used the term alexithymia to define me. He told me to draw my feelings as psychotherapy, and starting that day, I painted to manage the unknown."

I pinched my lips together, seeing the emotional blindness he went through.

"In your first letter, you called me a ghost, and you were right. That's why I chose to be named Spectre. I stopped existing. When my mother developed her sickness, I promised myself I'd immortalize the memories of others who could feel. I studied their faces and their emotions I couldn't describe or identify with. That's why I don't want to be visible to the world."

Because Spectre was afraid to be seen. Afraid to deal with his emotions that were unknown to him and afraid of the meaning behind them. It was like being lost in the middle of a dark ocean without being able to see what was underneath or when the next waves would come to ravage you. And I wanted to be his boat or the light piercing through the clouds.

"You think this is a weakness," I whispered.

He thought people would judge him for that, that he wouldn't be understood.

"Just like you think showing your emotions is a weakness, but it's not."

For him, it was a strength because he couldn't show them and wished he could. That was why he painted *The Sad Girl*. My pain was so strong it had gotten to him.

I made him feel.

I was the boat.

"Most of the time, I feel empty, and if I were to feel, I don't express emotions the same way others would," he continued. "I always isolated myself. It's for the best. I never liked or sought contact with people."

"Who cares?" I smiled. "It's like those fairy tales that want to make us believe we belong to categories—the villain, the pauper, the princess—but we are all human. We're all worthy of being the main character. You may not be exactly as people expect you to be, but you're you. Someone unique, who feels in a unique way."

He knitted his brows. "This doesn't scare you?"

"No, just like it didn't scare you the way I feel my emotions." Which were a whole lot messier.

"With you, it's different," he said. "You have so many emotions in you that I understand them, I can feel them, even if sometimes I have trouble interpreting them. You create something in me, and that has never happened to me before."

My heart was bursting in my chest. "Before me?"

"Yes, my muse." He towered over me, a few centimeters separating us. "You're the first person who made me feel something inside. I was a fucking void. I painted because I desperately wanted to feel. To be like the others. And when I saw you, you showed me how it felt to be alive."

"You shouldn't be scared to tell the world who you are. Because Spectre is a part of you—you're both of them. The artist that I used to hate unfairly and the mysterious Ajax, a very good surprise." I smiled, his soul speaking to mine.

I was his boat, rescuing him from the dark blindness he was lost in, and he was my fortress, sending me to the tops of colorful clouds in a magical universe instead of rotting on the sad, brown, and empty ground.

"Can you tell me more about how you feel now?"

I nodded and brought his hand to my collarbone. "I have goose bumps because I'm scared. I'm scared to stop hating you, and where that would bring us." His fingers brushed over my heart. "My heart is beating really fast because of what could happen next. And then…" His hand traveled on my waist, pulling me closer to him. "I feel like I want you to sink me further with you and give in to this fairy tale, but…"

But he was dead set on leaving, and I was staying.

He was a man that couldn't have a relationship because he was a phantom, and I was his Sad Girl.

"You're overthinking." A tight grin tilted his lips. "I never watched a fairy tale until I met you."

And he'd done it for me.

"Which one did you watch?" My interest was at its peak.

"All of them. It was rather exhausting, and their way-too-happy, corny songs live rent-free in my head."

"And do you feel right now?" My voice weak, I pushed myself closer to him so nothing would pass between our locked bodies. "Do you want to?"

"I have always wanted to. Now, no more words."

His lips closed on mine, and this time, our kiss grew soft and slow. He was feeling, his body betraying the words he didn't admit. I'd always called him cold and heartless, but I was wrong. He had been the opposite.

"I want you." I let out a helpless moan.

We broke the kiss, and Ajax searched around him.

"Searching for a place for a quickie or something?" I joked, hiding my nervousness.

"It's not a quick fuck between us, Aurore." He seized my hand. "I'll have you whole, slowly and painfully. It won't be just a glance—I'll show you how much I crave you because I'm fucking burning inside."

"How?"

"Right now. We're going home."

CHAPTER 23

Aurore

The ride home was filled with tension. Ajax's grip on the wheel was so tight the veins on his forearms were visible. My knees buckled together, and my breath was ragged. He went beyond the speed limit, and I kept my eyes away from him, concentrating on my frantic heartbeat and the full moon shimmering in the night.

We had a limited time to give in fully to each other, racing against reality. And that's what we did the moment we crossed the main door. The world became silent, giving us the stage. We didn't even bother to turn the lights on, lips crushed together and tongues intertwined. We kicked the moving boxes to the ground, and I collided with the wall, Ajax's hands capturing mine. *Finally*

I circled my legs around his torso, and his hands roamed over my body as if they always belonged there before he lifted me up. We had an end date—our contract ended tomorrow, and we were both leaving—but tonight, it didn't matter. The side character deserved one night pretending to be the hero. One night of lust and nothing else.

I'd pick up the pieces of my shattering heart on the ground tomorrow but not today.

"Bedroom or atelier?" he growled between kisses.

"Atelier." I slammed my lips on his again, and he carried me to his universe.

We coordinated a team effort: he turned the handle, and I kicked the door open, still kissing, exploring each other's mouths like it was a whole universe. He carried me through his studio, and I made sure the sculptures and paintings wouldn't fall with our contact.

"Leave them, I don't care," he breathed, animalistic and rough, while several cans of paint spread out on the floor.

I laughed a little, and he positioned me on the ground where I'd posed for him.

"Just a minute," his lips whispered to me, the rustle of his breath making my heart jump in my throat, missing a few beats on its way.

He left me alone in the penumbra, and in the midst of the silence, he ripped down the curtain that hid the bay window in one harsh move. I slammed my hand over my mouth. Spectre was deliberately tearing apart his own studio, making a mess, and yet he still found the will to do something affectionate such as using the curtain as a blanket on the floor.

The full moon and the garden lights lit up the space in midnight-blue rays as Ajax invited me to join him in the dark waltz we had started, his gaze making me feel like I was an art piece he couldn't drift his eyes away from. I hesitated for a moment: I was no virgin, but with him, I felt naked in a way I never had before. I was exposing my flaws.

His eyebrows knitted almost instinctively. "You don't want to."

"I want it very bad—that's why I'm scared. It's been a long time, and you're you, and I'm me." It didn't make sense, but what I meant was that the meaning behind it was so much more painful than with the other men. "But it's just sex. It's not a big deal."

"Forget the other men." He spun me to him, and when his lips met mine again, he dissipated everything.

His skilled fingers traveled under my dress to the side of my leg in a slight caress. They reached higher and higher until meeting my panties. I inhaled deeply and held my breath as he continued his way to the inside of my thigh. He paused for a moment, his eyes searching mine before he reached where I'd been wanting him to.

He stroked me on top of my panties in a phantom touch. He was a tease, and I rocked my hips forward. One of his fingers slid under my panties, and he met my wetness, a thin line appearing on his lips before he pulled it back, leaving me frustrated.

"This…" He locked my panties in his grip and pulled them up, sending a delicious friction to my clit.

I bit on my lower lip to hold in a moan.

"This is not just sex." He continued his torturous friction. "It's more possessive and intimate. Sex doesn't get my core raging with the need to fuck every inch of you and taste you until stealing all of your breath. So no, Aurore, having sex is bland, boring, devoid of feelings—this isn't."

And I was hot. Burning hot. And needy. I wrote about sex a lot, but never in my life had I arrived to that state of angst, that need to collide with someone else's soul and, on another less poetic note, the need to be ravaged. Right after this statement, he ripped my panties. He fucking *ripped* them. The memory of my underwear found itself at my feet, and I was bared for him.

"I'll buy you ten others," he added as if he could read my thoughts and my huge eyes. "In fact, I'm not even sure you'll need those anymore around me. It doesn't do justice to you."

"Are you insulting my underwear?" I gasped, my repartee still alive. I didn't wear granny ones. I wore slutty ones like any good respectable villain.

"It was in my way." His voice, slow and deadly, made my clit throb.

"Your way?" I raised an eyebrow.

"My—" He made the word last, just as much as he made the pleasure last when his fingers stroked my wet folds. His jaw went rigid, and he brought one of his fingers to his lips, tasting me shamelessly. "—way," he finished.

He unbuttoned his jacket and let go of it with lethal calm, his dress shirt clinging tight to his Greek warrior muscles. As he readjusted his cuffs, his eyes slid straight to mine.

"Would you strip for me, Aurore." His voice kept his usual dryness and control while his dark eyes betrayed the hunger submerging him. "I want to take you in fully."

He tilted the mirror beside him in my direction, as if hoping to see me from every angle at the same time. He stood behind me, my back brushing his torso, and I felt his hardness pulsing behind my butt cheeks. Despite the fairy-tale dress, I looked like an animal with flushed cheeks. He pulled down the zipper of my dress, and his sinful lips landed along my neck. His fingertips brushed the valley between my breasts, and just then, he took a step back.

Our eyes met in the mirror, and I lowered the strap of my dress and made the other follow right after. I lifted my chin and let the dress slide to the ground, exposing the shape of my body without shyness. His gaze detached from mine to take in each of my curves, those of my breasts to my belly, to my hips. At that moment, it felt like I was posing for him. He approached me, and his hand brushed my bare back, still controlling himself.

"Can I taste you." The rasp of his voice, half filled with need, half with lust, was torture. "Please."

Him begging made the wetness between my legs pool even more. He screamed dominance in a way that aroused me while pleading to me without shame, and that was hot.

"Yes," I dropped.

His fingertips went to circle around my breasts and closed on the bud of my nipple. He rolled it between his forefingers, and I gasped. He continued, cupping my breast fully while kissing the spot right below the lobe of my ear.

"You're even more beautiful than I imagined you, and I did. A lot. You haunted every part of me for years."

My hands reached to grasp his hardness from behind, but he stopped them in their course, locking both of them with one of his hands. "You'll make me explode if you do this now. I'll take my time with you, just as long as you made me wait. So fucking long."

"I always knew you were cruel," I attempted a joke, giving him a truthful smile.

"Your lips, or more accurately, your smile, is one of the things I prefer about you." His hand dipped between my legs and closed on my clit. "You have a different way of smiling, which betrays what you're thinking."

I gasped, and my hand collided with the mirror in front to keep me steady. "What are the others?"

"Your freckles." His pace around my clit was slow and teasing. "They tell a story." His other hand closed around my throat, and I tilted my head back. "Your eyes—those are the first things I drew of you." He kissed me, his thumb still circling around my clit. "And now your body, but I want to keep it to myself as a secret. My muse."

"It's unfair I'm naked next to you, and you—" I gasped when he intensified the pressure around my clit, the mist of my breath and the mark of my hand taking shape on the mirror. "I hate you, you know that?"

"Never stop hating me, Aurore. I'll take everything from you apart from your indifference." He kicked apart both of my legs so I'd spread them wider. "Don't move so I can taste you properly."

I used to be a combatant, but facing that adversity, I caved. Ajax spun me around and teased the soft spot below my ear. He dipped lower and left a trail of kisses from my breasts to my belly until he was kneeling in front of me. He, the epitome of untouchable, was kneeling for me. My lips parted, and my clit throbbed in angst of what was coming next.

He adored my inner thighs by depositing light kisses, like a phantom touch on my body. My hands passed through his sleek hair, and his mouth finally closed where I wanted him to. I moaned. He kissed and sucked on my clit, holding me in place so I wouldn't move. I rolled my hips to meet his pace, which intensified, tasting me with eagerness. My belly tightened to the point my breaths were ragged and my knees buckled. His hand grasped my butt cheek, and when he pushed one of his fingers inside of me, I leaned forward, losing control.

His tongue flicked over me again, holding me under his mercy like a prisoner until the last minute. He slapped my butt cheek and pumped his finger into me, again and again. I swore my eyes had rolled behind my head the moment my orgasm crashed in a burst of fireworks. I came without warning, my legs shaking. He didn't pull away at first, encircling me with his arms.

I eventually regained my breathing, and he stood up, unbuttoning his shirt to display his hard abs and defined muscles. Then, his belt followed, which he rolled in a circle before carefully placing it on the desk next to him. *That maniac.* Pants and underwear followed until there was nothing left but his hard erection rising in front of me.

"What are you thinking?" he asked, coming to me, breaking the few centimeters separating us.

"That my nickname for you, Greek warrior in a suit, was appropriate." I didn't mention where my perverted mind went.

He lifted me up, giving me a feverish kiss, my legs wrapping instinctively around his torso. Carrying me with one arm, he tipped over everything he had on his desk with a single gesture. The glasses that carried the brushes shattered on the floor, and some of his tubes of paint spilled onto the desk. As for the pieces of paper, they flew around us before gravity brought them back to the ground.

"You're all I fucking *feel* about," he cursed, and my heart lashed across my chest.

He put me on top of the desk, and I opened my legs as he captured my waist. The paint came up to my thigh and down his leg, but neither of us moved.

"You're all I *think* about," I admitted.

And it was after those confessions that we were muses to each other and he was everything I never knew I wanted, that Spectre and I had the same idea bouncing around our minds. He picked up the blank linen canvas next to him and posed it right behind me on his desk.

"Let's make art," I said, taking the paint off my leg to trace a path on his biceps.

He followed the movement of my hand, his chest lifting up and down as if he, too, struggled with breathing.

"I'm clean," he said out of nowhere, as if his brain was calculating all the possibilities. "Do you—"

"I am too," I cut him off. "And I'm on the pill."

"I have never done it without a condom. Never wanted to. But with you, I want to feel you properly."

"I do too."

Once things settled, it all then happened so fast. We made art, Spectre entering me slow and deep and igniting my world in the shapes of a thousand words and colors.

"You're mine, my fairy, just like I'm yours."

He cupped my face and thrust inside of me harder this time, to the point I could feel him in my belly. My nails raked behind his back, and our hips rocked in harmony. My heart couldn't handle this conflict of emotion. I offered him my neck, which he claimed, and our moans melted together. He was right—this wasn't just sex; it was a mix of hunger and fate, of need and hatred, of passion and tenderness. A mix of us.

I lay down on the table, and he pulled my legs toward him before taking the smallest tube of paint that he carefully chose and poured it down my chest. It was purple. A lavender type of purple. I bit my lip. He was eating me up with his stare, and feeling me with his skilled fingers, spreading the paint along my lustful body. My chest heaved, searching for my breath under his slow but deep thrusts.

He pulled one of my legs over his shoulder and kissed my ankle, his strong arms circling my leg to keep me steady under his embrace. This time, the playtime was over. Goose bumps erupted over my skin. His body tensed. And then, he pulsed into me, and I bounced against the desk. His pace intensified, and he pounded into me harder, keeping my hips locked in place as I laid my arms behind my head. My hands dug into the canvas, trying to hold on to something under the intensity of his merciless drives.

A helpless moan came from my lips. "Ajax, it feels—"

"I know, my fairy," he cut me off, reading my mind. "I know."

All of his muscles worked and tensed, and behind him, the mixture of moonlight and dust formed sparkly particles of blue floating in the air. He leaned forward, his hand closing on mine, the shapes of them immortalized on the canvas behind us as our bodies full of paint merged together. He squeezed my bottom, and I shut my eyes for an instant. This was like nothing I'd ever felt before, a mix of bliss, of pain and pleasure, of love and heartbreak.

We switched positions, knocking over his easel. Ajax sat on the floor, carrying me on top of him so I'd sit on his crotch—gentlemanly enough to not make me collide on the harsh floor and let me on top, but not so gentlemanly with the way he filled me to the point he'd own my screams and moans. His hands skimmed over my skin, tightening on my flesh as if I was only his. A carnal burning heat inhabited us; it was like we had been a silent volcano all along, erupting together, and it was messy and beautiful in our own weird way.

"Oh god—" I moaned.

"God is for nothing in all of this, my love." He pulled a strand of my hair away from my face. "Say my name."

"Ajax," I breathed.

He gave me a hard, forceful thrust. "The one you loathe, my fairy." "Spectre."

A thin line drew on his features. *That bastard.* He even possessed my hatred.

His eyes assessed me fully, darkening to a pitch-black intensity as I offered him a full view of my body, riding him to my pace with a daunting smile. I worked my fingers over his muscular chest, but he stopped them in their tracks and brought them to his lips. He kissed them with adoration and eroticism right before his lips explored my breasts and captured my nipple between his teeth. I leaned forward, giving in to him, tangling my hands in his silky hair. Ajax gripped my waist and cupped my jaw so he could drink me in with his burning eyes. Strands of my hair fell beside his face, like a curtain enclosing us in our moment. Moans echoed under his forceful, slick thrusts, and he took back control of our pace, savagely and hopelessly.

We were a mess, paint all around our bodies, and if this wasn't enough, Spectre hooked an arm around my waist and switched positions.

"I want to worship and see every inch of you. Is that okay?" he pleaded from the sultry rasp of his voice, and the moment he withdrew from me, I missed him.

Not like I had a choice. My body was burning to the point of eruption. I needed more. "Yes."

"Show me your back and your ass, my fairy."

I did, brushing my breasts on the canvas as I stood on all fours. A guttural grunt escaped his lips, and he brought me back to him so my butt cheeks grazed his hardness. Kneeling behind me, he bent down to kiss my shoulder, his hot breath teasing my neck, to the point the hair on my skin hissed.

His hands clasped my breasts, then traveled the length of my spine to finally settle on taking a fistful of my hair and pulling my head back. I craned my neck to meet him for a kiss, his tongue demanding entrance. My wetness pooling between my thighs, I was in angst, the feel of his hardness pulsing behind my back, bringing me to the edge.

He slammed into me, and I screamed a helpless moan. He kept me steady against his torso with his arm wrapped around my stomach. He seemed even thicker than he already was, and I dug my nails into his grip. My brows slithered into a hard line, and I lost complete notion of time.

He released me from his torture, his hands clamping down on my hips, and I leaned forward, my breasts brushing on the canvas, my bottom up. I curved my back, feeling him pulsing inside my belly. Under the roughness of our exchanges, the wood creaked, the once-stretched canvas loosening. I held on to the very end of it, my cheek brushing against it. My eyes searched for Ajax, and the view of him, on the verge of losing control with his eyes eating me up, created a new wave of heat inside of me.

He slid his hands down my stomach, and he towered over me to deposit soft kisses along my spine. My belly contracted. My clit throbbed. My mind went into delirium. This was all too intense. Too good. Too—

"I can't take it anymore." I gasped for air. "I need to—"

Come. I swallowed my last word, and he accelerated his frenetic pace to a rhythm that let me know he was close too. I moved my bottom against him, again and again, right before he sent me into oblivion. My strength vanished, and we exploded together in one last intense thrust. He kissed my nape, and we both collided next to the canvas that illustrated our first time. We remained on our backs, taking in the mess we made inside his studio as we regained control of our breathing.

Our heads turned toward one another. I was probably flushed, and he was gorgeously untidy for once.

"You know I won't let you get away again," he said with certainty, probably referring to our contract ending tomorrow—not that it mattered.

The anxious knot around my heart formed again. "Our situations are complicated."

"I know." He didn't insist. "Do you want to stay like this for a bit more?"

"Yes." I smiled, and he opened his arms so I'd lie on his chest, wrapping myself under his embrace. "But just for a moment. We can't pretend this is real, or it'll hurt too bad when we wake up."

"I believe it's too late for that."

I closed my eyes. "I know."

"You did it, Aurore. You inspired me," he whispered. *You inspired me.*

The moon disappeared through a dark cloud, and this felt like the end.

CHAPTER 24

Ajax

I stormed across my studio and pulled out Aurore's sketches I'd made from a drawer, a weird and unstoppable feeling devouring me from within. It hurt. It felt like a bomb had exploded into something messy, painful, and somehow blissful.

"Fuck it." I tried to ignore it by balling my hand, my pencils falling on the floor. I didn't even bother about the mess. It was alive.

A landscape of colors was tearing up the black void inside of me, and I stepped in front of Aurore's sketches I had displayed on my board like some sort of serial killer mood board. She went back to her bedroom a couple of hours ago, but her scent and the memory of her were still very much vivid. She said she'd continue writing her novel all night long, and I said I'd do just about the same.

I grabbed the palette and threw various colors, from cobalt blue to dianthus pink to cadmium orange. The flow of colors almost hurt my sight; it was bright and uncommon. As a child, my therapist had advised me to paint to channel the unknown emotions that engulfed me, those I could not describe or understand.

In a way, it felt as if I was blinded by the dark night where ghosts haunted me through my journey. Weakness, my father called it. Real men didn't paint. I lost the capacity to feel, the inability for emotions to pierce through my mask. The day my mother was diagnosed, I didn't feel—it was a numbness. The ache in my vital organs disappeared in two seconds. The day I became homeless, I wasn't angry. The times I'd had sex, it felt mediocre and boring. The words and punishments from my father didn't hurt me.

I thought I couldn't feel. That I was born with a malfunctioning heart.

And now with Aurore, it was years of holding emotions inside of me emerging to life in a rush. It was all too much like a tsunami you cannot control.

She awoke the dormant feelings in me I'd taught myself to ignore.

Contrary to popular belief, I wanted to feel. I wanted to be able to feel emotions, but having them was like hellions I couldn't see attacking me. I did another stroke with my brush on Aurore's dress, making a mental note to add one of the ribbons she wore because Aurore always had something in her hair. I always thought I was better left alone. I believed I couldn't create a link with someone, or I'd hurt them just like I did with my family because I was unable to love, or care, or something another human needed and craved. But with her, it changed everything.

I was leaving. She was staying.

My hand fisted, and I painted my emotions away in every shade of color. I had a mantra: never paint what people did but what they thought instead, through each of their expressions. Spoken language wasn't the only way to communicate with someone; the unique body language of a person spoke for itself even more, and in Aurore's case, it was a language I would gladly lose myself in and translate a thousand ways, again and again.

For hours, I devoted myself to focusing on the task. I had

everything I ever wanted, focusing on my personal success and finding security through routines, realistic thinking, and control. Yet Aurore had always been here, haunting me with her capacity to make me feel and want more than all of this.

I felt like I was ripping apart. I had to ignore what was happening to me from within and focus. Focus on each stroke and color, and ignore Aurore's lips, the feel of her, the shape of her. Her true self created an intoxicating flux within me, growing like a tumor. And as the tumor grew stronger, my brows creased harder. My heart was like a ticking bomb about to explode at any moment.

And so I painted until the sun rose with a tight feeling in my chest that felt like a glass shard that I couldn't pull away. I was barely looking at my canvas, the shades choosing the final destination for me. My hand was numb when I felt a movement in the back. I turned around to see Aurore wearing only my shirt, with a plate of food.

The tightness in my heart intensified like a knife planted in my chest, blood spreading.

"Good morning." She took in my whole atelier with a laugh. "We really did make a mess here. I made a typical French breakfast, croissant and everything. By 'made,' I mean I bought it because I don't want to poison you anymore."

I swallowed, assessing her, a wave burning me.

That woman had resurrected me.

"Thank you, but I'm not hungry." The idiot in me had to lie, incapable of being next to her again right now. My cock pulsed in warning of everything I still craved to do to her.

"Too bad for you. I'll eat everything, then." She dug her long fingers on the plate to bring a croissant to her sultry lips. *I wish I could be that damn croissant.* "Are you sure you don't want one?"

I want you, my brain screamed. *I want your lips wrapped around my soon-frustrated hardness. I want to bury myself deep in you. I want your moans and breaths.*

"Yes." And here I was, a cold bastard again.

She wiped her hands between them, swallowing the last piece.

"Do you need me? Oh wait, I need to change unless you want to paint me naked or something."

"Yes." But what did I say yes to? The naked part. Obviously, the naked one.

She chuckled. "You're strange this morning. If I didn't know you, I would even say you're embarrassed and shy, but I'm probably just disturbing your artistic mood."

"No, you aren't." I sounded pitiful. "You never disturb me, Aurore." At least, not the way she was intending.

"So you like having me in your private space?" She gestured dramatically with her hands before locking them together.

I didn't like it. At least, I think I didn't enjoy that feeling of tightness and vulnerability.

But I needed it. Needed her.

And if it were to disappear, I'd be nothing but void.

"I wouldn't want you anywhere else," I finally said, and she displayed a beaming smile I rarely saw on her features.

I rushed to hide the sketches of her in the desk drawer as she advanced toward me. It wasn't finished.

"I just sent the first ten chapters of my manuscript and a query letter and all the boring things to your email address, by the way, and no peeking! It's just a first draft, but I hope it'll be enough for Ever After to be intrigued by my story and want to read more, and pick me out of thousands of talented writers."

"I'll hand it over to them as promised." I cleaned up my hands with the towel. "Looks like our collaboration was fruitful."

"Very." She painted on a smile, one that was almost apologetic. Her hands rubbed together, and I read this as something someone did when they're anxious. "I can't wait to see your collaboration with Ever After." She handed me a check. One I had given her. "I can't accept the other fifty thousand. You can keep it."

I pushed her hand away. "It's yours. It's part of our agreement."

"I won't accept it. I won't touch it." She made a face and put the check back inside her pocket. She knew arguing with me was a lost cause. "Well, my ride back home will be here soon."

I should have been busy cleaning up my favorite brushes before the paint dried and clogged them, but instead, they met the trash can. I had no time for them, devoted to the woman in front of me.

"You could stay." Here the words were. I could still make another contract. Relationships were all about contracts, after all. Marriage. Moving in together. Divorce. Death. Birth.

Her fiery eyes met mine, and I kept the new rush of emotions in check. They burnt me as if I was wood consumed by fire. My black-and-white movie became colorful. My stare roamed over her with a newfound desire, my hardness pulsing behind my trousers. She parted her lips, slowly wetting them with that tongue of hers. I missed her taste. The sun warmed up her skin in blooming, hopeful rays as one does after the battlefield that we had been through. The only sound breaching the void was our breathing.

The world was cold before her.

At that moment, the sleeve fell off her shoulder like a phantom touch, and my gaze instinctively snapped back to her. Neither of us moved; her breast was almost exposed to me, and the desire to suck, claim, take was stronger than anything. She readjusted my shirt to the greatest disappointment of my hardness.

"I want you to be my muse." I stepped closer. "Full-time."

"You'll be leaving in a couple of days," she pointed out that annoying fact. "And I'll be back home."

"Why don't you come with me?" I felt a spasm tilting my lips, not thinking of the consequences this could have for both of us. "Your sister could come too."

"You're asking me to follow you to the other side of the world? But if I were to do this, it'd be only for you. I have nothing waiting for me where you're going."

I wanted to tell her she'd have me, but that somehow felt wrong. I was being selfish, wanting to have her for me. "I could inspire you.

We'll visit all the places you want. You'll write stories, and I'll listen to them."

Her lips smiled, but her eyes glistened. Sadness. It was sadness. "That actually sounds lovely, but I can't be selfish again. I can't let my family down. What we have, it's recent—we're not even sure it can last. And it's hard enough for Luna to fit in, and my mom, she'll be alone and—" She furrowed her brows, that spark of hope leaving her features. "It's not the right moment. Our lives are a construction site."

"It never is." I focused on each detail of her face, particularly on the feline color of her eyes.

All this time, did I choose wrong by not going after her?

"My sister needs me here. She'll be back to school soon, and I'm maybe on the verge of having everything I want with Ever After. I can't give up on my dreams or my family." She swallowed. "Just like you can't stay here with the phantoms of your past. You're running away."

The selfish idiot in me wanted to promise her I'd wait for her, as many months or years as she needed, because she was worth waiting for. But spasms crossed my brows for a reason I ignored. I couldn't tell her that. Not because it wasn't true—it was true. I'd wait a lifetime.

But what could I offer her?

I ruined the lives of all the people close to me. I made my father hate me, my mother forgot me, and I gave up on my brother. I didn't love the way normal people do. I didn't express my emotions nor experience them the same way. She deserved better. Someone who could give her that. A romance. Someone worth flying across the globe for. I wasn't worthy of being cared for nor loved, and more importantly, could I make her *happy*? I didn't even know what happiness was until recently.

"I hope you'll find whatever you're looking for. The world isn't black or white; it's messy and colorful, and I want you to experience every bit of it."

"We still have some time left." Knowing that I didn't deserve her didn't stop me from wanting to spend as much time as possible with her until the last minute before I left.

"I could squeeze you in during my busy writing schedule," she joked.

We made a step toward each other when I heard the door slam. Damn it.

"Ajax?" The annoying voice of Eric echoed and couldn't have come at a worse time.

"That's my cue to go," she said.

"I'll be right back."

Aurore

Arriving in the living room, I came face-to-face with Eric, who was admiring Spectre's newest painting in the middle of the empty living room. A painting we had painted the night before with our bodies. It was contemporary, with hard paint strokes of each color crossing the canvas.

Eric turned and greeted me. "I didn't know that Spectre was getting into contemporary art."

Oh no. I gave him a strained smile, like a teenager caught in the act as I stood by his side.

Eric observed the painting, squinting his eyes. "I'm not sure what he wanted to convey. It's not really his style, but it's still… something."

I cleared my throat, playing the innocent, trying to ignore the marks of my hands or the one of my butt right in the fucking middle of the painting.

"Who knows." I shrugged.

I turned my head so I could see the painting from another angle and, more accurately, the shapes of our hands locking.

Eric continued to squint his eyes, and then they doubled in size. *No. Don't tell me he—*

"Is it?" He pointed a finger at what should be one of my butt cheeks.

I pinched my lips. "You don't want to know."

Eric did something I'd never have expected. He burst into laughter. "If I had expected this turn of events…"

"Not even the fates could have predicted it," I snorted. Me and Spectre—it was unforeseen.

"Thank you for what you did."

Was he thanking me for sleeping with Ajax?

"I meant, to inspire him," he corrected. "The project he's working on is huge for him. He had asked me to pack his schedule full for the next six months. He'd have no free time—it's a big sacrifice for him, but he knows it's what you have to do if you want to be legendary."

He did? A little voice in my head screamed, *What about me?* He had asked me to come with him, and I'd thought about it. I did. I had started making a one-year plan. I could stay with Luna and visit him, and maybe later we could be together? Maybe it was possible to have it all. But a knot formed in my heart.

He asked me as his muse, not his girlfriend.

"So I guess I won't be able to visit you guys, huh?" My smile was frigid. Fake. Tense.

Eric chuckled, not having the slightest idea of the heartbreak happening in my head. "I guess you could, even though from now on, he'll have to focus. I have to admit, you have been the parenthesis he needed, the breath of fresh air for him to find his inspiration again. You saved his career. I think we owe you a lot. Now he can focus on what really matters."

On what really matters.

I'd never expected words to hurt me that much.

I was a *parenthesis. A breath of fresh air.* Temporary. A means to an end. His life was all mapped out, and there was no room for me in the future.

I couldn't blame him—he was Spectre, after all, and he had sacrificed his life to be who he was. The artist who didn't want to reveal his identity, therefore, he couldn't have a relationship with someone like me. I was his muse, The Sad Girl, and if we were together, showing ourselves, the art world might recognize me as such.

"Right." I swallowed the bitter words, stuck in my throat like a wave of acid. "You didn't set up a relationship for him in his plans, right?"

"I'm only his agent, Aurore. I do what's best for him—businesslike, not personally." His forehead creased. "You inspired him as his muse. But you need to understand that if he were to have a relationship with you, you'd have to hide. It'd be risky. You wouldn't accompany him to any events, and he couldn't paint you again without people being able to trace his identity back to you. He'll be traveling, painting, and maybe someday... maybe someday, he could reveal who he is, but I..."

"But?" I continued, my voice breaking. "You can be honest with me, Eric."

"But I think having a relationship will distract him. You helped him get back on track, but right now, he needs to move on. And you need to, too." He tried to care, but Eric was a businessman, like he said. He was protecting Spectre's interests, not his heart. "You really think he could give you what you want?"

"I think you know the answer." *Yes. A hundred times yes.* "If Spectre's identity was revealed, what would happen?"

"Well, we can't be sure, but we can expect the worst. His artwork will lose its price consequently. Since he signed up with Ever After, he's been offered many big projects in the US and offers for huge collaborations. His international career will be like no artist ever had. I believe he'd lose all of that if his identity was revealed out of nowhere."

"Yeah, I get it. If you kill the myth, you kill the story." My voice quivered.

"In a way. He created a story around himself. We can't take risks at this stage of his career; we have too much to lose."

"You don't have to worry. Your secret is safe with me," I said at the same time Ajax arrived at the bottom of the stairs.

I knew Eric couldn't know how Ajax felt and what he felt for me. If I listened to my heart, I wouldn't even care as I knew he couldn't know him as I did. And yet, I couldn't be selfish here. I'd learned to care for Ajax and understand his soul and what drove him.

"Ajax," Eric exclaimed. "We have business to talk about."

"Eric," Ajax greeted in his usual coldness. "Don't go inside my atelier, or you'll freak out. I'll be right back with you." He seized my hand and slammed his mouth on mine before he said, "I'll accompany you to the car. You text me when you arrive, okay?"

"Of course." I displayed another smile.

The one I'd perfected for so many years.

The one where I pretended everything was perfect while my heart was already breaking.

CHAPTER 25

Aurore

"Halloween season is here soon." Even though it wasn't coming until next month, it was the arrival of the pumpkin flavor in every treat. I displayed a creepy face to Emma. "I hope your coworker is scared of the haunting spirit of a corpse bride, unless he prefers clowns. I can do clowns—"

"There is no need to frighten him. I already stood up for myself and won the approval of my team." Emma's eyes glittered with pride. "I've followed up on your advice, and I almost won over my hopefully one-day mother-in-law by doing exactly as you advised me."

I leaned over with a sharky smile. "You finally told her to fuck off and to mind her own business because her son is one lucky bastard to have a girlfriend like you?"

"No, the other thing," she chuckled.

"You splashed water on her face in the middle of a restaurant? Always dreamed of doing that." *With Spectre, we could have before hooking up in a—*

"No! And how on earth would I win her over that way?" She gave me a stop sign with her hands, shaking her head. "I just told her the truth. That I love her son and that she needs to stop making me feel like I'm not good enough, or else we won't visit her for the Christmas holidays."

"Oh, you're evil," I said with malice. "You're threatening to ruin Christmas already. You're the grinch."

She made a face. Emma didn't want to be the grinch, and knowing her, she was already regretting having spoken her mind. "And did you follow my advice?"

"You mean about opening my heart like a marshmallow and that true-love bullshit?" And here the words felt bitter across my tongue, devouring my pride within seconds.

"I saw the way Ajax looked at you at the gala... I like him, and he did nothing wrong. He's not Spectre. Not all men are the same."

"You'd be surprised how similar they can be." My heart contracted. I didn't like to lie to Emma, but I had no choice. NDA or not, I wouldn't betray his trust. "Speaking of Spectre, I decided to give the other half of the money to the L'espoir foundation. We're planning a big spectacle with the children, with costumes and all of that. I don't know how you do this; planning an event is such a nightmare. Plus, I promised someone I'd make her fly, and I don't know how yet. And don't look at me with those big eyes of yours. I'm doing it for karma," I added. "Because I'm selfish."

"Yeah, right." She burst into laughter, lifting her arms in the air as if we were about to party all night. "Looks like my fairy godmother is back."

"Wicked," I pointed that detail out. "Luna is coming in a week, and I'm proud to announce I have a semblance of a manuscript ready." And Spectre would do as he said—he'd hand my manuscript over to the big guys. I'd impress them, and I'd finally get what I'd always craved by keeping my promise to Luna. *See, it wasn't that hard after all.* And despite this optimistic perspective, my heart still ached.

"It's weird. Since you worked with Spectre, you're inspired." Emma was the only person who could give a warm smile while having a doubtful frown. "You hated him, and now, you seem... happy?"

"I'm not!" I could feel the crimson red creeping on my cheeks as the villainous traitor that I was. "He's not that bad when you get to know him."

And even better when you sleep with him. Get him to cook shirtless for you. Get him to sit on the sand for you. Go on a date with him and—

Emma clicked her tongue in her cheek. "Would there be two men fighting over you, Miss Bardot?"

"Don't tempt me with a good book trope." I switched the subject. "Anyway, I have to close the store, and we'll meet later, okay?"

She lifted herself from the chair. "Fine, but think about what I told you. Oh, and I heard something in the headquarters of Ever After about that Spectre of yours, since you obviously seem to like him and you didn't even tell me shit about it."

"I would tell you everything if I could." And that was the truth.

"I know. That's why I'm not pissed at you." She was the more sensitive and the better person of us both. "There is a rumor that Ever After will do a collaboration for their one-hundred-year anniversary with an artist. I'm not supposed to know; I just happen to have an ear everywhere, so I bet I'll be able to see how you inspired him."

The lift of my brows was the only answer I could give her.

"Oh, Léo is calling me. I have to go!" *Saved by the bell.* Emma gave me a kiss on the cheek and rushed outside as I tightened my grip on the spatula.

For the next few minutes, I heard the fireworks exploding in the sky and the applause in the distance. I closed the curtains and went to unplug my computer when a notification appeared on my screen. I had received an email among those of my mother's tarot divinations.

One that was titled: Meeting about our common friend.

I clicked to open it.

From: Bernard Dupont-Brillac
To: Aurore Bardot
Subject: Meeting about our common friend.

Hi Miss Bardot,

I must admit, it took me some time to replace you in my memory, my apologies. I thought you were familiar, but it was only at the gala I began to place the pieces together of the puzzle that you are, Miss Bardot. I indeed remember you: the strange girl with dresses who used to model for our school—or should I call you The Sad Girl?

My heart blazed at the sight of the attached photos. The first was one of Ajax and me dancing at the gala—from the moment I caught Bernard peering in our direction with his creepy smile on. The second was an incomplete sketch of me. Me, the day of The Sad Girl. I had the same dress on. Bernard had kept Ajax's drawings. They were signed under his real name before Spectre was born. He'd put all the pieces together.

I went to his latest exposition in Honfleur, which was a pungent bore, hoping to run into you, but unfortunately, we didn't, and I'm forced to send this email. As you can see, I have tangible proof attesting that Mr. Ajax Clemonte is indeed Spectre. Could you imagine: the great Spectre was a failure, one of the worst Beaux Arts students? One who didn't even have the money to pay his tuition in full, while he came from a very wealthy family? I bet the newspapers would kill for this news and the view of his mentor and teacher: myself.

I did not teach you anything. That's why I'd like to meet with you about an artistic collaboration: one of being my muse.

I'm expecting a response within the upcoming days if you care enough for our friend, or I'll be forced to release his true identity, and it'll be only you to blame, as it had always been from the start.

I trust you to keep this to yourself or I'll know.

From one artist to another.

My nostrils flared, and my heart pounded. The lights of the shop shut off like a loss of power, and I remained in the dark, my screen and the distant fireworks the only light. I did not react, my gaze remaining fixed on Bernard's words. So it had happened. I flipped the computer shut with trembling hands and sat down on the cold tiled floor, curling into myself. Bernard knew who Spectre was, and it was all my fault. Again. Because of the past we shared. It was another reminder, a sign of fate, we couldn't be together, and now, his happy ending could be jeopardized.

But in another way, if his identity was revealed, if Spectre chose me, we wouldn't have to say goodbye. It was selfish, but if I told him, we could have it all.

I needed to fix this.

I sent a text to the first person that came to my mind. My sister.

> **Me:** Question. 1) You could be happy, honest but selfish by hurting the person you deeply care for. Would you do this? Or 2) Would you protect said person and hurt yourself in the process? (It's obviously a plot issue.)

I bit my nails, waiting for her reply in angst.

> **Luna:** You're writing the backstory of the villain? Definitely the second option. The villain would never let the only thing he/she loves get away. So they'd do a heroic act at the price of being miserable.

> **Luna:** The right heroic act would be to give the other protagonist a choice though, so the first option above.

But that was it.

I dropped the phone on the ground and took up my notebook, writing a note of my reality disguised behind a fantasy tale.

The villainess would sacrifice herself because she knew the wizard would never choose her over his kingdom. It was a lost battle. And sacrificing herself for love was better than being rejected. Because no one had ever returned her love. No one knew how to love her. Perhaps, she wondered, she wasn't worthy to be loved at all.

And a tear coming from her bleeding, cold heart dripped over onto her cheek.

Like a day where nothing goes right—the kind where you miss your bus after sprinting after it, almost get run over by walking on the sidewalk through a green light, and get yelled at in the grocery store—I climbed the stairs to my apartment like an undead, and when I reached my doorstep, I was unable to find my keys. This little incident made me want to tear apart this page of my life and burn the book of my existence.

"Fuck it! Fuck this!" I screamed, finally getting a hand on those silly keys.

I laid eyes on a package on my doorstep. It had no name on it. At this point, I was almost sure it'd be a dead fish from the mafia or a bomb planted by destiny itself. That the thing had been sitting there for hours, and that no one had stolen it, it could only be bad news. Not that I feared bad news. I was the ruler of it.

I entered my place, shut the door with my foot, and tore up the package. The theory of the bomb placed inside dissipated when I took notice of what the object in question was after opening the package like a brute. The latest MacBook Pro, released a few months ago, one with a high processor and the kind of battery that could last a full day of work.

"Are you kidding me?"

It was the queen bee of laptops.

And it was on my doorstep.

"Oh my god!" It probably wasn't destined for me, but I couldn't care; I'd keep it. I'd use it. I'd make it my own.

I tore my eyes away from the computer only to notice that I had completely ignored the little card stuck to the packaging.

Your computer was ancient. Please throw it out and don't fight me over this. You deserve to write in the outdoors like the crazy lady that you are.

Another person would have smiled. Texted back something like "you're the best person I know, thank you so much," or they would have started using that computer already, but I remained blank.

Blank and sad. Terribly sad.

I had found the right person for me, and I had to let him go. I had to do the right thing. My phone vibrated like a sign. Not once, but three times in a row.

> **Veronique:** The theater room is booked for the gala with the children. Please, call me back!

I had people counting on me. People I wouldn't let down.

> **Mom:** Your sister will arrive Friday at 3pm, don't be late to pick her up! I'm so excited for you to be back home soon. Your old room is ready.

> **Mom:** Today mercury is in retrograde and karma is about to strike! One of my guides told me that we were finally going to get what we deserve. Wear some onyx to protect yourself just in case, honey.

Even my mom didn't believe I was on the good side.

And at this point, I didn't think having an onyx with me would help.

CHAPTER 26

Aurore

Seven years later, I was back at the place where it all began.

I passed by the French baroque architecture of Les Beaux Arts under the stare of the figures embedded within the facade. I was back in the long hallway full of arches leading to the studio where I'd posed as a muse. My boots echoed on the ground in a murderous drum. I had arrived at Bernard's atelier.

His door was already half-open as he was finishing up a painting on canvas. He took sight of me, and his sharky smile popped up, his green-and-mustard suit blinding my eyes.

"I'm happy you came." Bernard departed from his easel and took a seat behind the desk, showing me my place.

I remained stone-still. "What do you want?"

"What every mentor wants, of course," he said, giving me another gesture of his hand to join him in sitting. "To be better than their students and not let them surpass them with their mediocrity."

"You're still jealous of him." I didn't sit. "This won't get you anywhere."

"Life was easy for Ajax." He gave a dismissive wave. "He was born rich and granted his talentless, spoiled-child's desire to take lessons here. That explains his brilliant career at such a young age. His marketing strategy for the whole mystery behind him is immaculate, I must admit. Even I failed to recognize the link between Ajax and Spectre as painters. He changed his whole way of drawing. He thought of everything… except for you. He didn't hide you well."

This was what Eric was doubting—people judging Spectre for what he was born into and not for his art.

"Why am I here?" I cut in, folding my arms on my chest.

"I want you to be my muse for one painting, as you know." He made a face as if he doubted himself of his own desire. It's almost like the view of me was repulsive to him. "Not that I want you, I don't frankly understand what inspires him so much in you, but I want to prove to the world that I could do better."

"You want the same success as *The Sad Girl*. You want to copy him," I spat.

"No. I want to surpass him, to prove to the world he isn't as talented as everyone thinks. If I do this, my career will flourish and—" He leaned forward, offering me a creepy smile. "If you accept, I'll be quiet and won't reveal his identity to the public. Of course, I trust this will remain between us and that you understand clearly you won't be paid for that."

I pinched my lips together and curled my fist. I wanted to annihilate him and his smug face. But I didn't. This wasn't about me.

"I'd need a confidentiality agreement," I dropped, keeping my emotions in check. I wouldn't give him anything. As Ajax said, emotions were power. He'd have my indifference.

"Of course." He plastered on a fake smile. "But if you refuse, I'll have no other choice but to tell the world about Spectre, and you can trust me that I won't paint a positive image of him nor of you— you will be the girl who tried to climb the ladder, a nobody who had glory on a painting. I'll make sure no one takes you seriously. BDB, Spectre's mentor, has a nice ring for my career. Either way, I'm winning. This is your choice."

"You're pitiful," I cursed, my heart wanting to lash across my chest. "Even if you paint me, you won't succeed in having any recognition. You're not as good as him. You're nothing."

"That's where you're wrong. You have to be a shark if you want to make history, little girl, and you're here because you don't have a choice."

I rushed to his desk, slamming my fist across it and narrowing my eyes to his froggy ones. "And you have to have a heart to feel happy and content with yourself, and I doubt you have one. I'll do what you ask, and I'll be the one reviewing the contract because you won't mess with me or Ajax. But I promise you, you'll never reach the same level as him."

I rushed out of his office, wanting to get out of there as soon as possible.

"Looking forward to seeing you again soon. We'll keep in touch." His voice sounded from across the hallway.

I continued to move at full speed, my arms swinging along my body. "I hate this place. I hate—"

It was like an electric shock to me when I bumped into someone, and as always, I didn't do things halfway.

"Fuck!" I yelled, knocking the person concerned to the floor, her books falling to the ground. It was a woman with glasses and a long flowery dress. I crouched down to help her as she struggled to pick up her books… of architecture. As if by chance. I wanted to snort. Probably a teacher. "Sorry, it's my fault."

"It's nothing. I'm—" She lifted her head, and oh my fucking—"Aurore, is that you?"

"Violette?" My voice was strained.

Violette—as in Violette, who stole Augustus from me. Violette, the perfect main character material.

Her being her gave me a warm smile, looking effortlessly gorgeous. "It's been so long. How are you?"

"Terrible," I lashed out, on the verge of exploding right into tears in front of the girl I'd describe as the epitome of perfection. "My life is on the verge of falling apart, and you look great, happy, which is so not what I need right now!"

She swallowed and picked up a few books, which she folded to her chest.

"I'm sorry I'm rude. It's just, I was envious of you," I admitted, helping her to gather all the books before we could stand up. "You got Augustus, and I didn't, and now you guys are married. I stalked you because I'm that awkward, and I made my peace with it. I'm happy for you."

My oversharing monologues were back, and I had no idea why I couldn't hold back my emotions. I was going to unpack years of frustration keeping it all to myself.

"I understand." She readjusted her glasses, either hating me or gloating. "It's funny because I wanted to be your friend desperately back then."

"My friend?" I raised my brows.

She gave me a light smile. "Yeah. I felt stupid next to you. You impressed me. I even tried to copy you once and bought a hair bow similar to yours, but I looked ridiculous."

"Wait, what?" My voice echoed in the empty hallway. "You? You were jealous of me? But you're perfect!"

"Do you know how exhausting it can be to try to be perfect?"

Her sentence slammed right back at me. Violette and I weren't that different after all. Sure, she was the opposite of who I was, but deep down, we understood each other, on the same impossible quest for perfection.

"Are you happy?" I asked her. "Are you still in love with each other? And please, be honest. I've moved on."

"Yes, we're very happy." She shrugged and gave me an apologetic smile. "I'm sorry we hurt you. We didn't mean it."

"I know." I lifted my chin. "I could tell he was in love with you at first glance. Every story needs a villain."

"I didn't mean to be the villain in yours," she apologized.

"Oh no, I meant me!"

"You?" She frowned. "I never thought of you as a villain but as someone I aspired to be. So bad that I asked the principal to close the storage room out of spite back then."

"You were the one responsible for it?" *I knew it! That bi—*

"Not my best moment." She stroked her arm. "It's even me who locked it with the keys. I almost locked a weird guy inside. I tried to talk to him to apologize, but he was the rude one who told me my hair bow didn't suit me and that I was a pitiful copy of someone incomparable. Trust me, I put that bow into the trash right after."

"I'm not surprised, coming from him," I chuckled, knowing this could only be Ajax, and suddenly, I was ready to draw a line under the past. "It was actually very insightful to see you again, but I need to pick up my sister. I'm wishing you lots of happiness, and I mean it."

"Same. If you ever want to grab a coffee or something, I'm available on the weekend while the kids are sleeping."

Right. They had kids. I couldn't help but grimace, and couldn't be more sure we'd never meet again or be friends because that'd be way too weird, and I had no desire to. On a positive note, I didn't feel like a miserable wreck talking to her. I felt somewhat powerful.

"I'll call you!" I rushed away from the hallway, already late to pick up Luna.

I didn't have Violette's phone number.

I just ditched her.

I should have felt bad, and a slight part of me did, but the other with the devil on my shoulder was smiling because I had let the past go.

I was waiting for Luna at the station like a lonely housewife watching the neighbors fighting with a heavy frown plastered on my face and my arms crossed. It'd been five minutes since her train had arrived, and she still wasn't here, while the big family with their ten kids was already getting into a taxi. I even decided to take matters into my own hands and went to see the people working at the train station. I had asked them if I could step inside a train car to find her, which they obviously refused.

I was ready to go full crazy on them when a voice pulled me out of my madness.

"Aurore!" That voice, I'd recognize her everywhere. My little sister was the last one getting off the train, wearing her strawberry dress and holding her suitcase. "Sorry, I just don't like to exit first. Everyone is screaming and yelling."

I wasn't one to give hugs easily, but I hugged her so close to me, as if she was on the verge of losing her life. "It's okay. I'm so happy you're here."

I smiled so hard my cheeks hurt, and I took her luggage, already hurrying to find a ride back. "I made a list of things we can do while you're here. It's gonna be awesome! I just have some rehearsals to go to with the foundation L'espoir, and you need to help me. I need your talent."

Her green eyes squinted, analyzing me. "Something about you changed… You're full of life and, at the same time, sad."

"Sad?" I faked a laugh. "I couldn't be happier. You're finally here."

"Your eyes glow." She raised an eyebrow, giving me that little sister look where you cannot refuse her anything. "Plus, you're so hyperactive that you didn't even realize the exit was on the other side. But that's okay. You've been living here for like, what, seven years?"

I snorted, heading in the right direction this time. "You're way too smart—it's annoying. But don't mess with me again, or I won't let you read my manuscript."

"I better have a nice dedication page," she commanded, pushing a strand of her blond hair to text on her phone. "You have to tell me, at least, what it's about."

I thought it through. I couldn't do one logline to save my life. I could tell her it was the story about the evil queen living in a reclusive castle and about the wizard whose magic was like art. A wizard that was dying slowly. The evil queen had been cast away by the princess long ago because she had fallen in love with the prince she should have married. A prince who broke her heart to choose the princess, who was none other than a simple commoner. The evil queen had grown embittered and took pleasure in unfortunate endings.

The wizard made everything die around him. He was feeling empty, living alone in a soulless manor. But one day, he was sent to the castle by the newly crowned prince to kill the evil queen alongside the fiercest female knight, inspired by my sister. But the wizard fell in love with the queen. And when he did, his magic glowed into something beautiful. The villagers saw that behind the monster, the evil queen wasn't the villain of the story; at the origin, she was the hopeful and kind godmother. A woman who wanted her happy ending. But the wizard, having recovered his magic, left her for the glory and the beauty of life in the golden palace of the prince. As for how the story ended? I had no idea yet.

I couldn't tell her all of that, so I said, "It's a love story with two antiheroes."

"Huh, I guess I'll have to read it because you gave me nothing there." I found her snapping a picture of herself when she thought I wasn't glancing at her, but I had eyes everywhere.

"Whom are you sending that to?" I sounded like a policeman, telling her what she could or couldn't do.

"Ryan, the guy I told you about… he's really cute, and he wanted to make sure my sister did, in fact, pick me up." Her cheeks reddened.

First of all, the lack of faith in this boy regarding my ability to pick up my sister made me cringe. Second of all, this was indeed cute. Obviously, I wouldn't be able to admit that out loud without rolling my eyes.

"You're not saying anything," my sister added. "I was waiting for one of your morality speeches about how I'm so precious for this world and that I shouldn't trust people because they'll hurt me."

"I—" *Did I sound like that?* Like this annoying grumpy person who was killing the mood? "I'm happy if you're happy, and I trust your judgment, but I'll need to know way more details about him to approve of him. He better treat you good, and don't do things you don't want to do, and—"

"Stop," she laughed. "I read romance novels just like you did. My standards are high, trust me. I recognize one who has the potential to be the hero."

Right, not like your sister.

I called a taxi, and it was a matter of minutes before we stepped inside.

"Did you know that Mom is going to be on the nature channel today? They're interviewing her with her bee sanctuary, so she wore her precious stones like a shaman, and don't get me started on her incense rituals," Luna scoffed.

"There must have been an epic vibe at home," I chuckled, imagining my mother welcoming the TV production with a namaste and her copper bowl to remove negative energies.

"Now, let's talk about you," Luna continued once she put her seat belt on. "The guy with the castle, what happened to him? And feel free to share everything. With all the gross details I read in erotica and—"

"You read erotica romance?" my voice snapped, and even the old mustachioed driver's eyes sparkled at the mention.

"You left a pile of very steamy books below your bed, Aurore. Of course, I read them." She raised a brow, that little snarky thing. "Anyway, you skipped my question."

I was about to lie to her again. To pretend that everything was perfect in my imperfect life, but for once, I couldn't. I couldn't be strong for her. I was tired of lies.

"I almost had my happy ending, but it didn't work out," I swallowed, watching her eyes stop glittering as if I had let her down. "But it's okay—I'm okay. I mean, there are other men and—"

"The story is not over. You're the writer, after all—you choose the ending." She seized my hand, making me feel like she was the big sister today. "You know you don't have to pretend everything is okay, right?"

I do. "But I'm fine. Everything is great and—"

"Aurore," she cut me off. "You know, I get why you're doing this act. You want to spare my feelings. You think I'm weak and that I can't handle anything because I almost..." She glanced at the cuts on her wrist, which she hid with her other hand. "But you're wrong. I'm healing. You don't have to be my mom."

"I never thought you were weak, Luna." I gasped. "You're the strongest person I know, and I admire the person you are so much. I love you. More than anything. You know that, right?"

"I know, and I do too." She glanced away. "But you sometimes make me feel like I'm... almost useless. Everything is always great with you; you don't let me in, and I feel like I'm not enough for you because you're always saying you're fine, while most of the days I'm not, and I feel like crap. And I'm like, 'if my sister can do it, why can't I,' and I'm—"

"I'm not fine," I dropped, the tears welling in my eyes. "I'm not, Luna, but I don't want to let you down again. I already did it twice and I—"

"I just want you to open up to me. The good and the bad. I don't want to be useless, please. I'm tired of everyone treating me like I'm a bomb about to explode, like I'm a mess." She raised her voice. "Please. Don't treat me like I'm a weight to carry."

I nodded, my lips shaking. "Fine. I'll tell you everything."

And so I did. I told her and the mustachioed taxi driver about how I fell in love with the man who gave me back my inspiration and how difficult these past years had been.

I exposed my lies, my vulnerability, and my fear, and after that, she hugged me. Despite all of my flaws, she didn't leave. She didn't stop loving me.

She was my little sister, the hopeful one, and when she told me that everything would be okay, I believed her.

CHAPTER 27

Ajax

I had to put my phone on silent.

Notifications were raging over it—news about my upcoming move to the US had traveled fast. Eric kept me busy with a schedule fit for a minister, and I had to focus on Ever After; this project, as much as I didn't want it, would be a new beginning in my career. Work had kept my mind away from thinking about Aurore and her lack of notifications. She had bluntly ghosted me. Maybe it was for the best. I didn't insist. I wouldn't be selfish with her.

Here, there was that void again that could only be filled with work.

I arrived at the address of the theater, hidden in a small alley in Paris. I stepped inside, and the overwhelming noise of people talking and laughing stung my ears. It was not my place. I took it upon myself and continued my way through the crowd, already feeling my fingers tingling with the need to get out.

It was filled with the kind of people everyone would instantly love: ones with cheerful outfits, radiant smiles, loving other people with ease for a reason that was unknown to me.

"Are you coming here to see your kids, sir?" A group of ladies, probably in their fifties, eyed me with an intrigued expression.

"No, I'm here to see—" *The one dressed in a black cape like the evil godmother in the back. The one who's rushing from corner to corner in the middle of the stage with a skull wand.* "Someone."

"Someone? Are you family?" one of them continued, blocking me with a creepy smile.

A knot formed in my throat, and I readjusted my suit, clearly uncomfortable by this interrogation. "No, I'm—" Desperate. Needy. Conflicted. "Just watching."

I didn't charm the group of housewives. They stared at each other as if they had encountered a pervert they wanted to get rid of.

"If you'll excuse me." I edged away from them and the crowd for what mattered.

I found a corner, exiled from the seats at the front of the stage, near the backstage and bathroom entrance. I would be free to be alone and still be able to watch my Aurore on scene. I had made a note on my phone that today was the day she was giving the spectacle with the kids from the hospital.

So I came to see her in a desperate and psychotic act.

She wasn't informed I was coming, and it was better this way.

"You're hiding too," a frail voice came from next to me.

I looked down and peered at the teenage girl sitting on the floor with something that looked like a notebook in her hands. Her fingers were blackened with charcoal, so I deduced she was probably draw-ing. A messy kind of drawing.

"Indeed," I replied, even more uncomfortable with kids than adults. They always looked so glowing and joyous, like they expected you to create fireworks just for them. "I'm not good with people."

That surplus of information wasn't necessary on my part, but that was meant to warn her: *please don't interact with me, or I'll scare you.*

"Me neither," she chuckled, and my plan backfired. She continued her pencil lines in her sketchbook. "I'm actually terrified of them. I'm afraid to look stupid or uninteresting. That's why I'm hiding here."

"People aren't that interesting anyway." The kid was the feminine, younger version of my old self. "You shouldn't care what they think. It's their problem if they don't like you. It's their loss, not yours."

"I want to fit in." She gave me a look with piercing green eyes before getting back to her drawing. "I'm supposed to be part of the spectacle, but I didn't say a word to the other guys. They probably think I'm a freak."

I took a look at her. She was wearing some kind of armor on top of a long, white, creepy dress, and a sword prop was on the ground next to her.

"A knight. You chose to be a knight or a ghost." I scowled. That teenager was weird, and she was probably the second most interesting person in this room.

"I'm the ghost of the first woman to be knighted, but I was obviously a princess before because who doesn't like a crown?" She chuckled, and I surprised myself by not being bored by this conversation.

"You remind me of someone I know." And my fucker smile was on again. "She's much older, obviously."

"See, you're good with people."

She gave me a look, and I leaned forward to see what she was drawing. I was expecting to find some doodles and had already prepared a polite smile, but this was surprisingly decent. Very good, even. She was doing a manga about some girl arriving at a new school full of what looked like vampires.

"Hey! It's not nice to look at it before it's finished!" She clutched her notebook to her chest and frowned. "Plus, it's terrible—it looks so bland. I'm bad at this, and—"

"That's because you're not focusing on how your final drawing will look. You want to make it pretty and perfect, but it shouldn't be. Each character has their own unique facial expressions that shape their personality. Use it to tell a story."

She went a couple of pages back and squinted at me as if she was processing whether my advice was that good or stupid.

"You're right, I didn't think of that. That's why they all look the same. But it's so hard to paint expressions." She gave me some weird puppy eyes. "Do you draw?"

"A bit." I felt uneasy, her eyes on me. "Do you want me to show you?"

She nodded. "You can try, but I'm not sure I'll succeed. I'm not good enough."

"Looks like someone made you believe a lie," I said, pulling up my trousers to squat next to her on the ground. "You're good."

She handed me her sketchbook and lifted a brow. "You're just being nice."

"If you knew me, you'd know I'm not known to be nice."

She drew a full smile as I sketched some facial expressions for one of her characters and showed her how to work with them. I used her and the info I gathered from her personality as an example. My little student did the same afterward, progressing really fast. She had the same ability to see the world in a unique way, giving birth to a whole new universe, just like Aurore.

"I got it!" she screamed, looking at her sketches as if she was holding a masterpiece. "It's so much more powerful now. This is the best advice someone has ever given me! You're actually good at drawing. You should do that for a job."

"I'll think about it."

Her eyes bulged as if she had just come up with some crazy idea. "Perhaps now you can show me how to—"

"Luna? Where are you?"

We both recognized that voice coming from the scene, turning around at the exact time. *My fairy.* Her gaze roamed the stands.

Wait. Does that mean—

I took a step back and parted away from the ghost knight teenager. This was her sister. Although they didn't look exactly alike physically, I should have known. I'd been talking to her sister. *Fuck.*

"Shit, that's my sister, who probably wants to include me in the group or is worried because she thinks I'm still eight." The girl rose, and I was probably staring at her like a freak.

"Better not be late, then," I managed somehow to say. "And, Luna, you'll fit in—they would be stupid not to accept you. You're the second human or, more likely, ghost knight in this room I liked having a conversation with."

"Thank you." She gave me a beaming smile. "You're not as boring as the other adults. You're fun."

Fun? I'd never been described as fun.

That little ray of sunshine waved at me before she went away to meet with her sister. "See you, Ajax!"

Ajax? I froze. All this time, she knew who I was, and she hadn't said a thing. I must have looked like a fool. I let out a sigh and a small laugh despite everything—Bardot girls were resourceful.

From afar, I saw Aurore introducing her to the others. In just a matter of time, they were all interacting together. I kept myself busy until the beginning of the show, with my fairy rushing from corner to corner as the seats were getting full, and with Luna, who was showing her drawing to the other kids. All was going well, thank fuck.

At the sight of her sister fitting into the group, Aurore, dressed up as the evil queen, was getting out of character by giving a tender look to them. It made me think of her story. The moment I had Aurore's manuscript in my hand, I decided to have a sneak peek at it and ended up reading the whole thing. Twice. I even added annotations and had it formatted like a full-size book. Although she hadn't attached the whole story; the ending was missing. I had never been so involved in a story as this, and there were a million odds to finish this tale. It was an impossible problem to solve.

The play began, and a horde of princesses, princes, villains, and heroes embarked on a story that only Aurore could have written. I freed myself from my place against the wall when the little girl in a wheelchair was secured with strings. She had an outfit with wings. She recited her text, and suddenly, the cables made her fly into the false sky. She was lifted into the air. Aurore applauded, jumping in her corner. She did it. She had kept her promise.

"You made me fly!"

I heard tears could mean someone's happiness was so overwhelming it couldn't be managed. This was what was happening to the girl who flew in the air and came to hug Aurore the first moment she landed. The parents were moved, and some had tears too. As for me, I had nothing. Not a single tear.

My phone beeped again.

New emails came in, including my plane ticket for my upcoming departure. My schedule was full with potential collaborations with huge brands for the future—if I didn't fuck up with Ever After and showed I could indeed produce more than gloomy and blank canvases. It was everything I believed I wanted.

But as I walked away in the middle of the theater show, under the eyes of the ladies gossiping about me and my rudeness, I missed the unknown and the unplanned.

I missed the mess she was making in my empty life.

"I can't believe you did all this." Eric roamed into my emptied atelier with a cryptic gaze.

His nostrils flared, probably from the aroma of oil paint that wasn't completely dry, and he faced my latest artwork positioned on tarps. This time, they weren't blank canvases.

The fact I hadn't slept for a week had helped my productivity, to the point that on the last stroke on the canvas, every fiber of my body was revolting. My body was as stiff as after having done intense training for six hours in a row.

"This one's my favorite." Eric craned his neck to look at the piece. "It somehow made me remember *The Sad Girl*. She looks like Aurore." Of course, she looked like her. It was her, despite the fact that I had played with contrast and was hiding part of her face from the public.

"It has a Mexican gothic inspiration. Her heart inside her thoracic cage is ripping, and birds, the ones that are flying away from her dress, try to sew off her heart with some fairy dust or something. You even worked with gold paper for contrast."

"I did." For all I knew, Eric was explaining better than I my own artwork. Words weren't my strong suit.

"It's excellent." He brought a finger to his chin as if he was already thinking of how he'd be able to market the series. "Each of your pieces is part of a story, so each piece is priceless. It's like holding a fragment of a story."

They all thought I was dead, so I'd give them enough to raise the dead from hell. "You can contact the exhibits, but I want them together. The highest bidder will win."

"Of course, of course." He stopped in front of the following painting. The woman was sitting like a regal queen, her skin ashen, on a throne of veils. She had chains around her, imprisoning the birds. "Huh, interesting."

I didn't bother to ask what was when his eyes stopped on what was essentially a self-portrait: a man, devoid of color, was living in a world of black and white and was being offered a four-leaf clover by that same woman. She was glowing in the dark like an angel, the birds waltzing around them in some sort of dance.

"I've never seen you paint anything like that." The following piece was the apparition of a hint of color on the man's heart at the contact of their touch, despite the barriers of thorns growing close to the woman to separate them.

In the next canvas, the man had ripped out his heart, the only colored part of him, to give it to her. She had accepted it, but the man became a statue. And the last painting was my own personal favorite. The woman hugged the statue, cracks appearing where she made contact as if the man wanted to break out from this curse.

I believed I had painted every shade of what Aurore and I were.

"For the first time in my life, I did something impulsive in contrast to my meticulous personality. You should celebrate," I said.

Eric wrote down the information about the size of the canvases on his phone. "You never party, Ajax."

"That's why I said you." I crossed my arms. The idea of a celebration was torture to me.

He chuckled. I'd never made him this content before. "This is great! It's your best work. But wait, if we send these for exhibitions, what about Ever After? This is not your project?"

"No." My tone was dry.

His smile disappeared as fast as it came. "No? Please, tell me you have something."

"I do." I paused. "I have something planned for Ever After. Something you'll strongly disapprove of."

He exhaled, shutting his eyes closed for a moment. "I knew that it seemed too good to be true. Why do you have to make my job harder than it is?"

"Don't worry." I readjusted my suit and walked out of my atelier, knowing what I had to do. "I'm taking care of everything."

CHAPTER 28

Aurore

From: Charlotte Lanza
To: Aurore Bardot
Subject: Appointment Ever After Publishing

Hi Miss Bardot,
   I'm Charlotte Lanza, the CEO of Ever After Publishing. I've come across your manuscript, and I'd like for us to meet. I've taken the liberty to book an appointment at our office from 2 p.m. to 2:30 p.m. this Friday.
   Cordially,
   Charlotte

I faced the premises of Ever After Publishing House, my heels hitting the ground at a murderous tempo. My hands felt moist as I re-adjusted my excuse for a suit—some of my only clothes that weren't packed in suitcases. Very soon, I would turn a page on Paris. As for today, there were several hypotheses as to why Charlotte Lanza wanted to meet me.

The first was that she loved my manuscript and wanted to meet the shadow worker with undeniable talent—Luna's words, not mine. Or, my theory, that I had disrespected the company by asking Spectre to deliver my manuscript to them and didn't submit an online application to their contest, nor was I referred by any agent, which resulted in them wanting to fire me in person.

"Miss Bardot, I presume?" The door slammed open before I could knock, and I faced a woman wearing a tuxedo. She had a square black haircut and gray eyes the color of a storm. She offered a hand in my direction. "Charlotte Lanza. Please come in."

I accepted her hand and stepped inside her office with some posters of bestselling books they had published.

She took her place behind her desk and pinned me with a look. "I have to admit the last few days have been rocky for us. I take it you're familiar with Spectre and are aware of our collaboration?"

Oh no, don't tell me she invited me here so we could talk about him. This was supposed to be about me. It was my time. "Yes, but I don't see how it's relevant to our appointment."

"It has everything to do with it." She raised a brow. "Spectre rejected our offer to collaborate together for more than a year, and a couple of months ago, we received a phone call from his agent. Isn't that weird?"

"I don't think it has anything to do with me."

"Just like the wizard in your story has nothing to do with him." She gave me a confident smile, the one that meant she had read my manuscript, which was a good sign. "I think there's something you need to see for yourself."

She gestured to me, pointing to an easel covered by a sheet. It was probably the artwork Spectre had done for Ever After. There was a security guard literally guarding it as if he accompanied a celebrity. This looked serious, intense, and I had no idea what my place was in this story.

"Please," she insisted.

My heart beat wildly with every step I approached. My hands met the material, and I lifted the veil, unmasking Spectre's piece. A dull noise echoed in my ears, and my knees buckled. I didn't expect any of that. Tingles ran through my core, my body expressing the words I couldn't find.

"It's… *The Sad Girl*," I whispered.

Spectre had given *The Sad Girl* to Ever After. His most precious and by far most expensive painting. The one he said he would never sell, and which was valuable. I was sure Eric must have told him it wasn't reasonable, but why…. Why would he have done that?

As if magnetized by the painting, my finger almost grazed the canvas. I didn't know what came over me, but I seized the canvas in my hands, wanting to observe it more closely. Wanting to feel closer to this part of him and of me. The security guard walked over to halt me, but Charlotte gestured for him to stop.

"She's The Sad Girl. She knows what she's doing."

I nodded to her as a thank-you and observed each detail of the painting. I had never been face-to-face with it before. The paint was in several layers, as if he had repainted it a dozen times to get it perfect. The colors between midnight blue and crimson red battled between nostalgia and sadness, and at the same time the passion and eagerness to continue fighting. Life—anything but a monotonous line.

I found it magnificent.

He had illustrated my pain, my tears, but he had seen me underneath all the layers I'd created to protect myself and feel invincible. He had laid bare each of my thoughts by reproducing my expression to perfection. He knew me better than I knew myself, and for that, I no longer hated this painting. On the contrary. Despite the sadness, it was magical. It was a turning point in our history and the day I broke down all the barriers around me. Luna was fine, everyone was fine, the future would be bright.

"He was supposed to deliver to us our one-hundredth anniversary piece, but instead, he had left *The Sad Girl*, along with a manuscript and a note that said, 'If you want to know her story, read this manuscript.' I have to admit it caught my attention." Charlotte crossed her arms, analyzing the painting that I had laid back on the easel. "The resemblance is striking. This painting has the greatest storytelling of our century; giving us the words behind this art is a gift to us. Even though he played us, it was an inflated act. I think you inspired it, Miss Bardot. Any artist is nothing without a muse, after all."

Of course, he did it for me.

He did it so I could voice my story.

He made me the main character.

My eyes met those of The Sad Girl. I wouldn't disappoint her—I wasn't going to lose it. I was going to do everything I could to make sure we all got the happy ending we deserved—her, me, Spectre, Luna, everyone.

"I'm going to cut to the chase." Charlotte leaned over her desk, intertwining her fingers together. "I have a question. Does it end happily, or does it not? Just like Spectre, you have a talent for the unexpected, and you took a risk not handing over the end of the story. I'm sure you can imagine how many manuscripts we receive per week? The question is, why should we believe in yours?"

I remained calm, trying not to show my excitement.

"If I'm here, it means you already do. I don't need to convince you; I only need to be honest." I wet my lips, the words coming in a wave. "I'd say it's not your typical ending. We all have different conceptions: for some, it'd be marriage and kids; for others, career accomplishments, and for them, it's... the freedom to exist as they want to. Neither the evil queen nor the wizard dream of a big wedding, nor do they want to move to a small village and quit their ambitions. They're both grinding hard, building a kingdom of their own outside of the prince's realm."

"I see." She brought a thumb to her chin. "We'd like to publish your story within our company. You'll keep your rights, of course, and we'll settle a partnership contract. You'll work with an editor, and the ideal would be to market it as soon as possible. We'll see how the public reacts at the release of the novel, and then we'd probably move to the next step by making it through animation movies if it's a success."

"I—wow." I didn't have the words. I'd been dreaming of this moment for so long. "This is huge. But I want to make sure you won't modify my story. I want it the way it is."

"You are the author—you will have the last word, and we'll stipulate it inside a contract." She gave me a sideways shark smile. "My team suggested that we make the evil queen a bit more…" She searched her words. "Likable. She's too hostile; they believe she needs to be sunnier and lovable, into the line of the pure virgin heroine or with a stronger redemption arc. A grumpy heroine doesn't sell."

"But she's not," I protested, defending my character. "She's like every other woman on the planet, because yes, we're not that different. We struggle. We try our best to be that perfect hero you're portraying in your stories, but we're not. We're not all sunshine, lovely, sparkly, and perfectly good-looking every day. No, we're messy, and sometimes we're just not her, but we still want someone to believe we can be a main character too. We just want to be loved and feel worthy too."

I leaned forward, a fist on the table. "Every woman in this world deserves her happy ending. You know, some of us feel excluded because we don't feel worthy of it, because we're not the typical main character that has it all. But we are. There is a happy ending for the misunderstood villain, the sidekick best friend, the freak, the busy mom, the introverted reader, for all of us. We have to stop stereotyping women and telling us how we should be able to find love."

I knitted my brows and found my strength, a tension raging through my veins. "I want people to read about a woman who overworks herself to be as successful as a privileged white man, just as you are right now. I want to write about her fears, her failures, the way she protects herself because she cannot trust anyone, even if she appears cynical and grumpy. I want to write about that kid who was bullied in school because she was in her own damn world. I want to tell her it's all going to be okay. I want to write about that little girl who one day wishes to fly because she will never be able to walk and still finds the strength to smile every day. I want to write about that man who stopped living and acts like a phantom because he thinks he isn't worthy of love, while I do fucking love him! I want to write about all of them because a novel may be fictional, but the impact it leaves on us and the emotions we feel while reading it are true. It stays with us."

Out of breath after lashing out my most hidden confessions, I relaxed my fisted hand. "You identified with the evil queen, didn't you?"

She readjusted her suit, poker-faced. "Yes, I did."

"That's why we have to believe we're not the only ones on the bad side of the story. A side character doesn't have to turn out to be the villain or be left in a corner. It has to shine. Those characters have the potential to be the heroes of a captivating story." I finally found my voice, my gut showing me the right way. "I'm sorry, but I'll not change the evil queen. She's authentic, and I love her the way she is."

"And I didn't ask you to." She gave me another full-tooth smile. "I see the potential in your story, and I'm interested in your voice, in that passion of yours, even if you nearly destroyed my lucky pin underneath your fist."

"Oh, sorry." I retracted my hand from the wooden table and the squashed cat pin.

"I want your story, and I'm ready to fight for it." She stood up from her desk. "Do you have a title?"

"*Nevermore*."

"This is a twist to the tale." She grinned. "Miss Bardot, I hope we'll collaborate. If you have any questions, I'd be pleased to answer them."

"I'll review your contract with my lawyers"—I didn't have any lawyers—"and we'll go from there. I appreciate the opportunity you're giving me."

Especially since I had handed over my resignation from the ice cream store at Ever After yesterday. The offer I had been waiting for all my life had finally come, right before my departure to return home. I finally accepted who I truly was without trying to be someone else. We shook hands once, and when I exited her office, my heart was burning in my chest—a mix of adrenaline and fear of the unknown. I took sight of Luna wearing a pink headband and a cute ballerina dress from my closet, waiting for me in front of the entrance, her foot hitting the ground at full speed. She was even more anxious than me. I did not keep her waiting and hurried to join her, trotting in stilettos.

"So?" Her voice was breathy. "How did it go?"

"I believe it's your birthday, and it's time for me to show you around Ever After." My lips curled, leaving the suspense at its peak. "Shall we go now?"

"Aurore! Tell me!" She crossed her arms and pouted.

"'To my sister, the greatest warrior I know, who showed me that villains, too, could get their happy endings.' That's my dedication to you," I hinted.

"Wait!" Her eyes bulged out from their sockets with that glee I knew so well. "Does it mean—"

"Yes." My smile was truthful. "I may have conducted a deal with Ever After Publishing. We did it!"

She took me by surprise and jumped into my arms. "I'm so happy! I can't wait to read it, and I'm not gonna do like your bad habit of reading the ending first."

For a moment, I let the wave of happiness wash over me, and when my phone rang, I secretly hoped it'd be Ajax. I craved to tell him everything. I missed him, and I hoped with time, the ache in my heart would stop. Except that the person in question was none other than Bernard Dupont-Brillac.

> **BDB:** I hope you haven't forgotten our meeting tomorrow afternoon. Don't forget to wear a dress. Artistically.

A knot formed in my throat.

Luna seized my hand and rushed us on our way to Ever After with excitement. "I think this is gonna be your happy ending! All's well that ends well!"

CHAPTER 29

Ajax

I thought for the first time in my life I was sick, a mixture of migraine and maybe heart trouble. Every breath was painful, I had a shard in my guts that never left, and I hadn't gotten more than two hours of sleep in a week. But it turned out to be absolutely nothing, just a figment of my imagination. The doctor or most likely my surgeon brother, had asked me if I was going through a painful event, but I was fine. I was always fine.

All of that didn't explain why I was standing like a fool in the middle of an amusement park, holding a bouquet of flowers to help my case. Maybe because I wanted to silence my ills for a moment. My plane was leaving in a couple of hours, but I had to see Aurore one last time before leaving. I had to be sure she'd be okay. This wasn't rational, but the world had never seemed so cold without her.

I crossed the door to her workplace and gave a quick glance around the room. Aurore wasn't there, but two other women I'd never noticed before had taken her place.

"Excuse me, do you know where Aurore Bardot is? She usually works here on weekends," I asked bluntly, not caring about the queue of people.

The gaze of the woman with purple hair pierced me before narrowing on the bouquet as if she wanted to burn the blooms in hell. "She quit working here, and she didn't even show up for her last working day, that snarky girl."

I remained stoic. It wasn't like Aurore to miss her last day of work.

"Ajax." Anyone calling out to me other than Aurore in this place seemed improbable and unrealistic, but it happened.

Turning to the voice, I recognized the blonde woman from the gala—not for the fact that she couldn't be dressed more touristically as she was for an amusement park, but by the sound of her voice and the way her eyes took me in as if she was shocked by my own existence.

"We've never been properly introduced," she continued. "I'm Emma or, as you know, Aurore's best friend, who strongly advises her on what's good for her."

"Ajax." The teenage girl next to her, holding a huge candy like a sword, shot me a smile. "It's nice to see you again."

"The ghost knight, or should I say Luna. Aurore's sister," I replied to her before focusing my attention back on Emma. "I'm Ajax. The one she probably described as an asshole, and we both know Aurore never listens to advice."

Apparently, I was either funny or truthful judging by the way Emma chuckled, and Luna pursed her lips to the side in a mischievous grin—just like Archi when he knew something I didn't and tried to blackmail me.

Emma crossed her arms. "What are you doing here? Are you searching for Aurore? She didn't come to work today."

"But it's the weekend. She's always working here on the weekends." I didn't like this nor the muscle working in my jaw. "Is she okay?"

"She asked Emma to show me around the park because she was… busy. She's not answering our texts right now." Luna shrugged.

Emma didn't miss a beat and bit on her inner cheek, her cold eyes on me. "Perhaps, because you broke her heart in some way."

She was blunt, which took me by surprise. "I wouldn't."

"Aurore is the kindest and most protective person I know. I don't know what happened between you guys, but if you don't fight for her, you may lose her because she's coveted by someone else."

Something bitter ravaged my cells as slow, deadly words escaped my lips. "Someone else?"

"Yeah, and I'm not a huge fan of his. I was rooting for you."

Luna let out a chuckle while Emma didn't budge, like a referee announcing the start of a fight.

"Who is he?" I articulated in a rather murderous way. *Did she start dating someone else? Why did I have no clue about this?* I had no right to be jealous—she wasn't mine, and I wanted her happiness, and yet… and yet I was ready to fight like a caveman with this moron, whoever he was.

"Look at the look of jealousy on your face. Nice." And now she was smiling. "Let's say he's an artist and the kind of jerk who always gets what he wants."

"I like him," Luna continued, her stare juggling between the both of us. "He actually did something huge for her yesterday. Something better than… peonies."

And now, it was my flower's turn to get insulted. I readjusted the sleeves of my dress shirt. They were both part of Aurore's life, and I was doing a terrific job at being liked by them. Charming people was not my forte. Human relationships were too complex and difficult.

"You're talking about Spectre?" Which meant I'd been jealous of myself, not forgetting that I'd been described as a jerk. The opposite would have surprised me though.

"You knew?" Emma opened her mouth agape. "Well, she's probably with that jackass right now."

Jackass. I cleared my throat. "Impossible."

"How do you know that? She can only be with him."

"Yeah, how do you know that, *Ajax*?" Luna gave me a twisted smile, gunning her eyes on me in an almost scary way.

Because I'm the motherfucker you all hate. "Do you know where she is?"

"I won't tell you. I don't want to betray her trust." Emma was a pain.

"What makes you believe she's with him?" I deadpanned, losing my patience. I made my knuckles crack. At this stage, I was almost sure to smother the flowers.

"Because!" she hissed. "If you know about Spectre, you should know she's his muse, and apparently, they are still collaborating together."

"Impossible," I repeated.

This whole situation didn't make any sense.

"Look," she sighed. "I know you're jealous, but I'm very well aware of what my best friend does—"

"Emma. She's not with Spectre, I can assure you. Please." I articulated each word painfully between clenched teeth.

Emma's mouth parted slightly as she pointed a finger up at me. Her face went white, and I succeeded in muting her. *Fuck it. Fuck everything.*

"Uh-oh, I think she guessed it." Luna gave me an almost apologetic smile. That vicious, smart teenager. She knew who I was all along.

Emma swallowed the news. "You are—"

"Emma, please." I didn't acknowledge what she had already guessed: I was the jerk in question.

"*Scheisse*, I should have seen that coming." She took a deep breath. "She went to the school of art or something, and when I asked her if she would be meeting with Spectre, she nodded. She said she'd be late, while we were supposed to—"

"She wore one of her dresses," Luna added, and that piece of information made me lose it.

"Take the peonies." I offered the bouquet to Luna, who frowned, definitely having a thing against flowers, and I rushed away from them in a not-so-polite way to head to the only place that crossed my mind.

Les Beaux Arts. *But why was she there again?*

"Wait! Where are you going?" Emma screamed after me.

"Wait, Ajax." Luna stopped me. "She's there to protect you, silly, and she'd kill me if she knew I was telling you this."

I tightened my fist and turned around, gritting my teeth. "Telling me what?"

"Who she's really with and why."

Time was against me.

I had my plane and a new life to catch in less than two hours.

CHAPTER 30

Aurore

"Sit," Bernard ordered, readjusting his glasses as he took his sweet time installing his canvas on his easel.

I sat without a word, my lips pinched together and my eyes vacant. I always thought Spectre was meticulous and organized with a routine of his own, but when it was about his art, he was messy and in a trance. Bernard was old-school, kind of boring, and ridiculously slow. It had been half an hour since he'd started placing the pencils in some sort of order, after having sharpened them to the limit of breaking. Pencils he was not even likely to use and which, without a doubt, were the most expensive on the market.

I eyed the apogee of white enveloping the room, with a dead silence for melody. Bernard glanced at me from behind his canvas, but I remained emotionless, not giving him a glimpse of my soul. The agreement was that I would model for him, not that he'd have more of me, and he knew it.

"You're giving me nothing," Bernard spat.

"I have nothing to give you," I quipped back, lifting my chin higher.

He sighed with annoyance and narrowed his froggy stare at me as if that was threatening enough for me.

"I want you to do something." A thin smile sketched his lips. "Cry."

Cry.

All my muscles tightened. That word alone made my heart skip a beat and my skin rise in alert.

Cry.

No one would have my tears again, and certainly not him.

"I won't."

"You're my model. You'll do as I ask." He mumbled something inaudible as he rushed over me.

Without asking me, he grabbed me by the arm so I'd switch position, arching my back like Notre Dame's hunchback. His hand above my head, he made me lower my chin, and it took all the will in the world to not fight back. I looked defeated, helpless, ugly. Spectre had sublimated my emotions in contradiction to Bernard, which lowered me to less than nothing. Their vision was opposite.

Bernard sighed with an expression of disgust and went back to his seat, on the verge of losing his patience. "Now, you cry. Be a good actress. Give me your pretty tears, Sad Girl."

My hand curled into a fist, ready to strangle him. I wanted to yell, but I couldn't, because if I defended myself, then it would have been all for nothing. I had to take it. I had to be stronger than my feelings.

"Don't make me do this." I wasn't going to implore him, but my shaky voice was weak enough to betray how uncomfortable I was.

"I touched a sensitive chord." His pencil strokes on the canvas were like stabs in my heart, and I didn't take my eyes off the ground. "You've done it before, you can do it again. Tell me why you cried, and I'll capture your sadness better than he did. I'll capture the ugliness of your pain."

"Anything but that," I articulated, one of my hands already shaking.

"You'll cry, Aurore. I have my ways," he said, and only my gaze moved in his direction, witnessing his eyes shining with something twisted. "Was it because of a broken heart? Did someone die? Had you lost your job? Was someone sick? Why did you cry?"

My chin trembled, and I had to bite on my inner lip to make it stop. I would give him nothing.

"Look at you. You're nothing." He kept trying to hurt me with his words to get me to give him what he wanted, and I'd resist. And I did until he said the words, "You look so helpless. How do you think Ajax or your family will react when they see the painting I'm doing of you? The beauty of The Sad Girl was a lie. I'll be painting you just as you are."

My eyes watered. *Ajax.* It'd hurt him. I was doing this to help him, and in the end, he'd be destroyed. *Luna.* She couldn't see me helpless. I couldn't be the victim. I couldn't.

"Here, you're finally giving me what I want." Bernard's voice seemed distant.

A tear fell. One single tear. "I—"

Students yelled in the hallway, snapping me out of my downfall, and I blinked away the tears, erasing them with my hand.

"What's all this again!" Bernard complained, close to breaking his brush.

It wasn't long before a student knocked and clenched the door open to tumble into the studio. "Mr. Dupont-Brillac! Have you heard what happened?"

"As you can see, I'm busy creating my next masterpiece, Friedrich. What on earth could be more important than that?" Bernard's irritated tone couldn't be missed.

"Sir, you don't want to miss this." The student rushed to Bernard's side to show him something on his phone. "Spectre just made a tweet twenty minutes ago, and everyone is going crazy!"

What? I jumped out of my seat and straightened my posture. At the mention of his name, my whole body seemed to have regained strength, the blood in my veins surging twice as fast. He revived me.

Bernard did a yoga mudra as if trying to calm down. "And why do you think I care about that incompe—"

"He just dropped his identity just like that! In one fucking sentence!"

"What!" In no time, I threw the chair back and raced toward the student in question, grabbing his phone without even asking for permission.

I read the tweet, my eyes widening. *Oh my—*

"Done playing games: my name is Ajax Clemonte, and I'm Spectre."

It was simple, effective, direct, blunt, and he still didn't master the communication touch, but that was him. *The man I freaking undoubtedly love.*

"What! Why would he do something as stupid as that!" Bernard made dramatic hand gestures, almost kicking his easel.

"It's brilliant," I dropped in a half laugh. "And so fucking courageous. He's so courageous—I can't believe him. I—"

"Leave us, Friedrich." Bernard snapped his fingers for the student to leave—which he did right away, faster than he came into the room.

"You know what?" I displayed the biggest grin. "I'm out of here. Now our contract is worthless. You have nothing against him, and I can tell you to fuck yourself gladly!" I gathered my stuff in a rush and headed toward the door. "You lost."

I need to text him. I need to—

"Wait. He can't get away with this!" He stomped in my direction. "He threw all of my teaching away because of a silly girl wearing dresses fit for a whore, and now he's doing it all again."

I snapped my eyes at him and ignored the insult he just gave me. "Stop it, Bernard. You're making a fool of yourself."

Bernard held my forearm, this time with a firm grip, and kept me locked with him.

"Let me leave," I gritted out between clenched teeth. "I'm not some defenseless girl, and I won't hesitate to kick you in the crotch."

His face had reddened with anger, his lips pursed together. "You'll stay, and you'll do this fucking painting as we agreed on."

"Let. Go. Of. Me." I was about to explode and teach him a lesson of my own when something snapped like a tornado of darkness.

Bernard's grip left my arm. A draft passed. Objects shattered on the floor. Bernard flew across the room against a very aggressive Ajax, who had just eclipsed himself into his studio. He sent him a blow before grabbing him by his collar and throwing him against the wall.

"That's the last time you try to touch my girlfriend and go behind my back." I had never seen Ajax so pissed off. Veins protruded from his forearms, and his gaze was pitch-black, his forehead creasing with the emotions ravaging him inside.

In a blast of ten seconds, too much had happened. It was all unexpected. "Ajax? What are you doing here?"

"I'm teaching," he said as he sent Bernard crashing to the ground.

He readjusted his dress shirt casually and took one deep breath, cracking his neck to the side, while Bernard was crouched, gasping for air on the ground.

I fucking smiled.

"I'll make sure you never teach again. You certainly won't bully anyone else, and I promise you that your artistic career is over." Ajax gave him one last dismissive look before grabbing my hand and dragging me out.

"You just revealed who you are. You're done just as much as me, Spectre," Bernard coughed, blood dripping from his mouth.

"Maybe, but I'm used to rising back. You're over, Bernard." It was the last sentence that Ajax threw at Bernard before we escaped his atelier. He seemed determined to direct us somewhere in a rush.

"Ajax, wait!"

He didn't, but when I noticed the wooden door of the storage room, I knew he was going where it all started. He pushed it right open and ushered us inside. It hadn't changed. The smell of wood and books remained, and the shelves held globes, mannequins, and canvases. It was a mess where you could find whatever you wanted, more spacious than I remembered. The broken window was still there. It was as if time had stopped flowing in this room.

I folded my arms. "Why are we here?"

"Because if I were to go outside and have a private conversation with you, I wouldn't be able to because everyone in that fucking school knows who I am now, and I won't find peace ever again," he roared.

"I'm not the one who forced you to make an impulsive tweet! Why did you even do that?" I raised my voice as high as his.

"Because of you, Aurore!" The palm of his hand rested on the shelf, which shook at the contact of it as he took a deep exhale, hanging his head down. "Because you went rogue into Bernard's fucking trap without talking to me first about it!"

"How did you even know about it!" When he remained silent, I knew only one person was aware of the truth because I couldn't hide anything from her and her smart-ass brain. "Luna! I can't believe it."

I went back to the point, reminding myself to have a conversation with her later.

"I did it to protect you and your identity!" I pointed that out by making an overdramatic hand gesture. "I had to do the right thing! If I had told you, you would have rejected me and chosen your career instead of me. That would have been more painful than doing the heroic thing. This way, I could stay in that fucking fairy-tale dream you created for us and—"

"You're wrong!" He took his hand off the shelf and stared at me, his lips curving down. "I would have chosen you, Aurore. Always."

My mouth snapped close. This wasn't possible. Could someone choose me for once? I was never the one to be chosen in the end.

"After what you did for me at Ever After, I couldn't let you ruin your career," I whispered. "I had to protect you like you did for me."

Even if it hurt.

"You know how painful it would have been to see you pose for that asshole! You're making me sick. I feel like I want to explode and—" He curled his fist, all his facial features harsh. "I can't bear it. I can't bear you being someone else's muse or girlfriend. You'd have fucking destroyed me!"

"And I can't bear that because of me you're losing everything you worked for!" I took a step toward him, my high voice shaking. "I can't bear to be the villain in your story."

"And I can't bear someone to hurt you and have you!" he quipped back before imprisoning me between his two arms positioned against the shelf. "You'll never be the villain in my story, Aurore."

My pinched lips shook. "Because of me, you lost everything."

"Without you, I was nothing." His frozen stare hit mine. "I should be the one to protect you, rescue you sometimes, or even be there for you, but you're not letting me."

I swallowed. "I don't need anyone."

"That's where you're wrong. We all need someone. I need you. Desperately. Even your fucking heroes need someone to protect them. That's why the villain fails—he or she has no ally. I'm your ally, Aurore. We're a team."

I tried to keep my hammering heart in check. "Were you not supposed to be gone by now?"

"I missed my flight." His Adam's apple bobbed. "And now, I have things to take care of since I bulldozed my identity online."

"Do you regret it?"

"No," he deadpanned, pulling away from me. "I didn't think twice before making the post when I guessed you were about to do that ridiculous act of bravery for me. Eric, on the contrary, is very pissed, but at least he'll be fully busy with this mess. I'm not even sure my next contract won't retract with this announcement, but Aurore, it has always been you."

My lips parted so lightly, and I felt the corner of my stupid eyes water. "What do you mean?"

"I mean that the fucking world is empty without you. It's cold. Freezing. Austere. It feels like I'm dead. It feels like nothing. But when

I'm with you, it's messy, sometimes infuriating and passionate, but so alive—"

"Is that a compliment?" I snapped.

"Yes, because when I'm with you, I don't feel empty. You left a shard in my gut that never leaves. And my thoughts, you haunt them. It's like you're at the center of everything, and I don't know what's happening to me—maybe I'm sick, but I can't breathe without you. I feel like an idiot and weak, like I can't control anything, and I'm constantly worried about you if I'm not near you and—"

"You love me," I dropped in a whisper.

Ajax was in love with me. He loved me. He loved me more than anything. Me. And I loved him, more than I loved myself. So why on earth did love have to be so painful?

"What?" He cleared his throat, taking a step back as if the word "love" was the sight of a shark swimming in a bloody pool next to him.

A beaming smile radiated on my face. "That's love. Everything you're describing. That's love."

"I don't know how to love," he lied from the rasp of his voice.

"How can you believe that?"

"I—" He shut his mouth, retracting whatever he was about to say.

We didn't tear our eyes from each other but let our emotions communicate through a long silence.

I didn't even realize that tears were streaming down my cheeks. I cried with every beat of my heart, water purging my scars from the past. I was crying, yes, but I was not sad. I was alive.

"What I feel for you will never go away. It's strong and consuming," Ajax said, leaning on the shelf across from mine. "Seven years ago, you stole my soul."

"Ajax, I—"

"Let me tell you the story of how I fell in love with you while you didn't even know I existed."

CHAPTER 31

Ajax

7 years ago

I didn't know how long I'd be able to afford the overpriced classes I was taking at Les Beaux Arts.

I was juggling between jobs, one at some fancy, rich-ass restaurant, serving men just like my dad, and the other at the reception of a night hotel where married men were accompanied by escorts for the night. I was saving every penny by living in an apartment with a weird dude named Isaac—he was everything I wasn't, slightly annoying and extroverted, sleeping until noon and partying all night long, but he was better than Léon. Without him, I'd probably still be sleeping in that train station.

The reason why I came to Bernard's expensive class wasn't because he marked each of my finished paintings with a red cross, nor was it for his motivational talk about how I'd never become a true artist because I didn't have that eccentric genius fever. It wasn't for the way his golden students treated me like a street rat and how I'd stooped to picking through the trash cans and storage room for their leftover materials. I was a couple of years older than most of them—despite that old dude living his teenage dream and a woman who thought she was a real-life renaissance painting.

The reason why I came to his class was something that'd make corpses laugh from beneath their graves.

Models came, all of them inspiring me with a deep constant void. My paintings were soulless underneath those technically perfected traits. I was reproducing everything I saw without a soul, without a detail worth exploring. I had no story to tell, no feelings to put into the light, no matter how hard I tried. And I tried to fit in so fucking hard. It didn't work.

Until there was her.

The girl who always arrived with a dress fit for a runaway bride. She had that smile. A smile so proportionate that the mere curl of her lips made her cheeks lift and her eyes squint. With a simple smile, her whole face expressed itself. And she had those eyes—feline eyes that could set the sun ablaze.

It'd been a couple of weeks since she'd been employed to pose at Les Beaux Arts, and I was making sure to never miss her. She invoked a peek at some unknown human emotions I couldn't classify—like the tingling in my fingers, my heart beating like an old record that blares, the temperature of the room changing abruptly. She created symptoms in me. But since then, my art had come to life.

Bernard was making it even harder on me until he'd purposely humiliated me in front of the students, asking them to correct my painting by adding a word that described the horror I had made. The words *freak, homeless, dead, filth,* and *incapable* came to engulf my canvas in the shape of dripping blood. And even then, I had felt a simple twinge but nothing more, and I walked past it every day; Bernard had hung it above his desk like some trophy.

I had talked to that mystery girl. Once. It was in the storage room, but it was in vain. I saw my reflection in the mirror. I knew what people were saying about me. Despite everything, she had written me a letter and given me a four-leaf clover. I was not used to receiving gifts nor people being interested in me. She called me a ghost, and since then, I'd been looking for a similar artist name.

In my usual place at the back of the class, I leaned against the wall and scribbled similar words.

Ghost. Spirit. Phantom. Spectre.

Spectre. I stopped at this word. It meant a ghost or a spectrum—a band of colors like in a rainbow. I erased what I had written. I wasn't Ajax Clemonte, rich heir. I was almost without a penny Ajax, whose fortune stopped at one luggage full of painting materials I hadn't even paid for myself and a pocket watch I stole from my father. From what I gathered, she had a preppy boyfriend in the architecture department. I wasn't enough to vie with.

I took out the pocket watch. She was late. All the students were waiting for her. Even Bernard tapped his foot. The sounds of shoes echoed in the alley, as if someone was running. I glanced next to my canvas. It was her. She seemed exhausted, crossing the main door with messy hair around her face and some makeup drifting down her eyes.

"I'm so sorry. I had an appointment that went on for so long, and I—"

"I don't have time to hear your pitiful excuses," Bernard cut her off. "Get on with it."

She nodded politely and threw her bag in a corner to step into the center, taking in a pose, her gaze lost on the horizon. This was my favorite moment of the day. I could admire every centimeter of her— from the mix of colors in her eyes, from burnt sienna to mars brown, like a work of art on their own, to her snub nose and the way the light hit her face like small crystals and reddened her cheeks. I could admire every corner of her while remaining invisible in the shadows.

My body had a brain and a will of its own. My pencil lines rushed, my eyes were going back and forth quickly, and my brain switched off. My hand clenched to the point that I could cut off the flow of my blood. I was in this phase where I forgot reality; I deformed it. My eyes roamed the material of her dress. The skirts were like a hidden identity, a mystery to be discovered.

A phone rang across the classroom, and I snapped away from that phase.

"Which phone is it?" Bernard complained.

"I'm sorry, it's mine. I—" She excused herself and left her place to the biggest sighs from the students to kneel down toward her bag. "I'm sorry."

"What a mess. This day is a complete mess!" Bernard whispered, bringing a hand to his forehead.

I turned my neck to the side to see her as she picked up her call. "Mom, I can't talk right now. What's—"

Her face went ghostly white, and she parted her lips, but no sound came out from them, as if she was disconnected from the world. My brows knitted together. She didn't even reply to Bernard's complaints and the other students' stupid laughs.

"I—" She turned around to meet Bernard, but her chin shook. "I'm sorry, I need to—"

A tear welled up in the corner of her eyes, and she rushed out of the room. It stirred something in me. I wanted to follow after her.

"What's wrong with this girl! That's it, she's fired. I'm done with all of this!" Bernard yelled.

"Maybe something happened to her," I dropped, loud enough apparently for everyone to hear.

"Like I care! Her job should come first!" Bernard tried to call someone in the hallway. "Look, I need a replacement for—"

His voice became more and more imperceptible as he moved away from the classroom.

"That girl is so weird, dude," Bernard's favorite student whispered.

"At least she's kinda hot, if we omit her killer eyes," another one continued.

A nerve in my jaw twitched at the comments. I wanted to be the only one to paint her, the one to see her, and not them. They were unworthy.

"At her first class, she brought cookies as if we were in a fucking old country movie. Did you know she's dating Augustus, apparently? But he's just in it for fucking. We all know he's crushing on someone else."

My fist balled as I listened to more of their gossip. I bent down to search my bag for my headphones. I didn't want to hear them.

"Guys, I bet you there is a unicorn or something inside her bag." The same favorite asshole spoke as if he was some jokester making everyone laugh.

Some girl bounced her way back from her chair to peer at the mystery girl's opened bag. "There is a manuscript there. Something called *Romance at Sunshine Lake*."

"Let's hide it from her."

My grip had tightened on my headphones, and I put them down on the floor. *Bunch of morons.*

"Do that and I'll brand the wall with the shape of your ugly-ass face." I gunned my eyes at the bully and former favorite teacher's pet.

"Relax, freak." He looked down on me as if I was that sociopathic man no one dared to approach. "I preferred you when you were mute. Didn't you understand the lesson we gave you last time? Looks like the freak has a crush on that bitch."

Last time. He was referring to the time they had already rummaged through her bag and I had gone to retrieve the mystery girl's notebook after meeting her in the storage room. This jerk and his group of friends had pushed me so that I was tripping on the ground. I hadn't said anything because if I had acted, I would have been expelled, and all hope of achieving a career in art and seeing her would vanish. I had to be patient to take my revenge on all of them. But patience wasn't something I had in my disposition today.

I displayed a deadly scowl. "Bitch?"

"What, you're offended? I'm sure you're going to the bathroom to give yourself a handjob like a freak." People laughed. "Why don't you just quit, loser? Go buy yourself some clothes. You smell like trash."

"I won't quit because I'm better than you," I said, crossing my arms.

"Oh yeah?" He tapped his pencil like some cheap-ass gangster. "How about I go after your whore and fuck her like the cheap one she is in a corner, huh?"

An infernal tide consumed me whole.

It burnt like acid.

My breathing quickened.

My muscles tensed.

Bernard entered the room again as that bully showed me a sexual image on his phone of what he intended to do with her. "They are all incompetent, so we'll work on—"

I snapped.

I rose up from my chair and headed straight for the bully. I knocked down his easel and threw him against the wall in a murderous impulse.

"Ajax!" Bernard screamed like a five-year-old kid seeing a mouse.

I didn't understand what was happening to me. I was possessed. My fist clenched at his polo shirt. I took a breath. And another. Clenching my jaw, I pushed that piece of shit away from me. He wasn't worth it. "Show some respect."

The student made a look of disgust. "You should tell that to Augustus, but maybe he's willing to share with a rat."

He tried to hit me back, but I intercepted him and knocked him down, landing a blow on his jaw. Blood dripped down his mouth, and when he spat to breathe through his bleeding mouth, he sent his blood flying, hitting my shirt. *Great, now I have to buy new clothes.*

"You incompetent fool. What did you do?" Bernard came to the side of his protégé, pushing me away. "You're worthless. Get out of my class before I call the police!"

"Gladly." I didn't even bother to take my stuff.

"I should never have taken pity on you and taken you into my class."

Pity. If only the school knew the learning methods that Bernard had inflicted on me; he would be automatically fired. I rushed away from the class, never looking back. I would never enter those doors again.

I rolled up my sleeves and paced through the corridors in the hopes of finding her. I went outside, and scanning the night, I distinguished a woman underneath the light from the lampposts on the Alexandre III bridge. She was leaning into it, alone, as if the world had fallen silent to give her the stage.

I got closer. Mystery girl was throwing pieces of paper away in the river, but her body wasn't racking with an onslaught of sobs and tears. No, her eyes were filled to the brim with tears that gushed down her ashen cheeks. Her bottom lip quivered, but her chin was high and proud, no other parts of her moving. The void seemed to call her in an invitation to jump, but she didn't. Even the breeze was silent.

I was hypnotized and fascinated. Her emotions were so powerful they stirred something in me. My stomach twitched. My heart threatened to flee away with maddening beats. My throat dried. The blood coursed through my cells. I memorized the scenery with one promise.

I have to reinvent myself.

I'll show them.

I was tired of wanting to fit in. I'd create a new identity that no one knew. I'd be a Spectre. And I'd take my revenge, making her a legend. I'd paint her and immortalize her emotions to share them with the whole world. I'd show them that a nobody could rise above.

She'd be my masterpiece.

I stepped forward to her, but what would I even say? I had never been good with words, let alone emotions. I didn't even know her name.

But one day... One day, I'd have everything.

And that day, I'd be enough.

CHAPTER 32

Aurore

Present day

"I can't believe this." I blinked twice, the hair on my skin rising. "Ajax…"

I lifted my eyes to him, and he was just as I remembered he was back then. One messy strand of his raven hair fell over his forehead. His arms were crossed. He leaned on the shelf, looking bad-boyish despite his well-shaved jaw and expensive suit. It was the same soul, the one who always saw me.

I inched closer to him, and his dark eyes finally assessed mine. My heart was beating an extreme symphony, and my hands roamed across his chest, wondering why I had made the wrong choice all along.

He was right next to me.

The one who thundered my heart.

"How could you have thought you wouldn't be enough?" I

breathed, and when his fingers grasped my hand to bring it to his mouth and kiss it, I knew I had already fallen too hard.

"I had nothing to offer you. I was so broke that I couldn't afford anything, on bad terms with my family, unable to evaluate my feelings. I had accomplished nothing and gave up everything I ever did."

For the first time, in his eyes, I could see pain. A long, everlasting pain, probably the reason why he wanted to run away from all of this. My gaze mirrored his, and my eyes glistened.

"You don't see yourself as I see you," I said, giving him the exact same sentence he had told me once. "You're the man who madly, deeply, incredibly captured my heart." I jumped on my tiptoes in an attempt to match his height. "You're perfect to me. You don't have to change anything."

"And you're perfect to me." His hand captured my waist as his other cupped my nape. "You're a character coming out from a fairy book, and I don't care if it's the sarcastic evil queen or the fairy godmother, as long as you're you and mine. I found you again, and you found me with that magnificent letter of yours."

"I'm so glad I sent it," I chuckled, and the moment our eyes met, it felt like a bolt of lightning had struck us together, and we knew what would happen next.

Time flew by at full speed.

We had one timeless moment.

Soft and moist. Hot and breathy. Electric and delicious. This kiss was two not-so-opposites fitting together in an explosion of unknown flavors.

Fingers carded through my hair, and we breathed each other in. The hunger within my heart couldn't be satisfied. I needed more of him and of what we could be. My eyes closed so my soul could speak, and our tongues tangled, battling madly like the first day. As if we shared one mind, he pinned me against the bookshelf, and my eyelids fluttered open. His were black, full of desire, and his breathing animalistic and rough.

"What are we doing?" I moaned, a feverish heat taking control of me. "What do you want?"

"You. To give you everything if you let me." He pressed kisses on the column of my nape. "But for now, I think it's about time I fuck you right on this shelf."

He pressed his pulsing shaft against the fabric of my dress, growing thicker by the second. My body seemed to exist only for his touch, demanding more and more, responding to him like a magnet.

"It's about time, indeed," I muttered, and I caressed him over the top of his trousers, slow but teasing enough, my lip bite promising him a memory the old Ajax and Aurore would have remembered for their entire lives.

He let out a low growl, and I worked on his zipper. It was my turn to torture him as much as he did with me. I wrapped my fingers around his velvet flesh and stroked him.

His throat bobbed, and he cursed. "You can go harder, my fairy. You won't break me."

I tightened my grip around his length, and I quickened my pace. He jerked his head backward. His breathing quickened. Blood coursed to his tip. His eyelids closed, and my clit throbbed with anticipation. I stroked him faster, and this time, the intense dark of his eyes met the fiery brown of mine. He wet his lower lip, and an almost imperceptible chuckle escaped him, dark and seductive.

"You're already killing me, controlling me with ease. It's unfair." Ajax dipped down, kissing me again.

I raised a brow, challenging him. "Wait until you see what my mouth can do."

I bent down so I'd be at the height of his length, and I took him in fully. He snapped a fist to his mouth, and I took his animalistic groan as encouragement. Locking my eyes heavenward on him, I thrust him inside my mouth, moving in and out. He twisted his fingers into my hair, and his palm pushed me further onto him. I licked him from the bottom to his tip, circling the head of his hardness, as he growled, his whole body tensing. I used my tongue on him, swirling around his velvet flesh. I quickened my moves until I tasted the saltiness of his precum oozing from his tip.

At this moment, Ajax made me stand up, locking my body with his, and pulled a strand of my hair away from my face. "I'm yours, and you're mine."

"I missed you," I panted with a fluttering stomach.

His skilled fingers worked their way under my dress, and he pulled my panties up, causing a delicious friction that made my clit ache with need.

"And you've possessed me," he growled, pulling the fabric to the side so he could meet my wet folds.

And he did, a muscle clenching his jaw as if he was containing himself. He plunged a finger inside me, and I gasped. My walls quivered around him, and I rocked my hips forward, rubbing myself shamelessly against the pump of his finger, biting my lips together so I wouldn't shriek.

He withdrew his finger from me, leaving me frustrated and flushed right until the moment he licked the taste of me, and a new wave of heat thrummed through my center.

"I've fantasized about the taste of you. I had to fuck myself in the shower at the bare thought of you," his deep voice teased in an agonizing whisper. "I think I'm going insane."

I wrapped a leg around his torso, a few books coming down at the contact of my back pinned against the shelf. "I did that too."

"Next time you do, can I watch? Please," he begged, lifting my dress up as I braced my other leg around him.

"That depends. What did you fantasize about?"

"I thought of waking up in the morning spooning you, your butt cheeks against my hardness, and making love to you. I thought of thrusting inside your sweet mouth before coming on you—breasts, mouth, I imagined it all. Tasting you as you ride me. I've thought of sixteen positions I want to have you in. So many probabilities that I couldn't even make a list of them, and right now, I don't even have enough time to appreciate you like I want to."

My heart skipped a beat. "Don't miss another second, then."

He sealed his lips possessively and roughly on mine, our tongues intertwining. My arms curled around his neck, and I spread my legs wider, pressing my hips up to his. He knocked off the strap of my dress and lowered it, exposing my breasts, my nipples hardening under his stare. "Fuck, you're not even wearing a bra."

He locked my hands with his above my head on top of the shelf, my nails instantly digging into his palm. He cupped my breast, his lips closing on it. His tongue lashed out on the bud of my nipple and a tendril of pleasure that couldn't be tempered unfurled through me.

"You know how perfect you are?"

This was his last statement before he drove briskly into me, and I bounced against the shelf. I gasped, trying to keep my eyes open. The items from the shelf fell beside us, but that didn't matter. He tightened the grip of his palm, pressing on my wrists harder until my hands tingled. My arousal pooled between my legs. His forehead creased, and a drop of sweat drifted down from mine.

"Is it deep enough for you, my fairy?" He hit the end of me with merciless thrusts, and I shrieked, pain and pleasure melting as I adjusted to his thick length.

I nodded, unable to speak. He grasped my butt cheek, pounding inside me harder than our first time, his balls slapping against me. My nails scraped his back, and it was as if we were punishing ourselves for the love we felt. Our raspy breaths tangled, and I lost myself in the lust flaring in his irises.

"Spectre," I moaned.

He nibbled and sucked on my bottom lip. "Good girl. You learned the lesson."

Spectre held me up with the sheer strength of his arm hooked around my waist, continuing to pound inside me as he pulled me away from the wooden shelf. We were giving in to one another in the penumbra, and I was set aflame in the middle of the aisle that had changed our lives, sheltered from the rays of sunlight piercing through the broken window.

I bit on my lip so hard. "It feels so good."

"Only 'so good'? I guess I'll have to make you change your mind," he whispered on my neck, and I was certain he was inhaling the scent of my hair.

"I don't think I can hold on much longer," I begged.

"You can hold on, my fairy. I'm not finished with you yet. Give me more time."

He gave me a mere second to catch my breath before my chest collided with the shelf, and his tongue lapped down the curve of my ear. My back arched, and he lifted my dress again so my ass was exposed to him. From behind me, he slid inside me again, and our moans echoed, the scents of parchment and wood mixing with his clean, fresh-out-of-the-shower fragrance.

His hands grasped my waist, and I moved with his motion. My legs shook, and if it wasn't for Ajax holding me, I would have probably lost my equilibrium. My chest heaved. My stomach contracted with each of his drives. A pain rose in my chest. I had never felt something so powerful that it could tear me apart in a draft. *Love—what bullshit.*

He snaked his hand down the valley between my breasts before he thumbed one of my pebbled nipples. My hips swiveled the faster he moved against me, and when his fingers teased my clit, I lost it. He circled around it, his thrusts growing harder and more desperate. This time, I couldn't contain the way my orgasm crested and the longing to come, racking my every nerve. He rocked us to the crescendo we both craved, and our orgasms wrenched us at the same time, consuming us whole. A loud cry escaped my lungs, and his arm hooked around me held me in place.

We remained breathless, his head buried in the hollow of my nape. Ajax placed a soft kiss on my forehead and pulled away from me. I turned around, still gasping, having the view of him buttoning up his dress shirt, adjusting his trousers, and tightening his belt. His face didn't display anything, not the passion that had inhabited us a couple of seconds earlier nor the consuming feelings that might have been tearing him up inside. His face didn't show any of that, no, but I knew his heart had felt it all.

I readjusted my messy hair that screamed of raw sex and tried to turn off the heat that flushed my cheeks. I held the strap of my dress, about to dress myself up like someone does quickly after a one-night stand.

"Let me do it." This wasn't a question, and there was not an ounce of hesitation in Ajax's tone.

Not leaving me another choice, he prowled toward me and pulled the straps of my dress back up my shoulders. He ran his hand over my dress to smooth it out, readjusting each of the folds to perfection with dedication. He even brushed out some strands of my hair and erased the mascara that must have dripped down my cheek. Ajax may have fucked the hell out of me and be poker-faced by nature, but his gestures showed he was just as heartbroken as me about what needed to happen next. A slight smile formed on my lips. It was nice to be loved and cared for, for once.

"What now?" I broke the silence.

His jaw clenched. "We face reality."

"You're still leaving, and I won't tell you to stay," I said, swallowing away the pain trying to rip out my heart. "Not because I don't want to, but because I care about you too much to hold you back. You have to do this. In a small-town romance, the hero changes, and he quits everything to live a simple life with his significant other, but I want more for you."

"I know. Just like I won't beg you on my knees to go with me because you need to figure out what you want like the fairy queen that you are." He took a deep breath, his eyes assessing each detail of my face as if he wanted to remember everything about it.

"What are you going to do now that your identity has been revealed?"

He thought this through before a thin line sketched his lips. "I'll learn to be human as you taught me. I'll manage."

Our fingers intertwined for an instant.

"Congratulations on your deal with Ever After. I never doubted you."

"You were the first person I wanted to call," I said. "I wanted to share it with you."

"I know." His thumb struck my bottom lip as if remembering the taste of my lips, and my stomach tightened even more. "At the thought I'll have to board my fucking plane, it feels like I'm swimming against the tide."

"And it feels like I'm drowning without you. Sometimes the right choices tear us apart, the way we have to sacrifice some things to have a quarter of the happiness of the hero."

"But I refuse for it to be the end, Aurore. Even if I have to swim against a whole storm to go to that kingdom of yours, I'll do it." This was a promise.

"And perhaps, I'll jump from the cliff to find you in a fall of life and death," I continued.

"This is not our ending," he repeated, articulating every word.

I nodded. "Not our ending."

Heartbreaking, this was a goodbye. For now.

But in my world, goodbye turned into forever.

Because I knew how the story ended for people like us.

CHAPTER 33

Ajax

"It's been days since I've been dealing with the stunt you pulled on me," Eric complained on the phone. "My phone is blowing up, everyone is asking for answers and want an interview with you, we need to—"

"I can't talk to you right now." I parked my car like an asshole in the middle of the Clemonte family residence in another impulsive act. "I chose to work with you for a reason. You're good, Eric. You're even the best at what you do, and I trust you to make the right choices to handle that shitshow."

I grabbed my keys, closed the door of my Aston Martin, and walked with heavy stomps toward that manor of misery. "Plus, for now, none of our contracts backed out. I'm sure we'd have a year booked with commissions."

"Since when are you optimistic?" he grunted. "I hate to admit this, but your impulsive act is maybe the best marketing strategy we could have ever thought about. You're back in the spotlight with your newest paintings. The way the public perceives those will determine your career."

"I have faith in those." I couldn't be more disinterested in having this conversation right now. "Now, I have to go. We'll talk later."

I hung up, not letting him have the time to complain more as my brother slammed the front door open before I could mouth a semblance of politeness.

"You asshole," he greeted me with the family snarl and crossed arms. "I can't believe you lied to me. I mean, I'm your brother. I can keep a darn secret."

I believed he was referring to the reason for my arrival here: the fact that I was the man behind Spectre.

"You were a real pain when we were kids. A temperamental one who could act on purpose to get me in trouble, and I was the one paying for your mistakes," I dropped.

"You mean you were the cold, emotionless, favorite, perfect one while I was the constant failure who couldn't stand up to you as much as I tried," he deadpanned. "I had to decompress somehow."

I knitted my brows, having no idea my own brother disliked me that much. "I tried to protect you from our father."

"You mean you abandoned me with him while I had to collect all of the broken pieces. All I ever wanted was for my fucking brother to trust me and be there for me like a friend when I was a kid." Archi gunned his eyes at me, his tongue working across his cheeks. "But you didn't seem to care about friendships or any human interactions. You never asked me if I was all right after I took Father's beatings because I wasn't as perfect as you. You only thought of yourself. You cared only about achievements, just like him."

"I'm—" I swallowed, a knot tightening in my chest. "You're right, I failed you. I didn't tell you I was Spectre because I thought you'd resent me the same way our father did. I thought you'd be better off without me because Father had pitted us against each other. Contrary to popular belief, I'm not a humanoid incapable of emotions."

"You have to stop pushing everyone away. I'm not Father. I'm better than him—and not only in the medical field. I don't need you anymore. I'm not that weak, and I thank you for that. Now—" He laid a hand over my shoulder. "That stunt you pulled about revealing who you are was genius, by the way. Very cool. So unlike you."

"Of course, you'd approve of me almost burning my career to ashes."

"I wouldn't be so sure about that, but one thing I'm sure of is you owe me an art piece I can put in my penthouse, and that's not negotiable." Archi pointed his finger at me and entered the house.

"Knowing you, it's going to be something megalomaniac like your close-up portrait," I mumbled.

"Exactly, and I can promise you, you'll hate doing it." Archi flashed his dimples. "Mom! Look who is here!"

I set foot in what used to be my home for the first time since the angry dinner with my father. I stood frozen in the hallway, waiting for one of my parents to arrive, preferably my mother.

"You have to know, Ajax, that her dementia and chronic condition progressed last month. It was pushed by a virus she contracted." Archi's jaw clenched. "I just want to prepare you. I'll go get her."

Get her?

Archi headed in the direction of the kitchen. Long minutes passed, and only the sound of Archi's whisper came through it. I took a step forward, and that's when he came out of the room, rolling my mom's wheelchair. A frozen wave lashed across my spine; it branched across my back like lightning. My mother seemed completely lost. A prickle of something unpleasant squeezed my head.

She, who used to be so carefree, was in a wheelchair, unable to walk on her own. She had lost weight, her bones were visible, and she was as white as a ghost, almost blue. She, who was always so clean and proper, was wearing an old dress that was way too large for her. She'd hate it. She laid her eyes on me for a moment hesitantly.

"It's Ajax. Your son," I told her, trying to appear friendly in front of my own mother because I knew I wasn't talented at making a good first impression.

"I have to pick up my baby from school. I—" She still smiled the same way, with care and generosity. "I—I'm—" She searched for her name, and she stared at the ground for long minutes. When her eyes went back to me, she frowned, one of her fingers jerking. "Who are you?"

"Two weeks ago, she attacked Dad in the middle of the night, thinking he was a stranger, and now—" Archi muttered. "She's unable to move on her own. She doesn't even want to eat anything or drink."

"Ajax," the voice of my father echoed behind my back. I turned around to take him in. He was actually gardening, judging by the gloves he wore, the boots, and some pants with pockets. He was planting flowers. *Lilacs.* My mom's favorite. The ones he held in his hand. "I—You're here because you're Spectre." He cleared his throat with his usual pride. "You can leave. We won't say anything to the media. This will pass eventually."

"You're not working." My father always worked. I didn't even recognize him. If my father and I shared something in common, it was the perfectionism for details, and right now, it was the first time in my life I was seeing him with a beard, badly shaved, not dressed in his typical polo or fancy suit.

"He retired," Archi continued. "He's spending some time with Mom because she's—"

She'll probably leave this world soon.

Our father had finally understood these were the last moments he had to live with his wife before she died.

Something burnt my heart like a poison spreading at a slow, agonizing pace. "Can I speak to you, Father?"

He shot a glance at my mother, then at me, and nodded in agreement. We headed to the veranda near the gardens to continue the discussion.

"I know we don't have the best relationship." I paused. "I'm leaving soon."

"You know—" He knitted his brows, his gaze resting on his garden. "I expected so much from you, Ajax. I've always been hard on you because I wanted what's best for you and your brother. I didn't want to be kind because I knew life was hell. I made you strong and the man you are today. I gave you everything so you'd succeed in life in a way I wasn't given those things."

"You did," I said. "And we're more alike than I would like to acknowledge. I pushed Archi away because I thought that was what was good for him. I closed myself off from emotions and focused on work and achievements because I could control it. Just like you, I was self-made, disowned by my own father. And in the end, we both screwed up, and we're alone with our mistakes."

"I'm nothing like you," Léon spat. "If I had your chance, I would do so much more and not waste it on art. You had everything, Ajax. You were smart and talented, and you gave up everything for—"

"For my dream, Father. This vision of me you wanted me to be, it's not me. It never was." I stiffened. "I'm not saving lives like you and Arch, but I help immortalize memories and make others feel, and that, Dad, that's a gift."

He let out a slight, dark, mocking laugh. "You never felt, Ajax."

"I felt. Everything. I just never expressed it. I never knew how to share my emotions. Just like you feel for Mom, and yet you still pretend you're stronger than your feelings, but no one is. Last time you asked me what pain was; now I know. It's like stabbing. An ache that won't go away. A shard in my gut. You can't sleep. You feel like you're sick. The world's so cold that even breathing is agony when you're in pain."

Being on the verge of losing Aurore had taught me pain. Heartbreak. Love.

"I can't accept who you are." He pinched his lips together, still not looking at me. "You remain my biggest disappointment."

I nodded. He would never change. "And what did you feel when you learned I was Spectre? What's the first thing you did? If you ever had some love for me once, you'll tell me."

He thought this through, and he took a deep breath, closing all the features of his face. "I smiled."

He smiled.

That meant everything.

I had made him feel. We might never see eye to eye or have a relationship someday, but I knew, deep down, there was some love left inside his heart for me.

"I'm gonna see Mom, and then I'll leave." I cracked my knuckles. "I'm sure she's loving that you're planting her favorite flowers."

His gaze lingered on the lilacs around him. "When she was still conscious, she said to me she didn't want to die in a hospital. She said she wanted to be surrounded by her family in her home, just like a flower blooming in her habitat. I'm just honoring her." He tried to act soulless. "I'm powerless."

"You're not powerless. You may have been cruel sometimes to Arch and I, but you've never been powerless." Aurore would probably say he was a villain who made the wrong choices but had a good heart deep inside. "You're doing everything you can to create memories that you will remember. You're making her live through you."

I took my pocket watch out of my jacket and put it on the table on the veranda, next to my father. "Your watch. I stole it the day I left."

My father's eyes doubled in size at the sight of the pocket watch, as if he had seen a ghost from the past. "It's been years… I thought I lost it." He took it in his palm as if it were a weak puppy, and even then, my father wouldn't show as much care as he did now. "I confiscated it from you when you were a kid. I was afraid you would break it."

"I remember." That was one of the reasons why I had stolen it. It was the most precious thing to him. To the point that every time I dared hold it, he'd slap me in the face, and I had to stay in the basement to pass my tests one hundred percent, or I wouldn't come out. "You said I'd never deserve it."

"It was your mother who gave it to me thirty years ago to celebrate her pregnancy."

I furrowed my brows. Thirty years ago. I wasn't born yet.

"She said it symbolized the years of happiness to come," Léon continued the story. "She had a miscarriage. Your brother, Achille, was never born. She could never bear to have lost your brother— that's why I did everything I could for you and your brother to not be weak. We never told you about it, but that watch was the only thing we have left of him."

My jaw clenched, and I balled my hand. I had a brother. Another one. That was the reason my father had a stern heart. For someone who had dedicated his life to saving lives, he was unable to save the one of someone he once loved.

"I'm sorry." I turned around, ready to step away from the past.

"Keep the watch." My father handed me the pocket watch while his back was still facing me. The moment I grabbed it, he continued. "Your mother left a letter for you some time ago. It's in your old room. I didn't open it."

It was the last conversation I had with him as I went to get the letter from my old bedroom. Coming down, I went back to my mother's side, who was facing the window without moving, her eyes vacant.

I kneeled next to her. "Mom, I'm gonna take you to see your lilacs, and we'll talk, okay?"

She turned her head slightly at the sound of my voice, and when her gaze rested on me, her eyes bulged as she panicked. "Help!"

I parted away from her the moment she screamed, but she struggled, her gaze shifting to every corner as if looking for a way out. "Let go of me! Help!"

I remained blank, and Archi and Léon pushed me on their way to reach for her.

"Come back later. She's having an anxiety attack!" Léon roared, trying to calm her down, but she was still struggling, slapping him.

"Go away!" My mother continued screaming, and I did not insist, rushing out of the house.

The moment I walked through the door, I leaned my head against the wall and closed my eyes, ignoring the slamming of my heartbeat. My grip tightened on the letter locked in my hand.

I couldn't leave just yet.

I slept in my car.

I couldn't enter my old house, especially not when my father was glaring in my direction through his bedroom window and double locking the front door so that I couldn't get in. I couldn't leave either, the screams of my mother still haunting me. My plane was late this afternoon, and Eric had already scheduled three appointments upon my arrival, thanks to the time-zone difference.

I looked like shit, and the first ray of light piercing through the mist blinded me. I got out of my car, took out my drawing board, and headed to the veranda, where my father was wheeling my mother out for her favorite moment of the day near the freshly planted lilacs. From afar, he seemed almost caring and gentle, tugging her robe closed and preparing her favorite breakfast—breakfast she didn't want to eat.

"She's calmer today." He zipped up his silky bathrobe; Léon was wearing the embroidered slippers we had given him for his birthday a long time ago. "I'm trusting you to leave afterwards."

"Yes." I displayed the same coldness as he as I sat across the table next to my mother.

She was silent, regarding the horizon with a very light, almost imperceptible smile, probably feeling at peace. I set up my materials on the table and hooked an ankle around my knee before grabbing my charcoal and pulling out a drawing paper. I observed the sunrise trying to break through the branches of the trees in a cadmium-red light and deep hansa yellow.

"You wrote me a letter, but I wanted to open it next to you," I said, but she didn't react. "I'll read it out loud, okay?"

"Aurore," she whispered, her eyes reflecting the dawn. She used to wake Archi and me during the summer mornings so we could all witness the dawn.

I started to draft everything around us, a pencil in each hand to sketch faster, immortalizing this moment in time. "I know a woman named Aurore, and she's just like that. You actually loved her when you met her, but what's not to love?"

My mother parted her lips and shut them again. Once the landscape was drafted, I observed every angle of her to translate her benevolent expression into my drawing. I wasn't good with words, but I'd let her see what I saw. I'd communicate through art.

My mother's gaze fell on my sketch, and her smile deepened into an almost real one. "Who?"

"It's you," I said, working in the way her eyes squinted. "But wait until you see the colors."

I took out the tubes of watercolor paint, and I made my color palette under the supervising eyes of Hélène. She observed my every move, the way I applied colors to reproduce the landscape and mixed opposite shades to work contrasts.

"You've never seen me paint." I painted the way her cheeks blushed in the sun. "With all those dawns, I never painted any. I always preferred the night, but it made you feel sad." Just like Aurore, she was all about happy endings and seeing the beauty in a world I was blind to see. "I get it now. The dawn is the promise of something new, while the night announces... the void to come."

I finished the details, the final touch of the artwork being the shades of purple of the lilacs she adored so much. Sometimes, a nurse would assist her or feed her between the breaks, but I didn't stop or acknowledge anyone's presence.

"I'm done." I cleaned the pencils and left only the painting on the table. "What do you think?"

She looked at herself through the artwork as if trying to guess who this woman peacefully installed in her garden was.

"I woke up happy," she responded, having trouble speaking as if her throat hurt her. "No more pain, leaving happy."

I tried to make sense of her sentence but didn't. I only deduced it was positive because of her illuminating features.

"Thank you." I almost reached for her hand but retracted. "I'll read your letter now."

I unfolded the piece of paper and read everything out loud in one go.

Dear Ajax,

If you're reading this, it means you came back home, which makes me tremendously happy. It also means I'll quit this world anytime soon, and please, don't blame your dad or yourself. I'm blessed to have lived a fabulous life. I have no regrets, and now it's your turn. Life is too short to have remorse or feel sadness over me—and I know you feel, Ajax. I always knew you felt more than everyone else. A mother always knows.

It's like that time when you were eight and you tried to stand up for your brother when he broke your father's antique vase. You said you did it, and then you pushed your brother on the ground, provoking a fight, so your father would believe you were responsible. Archi insulted you, thinking you had rejected him, and you took it. You said nothing. Later that night, when Archi and your father were together on the veranda (because there were so many good memories, honey, don't look only into the bad ones), I went to see you in the attic. Your father had torn away your drawings, but I glued them back together. I still have them. When you looked at me, you had a tear wetting the corner of your eye. You didn't even feel it—your face didn't show your pain except for that single tear. That's when I knew you were so strong, but I also feared you'd become lonely.

I don't blame you for leaving, Ajax. You had to fulfill your dreams, and every time I watched the dawn rising, I knew you'd do splendidly. You have a unique way of representing the world. I'll always live through your heart: remember, memories last forever. But if there is one piece of advice I could give you, it would be to love with your whole being and live with such passion and energy. Don't close your heart.

The letter had been written in two different sittings; the pen was no longer the same, and her handwriting had changed. It seemed that her hand was shaking between each word.

I was about to sign this letter a couple of years ago, but today, I met your Aurore—I love her. You finally opened your heart, and I can now depart to the other world in peace knowing you'll have the happiness you deserve. Don't be lonely. You have so much to give.

We can't control life, Ajax.

I'm demanding you not watch me die—let that be your father's burden. Don't be here. Live for me. Remember the good memories, and don't pity me. I'm not scared of death. Let me go. Live for me.

I forgot what I wanted to write to you… but know that I love you. You were always enough and worthy of love. Follow your heart.

Ps: Don't watch the dawn alone.

Your mom,

Forever.

I folded back the letter, and it took me by surprise when I felt my mother's fingertip on my cheek. She gazed upon me, and for a moment, I thought she had recovered her memory back. That she understood everything I had told her. She withdrew her finger in a small stroke, and her eyes fell on her thumb. There was a single teardrop.

One.

Sadness.

This was sadness. None of my expression budged, but the stirring *pain* of emptiness was still present.

"Are you an angel?" she said.

"Yes, and everything will be okay." I tried to smile. "Thank you for trying to teach me how to live."

She frowned, and then she was gone as if we'd never had this conversation, her defenses weaker with the disease. My phone vibrated again and again in my pocket. My plane. I had to catch my plane.

"I have to leave. I can't stay." I lifted myself up from the chair. "I'll do as you said to me."

My Adam's apple bobbed, and I took the courage into my hands to depart from her, leaving the painting on the table.

I raced to my car and revved up the engine, my lips twitching.

I had to leave.

She asked me to leave.

We can't control life, Ajax.

As for Aurore and me, I wouldn't read the ending yet.

I would watch the dawn and make a new one.

CHAPTER 34

Aurore

I landed in my hometown with my two suitcases in each hand and my heels planted on the damp floor.

"Welcome home." Luna gestured demonstratively as if the landscape in front of me was a work of art. "As you can see, that hasn't changed. The next store is a fifteen-minute walk away, and the six neighbors are still the same but older and nosier."

I winced, seeing the horror in front of me. The neighbors were already attached to their cottage window, spying on my arrival as if a black and involute shadow was crashing on the city. I was back for Luna and nothing else.

"The little Aurore," an old couple intercepted us. Two of my high school teachers—of course they'd remember me; we were no more than a hundred students in the whole school. "It's been a long time. You've certainly become a young woman. Very…"

The two stared at me with a lack of adjectives to describe me, and

I crossed my arms, wondering if they'd find at least one compliment. Luna sighed, and the traitor went inside, letting me deal with them.

"Certainly different," the old math teacher finished, and I felt like a theorem that he didn't have the answer to.

"What did you become? Do you have children?" My former English literature teacher gave me a benevolent smile.

"Nope."

"A husband?" the old man wondered.

"Neither."

Through their eyes, I could tell they thought of me as an old spinster.

"Depression?" She wanted to grab my hand with a pitying look. "With everything that happened to your family and—"

"Oh no. I'm fine." I bit my inner lip; I had to get rid of them ASAP. "I'm an author now, and I know you always told me it wasn't a stable job and I should focus on my studies, but here I am."

She did not react to my sentence. "Your mother told us you're going to move here for good?"

What? Me, end up in this rat hole? "What?"

"We all thought that with what happened to your sister, you should watch over your family. Poor you, to be abandoned cowardly by your father, and your poor mother, who had seen nothing—"

"You don't know anything about us." Only unfounded gossip. "Now, if you'll excuse me, I have to go join my family."

"You should have worn something other than heels. It's not practical." Look who had the science infused—the math teacher.

I towed my suitcase like a rugby player in a scrum. "Yes, well, you should have made roads. We are in the twenty-first century, after all!"

"Oh no, roads!" I heard them whispering behind my back. "It's going to hide our beautiful landscape and heritage."

The bad girl in town just came back. Hide your children and prepare your pitchforks.

I was mentally prepared to spend my days at home like a vampire in the dark, writing and editing like an old sorceress who had gone mad.

I went through the door of my house and released a deep breath. The only one in front of the door to greet me was Duchess purring at my feet, who I scooped into my arms. My mother was busy doing some… pottery. She had a huge smile on her face, and she waved at me in the midst of her mess, taking off her goggles, which I assumed were to prevent splashes.

"There is my talented bestselling author! You look… white. You should take in the sun—it's good for your mood! Coming back here will do you good, you'll see."

"I'm writing all day."

"Someone is grumpy," she teased me while chuckling.

Coming back here, in this room where I had so many memories with my father and my sister, wrung my heart. It belonged to the past, where I had buried a part of me. I was different now, and this place was suffocating me.

"Something wrong, honey? I smell bad energy over here," my mother asked, ready to dig out her purifying incense. The shape of her pottery vase was taking a weird form—more like a penis than an amphora, but hey, everyone sees what they want.

"Why didn't you break up with Dad when he first cheated on you?" I dropped bluntly, not expecting to have this talk right away with my mother. "You were hoping he'd change?"

"No, I did it for you girls." She stopped spinning her pottery, wiping her hands on the rag. "I did it so you could have a happy childhood. I wanted to protect you so you wouldn't miss anything. He was a good father, and he was financially supporting us. You were both so happy, and I wanted you to believe in love."

"But at what price." I took a seat in front of her. "Luna almost died because of the lies, and you always rely on me for everything now. And in the end, you got hurt—we all got hurt. You should have ended things with him, and we would have managed. You wouldn't have wanted either of us to stay in a relationship where we sob at night on our pillowcases. You deserved your happy ending, and we deserved the truth."

"Perhaps, but I—I've found it. I have the both of you, a nice house, a town I love, and I met someone…" She chuckled like some teenager in love. "He's a carpenter. We met online through the bee sanctuary you helped me build, and you'll see he's great. He lost his wife, but he believes in love too, just like I do."

At least I was Cupid, and she seemed happy, but why couldn't I be too? I had accomplished my goal, what I'd have sold my soul for, and here I was, grumpy and still with an aching, unsatisfied heart. "Then, I'm happy for you."

"I know I put a lot of pressure on you these past few years, but I—" She reached for my hand. "You're here now, in this town you love, and you have a book deal. It's everything you ever wanted. So smile and open your heart. Everything will be just like before."

"Perhaps this is not the happy ending I want," I said, more to myself than to her. "I mean, I don't think you realized the pressure I had on my shoulders for years. I had to earn money for you, for Luna, for me. I had to survive, to struggle every day, and maybe I grew cynical, but you don't know how it feels that I couldn't fail, or else you were all coming down with me. I was all alone, and yet, I had to pretend everything was great because you were counting on me. I was the parent, and now, I'm exhausted. I can't breathe in this town, even though I arrived just a minute ago, and you're already settling for me to spend the rest of my life here. I love you, and I love Luna, but compared to you two, the sunshine believers, I'm the antihero who is constantly fighting to win over her happiness."

At the end of my monologue, I took a deep breath. I had never said out loud how I felt, and now that I had started, I couldn't stop. It felt like the weight I'd been carrying for so many years had finally dropped down my shoulders.

"I didn't realize." My mother seemed disoriented by the news, pinching her lips shut and her pupils flaring. "You never talked to us about how you felt. You said you were happy."

"Because I made the same mistake you did with us—by pretending, to protect you."

"I'm sorry. I would have never—"

"I know," I cut her off. "It's not your fault. I don't blame you. I just feel like I lost my happy ending along the way, and I'm sad."

Ajax. The thought of his name alone would either make me flush, lose a heartbeat, or well up my eyes with tears. I had fallen in love with a man who had to leave, and now that he was gone, I was lonely. No achievements could possibly fill that void. I blinked away those thoughts. It wasn't in my personality to give up or mope about my fate.

"If there is one person who deserves to be happy, it's you. You always give and never ask. It's not too late. I shouldn't have implied you were coming back home for good. It's your life."

"I have Luna to take care of." I swallowed. "And afterwards, I will advise what I will do."

"And like you said, I'm her mother and—" The doorbell rang, and upstairs, I heard something tumble—probably Luna making a din. "Be there as a sister. She's doing great."

Luna sprinted down the stairs with lipgloss and a pinkish girly outfit on. "I got it!"

"Who is it?" I tipped the chair back, wanting to see who was coming.

"It's Ryan!" Luna jumped, and once near the door, she sighed before opening it with a sharp blow.

"Hi." The boy cleared his throat the moment he saw that the whole family was spying on him.

"Hi," Luna said back, hiding us from his vision with the door. Look at her, embarrassed, shooting us nothing more than a glance. "I'll be back home soon."

The boy handed her something that made her giggle. "This is for you."

"Thank you. I like gifts," Luna being Luna replied and slammed the door shut.

I found myself smiling, no longer feeling nauseated by the display of cuteness. I didn't even roll my eyes while I caressed Duchess, who had jumped on my lap.

"See? She's the main character of her own life. You, on the contrary, you're putting yourself second." My mother went back to her pottery and continued her vase—or, more accurately, her penis vase.

I gave her a kiss on the cheek before taking my things upstairs. "I'll settle and get some writing done."

"I think my vase is oddly shaped, but it reminds me of something," my mother muttered.

"It looks like a penis, Mom," I informed her through the bars of the stairs.

The clay penis in question at that exact moment split in two, my mother's eyes widening on me.

Welcome home.

After all, what's a villain but the hero who got denied her happy ending?

"Your wicked fairy godmother." My eyes settled on my phone with the certainty that I had written the acknowledgments during my walk in the middle of nowhere. I saved my novel, *Nevermore,* or rather the draft entitled "Draft67," on the drive. I was finally, utterly, completely done with it, and I tapped a quick email to my editor at Ever After. This morning, I even received the cover, which I had sent directly to Ajax for his point of view.

"Fuck!"

By having my gaze resting on my phone for so long, I didn't notice I had come across a tree branch that slapped me in the face. I had gone off the road. Again. I took off my lilac headphones, and the classical music left my ears—a habit I'd picked up from Spectre.

"I'm going to end up being lost by wanting to take a walk to breathe the fresh air," I grumbled for my fairy creatures to hear, but with my luck, I might as well attract a boar that was going to chase me or a poisonous snake.

I looked on Maps for a way to get home when I received a message from Ajax.

> **Ajax:** I haven't read the last chapter. I don't want to know how the story ends yet. But the cover you sent me is hideous.

I laughed, tapping faster on my phone, scrambling to get out of the weeds in my sports tennis skirt. It was true that it wasn't centered and that the color wheel palette wasn't taken into account, but it still wasn't that hideous.

> **Me:** Hideous? Wow, thanks.

> **Ajax:** Hideous.

At least he was dead set and left no room for debate. Point taken.

> **Ajax:** That's why I made you another one.

He sent over the cover he had made in the form of digital art. It was breathtaking. The cover was in a lavender tone, with a gloomy castle in the back and our two main characters in front, face-to-face, like an enemies-to-lovers trope, thorns surrounding them like an evil spell cast upon them.

> **Me:** You're a cinnamon roll.

> **Ajax:** That thing you eat?

> **Me:** No, the character. It means you're adorable. Too good for this world. A badass cutie.

> **Ajax:** I thought I was the grumpy austere kind?

I had to laugh, imagining Ajax's perplexed face.

> **Me:** Oh you definitely are, but I unmasked your true nature.

> **Me:** And about the cover, the one you did is incredible! If your artistic career doesn't work anymore, you know what to do next.

> **Ajax:** In all honesty, my artistic career sucks without you.

My heartbeat quickened. I'd followed every news story about Spectre like the good, trained spy that I was. Since the revelation of his identity, there were two camps that were exposed: one where the TV and the exhibitions craved his paintings and for his backstory to be told, the other camp filled with jealousy, ready to do anything to discredit him. But above all, Spectre's exhibitions to come were all announced complete, with a dozen new paintings. He was invited to gallery openings and to collaborate with prestigious brands. He did it.

> **Me:** It sucks without you too, but I'm informed of everything you accomplish. You're doing great, Ajax.

> **Ajax:** It's exhausting to talk to all of these people.

He attached a selfie, which made my jaw and that of the crows around me drop. He was at some ridiculously fancy event, with his three-piece tailored suit, clean-shaven jaw, and tenebrous eyes. I would definitely save that picture.

> **Me:** By talk, you mean brood in your corner, appearing busy by texting me and interacting at best with a head nod with anyone striking a conversation with you?

> **Ajax:** Obviously.

I sent a selfie back in the middle of my forest with some kind of smile, mostly looking like a madwoman who had just escaped from prison wearing a schoolgirl sports uniform.

> **Ajax:** Is that your fairyland? I want to steal you from it. I need you armed with your hair bow and killer eyes to get me the fuck out of here.

> **Me:** I need your deadly scowl to scare everyone away.

> **Ajax:** Deal.

With this promise, I had only one desire. It was to be at his side. I had become the pathetic character I used to despise.

> **Me**: Is it everything you hoped for?

> **Ajax:** It's what I expected. I shake hands. Make money.

Paint commission. Go to boring events. Sign contracts. And practice my deadly scowl. How is it back home?

Me: You'd expect me to talk with birds and dance as I'm going to the farmer's market, but I'm usually staying in my fortress like a vampire.

Ajax: You should be smiling, Aurore. Every day you should be happy.

Ajax: Every day I think of you.

I bit my lip, my fingers finding it impossible to reply for some reason, because it hurt too much. There was so much keeping us apart before that now, I was hoping this was real. We could be together. We acted as if we were, but we weren't. We were both on opposite sides of the world, on a mission of our own. And I was afraid. Afraid his messages would stop. Afraid he'd grow distant over time. And mostly, I was afraid the dream we had would end, because he was my happy ending.

Ajax: Every day I will.

At that moment, I felt really lost.

CHAPTER 35

Aurore

"Don't tell me you're still there," Emma's ear-splitting voice echoed over the speakerphone.

I ate the last cookie of the freshly baked ones I'd bought this morning. "Fine, I won't tell you."

It wasn't like I camped outside my sister's high school like some psychopath for more than seven hours.

The moment I said goodbye to her this morning at eight o'clock, I had a lump in my stomach. Her glassy eyes were terrified, and she kept eating her nails in angst. I felt like a mother dropping her child off at school for the first time, and I just couldn't leave.

"It's her first day at a public school, and I haven't seen her since the 10:00 a.m. break. I wonder if she's okay." I tapped my fingers against the bench, shut off my computer, and jumped up, ready to spring into action. "Do you think I should see if she's okay?"

"Of course, because it wouldn't be weird at all if a woman in her twenties infiltrated the teenagers. You would pass unnoticed and not at all humiliate her." Emma was full of sarcasm and seemed to run from corner to corner. Maybe she had invested in an exercise bike.

I frowned. "What are you even doing?"

"You're never going to believe me, but this morning, I was cleaning, and I saw…" She gasped, and I deduced that she had just thrown herself on her sofa. "A ring. A box with a ring."

"Which ring?"

"Princess cut."

Obviously.

"You think it's what I think?" Her voice rose up.

"That you just ruined his marriage proposal? Of course."

She started screaming and probably jumping on the spot. "I'm so happy! I compulsively cleaned everything."

"Just like a serial killer after a murder. Not at all suspicious," I mumbled.

"Finally!" She didn't pay attention to me. "Finally, Aurore!"

"Let him propose first because if he sucks, it's not even worth accepting." I couldn't help but share my unwanted thoughts.

"At this point, I might even propose to him first!" Her shrill cry pierced the loudspeaker. "I have to leave you—I have to channel my energy! Who knows, maybe it'll be your day soon too, my fairy godmother!"

"Yeah, right," I snorted. "Right. No way. No. Nope. *Nein.* I—" I breathed. This was ridiculous. "I'm not saying anything else."

She chuckled. "*Wenn du es sagst.*"

Before I could formulate a "what the hell," she hung up, and at the same time, the school bell that announced the end of the day rang. I packed my computer in my purse and posted myself in front of the gate next to the only bus driver in town. My heart hammered, hoping Luna had fit in, and I was ready to terrorize anyone who messed with her.

When I took sight of Luna, I almost crossed the gate myself or jumped over it like the students who skipped class. But Luna was not alone, and even more unusual, she was smiling. Two twin girls were alongside her, and they were all laughing together.

My lips curled, and I took a step back, positioning myself further away so I wouldn't act like the creepy sister waiting for her at the exit. Everything was fine. The past was behind us. The girls exchanged numbers, and Luna waved goodbye, directly finding me—she had noticed me from the start. She ambled toward me, and I acted as if I didn't even know she was already here with two raised brows and a big smile on.

"You didn't wait all day for me, did you?" She didn't buy it.

"Obviously not," I lied. "So, how did it go?"

"Actually, it was…" She searched through her words, biting on her lower lip. "It was good. Scary but good. I met those two girls. They invited me to their house this week for homework. I think I made some friends."

"Are you sure they can be trusted?" My mistrustful self couldn't be tamed, watching the two girls in the distance heading toward a tractor. *Their father had come to pick them up in a tractor?*

"They were very nice to me, and we had fun. Plus—" She shrugged. "—if they don't like me, that's their loss. Someone told me I shouldn't change who I was to please others and that I was great."

I could blush. "Aw, you're sweet."

"I wasn't talking about you." She smirked. "Ajax said that—and yes, I met him twice, and no, I didn't tell you about it because I thought you needed time."

Ajax. My heart skipped a beat. It always skipped a beat when it came to him.

I blinked. "Time?"

"Yes. To see you're meant to be together. Look." Luna seized my hands. "You see? I'm doing fine. I'm even thinking about applying to some fighting classes. I learned a lot. Here, this place, it's not for you. I think you came back for me and to help Mom, but you don't have to anymore. You need to be with him. The one you love."

"Maybe he doesn't want to be with me anymore," I said. "Time has passed. We haven't talked in days. He literally lives on the other side of the world. It feels too dreamy to be true sometimes."

"Maybe he does," she insisted. "True love is meant to be; it doesn't mean you don't have to work hard for it. You're both dreamers—of course it feels like a dream, Aurore. Have you seen yourself? Someone once said to me that our reality is forged by whatever we want it to be."

"And let me guess, I'm not the one who said that to you?" Moral of the story, I sucked at pep talk.

"No, it was Ryan." She had the prettiest smile on. "So, if you can't fight to get your happy ending, no one can, because I've never seen someone as stubborn as you, and I don't mean it as a compliment."

"Thank you?" A doubtful frown was plastered on my forehead. "You're actually right, but I—I don't want to leave you and let you down again."

"You never will," she laughed. "You need to continue to inspire me because that dedication was great, but I want plenty more of them, and if you don't chase after true love, you'll suck as an author. You're both muses to each other."

"Fine. I—" I dug out my phone. "You really think I should make that grand gesture when I fly off to meet him?"

"Yep." She nodded. "But you should probably text him first because we're in the digital age, and that thing about coming to see him unannounced only works in movies."

"Right." I pointed a finger at her. "Here goes nothing."

> **Me:** I'm coming to see you. I need you in my life, Ajax Clemonte.

I did. I sent the text to Ajax.

"Did he reply?" Luna's eyes widened.

"It's been a minute." A long, painful minute.

"Come on," she groaned, her whole body in turmoil.

"It's fine. We don't have to—" I screamed the moment a notification popped up on my phone. "He replied, Luna! He did!"

She urged me through gestures, jumping in place. "Well, open the message!"

> **Ajax:** Not if I'm coming first, my fairy.

"What!" I was certain all the school heard me.

"What did he say?" Luna screamed at her turn.

Ajax sent a picture along with his text.

He was in the middle of nowhere.

My nowhere.

On the road not paved.

On his way.

To see me.

"Oh my god. That man is crazy!" Luna brought her hand to her lips, letting out a laugh. "You have to see him! Oh, this is so good. This is like—"

"I need your help," I cut her off, carried away by a new energy. "You have contacts; I don't. And I need a ride."

Because running in heels in the mud just wouldn't do.

"Say no more."

We ran. I didn't know where we ran to, but we ran. It was only when we arrived by the twins that I understood what my resourceful sister had in mind. I arrived like a fury next to them and pointed my finger at their father's tractor, who stared at me as if I was the reincarnation of his great-aunt whom he wished to forget.

"Hi, I'm sorry, but can I borrow your tractor? It's a question of life and death."

"And happy endings," Luna added.

"Yes, that too, and you don't know how much I crave this one."

The old man's eyes widened, and for a moment, I thought I had paralyzed him to the spot. His two daughters nonetheless encouraged him. "She's the sister of our new friend. Help her, Dad."

He pointed to his tractor at his turn. "You know how to drive this old thing?"

I had countryside blood; plus, if there was one thing my father had taught me, it was how to drive a fucking tractor. It could not be that different from the one I'd received as a gift when I was four years old.

"Evil queens have dragons, so I can manage. Thank you so much—I owe you one!" I climbed the beast with my inappropriate heels, and once seated, I tried to figure out how the thing indeed worked.

I took a shaky breath and slammed on the pedal. *I'm one crazy fucking godmother.* I engaged the brake with my right foot and turned on the engine, releasing the tractor's parking brake. My hands tightened on the steering wheel. I had found my carriage.

"Go get him, Aurore!" From the sideline, Luna cheered.

I went in search of Ajax, leaning close to the steering wheel while doing jumps on the unpaved road. I tried to accelerate, but the engine was slow. I cut between the trees by the forest, managing to somehow not hit any, to arrive as quickly as possible. The sky rumbled, covering itself with blackness. I raced toward him as if my life depended on it.

In the distance, I saw a black car, his Aston Martin coming my way—the fluffy pink thing I had hung on its rearview mirror swaying from side to side. I smiled, strands of my static hair in front of my face. The sky rumbled again, the weather turning moist and humid.

"Fuck, how do I stop this shit!" I grumbled, switching the gears to neutral and finding the parking brake.

Ajax parked his car in the middle of the mud and got out with his ironed suit adjusted to perfection. His stare was upon me. He was frowning, a mix of worry and surprise as if he didn't think I was capable of arriving by tractor yet.

I passed on the rocky road and managed somehow to stop that thing by pressing on the pedal as hard as I could. I ejected myself from the tractor, my shoes with it, and barefoot I paced in his direction.

Lightning hit the sky, and I collided with Ajax's arms, the air wafting up my nostrils with the fresh, clean scent of him. He hugged me tight, and I swept him away so much when I landed like a rocket. Both of us displayed such a rare and true smile, and our lips met, wet and lustful. He invaded my mouth, and I gave in to him.

We kissed as if there were no tomorrow.

So that was the feeling of having everything you needed. The feeling of finally being on the right side of history because you were loved for who you were, simply and truly. Love—and to think that I had stopped believing in it once ago.

"You have my grumpy heart," I breathed in between kisses.

"You're sunshine to me."

I wanted to drown myself in his eyes.

"That's because you're even more grumpy than I am," I chuckled. "What are you doing here?"

"I want to see the world through your eyes. I don't care where I am as long as I'm with you. I don't want to live there without you."

I opened my eyes. "You left the US?"

"This morning, and I'm not going back unless it's with you," he said, caressing my cheeks. "I need you. I need to feel for you. Live for you. I want you to be my muse, my girlfriend, my everything."

"I love you," I said, the sky grounding like a bad omen to come. "I may not want the typical ending people would expect us to have, but I want our own happy ending. The one we'll make together."

"I couldn't agree more. I want to watch every dawn with you." He paused. "I want to see you wear all your dresses, my fairy."

"And when I run out?"

"I'll buy you new ones."

The rain poured.

The storm had hit us again.

A new page was turning.

"Did you read how the story ends?"

"You tell me," he said, already busy kissing me.

"They lived plentifully, being inspired and loving each other forever and ever with tons of steamy moments."

EPILOGUE

Aurore

Some months later

"**C**an you drive faster? I think we're late and—" I blew a lock of hair, somehow arranging my puffy tulle lavender dress. It was taking up all the space in the car, blocking me from viewing halfway up the road and even cluttering up Ajax's space. "Emma is going to kill me!"

"First, I can't because I'm already beyond the speed limit, and second, we're not late," my grumpy, unapproachable boyfriend in a beige suit drawled. "We're two hours early. I may have lied to you, knowing your taste for punctuality."

"What? You did that?" My anxious, screaming voice could have deafened him, even if I was somehow glad to not be late for my best friend's wedding. "You know I love you, right? This is very mean and sneaky, but I truly do. Your annoying punctuality saves me each time."

The last time was during our trip to the Dark Hedges, an avenue of creepy trees, and if Ajax's alarm hadn't rung an hour earlier than planned, we wouldn't have seen the dawn. Everyone came in summer-time, but I preferred the hostile fall. I remembered obligating him to sprawl with me in the middle of the road to take in the view, but the rebellious side of him didn't, focusing on me and the creative mad-ness of the second novel I was working on instead.

"You're anxious, and when you are, you're late and forget things."

Of course, on top of being perfect-looking and knowing me much more than I knew myself, he had to have the annoying trait of keeping his promises: taking me to all the places in the world I wanted to visit with my two suitcases packed with dresses, inspiring me every hour of the day. As for me, I made it a tradition to buy him a new pendant for his rearview mirror, each more corny than the other.

"I'm the maid of honor—of course I'm freaking out. I'm supposed to maintain peace between the guests and all of that. Have you seen me? I'm chaotic, not peaceful." And here I was lashing out another of my monologues at him. "Oh my god! The ring—did we get the wed-ding ring? We have to—"

"Breathe deep, my love. I packed everything. And you're all I see, my fairy. Even if I'm not content with the idea of people stealing you from me, I'll be satisfied to look at you freely and peacefully in a corner."

Ajax frowned, eyeing his GPS doubtfully as we sank further and further down a small path in the forest, surrounded by a river. Emma's wedding was at some castle, a two-hour drive from Paris and, if I re-called correctly, not too far from the beach coast. "Are you sure we're not lost or something? It looks like we're in an enchanted forest and—" I gasped. In the middle of the river, on a rock, there was a mewling ginger kitten. The hair raised on my skin. Cats didn't like water. What on earth was he doing here? A tendril of protectiveness squeezed my lungs, and I didn't think twice before screaming, "Stop the car now!"

Ajax suddenly swerved in the middle of the deserted road, and I unbuckled my seat belt, my big eyes on him.

"The cat! He's going to drown, look!"

The meowing kitten was trying to find a solution to outwit the

water and return to the land. Whatever happened before, he probably had to swim to the rock, and the current was too strong for an
animal of his weight.

Ajax squinted his eyes, assessing me and the cat in turn, as if he
saw a kinship or something. "He's a cat? How did he get into such a
situation?"

"I don't know, but this situation happens to the best of us! Maybe
he's clumsy, maybe someone evil dropped him there with his brothers
and sisters and he's the only survivor!" I shrieked as I opened the car
door and rushed toward the stream. "We have to save him—we can't
leave him alone, or he'll die! I can't let him die. I—"

My heart pounding with anguish, I was about to make the impulsive decision to cross the river in my floor-brushing bridesmaid dress
when Ajax stopped me, his arm blocking me from taking another step.

"Do you trust me?" he uttered, already taking off his jacket and
his loafers.

It was just four words. Four words that calmed me because I had
absolute trust in this man. He didn't say anything else as I nodded,
and he paced into the river, wetting his suit pants up to his knees.
Stern and perfectionist Ajax, who didn't like twists and turns, was in
the middle of a stream, stepping on rocks to not lose his equilibrium
to save a little kitten.

"You're almost there!" I cheered on the sidelines, the kitten scaring me to the brink of diving into the water. This cat was looking for
disaster. "And don't scare him. I heard that if you blink, they'll not
think you're a menace!"

Ajax turned to me and pinned me with a look as if I was asking
too much of him. I shrugged, and he approached the cat, holding out
a hand.

"Hi, little creature" was his definition of being sweet and unscary.

The kitten nonetheless seemed to have read into his soul and
jumped into his arms. My heart melted a bit more at the sight of the
animal cuddled up against him, his paw on his arm, despite the lack
of reassuring words or cuddles coming from Ajax.

"He's safe." He arrived at my side, being careful to not hurt him, nestling him in his suit jacket. "He's just a bit adventurous, like someone I know who likes to be wet."

I couldn't help but smile, holding the kitten soaked with shaggy hair on top of his skull and tiger eyes. Maybe that stray cat and I weren't that different after all. He was certainly unusual, with a tendency to attract drama.

"We have to see if he belongs to someone." Around us, there wasn't the shadow of an expectant neighbor. The only sign of life nearby was from some kind of manor hidden behind an alley of trees. A small path led there like a portal to another world. "We have to ask them."

We plunged into the path and came face-to-face with an imposing iron gate with a golden letter A on top.

"Ajax" was the only thing I could speak before I was muted.

Behind the gate, there were acres of gardens, with a huge weeping willow. My heart raced. It was a stone manor with ivy climbing the facade. The dark gray roof had peaks rising toward the sky, and the white stones of the manor brought in the light with large arched windows.

"Hi." A lady with a formal suit, who must have been some kind of worker for the manor, interrupted our contemplation.

I gave her the best polite smile I could. "Hi. We found a cat on our way, and we were wondering if he was yours?"

"Oh no, I'm sorry, and there is no neighbor within a two-kilometer radius. Someone must have abandoned him—it happens frequently. Thankfully, you were able to save him. I'm not sure his family had the same lucky fate." She gave the animal a look full of tenderness before focusing her attention back on us. "You're here for the visit, right?"

"The visit?" Ajax and I said at the same exact time, exchanging a look.

"Yes, the proprietor of the manor, Mme Duchemin, told me

you were coming as potential buyers. I wasn't expecting you before half an hour, Mr. and Mme Becsec."

"Oh, right." I let my voice drift away for a couple of seconds before pinning Ajax with a look full of malice. "The visit to buy this beautiful manor. That's why we drove here today."

Ajax knitted his brows, playing along. "Right. I like to be early."

"By all means, please come in." The real estate agent opened the gate and waved us in. "For a second, I thought you were part of a theater troupe."

Right—I was dressed in a puffy dress fit for a ballet, and Ajax's trousers still weren't dry. "Oh, no, we're just going to a wedding! After the visit, obviously."

"Oh, how lovely." She glanced at Ajax from head to toe and leaned forward with a light smile. "You're the tallest jockey I ever met. I did a bit of horseback riding during my teenage years."

"Jockey?" Ajax gritted out between clenched teeth.

"Yes, I've read on your file that you're a jockey. Jockeys are usually below one meter seventy, and you're, well, tall." She had to crane her neck up to evaluate his size.

I bit my lower lip to contain a laugh. Almost two meters tall, Ajax had stolen the identity of a jockey. This was all too good to be true.

"My horse is resistant," he deadpanned without an inch of emotion.

The real estate agent seemed destabilized, but she didn't dig for more information as we strode to the manor, and although having an intuition, Ajax and I were not prepared. We'd been searching for a place to call home for weeks in between our travels: not too far from the capital, remote enough to not deal with neighbors, bonus points if it was by the sea, and a place that would spark our creativity. I checked the mobile data on my phone because no data would have been a deal breaker. It worked, even better than I'd have imagined. We arrived inside the hallway. It was bright, with enough space for Ajax's marble statues. Another good point checked on the list.

"You can start upstairs. I'll get right back to you." The real estate agent beamed.

Ajax and I headed to the top to land in a room that would have been perfect for a period ballroom, giving a dark academia aesthetic, with vaults like in a gothic temple and chandeliers hanging on the ceilings. I whirled around with our newly adopted cat.

"I imagine lighting candles on a rainy day with the smell of pine trees and pumpkins. Us, dancing from one window to another like two memories in the shape of shadows immortalized into the stones, the sound of classical music lapping above the merciless rain." Phantom ants coursed through me, inspiration lashing in every fiber of my core. "And what do you imagine?"

Ajax readjusted the cuffs on his suit and deadpanned with his usual aloofness, "The sounds of your orgasm breaching through said rain of yours. Your hands misting the window as I'd savor the taste of you, and the fact that the heating bill will be terribly expensive since you will very often be naked."

Oh my—I gasped at the same time the realtor was making her entrance back with euphoria and enthusiasm, half out of breath after rushing up the steps.

"I see it'd be a perfect place for you, Mme Becsec. The flooring is hardwood." She gave me an instant look, her eyes bulging out of their sockets, and I had the feeling I was supposed to be somehow excited about this news.

She glanced from side to side, like one would tell a secret juicy gossip to her friends, "It's maple."

"Ohh." I didn't know what to say, so I bluntly knelt on the ground, and I hit the flooring with my knuckles like some woodpecker. "Unbelievable."

"I knew you'd fall in love with it since you're a tap dancer—this couldn't be better! You want to try it?" She encouraged me with a little squeal like a squirrel, and my lips curved backward, my smile vanishing far away for a more hostile expression.

"Yes, darling, you should try it." Ajax wet his lips, taking his superior air, and judging by the small grin on his mouth, I could tell he was enjoying my misery.

"Only if you ride a horse with your uniform, my knight," I quipped back, narrowing my eyes on my boyfriend as I gave a friendly tap on the floor like it was my old mate. "I don't have the right shoes, but this flooring sounds optimal. Top quality."

I lifted myself up, and we continued our visit, immersing ourselves into our new identities for snatching that manor from the Becsec family without an ounce of remorse. It wasn't heroic; this place wasn't meant to be for us, but we shaped our destiny. I wasn't ready to let go of an atelier giving way to the backyard, the smell of oceanic air perceptible from the balcony on the roof, nor the secret-garden vibes to be hidden from the tumult of the world to be inspired. It would be our corner of paradise before heading back to the madness of the world just an hour from here to live as many adventures as we craved.

But the moment I knew the Becsecs didn't stand a chance against us for this manor was the moment I squeezed Ajax's wrist as we arrived in the living room.

An enormous bookshelf with a rolling ladder painted in my favorite lavender color ran along the entire wall, rising to the ceiling. And they had dared to leave it empty and abandoned; in no time, I would have filled it with books, scented candles, and book geek things.

"Imagine how amazing your books will look on this shelf?" Ajax whispered from behind me, the rasp of his voice giving me goosebumps.

"Yes." In a flash, the life we would have together flashed in my brain, until the days when our skin would be wrinkled. He was my person, the one I'd have an undying love for.

"I think one of my favorite activities will be when you read to me, and I'll be immortalizing every world you're creating for us with drawings of you. I'll be human with you, my muse."

My eyes would have watered if it wasn't for the real estate agent interrupting us.

"The bookshelf can be removed. It's a bit spacy, and the color is—"

"Don't you dare do that!" I snapped at the poor real estate agent, my expression turning feral. "This—" I aimed at the bookshelf. "This is a piece of art."

"Don't touch her bookshelf," Ajax added. "She's not kidding."

"I'm so not kidding."

"Right, then it stays." She clasped her hands. "So, I'll give you two a minute, and then we'll discuss what you thought of the manor."

"What are we gonna do? We're not Mr. and Mme Becsec?" I whispered, watching her already preparing the paperwork.

"Let me take care of it."

Ajax displayed his deadliest scowl and cleared his throat, and just like that, I knew he'd strike a deal at all costs. And he did just that in less than five minutes, with intakes of very short sentences and a fat check.

And so we walked out of our new acquisition, Ajax's hand behind my back and my bridesmaid dress scraping the floor as I smirked, feeling invincible by his side. A luxury car parked right in front of the gate, and a couple got out.

The man, no less than one meter seventy, wore a fine brown checkered blazer, riding boots, and had a bourgeois attitude, walking in an austere manner. His wife, a tall woman twice his size, had a shockingly huge hat, a ferret fur scarf to accompany her red lipstick on her pinched lips, and a severe bun. The Becsecs. I raised a brow just when we were about to cross one another. They had the certainty this manor would be theirs, eyeing the way I was dressed with judgment.

"The house is not for sale anymore," Ajax dropped, cold and merciless, not sparing them a glance.

The Becsecs displayed an expression of disgust, twitching their lips backward, and their vile little eyes squinted.

I couldn't help but laugh. "You're villainous."

"Not as much as you are, my muse."

"You have to keep Lucky." Our newly adopted cat named after our four-leaf clover. "I need to find Emma and Luna. Are you going to be okay?" I asked Ajax in the middle of the wedding preparation.

I knew a wedding for Ajax was what a funeral is for others: the crowd already whispering while they took their seats in the chapel, the abundance of them already crying with joy or regret, the sweet words you have to come up with or else you'd be a jerk.

"I've lived worse than a wedding, Aurore." He was about to kiss me when his carved face shadowed with a dash of annoyance at the sight of Archibald coming our way with determined footsteps. "Scratch that—I'm not going to be okay."

Even Lucky meowed and somehow frowned in a grumpy way inside Ajax's embrace, despite the fact I had given him the ribbon that tied my hair so he'd look fitting for the event.

"What are you doing with a cat?" Archibald's forehead creased, analyzing our Lucky. "Wow, what a weird cat. He has a grumpy face just like—" He lifted his head to see his aloof brother without an ounce of friendliness. "He's lovely, just like you, Ajax. Did you even sleep? You look like an undead."

"Thanks, Arch." Ajax readjusted his suit. "In case you didn't know, it was my gallery opening in Miami before yesterday, which you were invited to, by the way."

"Next time, it'd be easier to come if you don't tell me a day after it's over, huh?" Archibald focused his attention on our newly adopted cat, who he petted. "And if only you weren't being your usual self, you would have known your own brother was indeed there, and he doesn't look like an undead."

A flash of surprise etched over Ajax's face. "You were there?"

"I can be a ghost too when I want to. It was your big day."

Ajax simply nodded, turning back to me and seizing my hand. "Be safe. If you need me, you call me."

"It's a wedding, Ajax, not a gun tournament. I'm perfectly safe." I kissed him on the cheek and rushed toward the fitting rooms with the bride's lily bouquet in my hands.

The first thing that captured my eyes when I slammed open the door was the view of my best friend in a sumptuous princess wedding dress in this castle-like scenery. It was a classical bustier but so pretty. She swaggered with a fan, exhaling shaky breaths with rosy makeup on, Rosalind lying at her feet with a cute pink tiara on.

"Emma! You're so perfect, oh my god!" I shook the bouquet with excitement and probably ended up killing all the new buds, so I put it on the nearest table. "But please don't cry."

"Aurore! I have something to tell you!" She squeezed my hands and exchanged a glance with Luna, who looked quite excited in a beautiful light pastel blue mermaid dress and butterfly hair clip.

"Don't tell me he canceled the wedding!" I was ready to pull off my shoes and chase him to hell with it.

"No, of course not!" Emma had tears trickling down her cheeks as she waved her hands, glancing to the ceiling to hold in her new waterfall of tears. "I've been trying to reach you for half an hour!"

"Sorry, Ajax is with Lucky, and we bought a house—well, a manor—and—" I paused, lifting a finger up. "Your big day. This story is for another time."

"What?" Emma's eyes widened, and her need to cry suddenly left her. Even Rosalind, that lazy dog, at the mention of Ajax straightened her ears and got into a sitting position.

"Who's Lucky?" It was Luna's turn to squint at me.

"We adopted a kitten we rescued. A grumpy ginger cat who likes to be wet."

"Oh, that's touching. You will start a family too." Emma seized my hand, almost breaking my bones with how tense she was. *Huh. Start a family too?* "And you won't be that far from me."

"What? Ajax is with a cat right now? This is too good!" Luna sprinted out of the room, already chuckling with mischief.

"Wait, you said *start a family too*? You're—" The words didn't come out of my mouth. "You are... He has you... are you going to have—"

"I am pregnant!" Her scream echoed so loudly that I believed she'd just shared the news with all the guests.

"Okay, I can't breathe with this corset anymore!" I bent over, a hand on my waist, trying to find some air in this room under the shock of the news. "That's great, Emma. You almost gave me a heart attack, but I'm so happy for you!"

"And of course, you will be the sarcastic but most incredible godparent." She jumped in the same spot, hissing a scream of excitement. "If you accept, of course! Léo doesn't even know yet. I'll surprise him on the wedding night."

"It's amazing. Of course, I'll give her romance novels so she'll settle for no less than a book boyfriend." This was my blessing to her child as the wicked godmother.

Emma chuckled. "And if it's a boy?"

"He'll know how to treat a woman the right way," I affirmed.

Emma would finally have her "they lived together happily and had lots of children forever and ever." The tale usually stops at this point of the story, but destiny had another outcome for me because my story was far from being over. In a certain way, it had just begun.

Luna popped into the room again. "You have to see this—it's excellent! Quick!"

We didn't ask questions and rushed to the door. We leaned behind it, each to a different level of height, to peer at the show in question by the chapel.

I had to burst into laughter. Ajax was surrounded by the guests, standing a head taller than everyone else, holding Lucky in his arms with a stoic, inscrutable expression. All of them were trying to pet Lucky and talk to my Greek warrior in a suit about how his kitten was adorable and where we had gotten him.

He who didn't like people and being under the spotlight was served. Even Lucky did not respond to any caresses and had eyes only for Ajax, pleading with him to get away from here.

"What wouldn't he do for love? It would be my nightmare too," Luna sympathized.

Archibald joined us, leaning on the door with his elbow. "I hope you never make him forget this memory."

Our eyes met from across the crowd, and I bit my lower lip. "I think I have to go save my boyfriend."

The End

ACKNOWLEDGMENTS

I've been there.

There, to the part of the story where you feel like the outsider, the side character who dreams it'll be her turn, or the one who puts so much pressure on herself she never reaches "good enough." What I can affirm is that you're a beautiful, talented, unique person who deserves to be the main character. You have so much worth, so enter the tale and never stop believing. You can have a real-life book boyfriend of your own. You can be the hero of your novel. You have a story to tell.

I witnessed and experienced bullying throughout my high school years. That's why I urge you to please speak up. Don't allow them to lower your self-esteem. Never let the bullies undervalue your worth. The world needs you and your incredible strength of character. You're powerful. Never doubt you are loved. You're a gift to this world.

My grandfather recently passed away. He was such a proud and strong person and had Alzheimer's. If you lost a loved one or know someone with Alzheimer's disease, remember: the person you love is still there. The memories last forever, as Ajax's mom would say, and she's right. Every loved one you have lost lives through you. Their soul is always with you.

To my own real-life book boyfriend: Lucas, you didn't inspire my Ajax because you're an artist too, nor because it took us six years to be together, nor for the fact you're listening to my crazy stories despite your grumpy self, but because you make me feel alive, and you're everything I didn't know I needed. I was dead set on giving up on real-life men, but you opened my eyes, and god knows meeting a romance author's standards is very complicated. Can you imagine he supports me by doing all the art scenes inside this novel?

To my bookish best friend, Naemi: thank you for inspiring my lovely Emma. Just like her, you're a force of nature. You can overcome every challenge, and one day, I have no doubt you'll become the best mom ever. To Juliette: a strong, hardworking woman, you're the proof a woman can thrive in a man's world. To Blanca: for always encouraging me to be creative from the start.

To my sunshine believer mom, who never stopped believing in love and truly understands the assignment of being a main character: thank you for inspiring me to do everything with passion and for your strength of putting your heart out there every time.

I always said I wanted to make my life a real-life movie or a book, and I did. Now, it's your turn.

An author acting like your very own godmother.

Made in United States
North Haven, CT
07 August 2023

40067137R00221